MASK OF
THE NIGHT

MASK OF
THE NIGHT

Mary Ryan

G.K. Hall & Co. • Chivers Press
Thorndike, Maine USA   Bath, England

This Large Print edition is published by G.K. Hall & Co., USA and by Chivers Press, England.

Published in 1998 in the U.S. by arrangement with St. Martin's Press, Inc.

Published in 1999 in the U.K. by arrangement with Headline Book Publishing.

U.S. Hardcover   0-7838-0380-X   (Romance Series Edition)
U.K. Hardcover   0-7540-1230-1   (Windsor Large Print)
U.K. Softcover   0-7540-2167-X   (Paragon Large Print)

The text of this Large Print edition is unabridged. Other aspects of the book may vary from the original edition.

Set in 16 pt. Plantin by Al Chase.

Printed in the United States on permanent paper.

British Library Cataloguing in Publication Data available

Library of Congress Cataloging in Publication Data

Ryan, Mary.
    Mask of the night / Mary Ryan.
    p.   cm.
    ISBN 0-7862-0380-X (lg. print : hc : alk. paper)
    1. Witchcraft — Ireland — Fiction. 2. Castles — Ireland — Fiction. 3. Large type books. I. Title.
    [PR6068.Y33M37 1998]
    813'.914—dc21   98-41388

For my sisters,
Eileen and Anne

ACKNOWLEDGEMENTS

This book owes its existence to much more than just the toil of the author. I am indebted to my family for their patience and support, to my agent, Bob Tanner, for his faith in me, and to my editor, Caroline Oakley, and copy-editor, Penelope Isaac, for their incisive and vital work.

The story of the Lady of Florence has no historical basis, although there is no telling what crimes of a similar nature were once committed in the name of truth.

Dublin, December 1993.

'Thou know'st the mask of night
is on my face . . .'

William Shakespeare: *Romeo and Juliet*

Prologue

Hotel della Principessa,
Venice
2 July 1914

My dear old chap,

I write propped up in bed — such a huge bed — in a palazzo overlooking a busy waterway. The building is a mixture of the oriental and the Mediterranean, built on a sunken foundation of oak piles. There are boxes of geraniums on the windowsills, and shutters admit shafts of light on to a mosaic floor. Outside, the water laps against the steps and a row of tethered gondolas waits like black swans. There are scents of herbs and spices in the air. Does that not sound like some kind of Shangri-la, beautiful and strange, instead of a city hotel on the Adriatic seaboard?

We arrived two weeks ago. Northern Italy is a land of contrasts, lakes like mirrors, mountains of snow-capped majesty, so different from the misty peaks and greens of home. We stayed at Como for three days. Then there was Milan, followed by the ancient towns of Verona and Padua and now Venice. We go to Florence next and then on to Rome.

I would like to describe the whole of our journey, but there is so much to tell that it must await another missive. We have as travelling companion a fellow countryman, Monsignor Dillon from Limerick, now attached to the Holy See. He is visiting the house belonging to his Order in Venice, and also some friends, people by the name of di Robenico. They are an old family of merchant stock, who own a great house on the Rio San Bernardo, where, as friends of the monsignor, we were recently conducted by gondola to dine in style. The monsignor will also accompany us to Rome, which is opportune, as he is fluent in the language and well acquainted with Italians of position. Your mother, be it said, is not overjoyed at this prospect, but I have pointed out how far the benefits outweigh the inconveniences.

She is bearing up extraordinarily well under the rigours of our travels, and undertakes everything with indefatigable zest. I, however, am in bed today; nothing serious, a touch of fever probably brought on by fatigue, but it gives me time to put pen to paper. I know I have been neglectful of you of late, and there is something I must tell you.

When I commented to Monsignor Dillon that the Middle Ages seemed to breathe down one's neck in this extraordinary city, he told me a little of the hidden history of this place, and intimated private knowledge of ungodly activities dating from the seventeenth century. He made much of this, pursing his mouth in the manner of one divulging only so much. He spoke of the position Venice once held as a free city; and then he dropped his voice and mentioned the presence here long ago of an inquisitor, a pillar of the Church who had forsaken his religion and turned to magic and the practice of the occult.

This man, said to have been a considerable mage, crafted, or chanced upon, a strange artefact, which he used as a focus for his power. This apostate priest is said, moreover, to have sold his soul for the artefact, which is presently being desperately sought by certain of the city's inheritors. It was kept hidden until recent times, when it mysteriously vanished, stolen by persons unknown. At least this was his story.

The monsignor told us this while we were at table in the dining hall of the di Robenicos', a room splendid with mosaic and hung with paintings. I was much more interested in my surroundings than I was in the ramblings of my neighbour, suspecting that his eloquence was due to a combination of the fine Antinori which he was imbibing in quantity, and the sweep of his Irish imagination; but I humoured him by listening. Then our host, a middle-aged man of distinguished bearing, pricked up his ears; my curiosity was whetted when he attempted to deflect the monsignor's confidences by changing the subject. I watched di Robenico carefully, somewhat astonished to find him agitated by a tale told by a prelate who was so obviously into his cups. Signore di Robenico speaks English well, and asked me what I had seen of the city. He spoke too of Dublin, which he had visited once in his youth. He was charming to your mother, who was seated on his right hand, and who was, I must say, looking particularly fetching. His wife sat at the other end of the long table, cooed at her husband *'Salvatore mio'*, and flashed her smile and her eyes among her guests, commenting in her heavy accent on some triviality, but with great gaiety so that everyone laughed.

Afterwards the monsignor, who was, if anything, in an even more inebriated state, whispered as we returned to the hotel that there was a secret society built around the legacy of this turncoat inquisitor. 'I assure you, this is a city which would have much to tell if cities could be brought to the confessional . . .' He nodded his head a little unsteadily in the gloom. 'They are looking for what has been lost . . . the focus of the old power. Great changes in the world may be pending. Now, if our Holy Mother were to have custody of this diabolical artefact . . .'

Your mother turned her head to look at me, and I could sense her exasperation. We glided in silence then, except for the whisper of the water, and were deposited at the hotel. The monsignor continued on his way to his accommodation with his Order, who have a church on one of the canals.

Pondering on the matter during the night, I found that my curiosity was greatly whetted. I

12

had never in my life imagined an apostate inquisitor; by definition they were the bastions of the Church, the hands, eyes and ears of the most Holy Inquisition, and the hammer of all — particularly women — who dared to deviate. I did not see the monsignor the next day, but I made as many discreet inquiries as I could. The answers were all evasive. When next I met him I questioned him, but he appeared embarrassed in the cold light of sobriety, and cautioned me against taking his conversation on the matter too seriously.

'But was there ever an apostate inquisitor?' I demanded, and he conceded eventually that there had been.

'Why did he turn his coat?'

He looked at me and curled his lip. 'Why do you think? He was brought down by a woman!' He rolled the word 'woman' on his tongue in such an offensive way that I was glad your mother was not present.

But I persisted in my questions. From where, I asked him, was this artefact stolen? What did it consist of? Why was the matter so important that Signore di Robenico evinced such malaise when it was mentioned?

He would not be drawn further, however, and bade me think no more of it.

But this proved impossible. I asked him later, having done some fruitless research, why this story was not chronicled.

'It was,' he said. 'A Jesuit novice who called

himself "a Witness" kept a diary of sorts, but it is not available for lay perusal.' And again he cautioned me to put the matter out of my mind. 'It's only a story,' he said.

As the days went by, though, I became fascinated more by the general desire for its concealment than by the story itself, which I regarded as little more than a myth. I have long been convinced that our own insular position on the fringe of Europe has fostered the restless Irish penchant for the shrouded and the mysterious. So my inquiry was more than an amusement for me; it was irresistible, a perfect holiday dalliance, if I may so describe it.

However, my 'dalliance' assumed an unforeseeable dimension last Wednesday night — a moment of serendipity, such as probably touches the lives of everyone at one time or other, though not, perhaps, in so definite a form. This is the nub of what I have to tell you — so pay attention, and when you have read my words you must destroy this letter.

On Wednesday night I found a ring. It was on the hand of a crumbling statue in a wall niche, a sculpture so old that it surely dated back several centuries. How the ring could have been put on that stone hand, what art, what craft, could have put it there, remains a mystery, for the fingers were bent and holding a stone book, to which they were joined by the skill of the artist. I chanced on it while wandering late and alone through the small shadowy piazzettas, over the little hump-backed bridges above the canals, where the gondolas emerge out of the night with a swish, and then vanish almost soundlessly into one or other dark waterway of this most sinister of cities.

The statue of which I speak was of a man in a long robe, wearing a cap (perhaps a lawyer's cap), and holding a book. My attention was arrested by the face, the expression of unbridled power and, even more so, by the underlying despair so subtly worked into the lineaments. Perhaps my imagination was heightened by the silence and the darkness but, being impressed by the genius of the sculptor, and acting on an impulse, I put up my hand to touch the statue. You can imagine my consternation when most of the arm came away and crashed to the ground, the hand still clutching the book. It was only then that I saw the ring, for the hand was hidden behind the object it held, and the ring was not visible to the passerby.

I looked around me, but the piazzetta, which was far from the Grand Canal — the principal thoroughfare — was empty, half lit, its corners dark. Only the quiet splashing of a small fountain nearby disturbed the silence. I must confess that my heart was racing as I took up the broken arm and allowed it fall again, so that the hand cracked and came away from the stone book and I was able, with surprising ease, to remove the ring from the severed finger.

Do not think ill of your father. My mind continues to be greatly troubled by the episode.

I brought the ring back to the hotel, promising myself that I would give it up to the authorities in the morning. I washed it. It is certainly gold. The signet is curious. I took a rubbing of it with a pencil and piece of paper and showed the result to Signore di Robenico when he and his wife were our guests for luncheon the following day. He evinced such wonder (and his wife gave cries of *'Che strano! Guarda, che meraviglioso!'*), asked many questions — which, being determined not to disclose the truth to him, I managed to parry with ostensible tourist ignorance.

I have resolved to keep the ring, for two reasons. The first is the fervid interest of Signore di Robenico, which he tries unsuccessfully to conceal. The second is because the monsignor, when I asked him why the signore should have been so intrigued, looked at the rubbing and informed me that it is the symbol of the secret society to which I have already referred. He also evinced great curiosity as to the source of my rubbing, and I told him I had taken it at night on impulse, and was not sure where. However, if what he says is true, it might lead me to the discovery of the old artefact used by this mage of the seventeenth century to focus his occult power. If the ring I have found belonged to the same gentleman, perhaps I shall continue to be blessed with fortuitous circumstance. It would indeed be amusing if a stranger to the city, a tourist, were to locate something which the city fathers have been seeking for some considerable time.

To tell the truth, I am also extremely reluctant to come forward at this late stage, for fear of aspersion on my character. Even on foreign soil, one must remember one's position as a member of the House.

There is also the difficulty that, although I tried to find the piazzetta the very next day, and have tried to do so each day since, I have not located it. I walked for hours, thinking that I might leave the ring back with the broken statue, and so salve my conscience and put an end to the matter. But I could not find the little square with the wall niche and the statue and the fountain. It is as though it has disappeared from the face of the earth. I can only conclude that it looked so different in the shadows of night that I cannot recognize it. But this city is like a maze and it is no great wonder that a foreigner would get lost.

I have sent the ring home to you. It will arrive in a parcel about the size of a chocolate box; the rest of the box is packed with newspapers and a couple of glass paperweights to give it substance. I hope I have not done wrong, but as God is my witness I intended no harm.

Your mother knows nothing of what I have just written — except, of course, that she saw the rubbing to which I have referred, and has questioned me about it with some anxiety. I have not shared the truth with her. I do not wish to burden her with what she would certainly regard as a wrongdoing on my part, but she seemed to sense anyway there is more to the matter than meets the eye. However, she is busy now with her sightseeing, and has let the matter of the rubbing drop. It would seem that Signora di Robenico has taken a great fancy to her. She invites her for tea and to visit friends, and is so kind as to send a gondola for her on each occasion; your mother is vibrant as I have not seen her for years.

Today, as I am poorly, she offered to stay behind to look after me, but I insisted that she honour her engagements. I have seen a great deal of the city, and have contemplated in St Mark's the pillar where the saint's relics were hidden until disclosed by a miracle; for Venetians it is the place where the past and the present are concentrated, as though it were the entrance to the world beyond our ken.

But now that I have written to you, I have no wish to do other than gaze out at the red-tiled roofs and the bustle on the Grand Canal. My mind is troubled, not only by what I have just told you, but also by the prospect of a war in Europe before the year's end, which *The Times* (available here but several days old) indicates as a repercussion from the recent assassination of the archduke and his wife in Sarajevo. Pray God this forecast is mistaken. We are at the dawn of a new age, a new enlightenment, and the prospect of it being destroyed by the carnage and the entrenched hatreds generated by war is too terrible to contemplate. It would also have adverse consequences in terms of the implementation of Home Rule for our country, which as you know is the dream to which I have pledged my political life.

I look forward to our reunion, when I will have much to tell you. I hope your examinations have gone well, and I wish you God's blessing in all your life's endeavours, my dearest boy.

Your loving,
Father.

PS. Keep the ring safe. Tell my dear little P. we send our love.

Nearly half a century later, Dee found this letter in the ruined library of the big house. She was nine. She read the stained document with difficulty before throwing it away.

Chapter One

'The woman has not recanted,' the cardinal said. 'Deliver her to the torture.'
The inquisitor bowed and withdrew.

Journal of a Witness

Summer! After a mild spring, an uncertain rainy April, high summer had arrived with everything going for it. Jenny was twelve. Tomorrow she was having a party. Today she was cutting the grass and looking around with pleasure at the garden.

The roses blazed, the lupine were all pink elegance, and the hollyhocks stood up like soldiers by the garden wall. Daisies sprinkled the lawn, but Jenny mourned them only briefly as she cut their heads off with the lawnmower. There they were, white-petalled, gold-centred, on delicate little stalks, and along came the mower with its busy rattle and all the little white-gold heads were flung up in the air and then lay crumpled. Fandango, the cat, a black fellow with white socks, stalked the garden path, lurked behind a hebe shrub, and occasionally dashed out to put manners on drifting wisps of grass. 'Waiting to spring out on Gramps,' her grandfather had said of Fandango in a letter, when Jenny had gone for a short holiday to the country, 'and carry him off

20

to his own private den!'

The sunshine was hot on her back, but her eyes were shaded under the white cotton sun-hat with its wide brim, dug out of her summer-clothes chest and pulled down over her thick brown hair. She concentrated on the grass, felt the satisfaction of the cutting blades, glanced at the portion of the lawn yet to be done. Beyond the lawn was the toolshed, swathed in morning glory. It was home to Gramps' tools, garden implements, potted plants, a roll of wire netting and a pair of thick black gloves. There was also a box of odds and ends in the shed, a gardening manual, a broken pair of secateurs, a roll of green twine, and a cardboard file containing damp, smelly pages. But there had been something else at the bottom of the box, which she had herself put there; an odd thing — a hard, enamelled silver mask. Jenny had found it some time before when she had explored the attic. It had been on its own in a leather case. She had taken it down to the shed so she could see it properly in the light. But the feel of it on her face had frightened her, so she had wrapped it in layers of paper inside a brown paper bag and left it at the bottom of Gramps' box. Sometimes she searched for it, unwrapped it carefully. It stared at her with empty eye-sockets; its open mouth wanted to speak. She had seen sneers before, particularly when she had changed schools and had run the gauntlet of her new class, but the faces of her classmates had never contained so

bloodless and inhuman an expression. She felt
that the mask knew her.

Once she made a drawing of it in her school art
book, painted it in with watercolours.

'What's this, Jenny?' her teacher had inquired.

'It's a mask, Miss!'

'I suppose it must be a carnival mask!' Miss
Rogerson said doubtfully. 'Where did you see
it?'

But Jenny had shrugged. It was a secret. She
did not tell anyone, not even Gramps. She did
not tell anyone what she had seen when she had
worn the mask.

Jenny did not remember her mother, who had
died shortly after her birth. There were pictures
of her in the photo album, a small-waisted young
woman in a summer dress, with her hair full and
swept up on top of her head. Most of the photographs had been taken in the same garden that
Jenny knew so well.

'Dat's my muddy,' she used to say to herself
when she was three, to remind herself that she
had a mummy like everyone else. Papa said that
Mummy had been the most beautiful woman in
the world. Jenny knew that this was true and she
felt very important because of it. But she also
sensed in her father a melancholy, a raggedness
of the spirit which was directed at her, as though
he blamed her, in spite of himself, for something. What this was Jenny did not know, but it
made her a little wary of her father. On his last
visit home he had sometimes been the worse for

drink, and this bewildered her. Her unreserved love and trust was for Gramps.

'My mummy was the most beautiful woman in the world,' Jenny told the girls in infants' class when she went to school. Later, having been informed by their own doting parents of the truth, they whispered among themselves in awe and compassion, 'Her mum's dead . . .'

She had been brought up by her father and by Gramps; the three of them lived together in Gramps' house. Papa was away a lot. He was secretary to Sir Michael, a rich man who wrote travel books. When he was at home, and in a good mood, he sometimes read Jenny stories, told her about Italy where it was very hot and where he had spent some time on his last trip overseas. He would open her school atlas and tap his finger on the long boot of Italy. 'See, I was here. It is so different to England. All the smells are different, the food is so different, the sun shines nearly all the time and people, even poor people, are very happy.'

But on his return the last time he had seen her painting of the mask, started. 'Where did you see that?'

'It's in the shed,' she said hesitantly. 'I found it in the attic.'

Papa had been very angry. 'You are not — do you understand me — you are *not* to take things out of the attic. You are not to play with that mask!'

'I only look at it,' Jenny said. 'I like to look at

it! I like to feel it.'

'You don't know where that thing came from, child!'

'It belongs to me!' Jenny said slowly in a stubborn voice, in which the wish to give vent to desperate tears struggled for concealment.

He had stared at her for a moment before turning to Gramps with ill-concealed irritation. 'She has become very wilful!' Then he had gone into the garden and found the mask, taken it away from the shed.

'Where did you put the mask, Papa?' she asked him later, because she needed to see and touch it, and he answered coldly, with grim parental satisfaction, 'Where you won't find it, young lady!'

'Please, Papa . . .'

He turned on her angrily, his eyes stern, his moustache bristling. 'No! I intend to sell it sometime. You are never to play with it again! Do you understand me, Jen?'

She looked away. 'Yes, Papa.'

Gramps had been consoling when he had had her to himself later that evening.

'That strange old thing is not suitable as a toy, Jen. I know where your father has put it, and it's safe. Don't think about it any more now.'

But this was not possible. Not only did she think about it, but she remembered what she had seen when she had put it on. Staring through the eye-sockets she had looked back along the length of the garden from the window of the toolshed.

But the house was silent, with dark, brooding windows, and Fandango was lying dead, eyes liquefying, bones visible under matted fur. The world contained neither Gramps nor Papa; it had changed into an intensely lonely place. She felt suddenly that she was being watched and she had torn off the mask, found that the house was still there with friendly, open windows, and Fandango sunning himself on the quiet windowsill; everything was normal. She had never looked through it again. But despite this there had been a sense of complicity, as though the effect of the mask, at some inaccessible level, was something she understood.

'Gramps,' Jenny asked the day after her party. 'When is Papa coming back?' She had not seen him for three months and there had been no letter for her birthday. She had been thinking that when he came back she would impress him with the essay she had written about the fox-cubs, which Miss Rogerson had praised and made her read out to the class. Maybe then he would love her and let her see the mask.

He might say, 'How's my sweetheart?' as Yvonne's father said to her when he came home. She fantasized about this, and also thought of the present he would bring, an especially nice one because she had had a birthday. He nearly always brought her something: a doll, sometimes a dress. Once he had brought her a little clock which had a wooden cuckoo behind two tiny doors. The clock had weights and the little bird would dash out on the hour and sing, 'Cuckoo, cuckoo.' It was broken now because she had let it fall one day when she was trying to find out how it worked.

But now her grandfather's face looked troubled and he took her on his knee. 'Jen, I got a wire this morning while you were still in bed . . . I do not know how to tell you what was in it.'

Jenny knew at once that something had happened to Papa. She waited, her breath stuck in her chest.

'My dear, your father had an accident . . . It happened in Paris . . . he was knocked down by a motor car.'

'Oh . . .' Jenny whispered, a whisper in which all the fantasies of a loving father coming home, laden with praises and presents, shrivelled and died. She knew from the pain she could sense in Gramps, and by his hesitancy, what was coming next.

'Jen, my darling, I'm afraid he's dead . . .'

Jenny slipped off her grandfather's knee, went to the couch in the sitting room and lay on it, curled up, her head against her knees, rocking herself. Gramps came and sat beside her in silence.

'I want to see him!' she sobbed. 'I wanted to show him my essay . . .'

The old face beside her registered melancholy disquiet. He reached out and put his arms around her. 'They will bring him home.'

Jenny smelt the tweed jacket, buried her face

in the angle of his head and shoulder, felt the warm, rubbery, slightly bristly cheek against hers. As always, there was the scent of pear drops, to which Gramps was partial, mixed with the scent of tobacco.

On the evening of the day following Papa's funeral, Jenny went into the garden, wandered into the shed. Her mind was full of her father. Where was he now? Was he looking down at her from Heaven? She thought of the mask. She knew Papa had taken it away, but she glanced into the box all the same. She wanted to hold it. It would make her feel that everything was possible, that perceptions were only opinions, that even death was not immutable.

She needed comfort. She had been feeling unwell since morning, a dizziness, a sense of being cold and shivery, a sore throat, difficulty in swallowing. She sat in the shed because she was so tired, and after a while went back into the house.

Her grandfather was in the hall. He was talking to Mary, the new maid, who was polishing the brasses on the front door. Mary had come from Scotland and seemed happy with them.

'Gramps, where is the mask? What happened to it?'

He looked at her over his glasses, glanced at Mary, and then back at his granddaughter. His grey eyebrows were tangled and met as he frowned. His eyes, which always twinkled, were speculative and still. He put his hand on her head, stroked her hair. For a moment she was afraid he might deny any knowledge of it.

'I have it safe,' he said after a moment. 'Don't worry; it's your mask now and I have it where no one will touch it.'

Then he asked, regarding her with sudden intentness, seeing that her eyes were glazed and her cheeks flushed, 'Are you sickening, child?'

Jenny nodded. 'I don't feel well; my throat is sore and my legs are all wobbly.'

Grandpa, looking suddenly afraid, glanced at Mary. She crossed the hall and put a hand on Jenny's forehead, felt the side of her neck. 'The bairn's burning, sir. She'd best be put to bed.'

She took Jenny by the hand and led her upstairs.

After that, Jenny lost track of time. Sometimes it was morning, and sometimes the night was there. The afternoons were lost. There were no days any more, just a contracting space in which she struggled to live. The doctor came with his funny bag full of little drawers and talked about her fever in low, professional tones. She heard words: 'potential brain damage if it stays that high . . .'

Mary sponged her; her hair was cut and the new sharp ends tickled her neck. She asked Gramps about the mask. 'Do you want it, darling?'

She nodded and he brought it to her. It stared at her with knowing eye-sockets. She touched it and pushed it under her pillow.

Later, as she lay bathed in sweat, she saw the carved wardrobe door assume a face and talk to her. It told her to put on the mask. She struggled to find it under her pillow, dragged it out and rested it on her face. Looking through it she saw a man watching her, looking down at her. He smiled, gentled her, said she would come back now and all would be well. 'Keep on the mask,' he said.

For a moment Jenny thought this man was Papa, and then she realized her mistake. Not you, she thought, recognizing him, not you after all this time!

She clutched at the mask. She had no strength left. She slipped towards coma, felt the life begin to drain from her, or rather with her, bearing her away. It was the easiest thing in the world.

Gramps, who had been out of the room for a moment, came back, drew his chair close and sat beside her, held her hand and removed the mask which had slipped from her face. He had attended enough death-beds to know crisis when he saw it, and after he had called to Mary to go at once for the doctor he turned on Jenny the whole of his will.

'Don't die on me, darling; don't leave your old Gramps . . . what would I do? And Fandango would miss you; everyone is asking for you. Yvonne and Mrs Stacey were asking for you today!' He sponged her forehead and his voice broke. 'Don't die!'

Jenny did not respond, but after a moment she murmured thickly, without opening her eyes, 'I think he's in the wardrobe,' and she moved convulsively.

Grandpa didn't turn a hair. He reached for the wardrobe door and opened it. 'It's empty,' he whispered. 'There's no one there . . . Stay with us, Jen.'

The morning came eventually, after an interminable night of hallucination. She felt cool. There was a long, healing sleep waiting for her, and she went towards it like someone coming home. She heard Mary's whisper, 'The fever's broken,' and Gramp's stiff response, in which control struggled with overwhelming relief. 'Thank God . . . Thank God.'

Grandpa took the mask and put it in his own room. Mary hung a picture in Jenny's room of a pretty young woman with very large and limpid eyes who was holding a lamp in her arms. Mary thought this a much more suitable thing for a young girl to look at than that frightful mask.

Jenny convalesced. She thought she was better, was glad to see her friends. Yvonne Stacey, the doctor's daughter, came to call, bringing her brother Andrew. They pretended not to notice how she had changed. Andrew repeated talk he had heard that there might be a war. 'I would like to go, if there is.' He was sixteen, far too young for the fray, Gramps said. If there was a war, he added, it would be over quickly. But Andrew did not agree. He said it would go on for years. He said this as if he hoped it would be the case.

They played gin rummy, then brother and sister went into the garden, teased and petted Fandango, who smiled at them from his sunny corner near the toolshed, taking the odd mock swipe at hands that became too impertinent. Jenny watched from her cane armchair near the back door. Gramps had installed her there, with a rug over her knees.

She wanted to tell her grandfather that she didn't want the rug, but couldn't. Since her illness she had difficulty in speaking; the words would trip and halt abruptly.

The doctor, having listened to her attempts to communicate, had shaken his head and turned to Gramps, drawn him into the landing for a whispered conference. She heard him say things like 'shock', 'anxiety', and 'damage can't be ruled out . . .' Gramps had come back looking even older.

Now Jenny said, 'Don't . . . want . . . rug!' She spat out the words angrily, but she knew that the crosser she got, the worse the problem would become.

The old man frowned, a frown full of concern, and he took the rug from her knees only to put it around her feet. 'Bear with me, darling. You have been very sick and I want to mind you!'

She knew she had become very thin and that

she looked terrible with short hair, like a boy. Yvonne said it was becoming. Andrew agreed with her, but she could sense his private dismay that illness could change someone so much; that they could have difficulty in speaking. He was friendly to her, like a brother, and he came frequently with Yvonne. He had sandy hair which fell in a straight, silken flap across his forehead, and which glinted when the sun caught it. He didn't say very much, relying on his sister to make conversation.

Jenny wept when she saw herself in the mirror. She thought of the mask which she had not seen since her illness, and searched in her room for it, but it was gone. Grandpa told her not to worry about it. 'I put it away again, darling. Best thing to do. But it's yours.'

Sometimes, that summer, Jenny would take the train with her grandfather and visit the zoo, spend time in St James's Park, feed the pigeons in Trafalgar Square, watch the Changing of the Guard. The weeks passed, became months, and then the winter came and yielded to spring and the months went on, changing from season to season and becoming years. During this time, Jenny's hair had grown long again, and the war, which Andrew and Gramps had spoken of, had come.

Jenny knew about the war. It was the fault of the Kaiser. England was going to win and big battles were being fought in France. She saw plenty of soldiers whenever they went up to town. Gramps said they were manning the air-defences. Once she had even seen a Zeppelin, a huge, cigar-shaped thing in the sky. It had been shot down by a small plane which went up and up and up, like a crazed moth, until the goliath had burst into a sudden sheet of flame. Jenny could only think of the men in it who had died, and for a long time its destruction haunted her dreams. These nightmares upset Gramps, who seemed to regard her as fragile ever since her illness, as someone who must not be subjected to any nervous stress. She still had difficulty in speaking, and when she wept because of it, Gramps held her in his arms and told her she would get better after a while. 'Be patient, Jen. Patience hypnotizes Fate.'

'Will the Zeppelins . . . bomb . . . us?' she asked.

'Good heavens, no!'

They went up to town less often as the time passed, and one year replaced another. Gramps was tired, and busy with his writing. He was a member of the Fabians, wrote for a periodical, and would spend hours in the dining room poring over his scripts, pages of densely written sheets spread out on the table, his round spectacles perched on the middle of his nose.

The road where Jenny lived with her grandfather was a terrace of red brick Victorian houses, each with a big garden at the rear and a smaller one at the front. Every morning she went to school, dressed in her pinafore, overcoat and muffler, with her books tied in a strap. She had left her old junior school, and now she was attending Miss Peterhall's Academy, a school for young ladies in Wimbledon.

Yvonne lived around the corner from Jenny, and they went to school together every morning. They would get the omnibus and, sitting together on the upper deck, Yvonne would talk of the war.

Andrew had run away to enlist; had lied about his age. He had done so just two weeks after their mother's sudden death from a stroke. He was now in France.

'Would you like to do something when you grow up?' Yvonne asked her. 'I mean, to get a job, or something. I don't want to stay at home! Too boring . . .'

Knowing Jenny well, Yvonne didn't mind if there was no answer, was used to interpreting for her friend the words she struggled to pronounce.

But today Jenny stared at Yvonne, saw her two red plaits, her pale blue eyes with stars in the iris, her cold sore on her upper lip, her quiet smile. A horse-drawn baker's van came around a corner with a clopping of hooves.

'I may not "grow up",' Jenny said, enunciating the words perfectly, as she sometimes did with short sentences. She saw the widened gaze of her companion, felt the strange, dream-like quality of the present, the stillness, the almost paralysed

sensation of time being frozen, as though someone had lowered a glass dome over her head. Her
own voice seemed to come from far away and in
that distance there was another vista, a glimpse
of sun-baked, red-tiled roofs, and dark waterways and flocks of house sparrows. She saw people in strange costumes, as though they were at a
fancy dress ball, but she heard nothing. The silence pervaded the present, made her feel invisible. She felt the tugging on her arm.

'Jen, are you all right?' and there beside her
was Yvonne's frowning face. The world was
back in sharp focus. Wimbledon Common, the
windmill, the ponds with the boys fishing for
tadpoles, the trees, the houses, were real again.
She felt terribly cold.

' 'Course,' she said, shaking her head.

They sat in silence.

'You said . . . you might not grow up,' Yvonne
said hesitantly after a moment. 'Why did you say
that?'

'Don't know. Am . . . grown up . . . for so
long!' She glanced at her friend, struggled for
words, became distressed.

Yvonne frowned and directed the conversation back to herself. 'I will be a nurse,' she said.
'I will wear a white uniform and a nurse's veil.'
Yvonne was now fifteen and longed to apply for
training; dreamt of joining Andrew in France.
But Jenny wasn't really listening. Her mind re-
played the sensation of a few minutes before,
and in the replay she heard the sound of water

lapping against stone and the thin, elegant music of a mandolin.

'Jenny Stephenson!'
Jenny started and gazed at her teacher. 'Would you favour us with your attention! Alternatively, if you are so interested in what is going on out of the window, out you go!'
Jenny gulped. 'Sorry.'
Miss Smith had a twist to her tongue when she was angry, and spared no one. She surveyed the class from her wooden dais, tapped her fingers against the lid of her desk. Behind her the blackboard was full of simple algebra problems. Through the window was the school garden, with its gravel walk and lawn where they played croquet in the summer. The sky was overcast, heavy with dark cloud; an intermittent sleet spat against the window. The fireplace was too small for the schoolroom. It was near the teacher's desk and the coals glowed in the grate with white ash. The girls at the back of the room shivered. They were all dressed in pinafores. Their coats were in the shoeroom, with their outdoor shoes. Near the door was a cupboard, painted dark green. This cupboard held the stacks of copybooks, pencils, ink, nibs, stacks of blotting paper and boxes of chalk.
Miss Smith was plump; she had dun-coloured hair which she wore pulled back and arranged in a loose bun at the back of her head. Her cheeks were red with tiny broken veins, and her brown

36

eyes were soft and flinty by turns. She was old, at least by her pupils' reckoning. Twenty-eight. She was being courted by a fellow teacher, a thirty-seven-year-old man who taught in the boys' school nearby.

'Jenny, come up and do that problem on the board.' Jenny looked around, saw Yvonne give her a tremulous smile. She did not want to go to the board and do the problem. She wanted to be back home with Gramps. She hated maths, especially algebra, to which the class had only recently been introduced; she couldn't keep her attention on it, and hadn't the faintest idea what it was about. But there was no gainsaying her teacher's command.

She rose, conscious of the small sea of faces, of the tall windows looking out on the garden, of the grey light from without, of the tense atmosphere in the room and the sudden small shivering sound as a few coals settled in the grate. She looked at the blackboard like someone from another world confronted by the unknown, took the piece of chalk in her hand. She moved forward to confront the problem she couldn't do, at least not through algebra.

'A woman buys two pints of milk and one loaf of bread for tenpence. Later she buys a similar loaf for sixpence. How much does one pint of milk cost?'

He was there again, without any warning at all, the man who had come to her when she was sick, who had stared down at her when she had worn the mask. His beard, which was cut close, hugged the lines of his face and outlined his mouth. It ended in a goatee. His eyes burned and the curve to his lip was the old quintessence of pride. Why is he back? she wondered dreamily, in the heightened awareness where she did not even register real surprise. His clothes were black, and the jewel on his left hand was as she remembered so long ago. He was in a dark place, but she felt rather than saw the light scintillate on the lagoon's water. Beside him was a black armillary sphere chased in silver.

She felt again the power of the old order that moulded every human life to its bidding, and she wanted, in an instant of weariness, to cry out in fear.

But his eyes despaired where once they had been hard with heaven's certainty.

'I will save you,' he said, 'if you will obey me. You must find the mask.' She heard her soul answer, 'I will never obey you. Do you think I am to be won to your lies, no matter what you say?'

The chalk moved in her raised hand and she watched as it finished the problem, knew that her teacher's silence was indicative of astonishment, felt the silent class behind her.

'Let the loaf equal x;
Let the milk equal y;
$\therefore 2y + x = 10d$
Also $x = 6d$
Find y.'

38

Jenny did not pause to think. She let the momentum of her strangely knowing fingers deal with the problem.

$$2y + 6d = 10d$$
$$\ldots 2y = 10d - 6d$$
$$2y = 4d$$
$$\ldots y = 2d$$

'Has she done it done right, girls?' She heard Miss Smith's voice. 'Hands up everyone who has the same answer.' Jenny knew, without turning, that the hands of all the brightest and best in the class were raised.

'Good girl, Jenny,' Miss Smith said. Jenny turned. She saw the twenty faces before her, some of them suety faces that would be old at thirty, heavy with jowls and disappointment. She saw the rain against the window. She saw her own place at the desk with the inkwell full of pencil shavings. The shavings suddenly seemed to represent what she could expect of life, all the years of it, dry and pointless like small wooden trimmings. She reached for him, one fear having overtaken another; if she could go back — to the place where life was hammered on an anvil, where the innermost reaches of the spirit were invoked as common currency, where she could speak with her old fire — would it matter what the price?

'Come back . . . don't go,' and again, but more distant, she heard the echo of his voice, 'Will you obey me now?' and again she answered, 'I will never obey you!'

That evening, Miss Smith spoke to her lover, 'I had a strange experience today!'

Frank Brinsley was lying back on the sofa in Miss Smith's sitting room. He was contemplating the curve of her hips, letting his imagination run riot. She was clever and respectable, but he knew that she was also human and he was prepared to wait.

'What kind of experience, sweetheart?' he murmured.

'One of the girls — Jenny Stephenson — did an algebra problem. She's normally quite useless at maths, but she did this so quickly that it was like lightning. It was idiotically simple, of course, but the format is still strange to them all. Funny girl. She was very sick some time ago, I understand, she's never been the same since — speech impediment . . .'

He stood up to put an arm around her. 'Poor kid. But children are full of surprises. Useless one minute, and struck with blinding illumination the next! Understanding comes like that! Being sick may have concentrated her mind in some way.' He stroked her arm, drew her towards the sofa. 'Maybe she's a child prodigy. Come and sit down and tell me about it.'

'She's no prodigy,' Miss Smith said. 'She's a bit strange in herself sometimes, has a vivid imagination, but she's no prodigy!'

'Is she pretty?'

She looked at him. 'For God's sake, Frank — she's a child. But she has something. Presence, perhaps. And a peculiar arrogance which I think is unconscious.'

She turned to him, felt his oh-so-gentle fingers suddenly on her breast. She removed them. 'I thought we were going out!'

'I am out,' he whispered. 'Out of my mind. How can you be so cruel?' He raised her face to his, stroked her lower lip with his index finger. 'Just one little kiss?'

Miss Smith heard the rain outside, heard the sputtering of the gas fire, felt the shiver of sexual excitement from breast to belly to toes, felt his leisurely tongue in her mouth, felt his wiry moustache against her upper lip. Discovery clamoured. His kiss became more urgent; his hands moved from breast to belly to the hem of her skirt. His breathing quickened.

'Don't,' she said, but he did not heed her and she made no further move to stop him. Afterwards she wondered if she had been mad.

'You're very busy this evening!' Gramps said to Jenny. She was bent over her homework, her hair alive in the gaslight, her slim white fingers holding the pen. Her hair had grown again and she wore it down her back, but its luxuriance made her face appear a bit pinched. She finished her essay, put down her pen.

'I'm tired . . . Gramps.'

'Hard day at school?'

Jenny breathed in, so she could articulate on the expulsion of the breath. 'I did . . . algebra problem . . . blackboard.'

He waited, knowing Jenny's aversion to maths. Fandango lifted his head from his basket and listened, his feral eyes half shut, his whiskers knowledgeable.

'I did it . . . right!'

'Good girl!'

Jenny saw the smile in her grandfather's grey eyes. She sighed and stood up. 'I'll go . . . to bed now!'

She went into the kitchen, where Mary filled her ceramic hot jar and gave it to her wrapped in a towel. Then she went back to the dining room, where her grandfather kissed her upturned face tenderly.

'Goodnight, Jen, sleep well.'

' 'Night, Gramps!'

In her bedroom, she knelt and said her short prayer, and then climbed into bed, shivering between the icy sheets, embracing the hot jar. Moonlight crept through the chink in the curtains. The hot, still core of her mind burned, but the fatigue of her body dragged her towards sleep.

Suddenly he was back. He was very silent, very dark. 'Obey me,' he said eventually. 'It will be all right, only you must come to me. I will never hurt you again. I will save you. I will restore you.

42

But you must find the mask.'

Something leapt in Jenny. She could go back. He would save her, if she went to him. And then a cold, tired watcher in her mind answered for her: 'No.'

'Then I must come to you!' he said softly.

'Fiddlesticks,' Jenny whispered in the mental world where she was perfectly articulate, ignoring the palpitations of her heart. 'You cannot! Do you think Time will do your bidding? Do you think the wheel of creation is subject to your will? What you did to me, and others like me, is over. The power that sanctioned it is not a real power in this land or in this time!'

'Nothing is ever "over",' he said mournfully. 'I love you and I am coming to find you.'

'You cannot,' she said.

But although she waited fearfully for an answer, he was gone.

Chapter Two

'She is young; she may recant in time.'
'There is no time. Presumption demands a penalty.'

Journal of a Witness

The war went on. Hundreds of thousands of young men marched into France. And France swallowed them, ground them into dust. There was the Verdun Mill, the Somme, Ypres, Flanders. The youth of Europe was broken, the blood of a generation poured into the soil.

'What is the war for?' Jenny demanded.

Gramps sighed. 'It's for greed.' There was a bitter line to his mouth. 'Capitalist greed and stupidity. I tell you this, Jen, after this war everything will change. No one will ever believe again in the morality of authority.'

He was thinking of young Andrew Stacey, who had gone to the war; of the insanity of accepting so young a recruit: they would have known he was under the minimum age and had turned a blind eye to it. Andrew's mother had died shortly before he enlisted. She had complained of feeling unwell and had retired to bed early. When her husband had returned home from a dinner at his club, she was already dead. Two weeks later, Andrew, desperate and running from his grief, had enlisted.

Jenny had grown. Breasts had started to bud. Body hair had appeared in private places, to her intense dismay. She was fourteen. Mary let her skirts down. One morning, to her terror, she found blood in her knickers. She told Yvonne, sure that she was going to die, but Yvonne said it was natural. 'It happens once a month. You just fix yourself up and get on with it!'

'I don't believe you!' Jenny said, aghast. 'I never heard anything so horrible!'

Yvonne shrugged. 'It's not horrible. It's just different to men. Mamma used to say it was a symbol of power. She said every woman should recognize that!'

Jen looked at her friend with compassion and love. She was only too well aware of the quiver of her friend's mouth every time she mentioned her mother.

'There's no power in bleeding . . . down there, or anywhere else,' Jenny muttered, feeling a sudden desire to weep with outrage. She paused. 'You mean all women have to put up with that!'

Yvonne shook her head, looked at her friend's furious face. She had never seen her in such a passion. 'Do you not know anything, Jenny Stephenson?' she asked in her calm, pragmatic voice. 'Women bleed so that people can exist, so there can be babies.' She paused before adding

45

with some satisfaction, 'Women make the world.'

Jenny looked at her suspiciously. 'Don't tell me you've started this, too?'

Yvonne smiled. 'Of course. You may be late because you were so ill . . .'

Some time after this, Gramps tried to talk to her. His voice went a bit squeaky.

'You're growing up, Jen. There are things you should know about growing up, about becoming a woman . . . Will I ask Mary to talk to you?' He dropped his pipe in his embarrassment, picked it up, fumbled in his pocket for his lucifers.

'I know everything,' Jenny said in a burst of furious fluency. 'I don't want to hear anything more about anything!' She stormed up to her room and threw herself on the bed, cried hot, angry tears. 'Why do things have to happen whether we like them or not?' she demanded of the moon-faced maiden in the picture over her bed. 'Things which interfere with our bodies? It's intolerable!'

The maiden looked back at her with limpid eyes devoid of intelligence. It was apparent at a glance that she could never have had a period. Jenny took down the picture. 'I hate you,' she said fluently and contemptuously, 'you look idiotic. I can't stand your silly smirk,' and she stuffed the picture behind the chest of drawers. In the kitchen, Gramps raised his eyebrows. He never mentioned the subject again.

Winter gave way to spring. In the trenches the

men endured the routine, stand-to at dawn, digging, wiring, keeping watch from the 'firing step'.

The fat lice roamed everywhere; the rats gnawed on the dead; there was the stench of faeces, trench-foot, carrion. The hurriedly dug graves were excavated by shells and the corpses lay with hands outstretched, as though beseeching a second opinion. Soldiers, inured to hardship and deprivation, acquired the 'thousand-yard stare'. Here and there young men went mad, refused to obey orders, became hysterical, were executed. The mud squelched underfoot; the cold, the noise of the guns and the interminable ennui made for volunteers, ready to go raiding on enemy lines, armed with knives and grenades and entrenching tools.

Andrew Stacey had been raiding the night before. He knew he had been lucky to have come back; one of his mates, crouching beside him, had been shot through the head.

When the letters were distributed there was one for him, enclosing a letter from his father, one from Yvonne, and a note from Jenny. A photograph fell out, and landed face upwards in the mud. It had rained in the early morning, and the ground was soft, with small rivulets and pools. He retrieved the photograph, wiped the mud from its back on his trousers, and took his correspondence to a quiet corner of the trench and read.

'Dear Andrew,' Jenny's note read, 'Yvonne

said she was writing and I thought I would send you a line to wish you well and say how much we all look forward to your return. Jen.'

Andrew reread this letter several times, and then folded it up with the others and put them into his pocket. He was just seventeen. He had lied about his age when he had responded to Kitchener's recruiting poster. He had told whatever lies were necessary to embark on this great adventure. His mother's death, sudden and without time to say goodbye, had decided him. She had left a void nothing could fill.

Andrew had not told the recruiting sergeant that. Neither had he told him that he was sixteen and that he had a toothache. He had not dreamt of the horror for which he had volunteered. He had not imagined what it would be like to put a bayonet through the heart of a boy not much older than himself and twist it, and then stick it in again and again until the flaxen-haired stranger lay still with blank, dead eyes open to the morning sky. He had never given any real thought to the prospect of dismembered bodies lying in the mud. He wanted to be home with a passion that filled the whole of his soul. He remembered his mother's insistence on neatness and hygiene; once he had resisted it, but now he longed for it. He wanted clean sheets and home-made bread and cleanliness; he wanted to be in a place where he would never again run a candle flame along the seams of his shirt to kill the lice. He wanted his illusions — that he was brave, that the war embodied the high romance of adventure — when he knew now that war was an invention of the devil and that he himself was merely a coward. Above all, he wanted the peace of his lost innocence.

He looked down along the trench. The mud was trampled; two bodies from the night before lay stacked to one side for removal. A rat with a long thin tail came scuttling, and gnawed dead fingers with straight front teeth. A soldier chased the rat, jumped on it with a helmet, sat on it until the rat was suffocated in the mud. When the rattle of the trapped animal ceased he lifted the helmet and took the dead rat away to wash and cook it.

Andrew took a piece of paper from his pocket and tried to write. He had an hour before he was back on watch. He thought of his father and his sister; he saw her freckles and blue eyes, remembered her wish to be a nurse, wondered what she would think if she could see the carnage. But knowing Yvonne she would endure it all with quiet practicality; think only of what could be done to alleviate the suffering.

He had never been to one of the field hospitals behind the lines where the nurses cared for the wounded and the dying. He had imagined it as a place with white sheets and green lawns, whereas now he heard stories of hospitals overrun with casualties; doctors performing amputations; men groaning on pallets and bleeding all over the floor as wounds opened on amputated limbs, or sinking into dreamlike silence as death approached.

'We are the young manhood of Europe: obedient, brave, foolish, unquestioning, we have marched into France to die,' one of his mates had said in a kind of chant on the night he was killed. 'I am not able for this!' Andrew told himself. 'I am afraid. That is the truth.' But he wrote to his father saying he was well; he was not to worry. He would be home on leave in a month or so. He put a normal face on things; his pencil stub pretended that he was the same Andrew with the same perspectives. It did not reveal that he was old, that he was a hundred years old and weary; that he knew things adolescents should not know; that, in the act of writing, he gazed across an infinite void to contemplate the heaven of home, as though he doubted its existence. He looked at the picture of his sister and Jen. He fixed his eyes on Jen as though he were an old voyeur and not the boy next door, devoured the picture of the two young girls sitting together. He saw Jen's face and neck and young girl's breasts with the ache of the aged looking back on Eden, wondering how he had ever taken such grandeur for granted. She was growing up. She had lost the starved, gamine look of her convalescence; her hair was long again, her face oval and perfect. Her beauty aroused in him the same awe that religion once had. But for him God had died in the noise of the guns, the whistle of shells, the sickening hot stench of blood and spilling guts. It was beauty that lived on; and it was to this that the mind turned.

Andrew was approached by a young officer who offered him a cigarette. The latter's uniform was mud-stained; his fingernails were caked with dirt, and the back of his hands were covered in dried mud. His name was Theodore O'Reilly, known as Theo to his friends; he came from County Cork in Ireland, from a limestone manor in the Fanagh peninsula overlooking the sea. He had often spoken to Andrew of his family, of his mother and sister, of Trinity College in Dublin from which he had graduated the year the war began.

'What did you read at Trinity?' Andrew asked, thinking of his father's frustrated plans for him.

Theo looked at him quizzically. 'History and English Literature. Why?'

'Just thinking how nice it would be to be a student . . . and not be here! Did you enjoy your studies?'

'Yes. History is fascinating, but we seem to learn nothing from it!'

'What do you mean?'

Theo gestured around him. 'We relive it, blindly, stupidly, criminally!'

'Yes,' Andrew conceded. 'I suppose we do. Were you interested in any particular era?'

'The Middle Ages, the whole epoch of superstition and cruelty. There was one episode in particular that fascinated me, although it came a bit later.'

'What was that?'

'It was something that happened in Italy. It was horrific. Don't ask me to talk about it!'

Andrew was silent for a few seconds. He felt the mud drying on his hands, smelt the stench of carrion and human waste and fear.

'Well, I suppose you had a good time, anyway.'

'A good time? Until the last year, I suppose I did . . .'

'What happened then? Too much work, I expect?'

Theo coughed. 'No. God, no . . . I joined a group of idiots — a sort of secret society . . . offshoot of a Theosophical Society.'

'Sounds like fun!'

Theo was silent for a moment. 'Not fun, just very strange, if you want to know . . .' He paused, dropped his voice. 'Horribly strange . . .'

'In what way?

Theo looked away. 'It started as a dare,' he said, almost in a whisper.

'What started as a dare?'

And then Theo told him how, to answer a dare, and because he was too reckless to refuse, and too proud to be true to his instincts, he had invited something he feared and regretted. Listening, Andrew did not know whether to believe him.

Now Andrew looked at the white face and the

eyes red-rimmed with exhaustion. He knew that this man was tolerated by his fellow officers as a mad Mick, his eccentricities ignored, his constant poetry-reciting no longer noticed. He took the proffered cigarette, noting how Theo's hand shook.

'I'm writing home,' he said. 'Just a note to the pater. What am I supposed to say? I've run out of lies. But if I don't write he frets himself sick.'

'Tell him it's a breeze,' Theo said. 'Tell him we seldom hear a shot fired in anger.' He gestured wryly and covered his ears as a shell whistled and exploded nearby. 'Tell him any damned thing he wants to hear. Makes no difference, because we're dead. The bloody earth is hungry for us, can't get enough of us. Open the grave, shovel the boys in. That's the ticket: shovel them in!'

Andrew felt the lump in his throat. Theo was going off the deep end. No doubt about that. They should ship him out and unscramble his brains. He had been in the trenches longer than most and it had begun to tell.

O'Reilly glanced at the photograph in Andrew's hand. 'Mnn,' he said. 'Very nice. Who are they?'

'My sister and a friend.'

Theo stabbed a grimy finger towards Jenny's smiling face. 'There's a deserving beauty! Is that your sister?'

'No. That's Jen . . . Jenny Stephenson.'

Theo nodded. 'Mnn,' he said again dreamily, adding, 'Jenny the brown, Jenny the brown, give us Jenny to burn or drown.'

Andrew turned on him angrily, but stopped as he saw the nervous tic shivering in Theo's face. The latter seemed unaware that he had given offence. He fell silent, and then added as he turned away: 'I'll let you get on with it. Your sister is pretty, but the other one's a beauty.'

Andrew watched his friend stumble away from him down the trench, heard his boots squelch in the mud, heard his brogue,

'Oh she doth teach the torches to burn bright.
Her beauty hangs upon the cheek of night,
Like a rich jewel in an Ethiop's ear . . .'

The sergeant came out of the fox-hole and stared after him uneasily.

'Mad Irish bastard,' he muttered, adding as he turned back, 'but he's still able to shoot.'

That night, Theo started out of his sleep and cried out.

'Shut up, O'Reilly,' someone hissed from the next bunk.

'Ask her about the mask!' Theo said in a thick, sleepy voice. 'Ask her where they put the bloody mask . . .' Then he went back to sleep, his mutterings petering out in incoherence.

Nearby, Andrew lay awake in his own cot, staring into the dark, listening to the booming of the guns, the taunts of the Germans in the nearby lines.

Theo dreamed. He dreamt he was at home in Kilashane. He walked up the avenue of elms and beeches to the front door, past the open, gravelled forecourt, and the lawn with the monkey puzzle tree. The door was open, and he went through the spacious porch and into the hall. His boots rang off the tiles. He saw the sunlight streaming into the library, picking out the gold lettering in the yards of dusty, leather-bound books, shining softly on the polished mahogany of the table and the walnut of the writing desk. He did not enter the room, but he knew it was empty. He turned to the drawing room, saw the chintz chesterfield suite, the sprawl of magazines on the occasional table, the display of dried flowers; he knew the polished brass of the tall fender with its leather top and seat, the marble clock and the family photographs on the mantelpiece. He knew this room too was empty. He paused in the middle of the hall and heard the silence. The silence came in waves at him, drowning him. He called out. His voice echoed back with mockery. The grandfather clock in the hall was still. The portraits gleamed dully in their frames. The waiting presence which filled the house was somewhere above him, up the curved staircase, in the landing, in the room that was his overlooking the lawn and the sea beyond.

'I should have destroyed it,' he thought dreamily. 'Melted it down, or something. Instead I managed to lose it.' He waited, unable to move, uncaring, dreamily resigned. But in his sleep he stirred restlessly and cried out again.

In London, Jenny woke with a start. Her heart was thumping, and the dread of something she could not identify subsumed her. She lay in the darkness, picking out the shapes of the chair where she had draped her clothes, the dressing table, with her hairbrush, the small wardrobe. There was moonlight against the flowered fabric of the curtains and, looking at the pattern, she thought she saw a face, repeating itself over and over in the intricacies of the design. She froze, telling herself not to be stupid, that her mind was playing tricks. For a moment it reminded her of something, the cold gape of a mask, and she remembered with a start that she had not seen it for two years. Where was it now? Gramps had brought it to her when she had been ill; but she had never seen it again.

'It's yours,' he had said. 'I have it safely.' She wanted to dive down under the blankets and forget the faces at the moonlit window, forget about the mask, forget the thought that anything might watch her with such calculation and inhumanity. But she forced herself to sit up, stretch out her hand to the bedside table and find the lucifers, strike a match. She got out of bed and lit the gas and it hissed and the blue flame lit the room. Then she went to the window and pulled the curtain back a little so she could examine the pattern on the fabric. She knew this fabric well, but she went through the motions of examination to answer a private dare, to answer unreasoning fear. The fabric was itself — pink flowers and green leaves — and only by dint of the wildest delusion could you imagine the features of a face in the gaps between the leaves. It was perfectly innocuous. She drew back the curtain and the black-out blind behind it and forced herself to look out the window. The suburban road was dark and deserted, except for a marmalade cat called Oliver which belonged to the Staceys; the cat was standing under an unlit street lamp and looking up, and its eyes shone with red fire as the retinas caught the light from the window and gleamed through the dilated pupils. The animal did not look like the daytime Oliver, and Jenny shivered and let the curtain fall, glad that she could shut out the night and the Oliver of the darkness who seemed so feral and different. She thought of Andrew Stacey at the Front, thought of his father and Yvonne and the way they scanned the casualty lists regularly. She liked Andrew; he was a bit proper and stuffy, a bit dull sometimes, but he was a friend and she hoped and prayed he would be safe.

After a while she turned out the light and got back into bed. She thought of her father who had died in France and been buried just before her illness. She thought of the mother she had never known; she thought of the peculiar mask and of the sense of recognition and of the odd experiences she had had. She thought reluctantly, forbidding herself to think of him but being unable to prevent it, of the man she had seen in a hallucination. But that had been two years before. She had recovered from her illness; her speech seldom halted now; she had worked very hard on it, forcing herself to eliminate the catch which paralysed her throat when she tried to talk, practicing ploys, like singing or speaking on the expulsion of breath. She hated how her mind would race and how her tongue would not obey her brain. She practiced in the attic where no one could hear her, weeping with frustration sometimes, elated with success other times. And one morning she had wakened to find that the tension was gone, that she could even articulate words beginning with 'A' without difficulty.

The room was suddenly very dark. As she lay back again on her bed she felt a kind of vertigo, and suddenly he was there, immediate, inside her head.

'Please go away,' she said.

'Find the mask,' he said. 'Obey me only in this!' The old ache was there again, the sensation of belonging elsewhere, of exile, of being the onlooker. And then the sense of asylum.

'I am safe here,' she said silently, eloquent in thought. 'And I will never obey you. You cannot come, just as I told you.'

For a moment she thought he was gone. Then his voice came again, gentle, searching, sad. 'You will obey me,' he said. 'I am coming soon and you will.'

Next day Jenny said to her grandfather:

'Gramps, do we have any books written by Sir Michael?'

Gramps looked up at her over his spectacles, his surprise evident. 'Who?'

'Sir Michael Philips: wasn't that the name of Papa's employer? I remember Papa showing me some of his books years ago . . .'

Gramps nodded. 'Oh, him. Of course. I think they are in the bookcase in the landing.'

'I looked there.'

'Try behind the first row on the bottom shelf. Why do you want to read them?'

'I want to find out about Venice. Sometimes I have . . . dreams . . .'

'What kind of dreams?'

'I see a man. I feel that I know him . . . and Venice — or someplace like it; a beautiful sunny place with lagoons and buildings — is there behind him in the background.' She paused. 'The dreams, Gramps, are not normal. The man is always the same, and he tells me to come back. He asks me to bring him the mask! I don't think I can stand it any more!'

Gramps paled, but his eyes never left her face. He saw the intensity, the introversion, the bookish focus of the eyes. Jenny read a great deal. She liked to paint, too, and had recently set up an easel in the attic where she had cleared a space under the skylight. There she spent as much free time as she could, talking to herself and brushing

59

surrealistic images on to the canvas. Though she referred to them as 'my daubs', and Gramps did not know much about art, he saw the brooding atmosphere in her paintings and wondered if she had real talent. He had suggested art college to her and she had been noncommittal. 'We'll see!' Now he felt uneasy and afraid. For four years he had observed her secretly, noting her struggle to recover the full use of her voice, the discipline she forced on herself, the breathing exercises she resorted to, the will which drove her. She could speak fully again, although he was aware that she monitored every word she said. The brain damage which Dr Stacey had feared for her when she had been ill had mercifully not materialized. But now, listening to what she was saying, he began to fear. It was like ice in his belly, this fear . . .

'These are nightmares, Jen, phantasms of the mind. You are too sensible to heed such things!'

'If they are merely nightmares, they ought to have the decency to wait until I go to sleep!' She sighed, aware of the uneasiness in her grandfather's eyes. 'Where is the mask, Gramps?'

'That old thing! I'd rather you didn't bother with it!'

She frowned, as though evaluating his dismissiveness.

'What do you think he wants it for, this man in your dreams?'

'I don't know. But I want to be rid of him . . . and if I had it, perhaps he would go.'

'What do you feel about him? Does he frighten you?'

'Yes and no. He seems to promise me something which I want very much, although I'm not quite sure what it is.' She gave a small, self-deprecating laugh. 'Too silly, isn't it?'

She paused, considering her grandfather's grave face, then asked, 'Gramps, did Papa find that mask in Venice?'

'I believe he did.'

Jen sighed, half in relief. 'That's it! He must be the ghost of the owner, looking for it back!' She smiled at the expression on her grandfather's face. He was silent.

'That's it,' Jenny repeated. 'But why do I feel I know him? Why do I sometimes long to go to him?'

The old man shook his head. 'It's a dream, child,' he said severely. 'You cannot apply logic to dreams!'

Jenny stared at him with sombre eyes. 'You think I am a bit strange, Gramps?'

'No. But harden your will. That man may follow you, Jen, in or out of dreams.'

'Why do you say that, Gramps?'

'Because,' he said bitterly, 'I sometimes suspect your father did not come honestly by that artefact!'

She stared at him angrily. 'What a thing to say! Papa was not a thief!'

He put a hand to his forehead. 'No . . . I didn't mean to say he was. But he did tell me once — he

61

was tight at the time — that the thing had come from a tomb!'

Jenny gasped.

'When I tried to question him about it further he was dismissive, said he had been joking. And he spoke of money, asked me how I would like to have a millionaire for a son-in-law, that kind of thing. But I would like to see the back of it, Jen. I would like to get rid of it! If it's worth something, why not sell it? Maybe then you would be free of these nightmares!'

Jenny shrugged. 'Get rid of it if you like. But let me see it before you do.'

Jenny went upstairs, knelt at the bookcase, rooted behind the first row of books on the bottom shelf. She drew out a few dusty volumes in hard, dark blue bindings. *Travels in Spain* by Sir Michael Philips (Bart), one volume said. The second book was by the same author: *Travels in Italy.* Jenny climbed the narrow stairs to the attic, threw herself down on the cushions she had arranged beside her easel underneath the skylight, and began to peruse the index. The fourth chapter bore the legend — 'Venice, City of Intrigue.' She turned to page eighty-five and stared at the photographic plate of St Mark's Square.

When Yvonne called she found Jenny still in the attic. Motes of dust danced in the light flowing through the skylight. The air was close and warm and filled with the smell of paint, linseed oil and turps. There were jam-jars full of brushes, and several paint-smeared rags.

'What are you doing?' Yvonne glanced at the half-finished portrait on the easel. 'Who are you painting?'

She stared at the emerging face on the canvas: the dark eyes, the saturnine brow, the pride and cold arrogance.

'I am painting a magician!'

'What magician?' Yvonne wanted to laugh, but something in the set face before her did not permit it.

'He lived in Venice.'

'What gave you that idea?'

Jenny gestured to the open book on the floor, and Yvonne took it up.

'While the city state gave the world a model of government, and the first system of banking, it also perfected the arts of intrigue and assassination by stealth, whether by the poignard or by poison. It was home to persecuted minorities, dared to defy Rome, and gave sanctuary to people such as Matthias Robertus, an apostate priest, magician, alchemist, necromancer, who followed in the tradition of John Dee, the great English magician, and who is reputed to have founded a secret society which branched into many different sects. They say he spent much of his life attempting to bring a woman back from the dead or, as he insisted, from the future.'

Yvonne chuckled. 'You're painting him!'

'Yes.'

'A dabbler in the occult? The founder of some secret society? A raving lunatic! Why him?'

Jenny shrugged. 'Because he knew his own mind; because he was a magician! Because he had the gumption to defy the great power of the time!' She glanced at her friend, raising her eyebrows. 'I find him interesting! He is himself: not mad, but not tame or over-civilized either . . . I think of him as possessing anger and courage and power!'

Yvonne shook her head and sat on the pile of cushions, observing her friend work and disliking more and more the emerging face with the goatee beard and curved moustaches staring out from the easel.

'He looks pretty beastly to me!'

Jenny smiled and said loftily, 'Does he disturb you? You should ascribe that to the skill of the artist!'

Yvonne felt that the room was uncomfortably close. 'Power at any cost, arrogance, evil, despair!' she murmured, echoing attributes inverse to those discovered by the artist. 'Yes, he disturbs me!'

Jenny glanced at her friend and then looked back doubtfully at the canvas. 'Is it that good? I think he looks mostly sad, like someone angry and betrayed.' She glanced at her friend with a mischievous gleam in her eye. 'You don't seem to like him very much! But maybe he would grow on you!'

Yvonne began to feel stifled. The attic was too

warm. 'Jen, will you come out for a while, get a breath of fresh air? It's jolly stuffy up here.'

Jenny stood back from the easel, saw how the hooded eyes of the portrait followed her; thinking suddenly that she had had enough for one day, she turned and carefully wiped the brush. 'All right.'

As they went downstairs, Yvonne, still thinking of what she had read, asked her, 'What is a necromancer?'

Jenny shrugged. 'I don't know. Shall we look it up?' She paused outside Gramps' study, knocked and asked if she could borrow the dictionary.

'Take it, by all means. What word are you looking for?'

'Necromancer,' Yvonne said.

Gramps frowned while the two girls perused the dictionary.

'Here it is,' Yvonne said, and read aloud: ' "Necromancy — the prediction of the future by the supposed communication with the dead." '

Jenny dreamed that night that she was standing in a small room. The walls were stone and one small window set high up gave some light. There was a stool and she stood on it and tried to see out, but the window was so high and the walls were so thick that she was not able to catch a single glimpse of the sky. When he came she was lying on her pallet. She watched him study her.

65

'Time has run out,' he said. 'What is the point of this defiance? I do not wish the devil to have you!'

'He stands behind you,' she murmured, 'but he cannot touch me!'

When he went away the light was leaving the window. From somewhere nearby she heard the sound of Vespers. *'Deus in adjutorium meum intende . . .'* The chant hung on the evening air, like a canticle to the night.

Chapter Three

'She will be mutilated by the torture.'
'What matter? Has the witch ensnared you?'

Journal of a Witness

Nineteen sixty-seven. It was her birthday and Dee was twenty-three. She woke early, listened in languor to the May dawn chorus, thought briefly of Ballyshane, her home in County Cork, and of her parents.

Dee's real name was Désirée. She had fallen victim to her mother's passionate relief at having at last, in her mid-thirties, produced a living child after a series of miscarriages. When she had demanded of her mother why she had saddled her with such a name, the latter had explained that, at the time of her confinement, she had been reading about Désirée Clary, an Irishwoman who, in the early nineteenth century, had married Marshal Bernadotte, and had subsequently become queen of Sweden when her husband was offered the throne. The name represented for her the fulfilled desire of her own heart, and the hope of an ambitious destiny for the fruit of her womb. It had never occurred to her that she was condemning her innocent babe to a childhood of taunts:

'Little baby Désirée,
Is too scared to come and play?'

The forces of conservatism had latched on to
Désirée right away. Her name was different; *ipso
facto* she was different, and this was unforgiv-
able. But she never called herself by her name:
its meaning 'desired one' seemed ridiculous; it
was French, foreign and pretentious. She called
herself Dee. But her peers all knew it was not her
name, and as long as she tried to evade its reality
they tormented her, giddy with pleasure that
they could draw blood.

She longed for escape. She saw pictures in
storybooks of witches with amazing powers of
locomotion. If she had a broomstick, what she
might do with it!

'What do you want to be when you grow up?'
the teacher had asked her one day.

'A witch!' Dee had replied, twinkling at her,
sure that her joke would be understood. But she
had realized immediately it had been a mistake.
The class hissed and her teacher raised her eyebrows as much as to say, 'Strange child.'

So Dee had become something of a loner,
minding her thin skin and her two stray kittens,
which had presented themselves in the plantation beside her home one day, as though sent by
Providence.

When she went to boarding school she had
said her name was Dee, short for Deirdre. She
knew that 'Deirdre' was all right, acceptable,

rooted in tradition. For a brief period she began to bloom, began to hope that she would never be rumbled, that she would never be the odd one out again. But the headmistress, Mother Anthony, had ruined everything.

'Désirée McGlinn — why did you say your name was Deirdre? It's here on your birth certificate: Désirée. What kind of a name is that?' The nun pinched in her lips. This was not a name in the calendar of the saints; it was not a name that carried the cachet of Irish mythology as did 'Deirdre'. And what was more, it had the whiff of something forbidden, something to do with the flesh, something touching the secret longings of the heart. All of which was anathema in a small closed community busily fleeing life.

So Dee had retired into her shell. She had read and studied, and only later made any real friends. If she had been contemptuous enough or secure enough to have brazened it out, she would have overcome in time to make her schooldays happy. Instead, riddled with uncertainty and with an existing history of being an outsider, she had bowed her head and given others the power to hurt her. She had turned to God. She loved the Latin psalms, '*Quid retribuam Domino pro omnibus quae retribuit mihi* . . .' sung in three-part harmony in the chapel on Sunday evenings. She would stand in a kind of ecstasy, partaking in the sublime, in a reaching up and away from everything that was merely human. Especially after the accident in the school laboratory. That had precipitated her into a withdrawal which had lasted for years, whose effects were with her still.

Now, a new twenty-three, no longer interested in psalms, she glanced around the bedroom. In the divan bed on the other side of the room was Laura O'Brien. Laura had been at college with her, and now shared a flat consisting of bedroom, kitchenette and sitting room, which was costing them four pounds per week. The flat was on the first floor of a Victorian house, with dividing doors between the bedroom and sitting room.

The place had been a mess when they found it, but they had covered the old dun-coloured wallpaper with white paint, pinned up some Art Nouveau prints, posters of the Beatles and the Rolling Stones, installed two lamps made from big chianti bottles, their shades festooned with wine labels, and had covered the shabby couch in big, bright cushions. The floor was stained and covered with an oriental cotton carpet which was the devil to hoover.

There were curtains on the bedroom window, but none in the sitting room, which faced south-east. They had put the dining table beside the window. The fireplace was blocked off, but an ancient green gas fire, which had to be fed with shillings, sat on the hearth. Above it, on the mantelpiece, which was white marble and very elegant, their books stood between two book-

ends in the shape of elephants, souvenirs someone had brought Laura from a trip to India. The
books included *The Essential Yeats*, *The Fear of
Freedom* by Eric Fromm, *The King Must Die* by
Mary Renault, *The Penguin Book of English Verse*,
a few history books, and a string of romantic pa-
perbacks which belonged to Laura, showing
beautiful busty heroines in various period costumes on the covers.

Laura was a history graduate, but she was addicted to historical novels, although she did not
hesitate to denounce them, for the most part, as
'delicious rubbish'. She was fond of saying that
anything was better than the truth. When ac-
cused of being disingenuous she listed events on
her fingers. 'Take this century alone: the first
war — ten million dead; the second war — sixty
million dead; five million Jews at a conservative
estimate; extermination camps; human beings
used as guinea pigs; the Churches unwilling to
do a thing: hiding Nazis in monasteries while
preaching about life; take Hiroshima, Nagasaki
— the shadows on the pavements of real people
vaporized, two cities in smoking ruins; fall-out;
take Bikini — the destruction of paradise, the
betrayal of trust. Take Stalin, Beria, the mass
murder of Russia. Take the phobias of every
filthy little monster who ever conned and wrig-
gled his way to power. Take the Korean and
Vietnam wars. Take Kennedy's murder. Take
the lies of every single institution about women.
Take any damn thing you like and give me fic-

tion. Unless something happens to redress the balance, we're all dead meat! They've enough nuclear stuff to blow the place to kingdom come and nothing at all to stop them. They'll do it for one idiotic ideology or another, but everyone will be just as dead! What does all that tell you about the thrust of history? Does the word "sheep" have a certain resonance?'

'Laura has a bee in her bonnet,' Ted said to Dee. He was a postgraduate student who had met Laura at a party and was taking her out. 'She has her little brains scrambled with all this effort at being intellectual!'

Dee stared at him. This was the guy Laura fancied herself in love with. 'It's no "effort",' she said. 'And they're not little. And they're not scrambled!'

Ted didn't seem to hear. 'For such a beautiful bird, it's a pity . . .'

'She's not a bird and it's not a pity!'

Ted frowned, then smiled indulgently, looking down at her quizzically from behind his bifocals, his eyebrows raised. He looked boyish and slightly taken aback, an innocent in hound's-tooth, charming by being charmed.

'Can't be a bird: no feathers . . .' Dee added helpfully.

Dee had a new job, public relations office in McGrath Limited, a successful Irish electrical company which had, only the year before, been incorporated under the umbrella of International Tele Utilities Inc. — ITU for short. ITU had its European headquarters in Brussels and its world headquarters in New York.

It was Dee's first real job. After graduation she had worked for a while with the University Press, and then had gone to London to work as a 'temp'. Her typing was good, thanks to a course she had taken with Laura and another friend, when, in their first year at university, they had attended typing lessons at Miss Flannery's Secretarial School twice a week after lectures. But temping was not a real job, and her parents had felt it was beneath her, now that she had graduated with a good degree. They would have liked her to teach, but this prospect did not interest Dee. Her father was a teacher, principal of the National School at home. The last thing she wanted was to follow in his footsteps, and was therefore very pleased to have landed the job in McGrath. She had been in it for two months and hoped to make something of it. It meant that she had escaped both teaching and emigration, the typical fate of the Irish Arts graduate.

She got out of bed and went to the bathroom, which was down the landing. When she had showered she returned to dress herself silently, so as not to disturb the sleeping Laura, who lay fervently embracing her pillow. Then she tiptoed into the sitting room to the kitchenette in the corner.

She put on the kettle, popped two slices of

bread in the toaster, and when it was ready brought tea and toast to the sunny window of the sitting room and drew a chair into the early morning sunlight.

From where she sat she could see the masts of the shipping in the Alexandra Basin, the gulls wheeling overhead and, below, the green sward of the small garden.

Once the garden had been a lot bigger, but a workshop of sorts had been built at the end of it, and this gave on to the laneway. The sea was not far off; sometimes she and Laura went for walks beside the estuary, watching the movement of the water traffic, the parr-ap parr-ap of the tugs, and the Isle of Man ferry as it approached the river to move slowly up the Liffey to its berth.

Dee felt that twenty-three was a good age. It was nicely poised between childhood and maturity. She anticipated with pleasure the arrival of the morning post; there would be a card from her parents — with a cheque — and probably one from her former flatmate in London and other friends now scattered since college was over. Colin, her boyfriend from her London days, might write.

She thought of Colin with longing and nostalgia. He was the most flippantly serious person she had ever met, with a worldly curiosity out of proportion to his years, his job (junior newspaper reporter), and his place in history. He took the whole socio-political situation of the world on board. But they had split up and she had re-

74

turned to Ireland and a career.

She was glad the days of studying were over; she missed college, but the prospect of taking life by the throat was the greatest challenge of all. She didn't mind if it was all work. Work kept away the sense of something dogging her which she could not evade, as though Fate, like a bloodhound, was following her.

Dee was from the Fanagh Peninsula, where the sea sang and whispered in summer and roared in winter, lashing the coast before the fury of the gales. Her home had thick stone walls. Part of it had once been a tenant's house, but it had been extended by her father, and was now a stout, two-storey building, sitting in a dip in the land. On the headland behind her home was the ruins of the former big house, Kilashane. Its gaunt remains challenged the elements, and the wind whistled around it in winter like a chorus of banshees. But Dee liked the din, the lonely wail of the wind and the beating of the sleet against the limestone and against the remains of a mullioned window in the old hallway. The roof had fallen in, and the floors crumbled over the basement and the remains of the once stately staircase. When she was still quite small she had explored this place, crept in through a basement window, parting the ivy and slipping through the broken window into what had once been the kitchen. The old range was rusty, the pots and pans long gone, the flagged floor slick with damp. The ivy had trespassed into the kitchen and grew its ardent greenery across one wall, from window to window, so that it was difficult to imagine what life must have been like before the Troubles and the decimation of the old family that had once lived and prospered here. But still Dee would sit in this kitchen on an old rickety three-legged stool and dream of the past. By the time she was nine she had explored all of the house, had crept up the broken stairs, whose banisters hung drunkenly over the stairwell, to the bedrooms above. She knew this was perilous; her parents had impressed it on her: the house was derelict, the floors might fall any moment, she must never go there. 'Keep away from the old house. It has dry rot and is about to fall down.' They took for granted that she obeyed.

Such strictures only made the place irresistible, as did the locked gate to the avenue with its sign: DANGEROUS BUILDING — KEEP OUT.

It was so easy to climb the gate or indeed slip through the gap in the old demesne wall and into the shrubbery. Other children kept away, frightened by tales of the devil and various certainties of an occult nature. But Dee felt the place draw her, and when she sat in the kitchen or crept to the upper storey she did not feel like a trespasser. She paid particular attention to the library, where books of yesteryear were strewn in soggy pulp all over the floor. The fine marble mantelpieces in the reception rooms had gone, been torn away from the chimney breasts by enterprising robbers who had recognized Adam fireplaces when they saw them. Cleaned up, their marble restored to its glory, the fireplaces fetched fantastic prices on the London antique market, while the bereft chimney breasts of the once great house hid the affront behind the encroaching atrophy, the ivy and the silence. The old wallpaper, with its Victorian block design, hung sadly away from the wall in flaps. There was the remains of some furniture; what might have been a desk with its drawers thrown on the floor and its wood destroyed beyond redemption. There were other items: old letters, a broken fountain pen, a blue glass paperweight.

Dee kept three of the things which she had found. One was a sepia photograph of two young girls in button boots and longish dresses sitting on a rustic bench and staring into the camera.

The second, found in the same drawer as the first, was a leather diary. The old photograph had curling edges and the diary had some of its pages stuck together. They were her window on another world, the private world of people who had lived and breathed and laughed in the ruin on the hill behind her. And from the day when she studied the photograph carefully in front of a mirror and fancied that the face of one of the girls, the darker one, was not unlike her own, she felt a kinship with the decayed mansion. Sometimes she was sure she had been somewhere before; that she had been many places before.

Her treasures she secreted away at the bottom

of her own chest of drawers at home, underneath a pile of old schoolbooks. She did not show them to her parents, afraid of the trouble she would get into, although her mother had commented that something in her room smelled musty and was about to embark on a spring-clean operation before she wrapped the diary in a hand-towel and sprayed it with her mother's Tweed. The smell of must disappeared.

But the third item which she appropriated was real treasure, and this she had happened on by accident. She had found it while creeping carefully through the upper storey, avoiding the rooms where the floors had fallen in. In a bedroom above the hall, where the edges of the floorboards sagged at a forty-five-degree angle, underneath a sprung board by the iron fireplace, something had caught the light. It was a ring, sitting against the rotten joist, a gold ring. Spreadeagled on the floor she took it out, examined it cautiously, and put it in her pocket. The floor groaned ominously. She crawled back towards the broken stairs, feeling the tension in the room, the certainty that something was about to happen. It was only when she had reached the safety of the overgrown front lawn and sat behind the monkey puzzle tree that the landing in the house behind her collapsed, sending a shower of dirt and broken plaster out through the open front door.

She took the ring out of her pocket and stared at it in wonder. It seemed to be gold, though she knew she could not be sure of that (she had once caused some mirth by assuming that the ring in the Hallowe'en barm-brack was the real thing). What surprised her about the ring was the emblem on the front of it, set there like the heart on a claddagh ring. The emblem was shaped like an M and had snakes twining around its feet, filling in the bottom part of the letter. In between the two uprights of the M was a face, or rather a mask, a bit like the mask she had found in a chest in one of the other bedrooms, but had thrown away. She remembered it well, had chanced on it while rooting among old clothes — strange, mildewed dresses with sequins, feather boas, shoes with ankle straps, a pair of patent-leather men's shoes. The mask had emerged from a chest, hidden under mouldy blankets and various garments. It had stared at her with such sudden lively ferocity that she had reacted violently and had flung it from her. She had gone back to find it a week later, but that part of the upstairs had fallen and mask and chest and sequinned dresses were all buried in the room beneath, under a pile of plaster and fallen joists.

The ring was another matter. She put the ring on her finger, from one finger to another, but it was too big for any of them. It ended up in a brown paper bag with the diary. She was very excited about it and longed to show it off, but the sense of having involved herself in an escapade that would worry her parents — and get her into considerable trouble — prevented her.

Sometimes on summer evenings, Dee took a homemade lantern to the bower she had made among the laurels in the demesne. Her 'lantern' was made from a honey jar with a screw-on lid. She half filled it with paraffin, and put a long wick dipping into the paraffin at one end and emerging through a slit in the lid at the other. She would sit in her bower in the shrubbery and light the lamp, watching the fire take the wick and illuminate the darkening cave of greenery she had around her. This gave her a great sense of peace, this feeling that she was hidden from the world. No one would look for her in the shrubbery of the old house because no one went there.

She liked to be alone. Because of her social failure she only felt she was herself when she was alone. Sometimes she tried to force herself to play with other children, those who occasionally forgot she was a 'green monkey' because they needed someone to make up numbers, but they would sense her unease and lack of commitment to the business in hand. Soon they didn't want to include her in their escapades. 'Here comes Miss Stuck-Up,' Treena Casey used to say.

They would tease her. In summer the other girls would strip to their knickers and swim in the Meena, which had deepish pools. She, on the other hand, would watch for a while, but would never take off her clothes.

'Come on, Dee, it's lovely,' someone might

shout, splashing bright droplets on to the bank, but she would walk away, looking down at her new Start-Rite sandals and white socks and hearing the insults. 'Scaredy cat, scaredy cat . . .'

I'm not scared, she told herself, knowing it to be generally true. I'm not stuck up and I'm not scared.

So it was almost to answer a private dare that she had stayed in Kilashane after nightfall. It would prove her courage. None of the other children would have the guts to emulate her. She thought of daring Treena Casey to join her, but knew that if she did, her mother would hear of it. Instead she settled down in her private fastness, which was comfortable with the old car rug and a cushion.

It was warm and close, with the overpowering perfume of honeysuckle from a nearby shrub, and she allowed herself to doze in the summer night. And then it seemed to her that she stood before the house itself. The building showed none of the ravages she knew: it was intact, brightly lit; someone was playing a piano and a man in evening dress was approaching her across the lawn. The notes of music tinkled out into the still, warm air, and the man walked as though keeping time, with an unhurried but uneven footfall.

She woke with a start to find her lamp still burning, although the wick needed trimming and the smoke from the burnt end was acrid. But she moved her head and saw, above the lamp, staring at her from the dark shrubbery and grotesque with the shadows, a human face.

Dee had felt her heart jump. For a moment she did not know whether she was in or out of her dream. She was too frightened to cry out. The face was still and studied her, terrifying in its immobility and the distortions from the flickering makeshift lamp. Then it was gone; the leaves shivered as it withdrew and she turned and tore through the shrubbery, stumbling down the incline to her home, racing to evade the sudden terror.

When she got home she bolted the door behind her.

'Where were you?' her mother demanded, her voice full of relieved anxiety. 'I told you not to be out after dark,' but she had simply fled to her room and shut the door.

Her mother had followed, hands on hips. 'Answer me when I ask you a question, young lady!' But Dee had simply muttered that she had been playing and hadn't noticed how dark it had become and then she had had a fright.

'What kind of fright?' Her mother's tone changed, became suddenly quiet. 'You're as white as a sheet!'

Dee shivered. 'Nothing.'

'You weren't up at the old house, were you?'

'No,' Dee lied. 'But when I was coming up the path by the wood I saw a man's face looking out at me from the bushes.'

Her mother froze. 'Did he speak to you? Did he touch you . . . ?'

'No.'

'Who was he?'

'I don't know. It was dark.'

Her mother pursed her lips. 'I told you not to be out after dark,' she repeated angrily, feeling the lot of mothers to be an intolerable burden. 'It was probably old Billy. If you're out after dark you wouldn't know who you might meet. They don't wear labels — you just never know . . .' She considered her daughter's stricken face.

'Old Billy won't hurt me,' Dee said.

'How do you know? He's a queer old yoke. Keep clear of him!'

Everyone knew old Billy, who'd had his wits scrambled long ago in the Great War. His house, a county council cottage, was further down the peninsula but he haunted the woods. Dee felt that he was harmless, childlike. Her parents had told her that he was called 'Old Billy' because he kept going on about Kaiser Bill who had lived a long time ago.

'Promise me you won't stay out this late again!'

'I promise. I'm sorry, Mam.'

Her mother kissed her then. 'Brush your teeth now, alanna, and go to bed.'

Dee hugged her mother. 'All right, Mam.'

Dee thought of Billy. Once he had stopped her on the boreen, jumping out suddenly from behind a furze bush, and frightened her by staring into her face. She saw his red-rimmed eyes, heard the words which came from his wet lips, saw the way his arm gesticulated, pointing to Kilashane and then around the whole of the peninsula like the big hand of a clock. His index finger pointed at her finally, as though the whole sweep of the landscape about had its focus in her existence. He gabbled something which rhymed:

'. . . Let us go seaward as the great winds go,
Full of blown sand and foam; what help is here?
There is no help, for all these things are so,
And all the world is bitter as a tear . . .'

She had watched him limp away, muttering and shouting out, lifting his fist at the seagulls which screamed raucously overhead. He turned in the direction of the ruined house. Although he had a cottage, Dee knew where he mostly lived, in the queer old treehouse he had made for himself in the grounds of Kilashane. She had seen him retreat into it many a time, while she hid among the bushes and the bracken.

But the verse so fiercely and garrulously quoted was only one of many she heard from him. 'I fled Him, down the nights and down the days . . .' she heard him mutter more than once, and when she came across a poem by Francis Thompson entitled, 'The Hound of Heaven', she recognized the words.

'I fled Him, down the nights and down the days;
I fled Him, down the arches of the years . . .'

'Who was he fleeing, Mother?' she asked the
nun who taught them English, producing the
book for her inspection.
'God, of course, Dee . . .'

Dee's reverie gave way to the pleasures of the
new day. The mist was golden with the morning
and it scattered as the sun climbed. The little
breakfast in the sunny window-niche was over.
The robins which had colonized the rowan trees
against the wall outside, stepped up their frenzied chirping. Dee collected the toast crumbs
from the table, scooped them into her hand, and
went to the kitchenette with her cup and saucer.
Then she glanced into the bedroom, but Laura
was still sunk in her pillow with the true passion
of the late-night activist. There was a world of
difference between Laura at midnight and Laura
in the morning.
'Rise and shine,' Dee said. 'You'll be late.'
Laura stirred, groaned. 'Oh holy God; it can't
be time to get up,' she said in genuine misery. 'I
feel like I've only just got to sleep! What time is
it?'
'Eight!'
'Suffering Jesus!'
She pulled herself to the side of the bed and sat
up, long legs sticking out under the bed-clothes,
blue eyes gluey with sleep. Tendrils of ash-

85

blonde hair were escaping from the large rollers. She pulled on her dressing gown and stumbled down the landing to the bathroom, calling back over her shoulder, 'You go on without me. But don't forget lunch.'

'I won't. See you at one.'

Laura stopped at the bathroom door, looked back at her friend, smiled sleepily. 'Dee!'

'Yes.'

'Happy birthday!'

'Thanks.'

Dee collected her mail from the floor of the hall downstairs and then she walked to work, opening the envelopes en route. There was a card from her parents with the predictable ten pounds, one from Sarah in London, but none from Colin. Maybe there would be one tomorrow: the thought rose to comfort her. There was always tomorrow. She rubbed her arm where the accident had happened. It still itched occasionally, although it was healed.

Chapter Four

'Well, Witch, where shall we put the brand?'
The witch wept.

Journal of a Witness

Dee walked down Bath Avenue in the shadow of the old gasometer into Haddington Road and down to the company's offices on the Grand Canal. The waterway sat there sleepily, green at the edges with weed and scum, indifferent to the ducks and the two swans. There were babies on the water, fluffy ducklings who scudded after mamma duck as though their lives depended on it.

Dee liked this walk, looked forward to it when the weather was fine. And as she walked and watched the canal she thought of what she had read in one of the Sunday papers some weeks back about conservation work being carried out in a city with canals for thoroughfares. After the disastrous floods of the previous November, repair work was under way in earnest in Venice. The heading of the article had been 'MYSTERY BODY DISAPPEARS'. A young woman's corpse had apparently been discovered, during restoration work, in a stone sarcophagus in Venice. Except for her face, the remains of the young woman appeared to be in an extraordinary state of preservation. Photographs were taken and the corpse hurried away for refrigeration. But it had never reached its destination. It had been stolen en route.

The corpse had been dressed in blue silk chased with silver. Her brown hair had been braided and was still shining when the tomb was opened. The obvious motive was ascribed to the theft; it was thought that there were jewels on the body. Its loss to historians and archaeologists was bewailed. There was a photograph of the sarcophagus and the house where it was found.

Dee had thought about this young woman intermittently since she had read the article. Embalmed, dressed in silk; she had died more than three hundred years earlier and her poor corpse had not even been allowed to rest in peace.

But what had disturbed her most about the article was the fact that the design on the sarcophagus had reminded her of the design on the ring she had found in Kilashane. She had compared both designs, the stylised M, wound with serpents and enclosing the masklike face.

Dee was in her office at a quarter to nine, was seated at her desk at ten to nine. Charlie, her boss, was not in yet; the door separating his small office from the bigger, outer office was locked. Liz, his secretary, came along at nine and opened it. Charlie might not present himself until ten, depending on whether or not he had been drinking the night before but when he did everything had to be ticking over, the mail opened, all systems going.

Charlie Kelleher had told Dee about his swift rise in the company. McGrath Electrics, while the biggest operation of its kind in the country, was only a minute part of the ITU empire. Charlie had joined at nineteen as a junior salesman. Determined to succeed, he had built up a network of contacts and, through hard work and excellent results, had made it to sales manager. But it had been a shock to be told one morning by his then boss, Joe McGrath, that the latter had sold the company to a Birmingham-based company. Joe had told him not to worry, that he had persuaded the Brits that, under their guidance, Charlie could manage the business. So, practically overnight, he became managing director. Two years later the British company was acquired by ITU.

And then his problems had really started.

'I need a dogsbody,' Charlie had said when Dee had presented herself for interview. 'Sorry, that sounds awful, but I need someone who can talk to a crowd of shitehawks I have to deal with in Brussels. They're on my back — endless bloody bureaucracy — a monthly business report: you could do that?' Dee had nodded. 'Good, good. And you're a university type . . . Fluent French? Better still. You can give the bastards back as good as we get: wrap them up in their own waffle! You're just what I need!'

Dee had been so overwhelmed by the enthusiasm of her prospective boss that she hadn't asked too many questions about a job description. It was only afterwards, when she was installed and trying to establish the parameters of her position, that she realized the vagueness of the job content.

Although she reported to Charlie, she quickly found she was actually working with Liam Dunne, the company's accountant. This had helped her to assume the Business Planning text, and also the writing of the monthly manager's and comptroller's letters, about which Charlie had fulminated.

Liam was a good teacher. Although she had no idea how to prepare accounts, or line up any figures, she did understand the reporting and budget control.

'Very good work,' Liam had said to her after her first month. 'You're coming along fine. If you could wangle a couple of weeks in the Business Planning Department in Brussels, you'd be the undisputed expert in McGrath!'

It had been while Dee was deep in thought one morning, her head bent over the contents of the monthly report, that she had met Peter Eggli.

He had walked stiffly into the office as though he owned the place. He was tall. He looked foreign, different, and obviously expected her to drop everything and attend to him. 'I'm from European headquarters in Brussels — Peter Eggli.'

'Oh hello,' Dee had said, realizing that Charlie was not in yet and that she had better do a cover-up job. 'Mr Kelleher is out at a meeting. He'll be back shortly.' She felt, rather than saw, Liz exhale in relief.

'That's all right. You're . . . let's see . . . Dee McGlinn? McGrath's new PR genius? Am I right?' His accent was strange, a mixture of French and American vowels.

She blushed. 'I'm Dee McGlinn all right. I don't know about the "genius".'

He smiled and caught her eyes, held them. His eyes were grey, and the expression in them belied the smile on his lips. There was nothing easy about his eyes. Dee realized that this man from Brussels missed nothing; that his bonhomie was not to be taken for granted. This was a man who would not waste time, mince words, or play games which did not tend to some considerable gain: that was her first impression.

'Perhaps we could have coffee, if you have a moment?' Dee glanced at Charlie's secetary, Liz, who, knowing that the man from European headquarters could not see her behind the door of Charlie's office, mouthed, 'Go on, go on.'

Dee glanced at the clock, got up. 'I can take my coffee break now.'

She had spent fifteen minutes with him in the canteen, and had been grilled in the most astute way she had ever experienced. Not like Charlie, who was a slob, this man had class and he had subtlety, which was dangerous.

She had begun to feel annoyed at the presumptuous way he thought he could plumb her. She knew that Charlie was no saint, but she owed him loyalty. She had begun to hedge her answers, to introduce irrelevancies. If the job was done, if the company thrived, what did it matter whether every 'i' was dotted and every 't' crossed? But when she looked at him again she had seen that he was smiling. The smile made him seem human, likeable, with a reservoir of wit. She realized that he found her attractive and this did not displease her. She was used to boys looking at her with this level of interest, but it was strange to be desired so by a man. He was surely married, though.

They had still been in the canteen when Charlie breezed in. 'Hello, hello. I was at a meeting . . .'

Dee had seen at once that more than one possibility had crossed Peter Eggli's mind as he'd studied the managing director of McGrath Limited. But he'd smiled, extended his hand. 'Your PR lady here has been taking care of me!'

That evening Charlie had taken her out for a drink after work. 'We can chew the fat over a pint,' he had said in a friendly fashion. Dee didn't like to refuse. She felt flattered, but also wary. She knew that Charlie was married and she hoped the drink was strictly business.

They went to Keenan's, sat in a quiet corner, he with a pint of Guinness and she with a glass. He asked her how she liked working for the company, and she said she liked it very much. 'You're a clever little trout,' he said. 'You managed Eggli very well this morning. He was singing your praises . . . Very good. And Liam tells me you have it all under control.'

His plump hand moved along the seat and accidentally touched her leg over the knee. She moved away a fraction, wishing she wasn't wearing a mini-skirt. Charlie asked her if she had made any holiday arrangements, talked of his own plans to take his wife, Maeve, and the kids on a camping trip.

'I'd like to go to Venice,' Dee found herself saying. 'I was reading about the restoration work there. Did you read the article in the *Sunday Press*?'

Charlie took a swig. The creamy head of his pint left a line on his upper lip and he licked it away. 'Jesus . . . Yeah, I saw that. Few weeks ago? Why are you so interested?'

'Well, appeals to the imagination, I suppose — the embalmed girl. And there was a design on the tomb, you could see it in the photograph — and it looked the same as the design on a ring I found years ago. That interested me!'

'Oh, what kind of design?'

'It had a stylized letter M!'

Charlie stared at her. 'That was strange. Well, well . . . Did you know there was a strange old berk in Venice once, who had that kind of thing for an emblem?'

Charlie had ordered another pint for himself

and a glass for Dee. 'Ah go on, you're only alive once', but Dee hardly touched it. She listened as Charlie became garrulous, rambling on. 'Yeah, he was some kind of wizard; he still has followers worldwide. They say he discovered some way of accessing the future. Are you sure about the ring? That's strange, all right, to find something with that device in Ireland.'

Then he had launched into world politics. 'The way things are going . . . Ah now, you see that Luther King fellow giving trouble in the States. If he gets his way the repercussions will be worldwide. And the next thing we know they'll be everywhere, black sambas traipsing around Europe as though they owned the place.' He turned to her. 'What do you think?'

'I'm a bit wary of jumping to easy conclusions about people. I detest hatred. Remember our own history!'

Charlie laughed. 'Yeah, that was different: the British propaganda machine. But nowadays white people have to stick together or we'll all end up brown as dogshite . . .'

Dee wanted to laugh. Charlie was disgusting enough to be comical. 'My mother is more concerned about Communism than anything else. She thinks that's the big threat!'

Charlie put down his glass. A dribble of Guinness foamed its way down the side of the glass and wet the small floater on the table. 'Jesus, yeah, Commies. No respect for God or man. But the day will come . . .' He glanced at Dee.

His demeanour suggested a man in his cups. But his eyes were calculating and in control. 'If the right men stick together,' he confided, 'there'll be appropriate action taken.'

'What kind of action?' Dee was puzzled.

'Blow the arse off them!'

Dee thought of Colin and his phobia about the Bomb. She felt desolate. It seemed to her that no matter where you went, so much was expressed in terms of power: the right to power and the use of power.

Charlie had gone on to tell her, yet again, the history of his rise in McGrath. He'd ended up by confiding that, unless he landed a coveted order from Erinview Limited, a company dealing with TV rentals for the domestic and hotel market, he would not reach his budget target for the year. This would mean no bonus and a question mark over his future.

'Those fuckers in Brussels,' Charlie said, 'think of nothing but bloody figures! No one is a human being in their eyes; they've got no feeling for the personality of the business. And the bloody Americans have switched the financial year to the end of June, which robs me of vital months! I've been on to Joe Corcoran of Erinview and he tells me we'll get the order just as soon as he gets his from the hotels. It's all on the cards, but it's the blasted time factor I'm worried about!'

'I'm sure everything will work out,' Dee said, becoming a little anxious as she saw that Charlie was all set for a good long drinking session. 'I have to go now. Thanks for the drink.'

Charlie had said he'd better go too: Maeve would be worried. As they left the pub he'd asked her softly, 'This ring you found years ago — the design on the signet — did it have . . . snakes?'

Dee started. 'Yes. How did you know?'

She sensed for a moment that Charlie had stopped breathing. He didn't answer.

Charlie had insisted on driving her home. He'd said she was a grand girl and had moved towards her when he'd stopped the car, but Dee, who'd had her hand poised for the door handle, opened the door and was gone before he could touch her.

Afterwards she couldn't help comparing Mr Eggli's compelling urbanity with Charlie's crassness. And in the days that followed she found that, despite the readiness she had had at the time to reject the former as presumptuous, his memory lingered. He was different. He had made her feel visible, as if her viewpoint was interesting, her femininity a forceful reality. But she also knew that it might be a long time before she laid eyes on him again.

Now Dee sat down at her desk. She had to get the manager's and comptroller's letters out. She wanted to do it herself, without either Charlie or Liam breathing down her neck. Charlie came in at a quarter to ten, barely glanced at her, went into his office and took off his jacket. The next time she looked through the glass barrier separating his domain from the rest of the office she saw that he was dictating to Liz.

Liam came around later and asked her to the canteen for coffee. He asked her advice about his girlfriend. How would he win her back; should he send her flowers? What did women like?

'Everything!' Dee said. 'Like men, they want the world!'

At midday Laura phoned and said she would meet her in the Saddle Room in the Shelbourne for lunch.

'It's too expensive,' Dee said.

'It's on me. Birthday treat. I got a tax rebate.' Later, in the restaurant, Laura ordered a bottle of the house red and toasted her friend. 'You're only young once!'

Charlie frowned at Dee when she returned. 'Have you been drinking?'

'I had a glass of wine,' she conceded with a polite burp. She waited for Charlie's cutting response, but he just grinned.

That evening, as Dee walked home along by the canal, she wondered again if there would be a birthday card from Colin. But she was sure that he had met someone else and, if so, the chances of him remembering her birthday were slim. She had fancied herself in love with him once; he was English, different, courteous in a way spoilt Irishmen so seldom were. 'I'll do that, love,' he would say when she got up to take the tray into the kitchen. You could wait all your natural life for an Irishman to so bestir himself.

And now he had presumably forgotten her. She missed him; missed the long kisses in his mini-car, missed the hands he slipped under her T-shirt, the walks in Hyde Park on Sunday mornings. She loved his understanding, his acceptance; loved him for the fact that when she said 'No', it did not end in a judo game. She admired him for his compassion, for his interest in endangered species; she smiled at his certainty that a great conspiracy was abroad, until this certainty became an irritation. He declaimed on the escalation of the war in Vietnam. 'I'm doing some research. It hasn't all happened by chance or the unabetted vagaries of international politics. You only have to look at the facts; I wouldn't be at all surprised if they do in Robert Kennedy like his brother, not to mention Martin Luther King!'

'Oh, Colin, don't be so bloody paranoid!'

'Don't you be such a green little leprechaun!'

'I'm not a leprechaun!'

He had sighed, smiled, but after several such exchanges she knew the end was not far off.

'Pretty woman,' the song said on the transistor radio the day they broke it off. The lyric reached its apogee in the invitation to share the nocturnal couch.

'That song drives me spare,' Dee said.

Colin did not laugh. 'Now who's paranoid?'

'Oh, piss off and mind your whales . . .'

She longed to phone him, but she had called

98

him last and pride was involved.

Phone me, you little bastard, she thought, smiling to herself at the incongruity of the phrase. Colin was six foot three. His own birthday was coming up at the end of the week. They used to joke about it — two Taureans, two stubborn characters.

Walking through the Dublin rush hour that May evening it occurred to Dee, and not for the first time, that she should have kept a diary. Her life had been touched by so many oddities — an introspective childhood spent haunting a forbidden playground, the discovery of strange curios there, the design of which had now surfaced in Venice, of all places; added to which she now had a boss who could be described as 'colourful', a job with possibilites and a sense of malaise she should try to both analyse and subjugate.

Once she had kept a diary at school, but Mother Anthony had confiscated it. Dee's horror that her private reflections were in the custody of the dreaded headmistress had ended her career as a diarist.

This experience had increased her diffidence about the diary which she had found so many years before in Kilashane and which was now at home. It was evidently a young woman's diary, written by someone who had neat handwriting and who had put a note of dire warning on the flyleaf, a bit like the threat on Egyptian tombs: 'I hope that no one will be dishonourable enough to read this diary!' The name of the owner was on the flyleaf; 'Yvonne Stacey', but the word 'Stacey' had been crossed out and 'O'Reilly' substituted underneath.

But in spite of everything Dee had recently taken an occasional peep inside. It was so long ago — 1919 was the date on the small journal — that it could hardly matter now.

She wondered about Yvonne Stacey, denizen of a world now gone. She felt suddenly lonely. So many people, a city full of them, and almost all of them strangers. No Colin; no one to share life with. But then, why would Colin want her; why would anyone? Laura knew why she always wore long sleeves. When Colin had found out his eyes had widened in compassion. She hated compassion. She wanted love, desire; she wanted to express the fire within her; she wanted whatever was unconsidered and unbridled. But they were not for her. She would always feel 'seconds', like the goods her mother sometimes bought in summer sales — bed-linen, china, curtain material — which had some hidden flaw. Others wouldn't notice it, but you knew it was there and were always aware of it.

Don't be such a maudlin God-help-us, she berated herself. Stop mooning. Stop feeling sorry for yourself. Forget him. But when she got home she wrote him a letter.

Dear Colin,
    Just a note to say Happy Birthday. I'm set-

tled in my new job — PR officer for McGrath Limited, which is a subsidiary of ITU (one of those international set-ups you are so fond of. I'm joking . . . I'm joking).

If you had the time it would be nice to hear from you.

Love,
The Leprechaun.

Why did she feel so uneasy? It was a bit like nausea, but a nausea of the spirit. It had nothing to do with Colin. It had everything to do with her life, with the sense that something was missing she could not precisely identify, like trying to do a jigsaw puzzle and knowing that a piece was gone. Who am I and why am I here? Who is Dee McGlinn? What relevance do I have to the year 1967? Is there any reason for the fact that I was born?

She turned on the transistor, fiddled with the tuner and stopped as she heard Joan Baez. The beautiful voice soared and lilted with the assurance that the answer was blowing in the wind.

Chapter Five

'Why do you torment me?'
'For God and the pleasure of it, Witch!'
'Is pleasure political?'

Journal of a Witness

'That's the ticket!' Theo said, as they cut open his blood-sodden trouser leg. Then, as the surgeon began to probe the suppurating wound, and the pain gnawed through him, up and up through his whole being until he trembled and was sick with it, he fainted.

The surgeon removed the piece of shrapnel and put it in a kidney dish. Then he cauterized and stitched the wound, releasing the tourniquet. The leg below the tourniquet was blue and swollen. The doctor looked at it doubtfully, pursing his lips. 'Keep an eye on that,' he said to the ward sister. 'I hope we don't have to amputate.'

He looked at the face of the young man, bloodied, with sutured wounds across his skull. 'Poor bastard,' he muttered, before he moved away.

The ward was long and wide and filled with beds. It was not really a hospital, but a barn pressed into service and managed by weary doctors and exhausted VADs, young women who had come from England to nurse the casualties in the field hospitals behind the lines. All the available space was filled with pallets where the wounded lay. Some slept, some slipped into comas, some stared at the rafters; some, the better ones, with nothing worse than trench-foot, tried to sit up and converse with their neighbours. The reek of carbolic and disinfectant filled the air.

The ward was cold; the boilers were run down because there was no fuel; the men had to be washed in cold water.

It was night when Theo woke; he groaned and then was silent. His leg pounded with pain. The sutures in his scalp were tight and hurting. He looked around at what he could see of the ward; he saw nurses hurrying, not running, but walking with speeds astonishing for women. He heard abrupt, guttural cries, petering into incoherency. A young nurse approached him, glass of water in hand. She held his head while he drank; he could feel her starched white apron, the softness of her bosom beneath it, the gentle rise and fall of her breathing. He tried to remember what had happened, to latch hold of his identity, his personal certainty of his place in the world, but as soon as he thought he had it, it slipped from him like a dream.

'What year is it?' Theo asked. 'Where am I?'

The nurse registered only a moment's chagrin. 'You're in hospital,' she said. 'The year is 1918.'

Theo drank, slobbered a little in his eagerness. She reached for a towel and wiped the drip from his chin.

'Why am I here?'

'There's a war on,' she said. 'You were wounded.'

She plumped the pillow behind his head. 'You'll be all right. You're one of the lucky ones.'

Theo glanced around. He saw the long shadows cast from the lantern; he heard the man beside him with the septic arm muttering in delirium. The shadows flickering on the walls, the sounds of pain, the little hard coughs from mustard gas, the atmosphere of mortality, the women in white aprons, were all surreal. This was Purgatory, or maybe Hell.

'I'm going to die?'

The nurse looked at him. 'Rot!'

Theo fingered the blue stripe on her sleeve. 'What's that for?'

'Efficiency!'

Theo's bitter laughter rang out in the ward. ' "Efficiency"! There's a word for you!'

The sister came hurrying and motioned to the nurse to go. She hoped he wasn't going to take on like many of them, irrational, trembling, starting at sudden noises. She took his hand.

'Take it easy now,' she said comfortably. 'You're safe now.'

Theo looked into her blue eyes. The whites were bloodshot and her face was hollow with fatigue. She was wearing a blue-belted grey uniform with white cuffs and buttons, and a white veil which was pinned tightly behind her head. On her breast was a brooch in the shape of a red cross.

'Safe?' he echoed, searching his mind in panic. 'Safe? I don't even bloody know who I am. Who am I?'

The sister picked up the chart which hung at the foot of the bed. 'Afraid we don't know — except that you're an officer of the Fifth Army. We rather expected you might be able to tell us! Your dog-tags were gone!'

Theo turned his face away. 'Do you know where do I come from?'

The sister smiled. 'You sound Irish, or maybe Scottish. But I know they are sending you back to England to convalesce — they'll make the appropriate inquiries for you, so you needn't worry. But you must start to get better for the journey. You must rest now.'

In the morning, while going over the events of the night with Doctor Warren before she went off duty, the night sister said, 'I'm a bit concerned about the Irish officer.'

The doctor frowned.

'Shrapnel wounds, especially in the leg,' she forestalled him, knowing that he could not be expected to remember every case automatically. 'You took out the shrapnel yesterday morning.'

The doctor nodded. 'It's too early to say about the leg.'

'I know. But he has amnesia; doesn't know from Adam who he is. I spoke to him several times: he's panicking.'

'Give him time,' the doctor said. 'Temporary amnesia is not uncommon.'

The ward sister knew that this was true; the reminder was unnecessary. 'It's not just amnesia. He has shell-shock. He shivers uncontrollably and calls out; sometimes he chants poetry. He's disturbing the others!'

The doctor gestured brusquely. 'We've nowhere else to put him. Give him laudanum.'

Theo was feverish. Nurse Watkins, newly on duty and still sleepy-eyed, came to take his temperature.

'I'll give you a present,' Theo rambled. 'What would you like?'

The nurse shook her head. 'Just get better,' she whispered. 'We like to see the boys get better! That's the best present of all.'

Theo tried to think of any present he had ever received, and could think of none, except a puppy which someone had given him when he was small. The puppy had a big tail and fell over every time he wagged it. Did the puppy grow up? He couldn't remember. But he could see the face of the man who had given him the puppy, like something through a distorting mirror. His father? It must have been his father, a man with a moustache and brown mole on his cheek with a single black hair. But he could not remember his father's name.

The nurse held his pulse and then removed the thermometer from under his armpit. 'Don't worry,' she said, 'you'll be as right as rain.'

Theo stared at her accusingly, his eyes glazed. He held up his hands, focused on them, frowned. Into his mind came the memory of a summer day, a ring in a box, a moment of trying it on. He knew the ring was important; he had lost it; where was it now?

'I had a ring. Where is it?'

The nurse lifted her shoulders. 'Did you have a ring? I'll ask sister.' She marked his temperature on the chart. One hundred and three degrees. They would have to operate if this went on. Only yesterday one of the men with a septic leg had died. The doctor had tried to save it, had postponed amputation until it was too late.

She felt the weight of all these lives, young lives clinging to survival in differing degrees of desperation; for some the effort became intolerable and they let go and died. Fight, she urged him silently. Fight! Even if you lose the leg there is still a world and a life to be had.

She asked Sister about the ring. 'He wants it,' she said; 'it might help him. It's probably from his sweetheart.'

'Check the cupboard,' Sister said, handing over the keys. She was referring to the cupboard where the men's personal effects were kept under lock and key. The only thing the nurse found in the envelope bearing the legend, 'Scalp wounds/shrapnel/Irish/Fifth Army', and the date of admission, was a photograph of two young girls. There was no ring.

She returned to her patient, looked down at him. 'Sorry. 'Fraid there's no ring. Maybe you lost it . . .'

He sighed, muttered, and subsided into the pillow.

She studied him for a moment, and wiped the sweat from his face. He was dark-haired and had very pale, waxen skin; the blue veins throbbed in his temple. His moustache was ragged. She registered that he was probably handsome, before her attention was distracted by a young officer vomiting two beds away and she hurried to help him.

In London Jenny read the paper. The Allied forces had launched a counter-attack on the Marne. She thought of Andrew. Every day the lists of the casualties grew longer. It was as though the war was a mincer and some diabolic plan had hypnotized the world that it should feed this mincer with its sons.

'Will the war be over soon, Gramps?'

He looked up at her from his paper. 'I pray so. You should pray too.' He paused, took her hand, rubbed the back of it affectionately. 'My guess is that the German front line will collapse, forcing them to retreat.'

'What will happen then?'

'There will be an armistice.'

'Would that mean the end of the war?'

'Yes.'

He smiled at her. She was seventeen now, willowy, pretty as a picture, he thought. She had become interested in the women's suffrage movement and often discussed the question excitedly with her grandfather.

'Do you think women should have the vote, Gramps?'

'The pretty ones should!'

'That is not a sensible answer!'

He looked at her: she was furious, her head to one side, her eyes intense. 'Of course it isn't,' he said mildly. 'I'm joking!'

She laughed, relaxing, lifting a long strand of hair which she still wore down her back. 'Be serious. Do you believe in it or not?'

'Of course I do!'

'Why?'

'Simple justice!'

She embraced him. 'Good old Gramps!' He smelt of shaving soap and his breath had the familiar aroma of pear-drops. She knew about the forced feeding of suffragettes and the 'Cat and Mouse Act' which had permitted the government to release the women prisoners when they were on hunger strike, and then re-arrest them when they had recovered.

Jenny was now attending art school. She worked at her drawings and at her painting in her studio in the attic where Gramps had had a second skylight installed. She had never finished her portrait of the magician, and it lay, with other canvases, propped against the gable end of the attic.

She spent hours wandering in the National Gallery, probing the faces of the past. She marvelled at the genius of the artists, to have portrayed envy and hatred and pain and arrogance, not to mention stupidity, vanity and calculation. But alongside these depictions there was compassion, wonder, joy, and such grace and light that she felt the past and the present had become one great, multi-faceted reality, travelling inexorably towards enlightenment.

I would like to be a great painter! she thought over and over. I want to set it all down, the fury and the tenderness of being alive.

Sometimes she looked in the mirror and wondered if Andrew would think her pretty when he came home. During his absence she had built him into a hero, invested him with certain grandeur of spirit and wisdom which Andrew, trench-weary and hardened by fear, would have had difficulty in finding in himself.

'Andrew will come back!' he said.

Jenny blushed. Gramps could read her only too well. She had met Andrew when he came home on leave; the last time they had gone to the pictures, seen Charlie Chaplin who had made her laugh.

In the dark of the cinema he had leant over and kissed her mouth. 'I love you, Jen!'

The words spun round in her head. There was

a mélange of emotions: sudden involuntary triumph in her own power, discomfiture, and then the sense of security. She was loved by Andrew. By loving her he became a niche, a spar in a turbulent sea. Jenny felt in herself the force of a passionate and assertive spirit, but she feared its manifestations, reserving it for her work. Assertive women ran into a lot of trouble. Men seemed to feel challenged and threatened by them, licensed to bad behaviour towards them of one kind or another. Jenny wondered about this. If women could not be who they were for fear of men, then men were not confronting reality either. Life simply became a game, played successfully by good actors; but for everyone else, the game turned into either a battle or a shambles. However, she was sure that Andrew was not the sort of man who would feel threatened by a woman. With him, she felt, she could be herself; he would accept her, anger, doubts, warts and all.

She had not mentioned Andrew to Yvonne, but the latter seemed to suspect anyway.

'Andrew's potty about you.' She said it almost conversationally, watching for her friend's reaction.

Jenny flushed and then she laughed. 'Don't talk such rot.'

Yvonne smiled. 'I would not object to you for a sister-in-law,' she said gravely, with a twinkle. Yvonne was eighteen now, freckled, gentle, about to start her training in Hurleigh House, a

111

convalescent hospital in Surrey, where her father knew the matron and the resident surgeon.

In September Gramps was proved right and the German forces began a retreat to the Siegfried Line.

Peace came in November. On the eleventh the armistice was signed; Germany surrendered thousands of heavy guns, machine-guns and warplanes, all its U-boats, a vast number of wagons and trucks. Britain went wild. Factories closed down, people danced in the street, there were fireworks and special editions of the papers and the pubs stayed open until they ran out of beer. The king said, 'The nightmare is over.' But ten million were dead.

Gramps, while embracing Jenny, appeared doubtful. 'The nightmare is not over,' he muttered when she taxed him on his dubiousness. 'In a way it is just beginning. I think this century will see horrors such as the world has never even dreamed of!'

Jenny shook her head. 'Oh, Gramps, don't be so down in the mouth!'

Her grandfather looked at her guardedly, then smiled and said he was a crotchety old crank, and that he was better off writing articles no one read than pontificating.

'What are you writing about now?'

Gramps put his head on one side. His hair was white and receded from his forehead and his whiskers were also white. His forehead was scored and his eyes were enmeshed in wrinkles.

'About power, my darling. How it manifests itself under many guises and behind so many lies.'

Andrew was coming home at last and Yvonne was throwing a party.

'It's a fancy-dress party,' she explained. 'Wear something different, dress up in something.'

Jenny was silent. She knew what she would wear — an old dress of her grandmother's which was in a chest in the attic and something else she had almost forgotten.

'Gramps,' she said, 'where is my mask? You remember, the old mask, the enamelled thing in silver — or whatever it was — that I used to play with? Do you still have it?'

He did not meet her eyes. 'I'm sorry,' he said, 'I'm getting old and forgetful. What mask was that?'

'Oh, Gramps, you must remember; I found it in the garden shed years ago. I want to wear it to Yvonne's party.'

Gramps remembered it well, too well. When Jenny had told him several years earlier that he could get rid of it, he had — in a moment of superstitious chagrin — taken it out to the garden with the intention of burning it on the bonfire. But the thing had not burned; it was there among the ashes when the fire was dead, staring at him. It was warm from the fire, smoke-stained, but when he washed it he found it was undamaged. He was relieved about this, having

113

vented his anger at the thing; it might be valuable, being obviously very old. But it belonged to Jen, as did everything her father had left, which amounted to six hundred pounds in the bank, a selection of leather travelling bags, some clothes and several pairs of men's shoes.

The clothes and shoes had been given away to charity, and Gramps had put the mask away and tried to forget about it. He did not want to have to make decisions about it. He did not want Jenny's blame; but neither did he want to be instrumental in bringing the curio back into her life. After their conversation years earlier, when she had spoken of her nightmares, she had never mentioned it again.

'I don't know where it went,' Gramps answered, coughing, 'but I'll look for it!' He was being economical with the truth, because he knew where he had left it. 'It's not suitable for a party, anyway, is it?'

Jenny accepted this readily enough. 'Maybe not.' She remembered the dreams she used to have once, which had started with her discovery of the mask. Better to do nothing to resurrect them, although she dismissed them now as the rag-tag of childhood fantasy.

'Remember the dreams I used to have once,' she asked her grandfather with a half laugh, 'dreams about a man who asked me about that stupid mask.'

Her grandfather's face assumed a careful expression. 'Yes. What did you say he was like?'

114

'He was . . . dark . . .' she said, 'the kind of darkness that has everything focused in it, in the same way that black is supposed to swallow every colour. He wanted me to wear it — the mask.'

'I see. Do you still dream of him?'

'No. I never dreamt of him after I painted him.' He straightened a little to look at her more carefully.

'You painted him?'

'A bad portrait. I imagined him as a magician of the seventeenth century. But I didn't finish the picture.'

'Why?'

'I suppose I didn't like him staring at me all the time.' She laughed. 'He's staring at the wall now!'

'How is Yvonne? Is she happy to be finished with school?' Gramps asked with an effort, wishing to change the subject and trying also to put from him the fatigue and the sickness which had inched itself upon him during the day.

Jen nodded. 'She's been accepted for training in a convalescent home. She's due to start next week.'

'Good. It's probably a nicer start than a general hospital. Her father probably pulled a few strings.'

'Gramps, are you all right?'

He closed his book. His chest was heavy and he felt light-headed, shivery, and when he tried to get up he stumbled.

Jenny shouted for Mary, and between them they got him up to bed. Then Mary went for Dr Stacey.

'Spanish flu,' the doctor said when he came downstairs. 'Keep him warm, plenty of hot drinks, soup; someone should stay with him as much as possible.' He looked at Jenny with concern, trying to tailor what he had to say, to prepare her without frightening her. The lines around his eyes and mouth seemed deeper than usual; his small professional smile froze her heart.

'I'll stay with him,' she whispered, struggling with the sudden overwhelming feeling that the very ground under her feet was about to be taken away from her. 'How bad is it?'

'He's not young any more, you know, Jenny.'

She saw him out. Gramps had once told her the doctor was a Freemason. As a child Jenny had thought that was why he never charged them a fee: he was Free.

In Hurleigh House, the converted stately home that now served as a convalescent home, Yvonne nursed Theo O'Reilly. He had lost a leg below the knee and had been shell-shocked to the point where he simply babbled inanities in bursts of horror and then was silent again. Yvonne tried to get him to talk. She tried to make him talk of his home. She assumed he came from Ireland; his accent was Irish, but she also knew that they had not yet succeeded in tracing his regiment or his people. He could remember nothing that helped, and still seemed to expect exploding shells at every hand's-turn.

She was allowed to dress his stump every day. It was an easy dressing; it was healing well and he had been measured for a wooden leg.

'Tell me about your home,' she asked him one day as she brought him, in his wheelchair, to his favourite window in the gallery, where he could look out at the winter lawn and the small artificial lake. There was a fountain in the middle of this lake, but it was silent now.

Yvonne picked up the woollen rug which had slipped to the floor and tucked it around him. There was something about this man, about the cut of him and his searching vulnerability which tugged at her heartstrings.

'Home is where the heart is,' Theo said.

Yvonne stood beside him and looked out of the window. 'Yes, especially when you are far away. You must long for it — Ireland.'

Theo seemed to start. He turned to look at her; his eyes were perfectly sane. 'Where?'

'Ireland. Isn't that your home?'

The patient stared at her without apparent understanding. Then he spat one word, 'Busybody!' and went back to staring expressionlessly out at the winter garden and the elegant stone balustrade of the terrace.

Yvonne was hurt. She had not yet learned to steel herself against the affronts of the unhinged. She had not expected it from Theo; in watching him she had allowed herself to project qualities on to him which answered hidden requirements of her own: the ache for meaning, the ache to love and be loved. She moved away, passing two other patients who were playing chess. They had heard the exchange and looked at her ruefully.

'Don't mind old Paddy there.' One of them shook his head and raised his hand to his head, tapping the side of his skull meaningfully and compressing his lips knowingly.

A dressing-trolley rattled down the corridor pushed by an orderly. It collided with a table and the instruments and kidney dishes clanged. One of them fell to the floor. There was a sudden commotion in the window niche where Theo was staring at the garden. He launched himself out of the wheelchair and lay, convulsed, on the floor, trying to burrow into the rug like a distraught animal scurrying for its warren.

Yvonne ran to him, called the orderly to help her, knelt beside him, soothing him, and then helped the orderly lift him back into the chair.

'Sorry about the noise, mate,' the orderly said. 'I wasn't looking where I was going.'

Theo did not respond. He shook while Yvonne rearranged the rug.

'You're all right,' she whispered, overwhelmed with pity for him. 'It was just a small accident; you're safe.'

Theo did not look at her. After a moment he turned perfectly sensible blue eyes on her and hissed, 'Why don't you all just bugger off?'

Yvonne turned away. She was tired and suddenly wanted to cry.

'There's no use looking like a week of wet Sundays, Nurse. If that's part of your training it's a poor show, a poor show!'

Yvonne looked back at the sane eyes. She answered him coldly. 'The war is over. Didn't anyone tell you? So shape up, Lieutenant — or whatever you are! I don't think you're as shell-shocked as you pretend. You may have been very plucky, you may be a hero for all I know, but that doesn't give you the right to behave like a pig!'

She turned on her heel then, feeling ashamed of her outburst. She was not aware that Theo had turned his head to look after her.

Later, she heard his voice. 'Nurse, I say, Nurse!' She came to him reluctantly. He had a photograph in his hand, pointed to one of the two girls smiling for ever at the camera.

'That girl is the spitting image of you!'

Yvonne felt herself pale. The photograph was of herself and Jen. How did this man come into possession of it? She remembered the day it was taken, remembered to whom she had sent it.

'Where did you get this?'

He shook his head. 'I can't remember,' he said in a low, unhappy voice. 'And, Nurse,' he added as he watched Yvonne's face study the snap, 'I'm sorry if I've behaved like a "pig".'

Yvonne smiled at him, seeing that his face quivered, that he was vulnerable, lonely, fearful, and also that, in spite of his confused state, the pulse of some gentle humanity beat in him. But where did he get the photograph she had sent to Andrew?

'It is me. I sent this to my brother, Andrew Stacey, when he was at the Front.'

He shook his head. 'So where did I get it?'

'You were at the Somme,' Yvonne said. 'Andrew was there, too.'

'Did he come back?'

She nodded.

He looked again at the photograph. 'Who is the other girl?'

'That's Jenny Stephenson. She is one of my oldest friends. She's practically engaged to Andrew . . .'

Theo sighed. 'Is she a nurse as well?'

'No,' Yvonne said with a smile. 'She wouldn't care for it. Nursing wouldn't suit her at all!'

'Why not?'

'She's not the type, that's all. She wouldn't have the patience. She wants to be a painter.'

'Is she good?'

Yvonne thought of Jenny's attic and of the canvases she had stacked there, of the strange portrait she had once watched her work on. 'She could be. I don't know enough about art to say.' She saw how he stared at Jenny, who smiled from the snapshot with all her innocence.

Later they came to fit him with his artificial leg. Yvonne stood beside him as he tried to stand, tried to take a step. He staggered and she grasped his arm, steadying him.

He put an arm around her and turned to smile into her face. It was the smile of the little-boy-lost, trusting, unguarded. He tried a few more steps, held on to the rails beside him, before the doctor sent him back to his chair and went away.

'And in case I haven't said so already, O lovely Nurse,' Theo continued when the doctor had gone, and he sat panting with exertion and triumph, 'I'm sorry I was so often rude to you. I've been a bit desperate.'

He paused to consider her reaction. 'I am a one-legged man trying to find out who he is. I suppose I've been trying out different personas to see if they fit.' He smiled ruefully. 'Am I forgiven?'

Yvonne looked into his eyes and fell in love.

'I'm not going to Yvonne's party,' Jenny told Gramps when he inquired about it. 'I'm going to stay and mind you.' It was a week later. Gramps seemed to be better. He looked frail but he was able to sit up against his pillows. His cough had improved and the doctor professed himself very pleased with his progress. 'For a man of his age, he has surprising reserves,' he told Jenny in the hall downstairs. 'But he still needs plenty of building up. The danger now, you see, is pneumonia.'

'He will not get pneumonia,' Jenny said. 'I won't let him!'

She handed the doctor his hat, helped him on

with his coat. He looked at her with a real smile, raised his grey eyebrows and told her to mind herself, not to tire herself too much. 'If you come down sick, what will happen then? I hope you are coming to Andrew's homecoming party? Be good for you — a break. I'll pop around and have a look at your grandfather!'

'Thank you, but I think I'd better stay with him!'

'I'm perfectly all right. I insist that you go!' Gramps said sternly now in his no-nonsense voice. 'Mary can look after me. I'm better. I'm fine. Off you go. Let me see you in your finery!'

Jenny demurred, but she eventually obeyed. Gramps had threatened to get up if she did not. She did not bother to look for the mask, because she knew Gramps would not approve, but she went to the attic to find the black velvet dress which was folded in a camphor chest with a few other old pieces of finery, which had once been deemed too good to throw out.

She had not been into the attic for some time, chiefly because of Gramps' illness, and she felt how it welcomed her, dusty and cold though it was, and how the winter light from the skylights was soft and mysterious. There was her easel with the new portrait she had begun: one of Andrew; it was still a charcoal sketch and she would need him to sit for her, but she had tried to catch the way he leant backwards when he sat down, and the asymmetrical slant of his face. She had tried to capture his confidence. She sat on her cushions for a few moments to study the drawing, and then she took the velvet dress from the trunk and carried it towards the narrow attic stairs. But as she did so she remembered the portrait of the magician, and she glanced at the spot where she had left it. It was there, leaning against the wall with some other pieces of her work, and she bent her head to move back beneath the rafters and turn it around. She was not prepared for the impact of the eyes, or the expression. The magician examined her, heavy-lidded, from a face which was complete.

I thought I had left it half finished, she whispered, gazing at her handiwork. 'I must be imagining things!' She tore her eyes away from the face and saw that the clothes, black silk with a broad grey collar, were also painted in. One hand, slender and aristocratic, lay on top of the other. A gold ring gleamed dully, reflecting light.

Jenny was fascinated. 'It's good. I did it well. I didn't realise I did it well . . .'

In her elation she forgot the cold. She stood, rapt in appraisal. She reached out to touch the painting, snatching her hand back in the sudden fear that she was about to touch something warm and living. She glanced from the portrait to the sketch on the easel. The figure drawn in charcoal seemed stiff, the work amateurish, the subject callow.

Jenny stood for another moment, rooted in indecision and stupefaction. 'I must have given it more time than I realized,' she muttered, taking the magician's portrait and turning it back to its survey of the wall. Then she thought: I must show it to Gramps.

It was only then that she realized that she was shivering with cold, and she took up the dress which she had let drop, shut the attic door behind her, and hurried down to the warm kitchen. Mary was blacking the range, and Jenny shook out the dress so she could admire it. Mary oohed at its portrait neckline, the bustle and tight sleeves, and then made her try it on, pronounced it too long, and spent some considerable time in taking up the hem, and in airing and brushing it.

Later, Jenny presented herself for grandparental inspection. The dress still reeked of camphor, but she twirled in it, sweeping the floor with its short train. The waist was tight and she had to hold her breath.

Gramps was misty-eyed, remembering a woman in it with velvet skin, and a time when everything was young.

'Have a lovely party. I remember when that dress was new. Your grandmother was fond of it; it showed off her lovely figure and her complexion!'

'It's a bit long for me, Gramps. Mary had to take it up. And it's a bit tight,' she added, making mock strangulation noises. For a second she thought of the portrait of the magician, and wanted to tell him how good it was, but she saw how he smiled indulgently, how he was happily thinking of days long-gone. Jenny followed his glance to the photograph of her grandmother on the mantelpiece, a woman who stood very straight with her head slightly inclined, as though she were shy of the camera. Beside her was a tall parlour-palm. She was holding a folded fan.

'You need a fan!' Gramps said. He told her to open the bottom drawer of his chest. Wrapped in tissue paper was an ivory fan, fretted with a filigree design.

'Oh! Can I borrow this?'

'Of course — it's yours! Off you go now!'

I hope I find someone as nice as you to marry, Gramps! she thought as she picked up the train and made her way slowly downstairs. Because it was dark, Mary accompanied her to the Staceys', even though it was so close. Jenny warned her at the door to send for her at once if there was any change in Gramps.

'He'll be all right,' Mary said. 'Don't be fretting.'

Yvonne met Jenny with a hug and complimented her on her dress. She was wearing a Grecian-style gown in pale blue, her red-gold hair was coiled after what she thought was the fashion of ancient Greece. She had looked it up in one of Jenny's art books. Jenny complimented her on her appearance. 'You look like one of the three Graces!'

'And you look absolutely wonderful,' Yvonne returned in genuine astonishment. 'Where did you find that incredible dress?'

'It was in a chest in the attic. Mary had to take it up.'

'You look completely different — a sort of *grande dame* — it shows up your skin and your eyes.' She paused. 'Come upstairs, I have exactly the thing to set it off,' and Jenny followed her friend upstairs and into her bedroom where Yvonne rummaged in a drawer and extracted something in a velvet bag. It was a diamond paste tiara, and Yvonne set it on her friend's upswept hair. 'There, now you look like a queen!'

Jenny saw herself in the mirror: slender, regal, a being from another age, dressed in rich black velvet, with a portrait neckline, tiny waist, and diamonds glittering in her hair. 'Oh, Yvonne, I don't recognize myself!'

'Andrew won't either! He's out but he'll be back shortly. It's all organized — a big surprise!'

'You haven't told me about yourself,' Jenny said as they crossed the landing to the stairs. 'About how you like Hurleigh House?'

'It's all right. Work is as I expected . . . much of it is awful. But I have met the most incredible man!'

'Who?'

'The original unknown soldier!'

Then came the sound of the front door opening, and Andrew's voice in the hall. 'Go on,' Yvonne whispered. 'Go on down. Knock him for six!'

Andrew was in uniform. He stood staring at

Jenny as she walked towards him down the stairs, holding her train in one hand and her folded fan in the other. His mouth opened and then shut.

'Jenny Stephenson! I don't believe it!' He moved to take her hand, and with a flourish bent to kiss it.

Jenny smiled, but she was struck by how much he had changed. Even in the last few months he had become older, a different person from the fresh-faced boy who had left them for the trenches four years earlier. His childhood and adolescence were over. He was twenty now, a young man with a war behind him. His sandy hair was brushed back from his forehead. He was in uniform; he projected the veneer of confidence which he had deliberately cultivated in the trenches; he was handsome, clean-cut, and he loved her. It was all there in his eyes, a pantheon of make-believe rooted in desire.

When the party was over, and people had drifted away with many 'Thank you, darlings', and 'Wonderful party!', Yvonne sat by the remains of the drawing-room fire with her brother and her friend, and told them about the young man she was nursing in Hurleigh Hall who had, incredibly, in his possession, the photograph of herself and Jen which she had sent to Andrew during the early part of the war.

'Good God, it must be that poor bastard O'Reilly. He begged me for that picture. I refused, of course, but later I lost it!' Andrew smiled at Jenny apologetically. 'So now we know!'

Yvonne blushed and said excitedly, 'Is that his name? O'Reilly?'

'Yes. Captain O'Reilly. They called him Theo. A bit off the deep end. Is he all right?'

'He was measured for his new leg today! He has amnesia, doesn't even know his name!'

'He was always a mad Mick,' Andrew said, and then he added, 'I suppose I'd better go and see him.'

Yvonne stood up to find a pencil. 'This means they'll be able to track down his family. Isn't that wonderful?'

Andrew frowned as she left the room and turned to Jenny. 'I hope she's not soft on this fellow. Do you know what he told me once: that he was possessed by the devil!'

Jenny recoiled. 'How horrible!'

'Well, no, he didn't say that exactly, but something like it! Still, mustn't talk about such tommy rot to a beautiful woman. We were all a bit mad in the trenches!'

'You seem perfectly sane to me. Will you sit for your portrait? I've already started it!'

Andrew professed himself delighted. 'Really, you've begun a portrait of me? That's simply ripping, Jen, I am honoured. To be painted by a goddess!'

Jenny felt that Andrew was being unnecessarily effusive. But she smiled. She watched the glowing coals in the fire. She was enjoying Andrew's words. She was enjoying being alive; she saw herself at one remove — a beautiful woman in a graceful gown being worshipped. She was aware of her beauty because it was reflected in Andrew's eyes. She was aware that it conferred on her a certain kind of covert authority, like someone who had been given the power to walk on water. But she thought of Gramps and murmured, 'It's late. I'd better go!'

'There something I want to ask you,' Andrew said, the timbre of his voice changing and his eyes full of adoration. 'I didn't mean to ask you now, but it's very important . . .'

Jenny glanced at him and looked back quickly into the fire. Andrew felt the remoteness in her, her inaccessability, and a combination of that and her beauty filled him with overwhelming desire. His expectations of the physical and the metaphysical had become one. He was unable to wait, to find the real woman behind the velvet dress and the shining hair. He was aware only of the thirst of his body and his soul.

'I want to propose to you, Jen. I want to marry you.' Now that this moment had come, this instant of affirmation, she felt firstly triumph and then chagrin. It was too soon, too demanding, too ready to crowd her life and commandeer it. When she made no response he asked anxiously, 'Jen? Will you?'

'I'll have to ask Gramps,' she said, turning to him, uncertain how to deal with the situation.

Andrew was ecstatic. Her lack of enthusiasm he put down to diffidence. He clasped her hand and when Yvonne returned said, 'We're engaged!'

Yvonne, who had deliberately spent an undue amount of time in her hunt for a pencil, came back with a fountain pen and a notepad. She threw her arms around Jenny and then around her brother, and congratulated them tearfully. 'It's what I've always wanted . . .'

She left the pen and pad with her brother so he could write down Theo's details, saying laughingly that three was a crowd and that she was going to bed.

Andrew pulled Jenny towards the couch and kissed her passionately, held her tight against him so that she felt his body erect and her breasts against his chest. Jenny submitted to his embraces in a surge of curiosity and new power. He thrust his tongue tentatively into her mouth. It wasn't a very long tongue, and was more an irritant than a cause of excitement. She wondered why she didn't feel excited. She thought the world of Andrew; Gramps thought the world of Andrew. She felt the bulge of his crotch press against her.

'What have you got in your pocket?'

'A naggin of whiskey. Oh, Jen, sweetheart, I'm joking! Do you know nothing? That's my cock. You can feel it if you like!' He unbuttoned his trousers, took her hand and put it inside.

Jenny felt the warm, stiff penis, felt the crinkly pubic hair on his stomach. She said nothing, but she moved her fingers along the length of his organ in gentle exploration. Andrew groaned.

Jenny withdrew her hand. Andrew saw her burnished hair in the lamplight, the soft outline of her cheek and forehead, and the sweep of her lashes. He put his arm around her, drew her face towards his. The tiara, which had already been unsettled by his previous embrace, came adrift and hung down over her temple. He removed it as gently as he could, but some of her hair came undone and a long tress spilled down on to her shoulder.

Andrew put the tiara on the occasional table beside the sofa, and looked at his love, who was busily trying to re-establish order in her coiffure.

'I can't wait to get you into bed.'

'What will you do with me in bed?' she asked a little archly, fixing hairpins assiduously to disguise how nervous this suggestion made her.

He laughed. 'I will make love to you. I will put that big fellow you've just been feeling inside you and move him up and down, backwards and forwards.' He waited for her squeals of delight, and when they didn't come he asked, 'Do you think you will like that?'

'I shouldn't think so,' Jenny said seriously, after a moment in which she had considered the prospect with dismay. 'There isn't the slightest chance that he'll fit.'

'Of course he will, my darling!' Andrew whispered, chuckling with pleasure at her naïveté; but he knew that the conversation had taken an improper turn, and remembered the respect due to his fiancée. He realized for the first time that she had moved away from him, and that her body was inclining, not towards him, but towards the other end of the sofa.

'I'm sorry, I shouldn't be talking to you like this . . . I've had too much to drink . . . Bad show, really. Shall I walk you home?'

That night, when she lay awake thinking of the events of the evening, she wondered again what had happened to the mask. She had almost forgotten all about it until the party had brought it back to mind. She remembered the strange feelings she used to get, the sense of being visible to someone she half saw, someone she saw without seeing. But her phantom hadn't troubled her for a long time; she wondered if she had been 'a bit strange in herself', as Mary had put it, to have imagined it at all. She had heard of adolescents being visited by strange occurrences. Yet, at the time, she knew that she had not been frightened; it had seemed natural, more real than anything in life she had ever known. Where are you, who were you? she wondered. She felt she had lost him; she felt an irredeemable sense of loss, but at the same time there was relief. She could live life at the pace and level she was born to now: nothing too exciting, nothing preposterous; the calm tenor of her future was already mapped.

She would marry Andrew in the spring; she loved him enough for that, surely; they would live out their days together. When the thought occurred to her that there was a portrait in the attic which was not entirely removed from the fantasies which had so troubled her, she put the thought away. It was a good portrait, and it proved that she had ability.

Yvonne's dislike of the thing made her reluctant, wondering if there was something as creepy about it as her friend seemed to think. If she could finish the one of Andrew with the same level of expertise, she would have proof that portraits were her true métier. But it was too soon to make such assumptions.

Gramps had been awake when she had come home from the party. She had gone in to see him. He lay there, barely visible in the gaslight from the landing. She saw his glass of water on the bedside table, and his book and his spectacles carefully placed on top of it.

'Did you . . . have a nice time . . . darling?' His breathing was shallow, and he wheezed as he spoke.

She sat at the foot of his bed. She was still warm from Andrew's kisses; still disturbed by the prospect of penetration by what Andrew called 'that big fellow'.

'Yes, wonderful time . . .'

'How's Andrew?'

'He's fine.' She paused, studying her grandfather's form beneath the bed-clothes. 'He asked me to marry him.'

She felt him tense, felt his sudden intake of breath. 'What did you say?'

'I said . . . I told him he would have to ask you.' Gramps was silent. His reaction, now that what he wanted had come, was that it was a mismatch. How can you marry fire with water? But she would, at least, be safe. To know that he would leave her safe was all he wanted.

He put out his hand and drew her towards him. 'God bless you, darling,' he said in a full voice.

Jenny bent down to kiss his leathery cheek, and found to her chagrin that it was wet with tears. 'Are you unhappy, Gramps? I won't marry him if it makes you unhappy. I won't marry anyone you don't approve of.' The comment shocked him, suggesting as it did a less than tempestuous desire on her part to take on Andrew for life.

'Do you love this young man, Jen?' he asked seriously, in his no-nonsense voice. 'He has a good inheritance from his mother, and he is eligible and decent, but there are other considerations.'

She laughed. 'I'm very fond of him, Gramps. I've known him ever so long.'

'Well, marry him, then,' he said, 'with my blessing. Marry him and good fortune to the two of you! It makes me happy, Jen, because I may have to leave you.'

'Oh Gramps — what do you mean?' The sudden tears burned her cheeks.

'Nothing, darling. I'm fine for the moment, but no one lasts for ever!'

'He said he would talk to you tomorrow,' Jenny said as she gently shut his door behind her.

Jen had left Andrew with the feeling that the die was cast and that it had happened too easily. Her life had been sewn up for her before she could blink. She had allowed the pressure of other people's expectations to make the most important decision in her life for her. She knew they were probably right; she was afraid of being selfish, of giving offence; she did not know her own wishes in the matter sufficiently to give a categorical refusal. Until the moment when he had popped the question, she had quite happily accepted the eventual prospect of Andrew as husband.

But Andrew was not quite what she had thought him. During the hours spent in his company she had detected in him a kind of presumptuous vacancy, but one she refused to think about. She also recoiled instinctively from the memory of having put her hand inside his trousers. It seemed indelicate of him to have engineered it, and indelicate of her to have accepted it. But I'm an engaged woman, she thought. Being engaged made it all right. There was a romance about being engaged. But as she thought of marriage a cold shiver blew through her heart. Somewhere beyond the reach of her consciousness she heard the prison door clang to behind her. She shook off this malaise, remembering Andrew's eyes, full of loving delight. She thought of his tongue with indifference; she thought again of the erection she had felt against her and the warm, stiff organ she had held in her hand. She thrust from her the thought that she was being swamped in the ordinary; an ordinary young man with a penis, remarkable only for his youth. That his youth would go, that the dynamic of it would degenerate into something set, and then what? That challenge and pain were preferable to what would be then.

Once she had known a presence that had challenged all her perspectives.

Where are you? she thought dreamily. You never existed, did you?; you were a figment of the mind. You said you would come for me, but I knew you couldn't. Anyway, it's too late now! She waited, being very tired and on the verge of sleep. But all she heard was the sound of a motor car coughing in the street.

Chapter Six

It was sensational . . . in its notable animus against the female sex.

The Catholic Encyclopaedia (1912)

The New Year dawned. It was 1919 and the world was at rest. In January the peace conference got under way at Versailles. Jenny and Andrew planned their wedding. Gramps was still not well. He had not recovered fully from the Spanish influenza and said he would like to see them married before he died. Jenny wept secretly, but she decided to humour him. She did not expect him to die, she could not even imagine it, but she did not want a big wedding either, so she and Andrew, who was only too willing to marry in haste, went to a registry office one cold morning and came back to say the knot was tied. Gramps was delighted. For days on end he seemed much better, and insisted that the newly-weds went away on a honeymoon. They went to Brighton but only stayed for a few days. When they came back it was to find that Gramps had had a relapse. A few days later he was dead.

Jenny grieved. She felt very alone. Yvonne seldom came home now, evidently preferring the ambience of Hurleigh House. Andrew had moved in and had taken up an accounting job in the City. Overnight he assumed the responsibilities of a husband, was well pleased to assume them, to see himself as breadwinner, head of his own household. But he never sat for the unfinished portrait. When he followed Jenny to the attic once, where she had gone to grieve for Gramps, the thing foremost on his mind was making love. He tried to comfort her, but he wanted to make love. Jenny resisted. She showed him the charcoal sketch of himself; he only stared at it and made a curt comment. Then he flicked through her work and found the portrait of the magician. 'Who's this cove?' he demanded dismissively.

'He's a magician,' Jenny said defensively, wiping away the tears of loss for Gramps that came in spurts no matter how she tried to stop them.

He turned to her with ostensible husbandly tolerance, which did not mask his disappointed ardour. 'Oh, Jen, when are you going to grow up? Painting magicians, I ask you!'

Jenny looked at the portrait. 'You don't think I did it well?'

'Oh, Jen,' Andrew repeated in growing exasperation.

He reached out suddenly and pulled her down on to the cushions, fumbling for the buttons of her blouse, hiking her skirt up. Jenny saw the way his face distorted, the carnal greed. She shoved him away, and stood up beneath the skylight, adjusting her clothes and breathing hard.

'Leave me alone . . . just leave me alone.'

'What is the matter with you? You're supposed to be my wife!'

'There's nothing the matter with me,' she shouted with a desperation which took her as much by surprise as it did him. 'I just want some time to myself without you perpetually following me around, pawing me. I can't stand it. I just can't stand it . . . Being a wife doesn't mean I should be pawed to death!'

Andrew stared at her in horror. He got up with as much dignity as he could and stormed down the attic stairs.

When he was gone, Jenny burst into tears. 'Oh, Gramps, why did you have to die? It would be all right if you were still alive!'

Eventually she dried her eyes and put the small portrait on the easel. The dark eyes seemed alive, looking back at her from the layers of her own painstaking effort.

'If you are a magician,' she said, 'why can't you do something. If I could only be with him again, just once . . . Oh, Gramps, why did you have to leave me?'

She stayed in the attic until night came. First the dusk crept quickly in through the skylights, and then it was night and you could see the moon behind some clouds and then a few stars. Her eyes were used to the dark, and she could make out the shape of various things in the attic: the old camphor chest to which she had returned the black velvet dress, the broken Singer sewing-machine with the foot-trestle, the cracked basin and ewer on top of the low chest of drawers. She lay on her cushions and covered herself with a rug which she kept on standby for winter days. After a little while she fell asleep, and when she woke it was to hear Mary calling her. The salt from her tears was dry on her cheeks; but she felt comforted and at peace. She smelt something in the air and recognized the scent of pear-drops and the faint aroma of tobacco. She tried to remember her dream. 'Gramps,' she whispered, 'was that you?' But the dream was gone and all that was left was the combination of scents and the peace.

In the kitchen, Mary had prepared supper. She looked apologetically at Jenny, drew a letter from the pocket of her apron, and said she would soon be going back to Scotland, that she was needed at home.

Yvonne went on with her training. Hurleigh House would close soon, and she had applied for a place in St Thomas's Hospital in London.

Theo remained withdrawn, but he was no longer an unknown quantity.

'Your name is Theodore O'Reilly,' Dr Perry told him triumphantly one morning, not long after Yvonne had spoken to her brother. He consulted his notes. 'It seems you are from a place called Kilashane. It's in Ireland — County Cork!' He watched his patient for the lightening of the eyes, the flood of recollection, the sudden rush of adrenaline. You are a captain — Second Grenadier Division; you are known as Theo to your friends!' He raised his eyebrows, waited.

'You don't say!' Theo said, looking more bemused than anything else, like someone who had been told he had landed a part in a play, or that he had been accidentally married by proxy to a stranger. 'Are you quite sure? There's no mistake?'

Dr Perry shook his head. 'No mistake, my dear boy. You've been rumbled. Your family are on their way to take you home!'

'You don't say!' Theo repeated, looking stunned. 'Who are these people? I mean, who are my family?'

The doctor blew a little air into his cheeks. 'Their name is O'Reilly, same as yours,' he said in semi-exasperation. He had hoped that his news would have jogged the patient's memory and he was disappointed. He glanced at his notes again. 'Kilashane House, Ballyshane. Does it mean nothing to you?'

Theo put his hand to his head. 'I don't know, I don't remember,' he muttered, angry at the disability which was keeping from him the full import of what the doctor was telling him, angry at seeming a fool, angry at the status of patient, or nut, or whatever you were when people could shuffle you around and give you away to strangers.

'Well, your mother and sister are apparently

141

en route to find you. When you see them it may do the trick. Don't worry about it in the meantime: never any point in worrying . . . So chin up, that's the thing!' He moved away, but turned back. 'I hear you're to be decorated. There's something to chew on!'

Theo lay on his bed, tried to think, to remember the war, the firing line, the trenches, the smells, the artillery, anything that would open for him a window on the past. It was night and supper was over. The other men talked; someone was yarning on about an incident involving Matron and there was laughter; then someone played the gramophone.

After a while, all sounds seemed to recede, and Theo slipped into a disturbed sleep. He found himself in Ireland, a different Theo, walking jauntily through the archway of Trinity College, aware of the bronze statues of Goldsmith and Burke behind the railings on either side, the hum of the city, the rattle of trams and the clopping of horses pulling drays. The porter was wearing his dark blue riding hat and coat and acknowledged him briefly. Underneath the archway, with its instant smell of academia, the cobbles were made of wood, hexagonal blocks set into the ground. There were posters advising of various outings, society meetings, boat-club venues, debates. Theo crossed the cobbled square under the campanile to his rooms in 'Botany Bay'. He climbed the narrow wooden stairs to the quarters he shared with Jonathan Foy. The latter was there, donning his undergraduate gown. 'Hurry up,' he said, 'we'll be late for Commons.'

Theo groaned in mock terror, took his gown from the peg behind the door. As they went back downstairs, Foy said, 'I say, O'Reilly, Rutherford and Kelly are on for it this evening. It's amazing . . . The fellow is probably a charlatan . . . But it's a rum business, all the same.'

Theo was intrigued. He knew Foy was referring to a medium who conducted séances in the South Circular Road. Foy had been to one of these the week before, and had returned confused and excited. Now Jonathan asked, 'Are you game?'

'Why not? I'll go and hold your hand!'

The dream began to whirl in and out of confusion. He was at a séance, holding hands around a table; objects moved without apparent cause; the medium spoke with a low, compelling voice, a male voice hypnotic with monotone and a certain kind of power. He heard his own name mentioned. He sat, too stiff with fright to move. 'Who dares give himself to me?' the voice said. 'Who dares?' Then Theo was speaking: 'Look, I've had enough of this.'

'Are you scared?' Kelly whispered. 'I dare you! I bet you haven't the stomach for it!'

'Don't break the circle,' Rutherford hissed.

Theo snatched his hand away, broke the human chain and with an effort at bravado announced, 'Right now I'd give myself to any ambient demon in exchange for a pint!' He waited for the laugh, but it did not come. 'Fair exchange is no robbery,' he said with an attempt at a guffaw. 'Come, Spirit, do your worst!' Still no laugh. The medium moaned, slumping into his armchair. Theo's fellow students faded backwards, as though they had been figments of the imagination. Theo felt as though the power had left his limbs. It seemed to him that he was on a moor at night, and that the coldest wind he had ever known was rushing at him, through him, blowing part of him away.

He woke sweating. There was only the breathing of the other men in the ward and a few snores rattling. The last thing he had remembered before he surfaced was being in a pub with the same students and finding a pint he had not ordered standing in front of him on the bar. 'Who bought me that?' he had demanded, certain that it was a joke. No one laughed. But they had all turned away from him, averting their eyes.

The morning after the dream, Yvonne came by to congratulate Theo. She was on the best of terms with him now. She brought him a few poetry books from home: Tennyson, Rupert Brooke, Swinburne. She hoped that they would make him focus on something outside himself. He looked through the volumes, quoted a familiar verse at her here and there with a smile. She thought he looked very pale.

'I heard the news, Captain O'Reilly,' she whispered in his ear. 'Now we know who you are —

so all your secrets are out. I hear there's even talk of a little medal — Military Cross — gallantry over and above the call of duty . . . You went back into the firing line for a wounded man.' She shook her head. 'You *are* a dark horse!'

But the badinage was lost on Theo, and the new certainty of his identity seemed to plunge him back into depression. 'I don't want a medal,' he said, his jaw working. 'I can't accept a piece of tin for something I can't even bloody remember!' He squeezed his eyes shut, knit his brow and shook his head. Then, to her consternation, she saw tears ooze from the corners of his eyes and his mouth pucker.

It's all been too much for him, she thought. To know he has a family, roots, must be overwhelming. Like being discovered on a desert island and brought home.

She wanted to put her arms around him and hold him close, but instead she said, 'I'll take you out on the terrace for a walk if you like.'

Theo did not reply and she took silence as consent.

She looked around for his walking stick, placed it across his knees, and wheeled his chair to the french window and through it to the Georgian terrace outside with its classical stone balustrade. It was a mild day for the time of year, a false spring. Some birds, deluded into thinking that winter was over, were chirping in the garden. It had rained earlier, and the air was very fresh.

Yvonne parked the wheelchair by the balustrade, from where they could see the shrubbery and the artificial lake and the line of bare, skeletal trees about half a mile away which marked the roadway.

'Don't you want to go home?' she asked gently. 'You don't seem terribly enthusiastic!'

He turned to look up at her. 'But how can it be home when I won't know it? No! Home is here, with you!'

She was silent, touched, but uncertain whether she should respond. 'Oh, Yvonne, you can't imagine how rotten it is . . . to have a blank instead of a memory. It's as though you were born a month ago; it's as though you weren't human. And bits and pieces come and go like dreams, but I don't know whether they're memories or fantasies. It's indescribable!'

'You must have patience,' she counselled. 'You will improve; little by little you will find it all coming back.' She tried to sound knowledgeable, which she was not. But she willed for him that he would recover, because she could not bear his pain.

He stared down at the garden. 'Will I? I wonder. It's not just the memory, it's as though there's something positively fighting my attempts to recover my wholeness. It's as though something or someone was trying to squeeze me out.' He turned to look at her again and she saw that the blue of his eyes had become very dark. 'Every time I think I have some concrete recol-

146

lection within my grasp, something very strong impedes my grasp of it. And I find it takes more and more energy and becomes more and more difficult. I'm being pushed against the shell of my own self; soon that will crack and then . . . what price me?'

Yvonne shook her head. 'You are allowing your imagination to run away with you. You are beginning to improve! Dr Perry thinks so . . .'

'That is because I talk . . . to you. He sees me reading poetry. He sees that as the beginning of my return to the world of real people. He does not realise that it is only an escape. I am not really improving, Yvonne! I know, because I live inside this body, inside this mind, and am aware of what is going on in it.'

Yvonne looked around. She was due on duty in the linen room. Any moment, Sister would appear, and she would get into trouble.

'You may be the only person who can get a response from him, Nurse, but you're behaving like a moonstruck ninny,' Sister had said to her only a few days before. 'The man is falling in love with you! I do not want to see you pay him such marked attention in future! Is that clear? You will give him only the same attention you give all the other patients.'

'Yes, Sister.' But Yvonne's heart sang because Sister thought he was falling in love with her.

But no matter what Theo said, no matter what despair he expressed, she knew that he had made some kind of progress. After all, he had stopped starting at sudden noises; he smiled more often; he had begun to take pleasure in the fact that he was mobile again. The recently fitted wooden leg was invisible beneath the trousers, and if he walked without the fluid movement of a young man, no one remarked it. There were all too many in the same boat, glad simply to be alive.

'I have to go in, the dragon will eat me!' Yvonne said. Theo always referred to Sister as 'the dragon'.

He looked up at her and smiled in spite of himself. Her cheeks had colour and her eyes were very blue. 'Delectable nurse! I would like to go to the shrubbery. Will you meet me there in half an hour, if you can. I want to talk to you in private.'

He wheeled his chair away to the specially constructed wooden ramp which gave wheelchairs access to the garden. Yvonne made sure he had negotiated this descent safely, and then she returned to the house.

She suspected he would try out his walking in the shrubbery because he could do so there in privacy. She had seen him a few times, crunching slowly along the gravel path, his walking stick at the ready, his wheelchair nearby. Then he would emerge into the formal sunken garden, his gait increasingly steady, until fatigue suddenly claimed him and he leant heavily on the stick, breathing heavily, at which point someone would hurry to his assistance.

She met Dr Perry in the hall. He was a man in

his late fifties, medium height, spare, with a bald head, bushy eyebrows, and an avuncular manner towards this young woman, the daughter of an old friend.

'Well, Nurse Stacey, how are we this morning?'

'Fine, thank you, Doctor.'

'Haven't had enough yet?' he demanded with a twinkle. 'Ah, well, I had a wager with your father, and it looks as if I'm going to lose!'

Yvonne smiled. She knew that Dr Perry and her father had been classmates a hundred years before when they were young. She could not imagine either of them as having been young, but they seemed to remember it as though it had been yesterday.

'I see you talking to our mystery Irishman a good deal. Does he confide in you?'

'Not really. His memory is too bad for confidences.'

'I think he'll snap out of it,' Doctor Perry said, 'now that his background has been established and he is going home. Physically he's making good progress. You know we're sending him home?' he repeated, studying Yvonne's face. 'Best thing for him. Nothing more we can do for him here! Glad that they found his people!' He looked at her curiously, and Yvonne knew at once that Sister had been talking.

Half an hour later, Yvonne got one of the other nurses to cover for her in the linen room, fetched her cape, and went to the shrubbery. Theo was sitting on a bench beside the statue of Artemis. She sat beside him and he took her arm. With his other hand he leant on his walking stick and poked it into the gravel, making circular patterns while he talked.

'When I have to go . . . home . . . would you consider coming with me? I don't think I could manage without you now!'

Yvonne felt as though she would choke. She looked at him, at his brooding eyes, his dark moustache, his wry, uncertain smile. He glanced at her and then looked diffidently away.

'I'm asking you to marry me,' he said. 'Don't give me an answer yet — not until I find out if I can support you. They have written to Kilashane and my family are coming. When they do come I'll know if I have anything worth a damn to offer a wife — if I possess property or money or what, or whether I have to make my way in the big bad world.'

Yvonne gulped. She knew that there could be no question of Theo making his way in the world, at least not for the present. Maybe in a few years he would regain the mettle the war had filched from him — assuming, of course, that he had ever had it. She watched him now, the despondent set of his head, the air of dejection mixed with optimism, the grim line of his mouth. He continued pushing at the gravel with the tip of the walking stick.

'I'll marry you,' Yvonne said simply. 'I love you!' She threw both arms around him and pressed her face to his breast. 'I've been in love with you for ages, Theo, almost since you came!' He dropped the stick, held her in both arms while his mouth came down to meet the lips she offered. Time seemed to stop for Yvonne; the touch of flesh on flesh made her feel as though she flowed into his life. When they drew apart, the winter day seemed brighter; she heard the interrogative chirp of a robin. Was winter over, the little bird seemed to be saying, because if it is I'm going to sing mating invitations from morning till night. Yes, she thought. The winter — of all their lives — the war — was over; life had a meaning; she would be with Theo for ever. She would mind him for ever.

'Come along, little Nurse,' he whispered after a moment. 'Or the dragon will be asking for you and there'll be trouble!'

'The dragon can go hang,' Yvonne muttered with the bravado of euphoria. She fixed her hair and cap, picked up Theo's stick, handed it back to him, and deliberately refrained from helping him to his feet. But she took his arm for a moment as they plodded for a few paces back to his wheelchair. As they moved away, she glanced over her shoulder at the bench beneath the statue of Artemis, as though to imprint the place on her heart. She saw the laurel bushes and the green bench and the stone statue and the watery sunlight. She saw the design Theo had marked in the gravel. It took a moment to register that the design which he had drawn at their feet was not just any old doodle. When she had deposited Theo in his wheelchair she went back to inspect it; she saw with a shock that she had not been wrong. She stared at the design drawn in the gravel before surreptitiously rubbing it out with her foot.

Sister said to her coldly when she came back, 'Where have you been, Nurse?'

'I went out for some air, Sister,' Yvonne lied. 'I felt faint.'

Sister regarded her severely. 'You should have asked permission, Nurse. I can't run a ward where my nurses take off whenever they feel faint. Where do you think you are? A finishing school for young ladies? I found Belling doing your work for you in the linen room. I shall put this on your report.'

Yvonne hung her head. 'Yes, Sister. I'm sorry!'

Theo became excited as the day drew near when he would see his family. He had received a letter signed 'Your loving mother', which told him how delighted she and Kate were that he was safe. 'They told us you were missing in action, Theo! We have been in mourning. But this is a reprieve!'

'I wonder what they are like — my mother and Kate? Who do you think Kate is? My sister, I suppose!'

This gave Yvonne a start. Kate could be anyone, a fiancée or sweetheart. For a dreadful moment it occurred to her that he might even be married, but then she remembered that his records said he was single.

'I have no pictures in my head to fit them,' Theo went on. 'One minute I expect a pair of gorgons, and the next I expect two charming women whom I shall instantly recognize.' He ran his hand through his hair. 'Do you think they will find me much changed?'

'No,' Yvonne said, her eyes very soft. 'You look wonderful . . . every inch the romantic hero! You are looking so much better than when you came here.' But she saw that he was sweating and added, 'Relax. They're your family. They love you.'

He caught at her hand. 'You will keep your word and marry me?' he demanded suspiciously.

She smiled. She had gone over this in her mind through several nights. At the core of her love was pity. It was pity which fuelled the fires of her passion, which spurred her to sacrifice. She was sure she could do something for this man which would redeem his life. His need of her filled her craving for purpose and love.

'Of course. Just try to stop me!'

A few days later, as Yvonne passed through the gallery on her way off duty, she saw that Theo's family had come. He was sitting in his wheelchair by his usual window niche. Seated beside him, holding one hand, was a very young

153

woman who seemed on the point of breaking into tears, while his other hand was being held by a middle-aged matron. Both women were dark-haired, although one of them was touched with grey; both were blue-eyed, and dressed in clothes which, while well cut, were also well out of fashion. Yvonne slowed her pace, caught Theo's eye as she passed. He put out a hand to stop her.

'Come and meet my mother and my sister,' he said. He turned back to his family, who inclined towards her politely. 'This is Nurse Yvonne Stacey, my fiancée. Yvonne, this is my mother and my sister Kate.' Then he added, turning to Kate, 'You are my sister, aren't you?'

Kate nodded and turned her head away. Theo's mother started. She had a strong, fine-boned face, lined across the forehead. She registered consternation and then disbelief.

Yvonne put out her hand. 'How do you do, Mrs O'Reilly?' she said nervously. 'It's nice to meet you.'

Mrs O'Reilly took the proffered hand. 'How do you do?'

'We thought he was killed,' Kate said, when she had recovered her composure. 'The wire came last week to say he was here . . .' Then she added, with a gulp, 'You're not really engaged to him, are you . . . ?'

Yvonne felt more foolish than she had ever felt in her life. She waited for a response from Theo, waited for him to say that of course they were engaged; that they loved each other and would get married as soon as possible; but he just smiled a closed, secret smile and was silent. So she did not answer the question either and managed a smile.

'Well, I'll leave you to it; you must have many things to talk about!' she said awkwardly.

As she walked from the gallery into the hall, she heard footsteps and then a voice. 'Nurse, Miss Stacey!'

Yvonne turned to find Theo's mother behind her.

'Can I talk to you, Nurse, for a moment?'

'Of course!'

Theo's mother came towards her across the hall, walking with a tired, preoccupied composure. She examined the young red-haired nurse with questioning eyes. Her voice had a soft lilt. A bit like a Welsh accent, Yvonne thought; do some of the Irish talk like the Welsh?

'How badly is he hurt?' Mrs O'Reilly demanded this in a quiet voice, as though sure that Theo was much more badly injured than was apparent. 'He told me he has a wooden leg. It's such a tragedy. He used to be so good at tennis and riding — very athletic. But there is more than that. He doesn't know us, doesn't know his mother and his sister! How badly is he hurt?'

'He has lost the right leg at the knee,' Yvonne said. 'But he must have told you that. He had gangrene and they had to amputate!'

Theo's mother regarded her bleakly, almost as

though she was focusing elsewhere and didn't see her. 'I understand that. What I do not understand is why he is so greatly changed. He seems forgetful of everything. Did he . . . suffer any other injury?'

'He had scalp wounds. He has amnesia, also shell-shock . . . But he is improving.'

'Shell-shock! Amnesia? Will he recover? What do the doctors think?'

'They think he is well enough to go home. But you must talk to Dr Perry yourself. Sister will arrange it.'

Mrs O'Reilly nodded. 'Of course. I shall do so immediately.' She considered Yvonne for a further moment or two. 'I would like to take him home as quickly as possible.'

Yvonne was silent. 'We are engaged,' she wanted to say; 'I have a say too in his future.' But the Irishwoman's tone of voice, the breath she brought with her of the real world and its sensible perspectives, forestalled her. What, after all, could she do with Theo? She could hardly bring him back to her own home as though he were a stray puppy.

'I hope he hasn't upset you with this engagement nonsense,' the older woman went on in a gentler voice. 'It's too bad of him, although you're probably trained to deal with it. Men in his condition must become so dependent. You probably find they are all in love with you . . . And when they get better they see things differently.'

Yvonne felt silly, and wounded to the heart. 'If he sees things differently,' she said, 'that is his prerogative. But I happen to love him very much, and if he wants me for his wife I shall be his wife.' She looked her prospective mother-in-law in the eye. 'Good day, Mrs O'Reilly,' she added, moving away.

Mrs O'Reilly hurried after her. '. . . I didn't understand. But, my dear girl, you can't really be serious?' and when Yvonne didn't reply she added softly, 'I can't help thinking that an engagement under these circumstances might be something everyone would regret. A man recovering from amputation and shell-shock, suffering from amnesia. A man who does not even know his own family! Do you really want to marry such a man?'

Yvonne said, 'I take your point, Mrs O'Reilly, you needn't go on,' and she turned the corner to the nurses' wing, found the room she shared with two others, and threw herself down on the bed. She hated the sense that she had been confronted with her own immaturity, the feeling of being the silly child who did not see things properly. She was furious, but only with herself. Theo's mother was right. She had spoken the truth. Theo was in no condition to undertake marriage. There was nothing for it but that they would bring him home. And where could she fit into all that? She was behaving like a schoolgirl with a crush. She was crying for the moon. She had broken the first rule of her profession; she had become personally involved with a patient. She loved and wanted Theo, who was hurt and vulnerable and who needed her. But who was the real Theo? And would the real Theo want her?

She would have to say goodbye to him. But would they be able to mind him, would they understand him and how frightened he was? She knew that he was terrified, much more so than anyone — including Sister or the doctor — suspected. And she thought uneasily of what he had scratched in the gravel earlier that day, which she had, in a moment of uneasiness, obliterated. Well, so what? It was only a five-sided star. It meant nothing. But no matter how she rationalized his behaviour, she knew Theo feared something, dreaded something.

'What did you think of my mother?' Theo asked Yvonne the following morning.

'She seemed very sensible,' Yvonne answered as she took his temperature. 'Did you remember her?'

'I didn't recognize her,' Theo said, smiling ruefully. 'I hadn't the faintest idea who she was. Wasn't that dreadful? Not to know your own mother?'

Yvonne sighed. 'Yes . . . But it all takes time. Do you remember her now?'

'Yes and no. It's as though she has filled a missing space, like a piece in a jigsaw. And I begin to remember the name Kate and I remember something she reminded me of: playing with her, at any rate with a girl a lot younger, in an orchard the day I fell from a tree and broke my leg!' He smiled again, tapped the wooden right leg. 'This one, I believe. I think the girl was a bit of a brat. I didn't remember the woman!' He reached out and put his arm around her waist.

'Don't, darling,' Yvonne whispered. 'If Sister sees you, I'll be sent packing!'

Some of the other men had seen Theo's movement towards his nurse. One of them began to whistle the air from a popular song: 'Oh they'll never believe me', but he shut up when Yvonne turned on him, flushing, and shook her head.

When Mrs O'Reilly and her daughter came in later to visit Theo, Yvonne nodded at them politely, but she did not speak to them.

'There's great shenanigans going on at home,' Theo said a few days later. He had been reading the paper, an article about how twenty-five newly elected Irish MPs had refused to take their seats at Westminster and had established instead a parliament in Dublin. 'What do you think of that?'

Yvonne sighed. 'I don't know what to think, except that they're probably making a lot of trouble for themselves!'

Theo regarded her quizzically, and a smile played on his mouth. 'Are you saying you have no sympathy with the Irish cause, my little Sassenach?'

Yvonne shrugged. 'I don't know anything about the Irish cause. All I know is that whenever people make trouble, that is precisely what they get!'

'My practical little nurse!'

She was examining the stump of his amputated leg. As she rubbed it with zinc ointment, Theo watched her with apparent detachment.

'It's perfectly healed,' she said. 'But the new leg is a bit hard on it, so go easy for the moment.' She anointed the stump slowly and carefully, knowing that Theo's departure was only a few days away. Dr Perry had confirmed to his mother that he could go home in about a week's time. Yvonne wanted to cry. He hadn't said a word to her about it, about their future.

'You'll have to continue rubbing in the ointment at home!'

Theo seemed abstracted, as though he hadn't heard what she said. Then he murmured, 'It seems I'm the owner of this place — Kilashane. My father died; the place was settled on the male heir. Strange, isn't it? To wake up and find I'm a man of property. I have a home to offer you . . . When can we get married?'

She turned her head away. 'When you're better,' she said. 'Come back for me when you're better!'

Theo seemed thunderstruck. His brows gathered together and his eyes concentrated on her fiercely. He grasped her wrist. 'Have you changed your mind? Don't want to marry a cripple — is that it?"

'Oh, no. Of course not. I don't think of you as a cripple. But it might look as though I am taking advantage of you, or something . . . Theo, you might feel differently about me when you are fully better.'

He sat up straight in the chair. 'In that case I'm not going anywhere until we are married. If my family who, as far as I'm concerned, are people I've never laid eyes on in my life, want me to go away with them, they'll have to get used to the idea of you as part of the equation . . . I'll talk to the padre, ask him to arrange a special licence. We can marry in the chapel here. I want to marry you. I want to wake up every morning and know that you are there. I want you for my wife!' He shook his head to forestall any protest. 'Don't worry about my family. I'll make it perfectly clear to them.' He smiled at her slowly and his voice softened. 'And that is that!' Yvonne felt the anxiety leave her. He seemed so clear-minded, trenchant, sure.

He rubbed his fingers against the palm of her hand. 'And, Yvonne,' he asked gently, 'will you do something for me?'

She looked at him. 'Of course! What do you want me to do?'

'You will ask your brother to the wedding, won't you?'

She laughed. 'Naturally!'

'And his wife — the girl in the photograph?'

Yvonne looked puzzled and then remembered. 'What girl? You mean Jenny?'

Theo nodded.

'My brother and my oldest friend! Of course I will invite them! Andrew is coming to see you anyway. He says you must forgive him for not coming before now, but he has been so busy, what with his marriage and his new job.'

Theo sighed. 'It's ten to one I won't remember him. Have you told him that?'

'Of course. He knows you were hurt.'

The following weekend, Andrew presented himself at Hurleigh House and sat talking to Theo for about twenty minutes. He was embarrassed and showed it. He ran out of anecdotes about the Front, which he thought would be common conversational currency. Theo listened but always shook his head. He couldn't even remember the Great Retreat of March 24th and the disintegration of the Fifth Army. 'I'm a dead loss, old fellow, a dead loss. They tell me it will improve. But I wonder, I wonder . . .'

Andrew made appropriately encouraging noises, and shifted uneasily in his chair. He wanted to ask Theo about his engagement to his sister, which seemed to him to be an utterly preposterous state of affairs. His father had already consulted with Doctor Perry, who had told him the prognosis was hopeful, but that there were no guarantees.

There had been no talking to Yvonne. 'I am going to marry Theo O'Reilly,' she had said in a voice of cold decision, 'and nothing in heaven or on earth is going to stop me!' Andrew disliked any form of drama, and this little speech, which he felt was uncharacteristic of Yvonne, had filled him with distaste.

'Is Yvonne looking after you well? She says you are engaged!'

Theo studied him, gathering his forehead into a scowl. 'Yes. Do you object to your sister marrying a wreck like me?' he demanded, studying Andrew's face. 'At least they have found out who I am. I do have something to offer her, you know. And I do love her.'

'Fact is, old chap,' Andrew said after a moment, 'it's a bit unfair on her. Could be quite a strain, if you didn't recover fully, and so on.'

When Theo did not respond and only regarded him balefully, Andrew added uncomfortably, 'Topping girl, you know. Very fond of her . . .'

Theo nodded, but he did not offer any counter-argument. Instead he said slowly, 'I should congratulate you. I understand you got married recently yourself.'

Andrew brightened. 'Yes . . .'

'To the girl in this photograph with Yvonne,' and he took out his pocket-book and extracted the small sepia snap.

Andrew looked at it and laughed. 'You asked me for this in the trenches, do you remember? You said that my sister was pretty, but that Jen was a "deserving beauty".' He paused, reddened. 'I think that was the phrase. I was struck by your use of words.'

Theo looked from the photograph to Andrew and back. 'You're a lucky fellow. You must convey my compliments to your wife.'

Andrew said he would and stood up to leave. Yvonne came along and walked with her brother to the end of the ward.

'What do you think of him? Isn't he wonderful!' she demanded in a low voice.

Andrew felt suddenly protective. 'He can't remember any of the things we all shared. Are you sure you want to do this, Yvonne?'

She looked up at her brother and nodded. 'Please don't disapprove. Please be on my side. Papa will agree if you are on my side!'

'Marriage is a serious business,' Andrew said wryly. 'It's not all wine and roses!' His tone was not lost on his sister. He saw the immediate frown of inquiry on her face and added, 'But as you're so frightfully sure about the whole thing, know your own mind and so on, I won't queer the pitch for you!' Yvonne embraced him and he left, thinking of his homecoming and Jenny, who would probably be in the attic with her easel, her peculiar paintings and her grief-stricken face, while the gulf between them widened all the time.

But then it occurred to him that, as she had been the one in the wrong, she should apologize, be the one to make up. He assumed a sense of grievance. She was his wife; she had to accept his

164

will. It was not as though he had sought anything from her which was not his right. When she came to her senses it would be time for him to indulge her whims. If he bowed to her now they would never have a marriage. Oh, Jen, he thought forlornly, don't let us be like this. But he knew this mode of thinking was weak and he put it away. Grievance reasserted itself. 'Treat women like horses and they will learn to take the bit,' he had heard one of the older officers once say. 'Otherwise they will carry you to the devil!' Yes, he thought. It was time he made a stand.

Yvonne went back on duty, giving Andrew the thumbs-up sign as she passed and slipping into his hand a card for his forthcoming birthday, which she had dedicated to the 'most wonderful brother in the world'. Later, she wrote in the diary Andrew had given her for Christmas.

Chapter Seven

'I am afraid,' she said, 'I am afraid that I will be broken.'

'You are right, Witch, to fear.'

Journal of a Witness

Charlie sent Dee a television set when he heard that she had none. 'We can't have that! An employee of McGrath Limited who hasn't got a telly! I'll tell Jim in Dispatch to send you one!'

'It's all right, Charlie, honestly!'

Charlie frowned. 'Don't worry, no strings . . . I have no designs on your virtue, you know!' He smiled then to show he meant no offence, but Dee sensed the undercurrent. She had refused all further invitations to go for a drink after work, and he was peeved. He would probably try some other tactic, she had thought, and here it was.

'You remember that story you told me when we had our little drink at Keenan's — the one about the embalmed tart they found in Venice? There's a programme on about it on Friday, BBC. Thought you wouldn't want to miss that!'

'Why do you say she was a tart?'

Charlie smiled, pleased. 'No reason. All dressed up and nowhere to go. Ha-ha . . .'

'Ha-ha-ha,' Dee echoed. She had been a

woman, so she had to be a tart. Charlie found that reassuring.

So the telly had arrived, a new model, the brand name 'McGrath' inscribed on a small metal disc below the controls. Under it again was the legend — SUPERLUX. This was the top of the range. 'It's just the bloody old box that's different,' Charlie told her. 'It's a good television, 625 lines, but exactly the same as the VISION range, except for the box. Price difference, two hundred pounds!' He laughed.

Laura helped her put the television on the coffee table and position it in the corner. They had a pair of 'rabbit ears' which only picked up Telefís Éireann, so Dee asked Jim in Dispatch if anything could be done. 'There's a BBC programme I want to watch.'

'Is there a roof aerial on the house?'

There was; some other tenants had televisions. So Jim had come out and fixed things up and lo, BBC came through, complete with interference, but good enough to follow.

The programme was a documentary. Venice was sinking. A fortune was required for the work of restoration and preservation. The wooden piles on which the city had been built in the salt lagoons could be replaced where necessary with concrete; protective sea walls could be built across the entrances to the lagoon. The camera dwelt on the water lapping against steps which had once been above the water mark, on the interior of old palaces, churches, on frescos and plaster-work which would be saved for posterity. There was a reconstruction of Venice in its heyday; a state of merchant princes, fiercely independent, holding its own against both the mainland and the Adriatic. There was a silhouette shot of the lion of St Mark on its pedestal, its stance representative of everything that was proud, powerful and free.

The programme brought the reader through Venetian history. There were one hundred and seventeen small islands built, for the most part, on wooden piles driven into the mud at the bottom of the lagoon. These were joined by hundreds of bridges spanning the myriad canals. It had a long and chequered history; it was a city of political and religious intrigue which had degenerated into a devotion to licence and luxury with masked balls, and every opulence. The camera dwelt on old paintings of masquerades, with all kinds of dominoes, plumed headdresses and rich costumes.

The camera followed an architect through the streets, the winding little alleyways, the small waterways, the doors reached only by gondola. In a crumbling mansion with mosaic floors, the camera pursued him down a short flight of stairs.

'This is a strange feature,' the architect said, 'discovered only recently. Here we have a once-watertight chamber which is now below the level of the lagoon.'

The door was half open and the darkness was cut by the lights of the camera crew. In the middle of the floor, now awash with water, was an empty stone sarcophagus, its lid lying to one side.

'This was a tomb. In this stone coffin a young woman was laid to rest. The body was embalmed, and seems, on the whole, to have been in a remarkable state of preservation, especially given its surroundings.'

The screen filled with the photograph of the corpse of a young woman in an elaborate blue gown. The dead girl had coiled hair. Her hands lay one on top of the other bent at a strange angle. The neckline of her gown exposed white flesh which was caressed by a double row of pearls. Her earlobes peeped from under the coils of her hair. Everything about her spoke of pride in her beauty and despair for her loss. Except for one thing which was at eerie variance with the rest. She had no face. Instead, where her face had once been, there was only a death's head — shining white bone, empty eye sockets, teeth in a horrible rictus only inches above the white neck, the apparently perfect body and the luxuriantly coiffed hair.

This impacted on the viewer; it was like opening a beautiful book and finding the pages blank. You were led to glimpse of a person's life, to glimpse the love which had built this tomb for her, and were denied the only telling evidence of who she was.

'This photograph was taken at the time of the discovery. Unfortunately the body disappeared while being taken to a laboratory refrigeration unit. Whoever she was, the lady was still young and was dressed in silk; her gown was bordered with silver filigree and the whole costume seems to have been in an extraordinary state of preservation. The dress was of the fashion of the early seventeenth century; it was most unusual that anyone of that time would not have been buried in a shroud. Her face seems to have been the only part of her that did not stand the test of time! Her loss in transit to the laboratory is a scandal. Not only has the body been lost to scientists, but the jewels she was wearing are also gone.'

Dee studied the photograph. There was something extraordinarily touching about the corpse, something eerie, something that conjured up tremendous suffering, that spoke of endurance and vulnerability. Dee studied too the design on the sarcophagus when the camera zoomed in on it, and knew that she had not been mistaken.

When the programme was over she turned the television off, went to the kitchen and plugged in the kettle. Laura was out with Ted and would not be back for at least an hour. She would come in, bounce around the flat, and try to engage Dee in conversation if Dee were still awake. Eventually she would reluctantly fall into bed and repeat in the morning her usual desperate resistance to the new day.

Dee took her tea into the sitting room and lay back on the couch. The summer night was fading outside. The window was open and she

170

could hear the laughter and screaming of children still at play in a nearby garden. The sound of play suddenly ended with a woman's voice calling. Then there was only the muted swish of traffic.

She watched the colour of the sky deepen from the warm blue of evening to the violet of night. The flat darkened around her, but her mind resisted sleep. It was full of what she had seen on television and full of a malaise she could not elude, an old dread, an old ache, an old uncertainty. What possessed her in some way was the design she had seen on the sarcophagus, the design carved in the stone. She was certain it was the same as that on the ring.

In addition, while examining the mysterious masked figures shown dancing in the selected paintings of the past, there had been the sudden recollection of that thing she had found in Kilashane, the mask. She had been very young and it had frightened her, staring at her with its empty sockets, its gaze very cold and the inhuman grimace on its mouth real enough to make her throw it away. Even now its contemptuous, joyless smile returned to her. It had the power to frighten because it was a travesty.

Where did I throw the mask, she wondered. I was upstairs at the time and found it in a chest full of old clothes. But the stairs in Kilashane were gone and the upper floor with them, and whatever had rested on that floor had crashed on to the floor beneath and was now part of a great heap of debris.

'It's under the rubbish somewhere,' she said aloud.

There was a sound behind her and a voice asked, 'What's under the rubbish?'

Dee jumped, looked behind her and, as the light flooded the room, saw that Laura was standing there, grinning.

'I didn't hear you come in,' she said, trying to re-establish the normal rhythm of her breathing, and squinting against the light. 'You gave me an awful fright!'

'You were talking to yourself: first sign of madness.'

'I was remembering something — a thing I threw away when I was a child.'

Laura went to the kitchen, found a Ryvita and a banana and began to slice the latter into small round pieces which she then used to decorate the rye bread.

'Men,' she said, munching. 'What did you throw away?'

Dee started to tell her, but was too tired for the full story. 'Ah, it was just an old yoke I found when I was playing!'

'Probably a priceless antique.' She looked at her friend. 'What was it?'

'It was a mask,' Dee said reluctantly. 'Just a mask. It looked a bit like those masks they used to wear in Venice! The programme reminded me.'

Laura indicated the television, speaking with

her mouth full. 'Wasn't it decent of your boss to give us a telly!'

Dee sighed. 'His intentions are strictly dishonourable!'

Laura stopped chewing. 'Has he propositioned you?'

'He never stops. He's an eejit . . . good at his job, but otherwise an eejit. You saw him yourself.'

Laura chewed speculatively. 'Yeah. He's about as attractive as a stale rock bun.'

Dee laughed. 'Did you see the news?'

'Some of it.'

'Anything interesting?'

'Oh, just the usual: famine, war, pestilence and death!'

'Jesus, Laur, you sound like Colin!'

Laura laughed.

'I seemed to have missed out there. Ted is all convention; his brains are in his gonads!' She paused, swallowed. 'We made love on the floor!'

Dee sat up. 'Go on!'

'We were watching the news in his place and one thing led to another . . .'

'I never did it,' Dee said after a moment. 'I never wanted to badly enough, because I was never sure enough that he wanted me enough.' She shrugged, flushed. 'Does that sound convoluted?'

Laura looked at her. 'You don't have to explain. For an attractive young woman you harbour a lot of doubts about yourself. But of course you are right. No point in doing anything you don't want to do!'

'It's also because I have this ghastly . . . mark. When Colin saw it I hated the pity in his eyes!'

'Dee, if someone cares about you he is not going to give a damn!'

'That's the theory! Anyway you seem to take it all — everything that life cooks up — in your stride!'

Laura sighed and looked suddenly vulnerable. 'Appearances can be deceptive.'

Dee permitted herself a smile. 'Well, the news can't have been very exciting anyway!'

'I turned it off at the bit about the recent antics of the Ku Klux Klan,' Laura muttered. 'We decided to make love, not war.' She looked wistful for a moment and her voice became a whisper. 'Well, I was making love and he was making war!'

'Oh,' Dee said, deflated, 'was it like that?'

'I wasn't a virgin and his majesty was miffed! When he asked I told him he was "numero due". He immediately wanted to know the identity of "numero uno"! In fact, he seemed much more interested in him than he was in me!'

'Do I know him?' Dee asked tentatively. Laura went to the window and drew the curtains.

'Numero uno? No. I was fifteen and he was thirty.'

'That's statutory rape!'

'It was a mistake,' she said shortly. 'I'm quite good at them!'

'You shouldn't let him upset you!'

Laura laughed unsteadily. 'All the "shoulds"!'

Dee did not sleep well that night. She lay awake in the dim room, grateful for the light from the streetlamps. She had never before thought to find a direct connection between the ring she had found so many years ago and the mask. Where was the ring now? She had put it into a cardboard box in the bottom drawer of her dressing table, along with other treasures; with a photograph in an envelope, assorted letters, a tortoiseshell comb, a medal for elocution she had won in school, and one for coming second in religious knowledge.

Before dawn she slipped at last into a dream-less sleep. When she woke she knew from the quality of the light in the room that she had over-slept. She rushed into her clothes and almost ran the whole way to work. But she was late. It was the first time it had happened. Charlie was in his office and looked at her over his glasses.

'The phone's been hopping, Dee. For God's sake get down to work!' he said in tones of cold exasperation when she tried to explain why she was late.

But later, in a better mood, he came by her desk and asked, 'Did you see your programme? Is the set to your liking?'

'Yes, thank you. I saw the programme . . .'

'So what's the low-down on the corpse?'

'They don't know. She's an enigma!'

Charlie brought his face down a foot or so. 'Like yourself. I love enigmatic women. They're a challenge . . .'

Dee turned away from him to look at her work. He stayed for a moment with his eyes fixed on her and then he said softly, 'Take your time, baby. I'm going to get a big, big bonus and then I'll take you to Venice! And you can see your enigma! And I'll see your enigma!'

Dee looked up and saw the double entendre in Charlie's eyes. There isn't the slightest chance, Charlie dear, that I'll go anywhere with you! she said to herself. But Charlie raised his eyebrows, as though he had heard her thoughts.

He joined her for coffee at eleven. 'Dee, I'm a pig. But not as much a pig as you think. Did you see the design you told me of, the same as the ring you say you found years ago?'

Dee was surprised he had remembered. 'Yes, as a matter of fact I did.'

'Will you draw it for me? I was always a bit of an antiquary — it was a hobby in the days when I still had time!' He took out a notepad from his pocket and put it down before her with a ball-point pen.

Dee drew the design — the M with the twining serpents, the gaping mask face inside. Charlie looked at it for a while, but his face was inscrutable.

'They did go in for fancy work!' he said with a laugh, but she saw that he carefully returned the notepad to his pocket. Charlie went back to his office. Through the open door Dee heard him talk to his prospective customer, Joe Whelan of Erinview Limited. Could he have a firm order for the five hundred sets? What? It was all right for him who didn't have a bean counter breathing down his neck . . . He motioned to Liz to shut the door.

While Dee was having lunch with Liam in the canteen, Charlie brought his tray over and sat down. Liam made room.

'Is there any sign of that Erinview order?' he asked his boss. 'We're a little behind budget.'

'They're in the bag,' Charlie said. 'You can make out that invoice for those five hundred sets!'

Liam sat back. 'Great. Give me the order. I'll get the shipment prepared and the invoice off.'

'Joe Whelan hasn't given me a written order. They're in a great hurry all of a sudden.'

'When do they want shipment?'

'Day after tomorrow! It's for the new Burkhampton Hotel!'

'Congratulations,' Liam said. 'I'll prepare the invoices. This means we're well ahead of budget!'

Charlie smiled. He looked at Dee and winked, and Dee realized that she had real news for the monthly report, a copy of which she would send to Birmingham and Brussels.

That night, when she got home to the flat, she found that it had been burgled. Every drawer had been pulled out and her own and Laura's clothes were all over the floor. Nothing had been taken except a small sum of money left in the communal food-money jar in the kitchen. They told the police, and two young gardai came and dusted the place for fingerprints, but said they found nothing.

It was a week later that Dee knew the truth about the Erinview order. Her piece about it in the monthly report had been leaked to the Press, and there had been an article about it in the *Irish Times*. Then Joe Whelan had come on the phone. There was a phone call from Birmingham, a long phone call, and Charlie's voice could be heard muttering apologetically through his half-open door. Later Liz whispered in the canteen that Charlie had shipped an order which the customer hadn't made. He was in deep trouble. He did it to make his budget and had sent the consignment into storage. 'Jesus, he's a right eejit . . .'

Charlie, looking pale and upset, summoned Dee to his office. 'What do you mean filling your monthly report with stuff about that Erinview order? Who authorized you to do that?'

'You told me to use initiative,' Dee said. 'You said the order was in the bag. Liam heard you. You got him to issue invoices!'

Charlie put his head in his hands. 'Oh Christ, I was just trying to make the bloody budget, otherwise no bonuses . . . jobs at risk — even yours.

178

And you have to do this to me!'

'I'm sorry,' Dee said miserably.

'What are you going to do about it to get me out of the shit,' Charlie said desperately. 'This is serious!'

'What can I do?'

Charlie looked at her stricken face and seemed to soften. 'There is one thing you could do . . . Well, you can't undo the mess, of course, but perhaps . . .'

Dee thought he was going to suggest a tête-à-tête, but instead he said, 'You remember you spoke to me a few days ago of a ring you had found with a curious design. Will you let me see it? I've become very interested in this Venice business . . .' He sighed like a defeated man. 'I'm not as thick as I seem, and if I'm going to be out of a job, I might try for a job in the antiques market.'

'Of course . . . But I don't want to sell it!'

'I don't want to buy it. Will you bring it in on Monday?'

'But what about the mess I've got you into?'

He sighed, and she found him suddenly pathetic and rather sweet. 'It wasn't your fault, Dee. It was mine!'

She left the office that evening alternately cheered and sick at heart. But it started to rain when she was a hundred yards down the street, so she went back. She knew there was an unclaimed umbrella in the cloakroom.

The office was quiet, the typewriters shrouded

179

in black dust-covers. Only Charlie's voice broke the stillness. He was on the phone and she heard her name mentioned. He was speaking French. Charlie, who had said he couldn't speak any foreign languages, was perfectly fluent in French. She stood outside the door. The whole timbre of his voice was different, fluid, devoid of tonic accent.

'Dee McGlinn . . . *Elle m'a dit que c'était exactement le même dessin. Oui, exactement la même chose . . .*' He was quiet, urbane, not like the Charlie she knew.

'*C'est une jeune fille . . . C'est extraordinaire, n'est-ce pas? Oui, oui, je comprends! Oui, la semaine prochaine . . . Bien sûr . . . Allez!*'

Dee went home for the weekend. She took the train to Cork. She leant her cheek on the palm of her hand and watched the houses and farms fly by. Then she read the papers. A fat bishop with a little hat and a long dress inspected a guard of honour. Jack Lynch looked out from a photograph with open-faced honesty. There was an article about the Beatles. She studied their picture. She liked Paul McCartney best. Of all their hits her favourite was 'Lucy in the Sky with Diamonds'.

Her father met her at the station. Dee saw him before the train stopped, standing there on the platform, a spare man in a tweed jacket with his grey, windblown hair and weathered face. As soon as she saw him Dee's world fell into place.

The job in the company became merely a job. She was back where she belonged. The drive home was conducted virtually in silence. The love between father and daughter did not require many words. She felt this love; it was a strength she came back to, resourced herself from. It was power and it was peace. But it was never spoken of between them.

'How's the new job?' He glanced at her proudly. He emanated the certainty that everyone would find his lovely girl as wonderful as he did.

'I don't know,' Dee said.

He turned to her, frowning, looked back at the road. 'Are you having problems?'

She sighed. 'Afraid so . . .'

His voice was gentle. 'What kind of problems?'

'Boss problems!'

He waited. When she didn't elaborate he said, 'If he's giving you trouble, dump the job!'

'Oh, Dad, I can't!'

'Why not?'

She shrugged. 'It's a good job. It's part of an international set-up. It could lead to other things. Charlie's a bore, but he's something I would put up with, all things else being equal. At least I thought he was just a bore!'

She longed to tell her father about the phone call she had overheard. But how could she tell him that Charlie had had a conversation in French in which she featured; in which he had recounted what she had told him about the design — presumably of the ring and the sarcophagus — being exactly the same. In retrospect she wondered if she had misheard; could someone else have been in his office? But it was his voice, she was sure it was his voice. What was so important about the design on the ring that he should speak to someone about it in French? Or could it have been anything else? Had she mentioned some other design? She didn't think so.

She paused. 'Dad,' she whispered, 'there's something going on which I don't understand . . .'

'Is it against the law?'

She shook her head. 'I don't know, Dad. I don't know anything about it. It's . . . just a kind of taste in my mouth.'

He was silent. The road was almost solitary now. They were into the countryside and had left the main road. The fields were warm with evening; the birds sang passionately of summer before bedtime; the hedgerows were bright with convolvulus and dog-roses.

'What should I do?' Dee ventured after a while.

'Trust your instinct. Get out. You'll always get another job! But make sure first that you're not just imagining things!' Her father's voice was stern.

Dee ruminated. 'Good jobs are thin on the ground. I can't get out just like that! I don't know what will happen, and I have no concrete evidence of any wrongdoing, except a scam which my boss dreamed up to keep the company within budget, but which does not involve serious fraud.'

'Maybe you are a little over-zealous,' he said.

Dee examined the countryside, waiting for the chimneys of Kilashane to appear around the next turn in the road.

When they arrived home, Dee left her father to bring in her bag and rushed into the house through the open front door. Her desire to see her mother was as intense as when she had been a child. Emerging from the kitchen, her mother kissed Dee eagerly, looked her up and down. Dee was wearing a beige safari suit, a belted jacket over a mini-skirt with a single inverted pleat.

'The jacket is nice, but I always think that —'

'— I know, "Mid calf-length skirts are most becoming on a woman," ' Dee finished for her, laughing. She followed her mother into the kitchen which was full of the smell of freshly baked scones. Her mother took them out of the oven and put them, flipped upside down, on a wire tray to cool.

'Tell me all the news from the big bad world outside.'

Dee perched on the edge of the table and watched her mother put on the kettle. 'Oh, Mam, it's good be home!'

Her mother turned with delight on her face. 'Did you miss your old parents then?'

Dee crossed the room and put her arms around her. 'You know I did. How are things with you, Mam?'

Her mother sighed, lowered her voice. 'Your father's retirement is not far off . . . end of July. But he doesn't want to sell and move to Dublin!'

Dee shook her head. 'But, Mam, you mightn't like Dublin — I mean, as a place to live! Your friends are here.'

'You're in Dublin, aren't you.' She sighed again. 'There's so much we could do there! He did promise, you know.'

Dee took a scone. It was piping hot, and when she split it with a knife the steam rose from the two halves. She spread butter on it and blackberry jam, sank her teeth into the crustiness, into the soft, hot centre.

Her mother made tea. 'Have another scone. It's two hours to supper!'

Dee groaned. 'Only if I can remove the calories!'

'Calories! A woman was meant to carry a little weight. You're getting far too thin! Is something worrying you?' Dee avoided her parent's eyes and lied.

Later she searched in her room, found the old cardboard box and, inside it, the envelope with the sepia photograph and the leather diary she had found at Kilashane. And in the corner, wrapped in tissue paper, as she had left it, was the ring.

She drew it out gingerly, unwrapped it. It was a man's signet ring, with the strange design on the signet exactly as she remembered. She rubbed at it with the tissue paper, sought for a hall-mark.

But there was no hall-mark such as she had ever seen. The inside of the ring was perfectly clear, except that the letter M was stamped into the gold behind the emblem and there were some characters beneath it which she did not recognize. M for masquerade, she thought. M for mercy. M for me. This made her smile. The ring was strangely beautiful. She put it on the thin gold chain which had once held her communion medal and hung it around her neck, next to her skin.

Then she took up the diary. She had inspected it superficially in the past, but the sense of intruding on someone's privacy, of being a sneak, had prevented her from delving too deeply. She knew that many of the pages were stuck together. She knew the name on the fly leaf: Yvonne O'Reilly, 1.1. 1919.

She turned a few pages. The writing was small and sloping. She had not read it for a long time. What had the diarist looked like? What had it been like to live in 1919?

She began to read.

Oh God, what is there for him? What will happen to him if I can't go with him? Forgetfulness, sweating, fainting, limping, jibbering.

Andrew came to see him today. 'Hello old chap,' he said.

I could see that Theo did not recognize him, and was sick with the sense that the world goes about its business and knows him after a fashion, while he doesn't know it. They talked briefly and stupidly as men do when they have nothing to say.

Afterwards he told me that he had never seen my brother before in his life, but that something he said brought back the winter evening and the merciless pounding of the shells. He even wrote me a note to say that he had made a breakthrough in that he remembered 'being lifted by the force of an explosion and flying away, as though I had wings. I saw the night sky and the stars and there was silence, as though the guns had stopped and nothing could reach me any more. Maybe I did fly away and what's left is only the dross, the scrambled bits and pieces. What can you do with that, little Nurse?'

What indeed?

There is poetry in him. I am not free where he is concerned. I never thought I could feel like this! I never thought I had that much ferocity. Andrew and Jenny are married, so I am not too young, as Papa tries to insist. I feel it is a consolidation, a hold on life, on childhood. The war has destroyed our youth. Things have been so strange, with so many friends being lost.

Jenny's grandfather's leaving her, dying so

suddenly, has devastated her. Marriage is a good idea.

I could do so much for him and it would be wonderful to do much for him. He loves me and that counts for everything!

Dee heard her mother's voice. 'Darling, supper is ready!'

She put the diary back in the box, replaced it in the dressing-table drawer and went downstairs. The kitchen table was set for supper; a candle had been placed in a small silver holder in the middle of the table.

'What's this for?'

Her mother smiled. 'We're celebrating. We don't see that much of you any more!'

Her father lit the candle, poured wine, and they sat down to table. Dee looked around the kitchen, luxuriated in being home. The dresser contained the same plates, the same copper frying-pan hung from the wall, the window sill had plants as always, the garden outside was getting the evening sun. Nothing had changed. Nothing except her.

'Who was Yvonne O'Reilly?' she asked softly.

There was silence. In the quiet the clock ticked and the leaves of the trees outside the open window shivered and nodded in the evening breeze.

Her parents looked at each other. 'She was an Englishwoman who married one of the O'Reillys of Kilashane,' her father said.

'What happened to her?'

Her parents looked at one another again and shook their heads. Dee assumed they didn't know. 'Did she leave? Did she have children? What happened to her?'

'She died.'

'How?'

'Nobody is sure. But she died young! Where did you hear about her?'

Dee shrugged. She wanted to say, 'I have her diary.' But how could she explain that, except by letting them know she had defied them consistently down all the years.

'There was a lot of superstition around about how she died,' her father said softly. 'There was a mask which was supposed to be bad luck. Some say it came from the sea people . . .'

'The sea people?'

Her father laughed. 'The seals. Irish mythology would have us believe they were intelligent beings, with agendas of their own!'

Dee smiled. 'Never mind the "sea people". What happened at Kilashane. Why did the place die?'

Her parents looked at each other. 'Who knows?' her father said. 'The Troubles probably had something to do with it.'

'Everything in this country is blamed on the Troubles,' Dee whispered. 'But I don't believe in the Troubles. There's always a reason for things; there's always some individual human agency, however much events may subsequently be pinned on the tide of history. It is the person;

it is the individual who makes and is responsible for what happens!'

Her mother looked stricken and her father said softly, 'What about the forces which propel people in one direction or another? They are not of any one person's making!'

'Are you saying they are diabolic?' Dee demanded. 'How useful it is to hive off our own misdeeds on the devil!' Her mother made the sign of the Cross and her father shook his head.

'The devil lives,' her mother said. 'Don't bandy words which invoke him.'

'I live too,' Dee said, 'and I have the right to question everything!'

Chapter Eight

'It will be Spring soon,' she said. 'I would like to see the sky . . .'

'You must learn obedience. Obey me and you will be free.'

But the witch only wept.

Journal of a Witness

There were crocuses in the border of the lawn. Theo saw them without remarking them particularly. He watched the robins pecking on the bird-table which someone had put near the fountain, and then he bent over the notebook on his lap and wrote.

'I'm a being without a past. If I have no past, how valid is the future? I am going "home". I remember the name, Kilashane, now that it has been told to me and I have had time to ponder it. And there are shreds of recollection — an orchard, a view across a lawn, the smell of the sea. When I think I am about to remember more, when I have something just within my grasp, something intrudes to block it. It's as though I'm occupied; a country of occupation. The fight in me is dying. Y is my one spar in the shipwreck. But when that is gone she will not be able to find me; she would need more than love for that.'

He glanced out again across the sward of the wet lawn. He felt with his hand the wooden leg in his trousers. He smiled grimly. A war behind him; what had it been about? It had been about power, wealth; he knew that now. It had been about cynical manipulation of the young to serve the greed of the old. It had been about contempt for life and love of status. For this, to preserve this, to ensure that Britain's trade remained three times the size of Germany's, the old had sent his generation out to die.

And now, because of the war, because of what it had done to him, a woman who called herself his mother and the young woman whose name was Kate O'Reilly were going to take him 'home'.

Dr Perry was on his rounds. His stethoscope hung from his neck, his cool hands probed here and there, his tangled grey eyebrows went up and down and he narrowed his eyes in concentration. He joked with patients and the ward sister smiled. Theo said he was fine in response to the usual questions. 'I see you walking in the grounds,' the doctor murmured as he examined him. 'That's good. The more you mobilize, the better. Gets the balance back; gets you used to your leg . . .'

He consulted his notes. 'So you'll be off home next week, then,' he added jovially. 'You'll find that will help the memory! Nothing like old familiar places, familiar personal belongings — your old teddy bear if you still have it — smells, small things!' He twinkled at his patient, 'Do you remember anything at all? Never yet knew a case which remembered nothing!' Theo frowned. He hated this line of questioning. It made him feel like an idiot.

'Snippets,' he said with more enthusiasm than he felt; 'I remember snippets.' Then he dropped his voice and added, 'I remember a ring . . .'

'Capital,' the doctor said. 'Capital.' He palpated Theo's stump. 'Capital. Think about the ring. Imagine it. When did you get it? What did it look like? That sort of thing! Get a handle on the past . . .'

Theo was suddenly withdrawn. 'It's the future which concerns me most. You can congratulate me, you know. I'm getting married tomorrow!'

The doctor knew this; Sister had told him. He had asked Yvonne and she had confirmed it. Her father was coming for the ceremony. The chaplain had obtained a special licence. He had questioned the doctor as to whether the man was fit to undertake marriage; whether he was fully compos mentis.

'He's all right,' Dr Perry had said. 'He just can't remember most of his life. But he's single, and he's free to marry if he wishes. It's the young woman you should talk to. I don't think she realizes what she'll be taking on! These young women are all full of romance and think the future is guaranteed by good intentions.'

The chaplain had spoken to Yvonne. 'I love him, Father. I just love him. I know it won't be easy,' she added, to show she was grown up and had given the matter due consideration. 'Is marriage ever easy? But I love him . . .'

But in her heart she felt that nothing could be easier. To love Theo, to marry him, was simplicity itself.

The chaplain observed her keenly. He felt sorry for her. So young, so ready for the noble gesture; so profligate with time! She knew nothing of how long life was, how it stretched and then contracted; she could not guess how she would feel in twenty years if this man, to whom she was about to entrust her life, was still full of absences, still rambling, still unfit for the business of living. No matter what she thought or felt now, the life in her would make demands on him. If he did not deliver, if it became clear that he could never deliver, the corrosion would set in whether she liked it or not.

'Think carefully,' he said. 'Think of how it may be in twenty years.'

Yvonne smiled. She thought of how it would be in twenty years. Her children and Theo's would be growing up around them. She would be with him, able to mind him, help him, talk to him, bask in the peculiar aura of his originality, soothe the ache of his vulnerability. He had a home in Ireland and they would live there. She didn't care where they lived. Ireland was probably a nice place anyway; people always gave her the impression that it was quaint and funny. She would become Irish and be happy.

'You will be going to another country, away from your family, with a disturbed young man you hardly know. He's a Roman Catholic, too . . . Irish . . . There's unrest in Ireland. Think carefully, my dear young lady.'

'His people shall be my people and his God my God,' Yvonne said with a full heart, smiling to herself and remembering Ruth in the Bible.

The chaplain knew when he was beaten. Well, he said to himself, one never knows. God moves in mysterious ways . . .

Theo's mother and sister Kate were there for the wedding. Andrew and Jenny turned up with Doctor Stacey. The latter was bewildered by his daughter's engagement, but had not the heart to prevent it. The young man was respectable, well set-up, and would probably recover. Those were the plus signs. The minus signs reminded him that he was Irish, Catholic, that Yvonne would be going to Ireland to live, that her husband was suffering from shell-shock and might not, after all, make a full recovery. But he had never seen his daughter so ecstatic; he had never seen her so alive, so bursting with happiness. He could not break her heart.

They sat in the small chapel with a handful of guests and patients while Yvonne and Theo took their vows. Jenny, wearing her own going-away outfit, sat with Andrew and his father. She saw the back of Theo's head. Then she saw his profile. Then she saw him almost full face as he turned to greet his bride; she saw the way the colours from the stained glass window touched him in a sudden burst of sunshine. She saw his eyes. She felt the floor of her chest constrict. She sat very still and Andrew eventually leaned over and whispered, 'Are you feeling all right.' She nodded. The marriage service commenced.

Mid-way through the service she excused herself and went outside. Andrew followed her. He saw her hurrying towards the shrubbery. When he found her she was bending over, retching. He ran to her.

'What happened to you, Jen?'

Jenny straightened, wiped her mouth with the handkerchief he offered her, turned to her husband. She had a greyish pallor and her eyes seemed large and bright and fearful.

'Nothing,' she said. 'Nothing at all.'

'Do you want to go home?'

Jenny's eyes moved to the building behind him. 'No.'

She went back slowly with him to the chapel. Andrew tried to be solicitous. His mind scanned the possible reasons for her indisposition, settled with mixed and bitter emotions on the one most likely to occur to anyone else.

Afterwards there was a small reception with a buffet in the nearby hotel — the Binnington Arms. There she met the bride and groom.

Yvonne embraced her. She was radiant and her cheeks were flushed. Andrew kissed his sister and congratulated his old friend. He stood up very straight, as became a gentleman, while he assessed the extent of Theo's injuries and his recovery. 'You're a lucky fellow, Yvonne is a topping girl.' He glanced at his sister, smiled teasingly. 'Even though I say so myself!'

Theo nodded, 'Yes.' He looked at his wife without focusing, like someone whose mind was elsewhere. He turned slowly to Jenny. He was very handsome in his new uniform, was clean-shaven except for the dark moustache which had been neatly trimmed; the scars on his forehead, which disappeared into his hairline, were now pale and noticeable only in certain lights.

'Darling,' Yvonne said, leaning towards her new husband, 'this is my best friend, Jenny. Remember, I told you all about her. We were at school together and she and Andrew got married recently.' She fed him fragments of information so that he would not look blank. His confused white face made her think, for a moment, that he had forgotten most of what she had told him. 'The girl in the photograph, remember?' She turned to her sister-in-law. 'Isn't it the most amazing coincidence — that he had a snapshot of us in his pocket through most of the war?' She knew perfectly well that Jenny was aware of this, but it was something to say.

Theo took Jenny's hand. For a moment he did not meet her eyes, and when he did the pupils dilated into dark pools of pain. The expression on his face changed from one of bewilderment to one of recognition and ferocity.

Jenny whispered, 'How do you do?' tore her eyes away and excused herself. She went into the ladies' room.

'Hasn't been quite the thing today!' Andrew said uncomfortably. 'Sick earlier.'

Yvonne followed Jenny to the ladies' room, found her sitting before the mirror and trembling from head to foot.

'Are you all right?' she demanded gently. 'I never saw anyone so white.'

'I'm sorry,' Jen said. 'I had a bit of a turn earlier. Don't feel too well.'

Yvonne regarded her carefully and asked in a voice full of anticipatory delight, 'Andrew told me you were sick. You're not . . . expecting?'

'No,' Jenny said shakily. 'No.'

While Yvonne was in the ladies' room with Jenny, Theo's sister Kate took charge of him. His conversation with Andrew about the war had deteriorated into monosyllables. It was plain that Andrew was extremely uncomfortable with someone who couldn't remember shared experiences. He distracted himself by privately assessing the young Irishwoman, Kate, whom he found very attractive. She reminded him of a fawn — innocent eyes, diffident — but with some kind of hidden agenda, some hard little nub, like a nut in a chocolate. In a way she resembled Jenny, because, although not a beauty by any means, she was individual; but she was of the earth and Jenny . . . Well, Jenny did not seem to belong anywhere, but to some private dimension of her own to which only she held the key. She had withdrawn into this personal space and he had been excluded. He blamed himself, because of what he had recently done, because in doing it he had overreacted, but he was angry too. He allowed his eyes to trace the length of Kate's skirt. Pity about the clothes; out of date, too long, although a nice little ankle peeped out underneath. For a moment he imagined her in a bathing suit, and smiled at her urbanely as he mentally undressed her.

Kate blushed. She knew her skirt was too long, but she had had no time to buy anything new. She also read something in Andrew's eyes which a secret part of her recognized and answered.

'Mother is so looking forward to going home,' she said hurriedly to deflect discomfiture. 'I hope Yvonne will be happy with us. She's such a darling!'

Too good for him by half, Andrew thought. But you, my dear; you could be a cure for frustration!

Andrew drifted away and Kate kept up some chatter, noting miserably that Theo was sweating and seemed confused. His eyes had assumed a glazed appearance and seemed to bulge a little, like someone on opium.

She glanced across the room to where their mother conversed with Dr Stacey. The older woman held herself well; she was laughing at

something the doctor had told her, some anec-
dote, and the sudden burst of her mirth made
her seem like a girl. Kate watched in amazement.

'I know Yvonne's a darling,' Theo said suddenly to Kate, switching back to a kind of normality. He indicated his mother with a wry
inclination of his head. 'Even Mother says so.
But I think she feels sorry for her. Poor kid and
all that, married to her wreck of a son!'

Kate searched in her bag. 'Theo, I have something I meant to give you. It might help jog your
memory. Papa sent it from Venice the year the
war began. He sent it to you . . .'

She waited for some glimmer of remembrance
in her brother's face, and when there was none
she took something small from her bag with an
air of suppressed excitement and put it into
Theo's hand. Theo stared at the gold ring in the
palm of his hand. 'I don't know where he got it,'
Kate went on. 'But he did send it to you! I know
that! Dr Perry says you mentioned it to him. Do
you . . . ?' Theo trembled. He grasped the ring
and with a strangled cry flung it across the room.

Almost immediately, Yvonne was back at his
side, taking his hand, soothing him. She made
him sit down. Dr Stacey and Mrs O'Reilly came
swiftly across the room. The latter put a hand on
her son's shoulder.

Kate went to retrieve the ring which was in a
corner underneath a chair. She drew Yvonne
aside and gave it to her, saying that it was
Theo's. 'I'm sorry. I think he's very tired. It

seemed to upset him. I thought it might jog his memory . . . I was sure it would because he mentioned it to Dr Perry. Did I do wrong?'

'Don't worry,' Yvonne said, aware that Kate was on the verge of tears. 'He'll be fine. It's just the day is a big strain for him.' She looked at the gold signet ring and put it in her pocket. 'I'll give it back to him sometime. I presume you meant him to keep it!'

'Oh, it's his!' Kate said. 'Father sent it to him from Italy the year he died! For some reason I have not been able to show it to Mother. I think she would disapprove because Father . . . did not return alive. So put it away somewhere, if you like.' Kate smiled tremulously. The smile lit up her grave face, showed her small white teeth. 'God bless you, Yvonne,' she said with a relieved exhalation of breath. 'I'm glad you're coming home with us. I so hope you will be happy with us . . .'

Yvonne glowed with pleasure. She turned to look at her new husband, and saw that he was staring across the room to where Jenny, who had returned from the ladies' room, was drinking a glass of wine and talking to Andrew. Her back was turned. She was slim and fine boned, wore a dark blue hat and a blue belted woollen dress. The curve of her arm and set of her body were full of grace. Her complexion was delicate English rose. There was nothing of assertive elegance about her, rather a quality of the ethereal; someone who belonged in a dimension where assertiveness was unnecessary.

Watching her, Theo muttered to himself.

Yvonne heard the garbled words and went to him at once. 'Jenny the brown, Jenny the brown, give us Jenny to burn or drown,' he whispered.

Yvonne frowned, wishing the day would end. How soon could they decently leave?

He turned to her, and grabbed the hand she slipped into his so that it hurt. 'Don't let me go, Yvonne,' he said in a small, tight voice. 'Hold me.'

She returned the pressure of his fingers. 'I will; you know I will.'

It came at last, the long awaited moment of departure, the moment when the door of their room shut behind them, the moment of finally being alone together, of lying down side by side together for the first time. It was, for Yvonne, inexpressibly poignant. She lay beside her new husband in her new nightgown, reached for his hand and kissed it. Then she waited for him to embrace her, caress her, speak the words she longed for, whisper his love.

But instead of the shared love and confidences she had expected, she found him taciturn, exhausted, and he made no move to touch her. She wanted to hold him in her arms, let him know that he would never be alone again, that her strength was his; glut herself on his happiness. But he moved away and gave himself up to an independent sleep — or what passed for sleep. Although she woke several times during the night and listened for his breathing, it was never the deep breathing of one truly asleep; but when she whispered his name there was no response.

For his part, Theo wavered in and out of sleep, a half sleep where he dreamed and woke and dreamed again. He felt himself rushing upwards, away out, until he was over London; he saw the lights below, the maze of streets and sleeping buildings, the sparse traffic, felt the cold air, saw the Thames winding towards the sea, the Houses of Parliament, Big Ben. It all looked like Toy-town, made of papier-mâché. He felt that he was escaping something; he felt that he was searching for something. He knew that the city below, that all the individual lives in it were terribly important; that each life the world contained possessed some morsel of infinity. He remembered a place in the country near the sea, a parcel, a ring, and how he had felt when he held it in his hand; how he had not wanted to put it on. He knew suddenly where the ring was and he wanted to call out a warning; he wanted to get back and warn her. But, when he tried, the force which propelled him high above the city seemed to close around him.

The following morning they had breakfast in their room. The waitress knocked and Yvonne threw on her new pink kimono and opened the door. 'Breakfast, madam,' the girl said, wheeled in the table and discreetly positioned it by the window.

Theo was awake; he sat up, reached for his wallet, and leaned towards the waitress with a ten-shilling tip.

'Oh, thank you, sir.'

When the waitress had taken her leave, Yvonne turned to Theo.

'Would you like it in bed, darling?' but Theo was already half out of bed, reaching for his stick.

'No,' he said. 'No, no. No, I'm not a confounded invalid.'

Yvonne's face darkened with surprise. 'I'm sorry . . .'

Theo sighed. 'For God's sake, don't be sorry. There's a difference to being a cripple and being an invalid. Your husband is the former but he refuses to be the latter.'

Yvonne smiled at him and reached out for his hand. 'I don't think you're a cripple, Theo. You are perfectly mobile now and will continue to improve. Don't be so cross!' She opened the curtains and saw the light touch his sleepy face.

He looked around the room. 'Where did you put the ring?' he demanded softly.

Yvonne started. 'What ring?' She was afraid of the repetition of yesterday's upset.

'Kate gave it back to you. I'd like to have it! I had it in my hand yesterday and now I remember it well.'

Yvonne went to the dressing table and took up

her bag, searched in it for the ring, tossed it to the figure in the bed. The gold glinted in the morning sunlight as it described a small arc across the room. Theo caught it, examined it cursorily, and shivered violently as he closed his hand around it. Then he slipped it on his finger.

Yvonne waited. She heard the movement of traffic outside, the clatter of a horse-drawn dray, the hoarse sound of motors going by, the sound of someone moving outside in the corridor, voices and a woman's sudden laugh.

Then Theo smiled, a triumphant smile which lit his face with sudden life. 'Don't look so glum, Yvonne. Don't mind me. Eat your breakfast.' He strapped on his leg, got out of bed and took his own seat, passing her salt and pepper, shaking out his napkin.

She cut into her poached eggs and the yolk spilled on to the moist toast. 'Hmnn,' she murmured, savouring the mouthfuls and searching for something to say which would return her to a sense of the normal, 'I love poached eggs!'

Theo raised his head. He was still smiling. 'Do you, my dear? I think you love many things. Perhaps it would be better if you loved less!'

Yvonne started, looked at him with a troubled face. 'What do you mean, Theo?'

His eyes met hers and she looked away. 'One loves for many reasons: out of choice perhaps, because it is better to suffer love than terminal ennui; out of a kind of poor necessity, a play; but there is also the love that is thrust on one, that burns fiercer than life, that allows for no escape, not even through death . . .'

He stopped, gave a short laugh. 'Never mind. You are not likely to be troubled in that way!'

Yvonne was silent. She felt suddenly that she was very young and Theo very old. She studied his face. He ate his bacon and eggs with a leisurely relish she had never seen him apply to food. There was no sign of the confusion which was his hall-mark; he had withdrawn to some perfectly self-sufficient citadel.

'Theo . . . ?'

'Yes?'

'You have changed!'

He raised his eyebrows. 'Does that perturb you?'

Yvonne retreated. 'Yes . . .'

'How have I changed?'

'You just have!'

She tried to work it out. He had acquired some kind of certainty, some brusqueness which was not his wont and which was at odds with his usual gentleness and confusion. She became silent, but watched him. Perhaps this was part of his recovery? She should rejoice if it was, but part of her was afraid. The fear stemmed from the suggestion that she did not know him, that she had married a stranger, that the dire possibilities his mother had forecast on their first meeting had indeed come to pass. A man recovering from shell-shock might be one thing, but the recovered man, the man with his personality restored, might be another and very different person.

'Don't be so bloody English,' Theo said suddenly, without raising his eyes.

'I am English,' Yvonne said quietly. 'You are being unreasonable.' After a moment she added, 'It never bothered you before!'

'What I find irksome is the way you people circumscribe yourselves. You're all attached to some kind of damn leash. Stop vetting circumstances, stop measuring them against the "done thing", stop rationalizing everything. Stop being so conquered by the bloody Norman ascendancy. Above all, don't be nice! It cloys!'

Yvonne sat miserably, struggling with anger and bewilderment. Then she said without raising her voice, 'The English use politeness as both shield and weapon. When we put the knife in it is done exquisitely. Don't bait me, Theo!'

He laughed. 'That is much better! Would you put a knife in me?'

'I love you. I know that. I do not have any knowledge of knives, nor do I wish to.'

'And you — a little Sassenach — coming to live with the wild Irishry! How are you going to manage at all? Surrounded on all sides by the quaint fighting Paddies! Dear oh dear!'

'Maybe I will undertake a new conquest of Ireland,' Yvonne said with a smile, deciding that she may as well enjoy being teased and turn it to badinage. 'You might be underestimating me.'

'Ireland was never conquered,' Theo said, his

voice returning to normal. 'That is the problem with the place. You can't conquer a nation of roaring individualists.'

'And they can't prevent you for the same reason!'

Theo smiled. 'Very good!' His face was suddenly very gentle, his blue eyes studying her. 'Are you glad you married me?' he demanded softly. 'You're not afraid it might have been a mistake?'

Yvonne gulped. 'No. I was just wondering why you are so different today!'

'Come now, the truth. Would you have secrets from me?'

Yvonne was suddenly tired. 'No, darling. Of course not!'

The word 'darling' had power. It conjured up rights and territories. She had the right to call him 'darling', she had the right to his respect and his forbearance. She used it as armour, as a badge of property, as a means of deflecting anything on his part that might overwhelm or hurt her. If she was too small for him, after all, she still had rights.

Theo smiled again as one might who addressed an anxious child. 'You see,' he said, 'I think that you do not know me . . . I do not wish to inflict pain on you! And I may not be able to avoid it!'

Yvonne's brows drew themselves together. 'Perhaps you don't know me either,' she said darkly, her pride unwilling to have him appropriate all the mystery between them.

He studied her for an instant. 'I know more than a little about you,' he said. 'And I shall prove it very shortly.'

When they had finished breakfast, Theo led his bride back to their bed. She clutched instinctively at her kimono, all her interest in lovemaking had disappeared. Theo had become a stranger, and the virginal instinct of her shy body was to escape him. Against that there was the sense of duty, now that she was his wife. But there was something else in her too: a wild, albeit shrinking, curiosity.

Theo sat beside her on the bed, looked at her calmly with an interrogative smile. 'Well, Mrs O'Reilly,' he murmured softly, 'what shall we do? Shall we dress? Go out for a while?'

He picked up her hand and turned it over, smiling a little, stroking the white skin on the underside of her forearm. 'How soft the flesh is!'

Yvonne moved away a fraction. Theo reached out and gently pushed back the silken sleeve of the kimono. He turned her underarm to his gaze, rubbed his right index finger softly along the silken skin. He stroked her skin very slowly, moved up her arm with tiny, unhurried caresses. He did not speak, or meet her eyes. His eyes were for her arm, where he traced the blue veins at her wrist right up to the inside of her elbow. He seemed almost disinterested.

Yvonne began to relax. The butterfly strokes on her arm were no assault on the fortress of her virginity. Whatever she had expected from the nuptial embrace, however dutiful or helpful she had imagined she would be, this demanded nothing of her. Theo's fingers began to stroke her arm higher, pushing her kimono sleeve back to her shoulder. He lay her back against the pillows and, although she tensed again, he resumed the small stroking of her arm so that she began to wonder why her left arm should contain so much to interest him. Her body, relaxed and once more feeling itself in control, began to respond. The skin at the top of her arm waited for his touch, became impatient. Eventually his fingers probed laconically into her armpit, stroked her underarm hair. This intimacy lasted unendurably. Yvonne lay quite still with half-closed eyes. The cool hand moved a little, and then fingers moved from her armpit and began to stroke the soft swell of her breast at the point where it rose from her rib cage. The movements were very slow. They moved upwards very slowly along the curve of her breast. The nipple erected expectantly. Yvonne closed her eyes. This intimacy was more delicious than anything that had ever happened to her in her life. She waited, shivering at the infinitesimal advance of his touch. But he did not touch the swollen nipple. Instead he suddenly withdrew his hand and reached for her wrist.

Yvonne opened her eyes.

His eyes were smiling at her with a heightened gleam. 'Your pulse is very fast,' he said lazily.

'But we will end the first lesson here.'

Yvonne turned away to hide the emotion in her eyes.

'A woman's body,' he said, 'is a highly tuned instrument, capable of all kinds of music. You see how I do not dare to trespass too far.'

Yvonne, feeling confused and suspicious, searched him for diffidence; but the smile in his eyes was assured.

Later, as she got dressed in the small dressing room, he said, 'I would like you to tell me all about your life. Tell me about Andrew and Jenny.'

'Nothing much to tell,' Yvonne said. 'I've told you before, anyway. You know that Andrew is my brother. Jenny lived a few doors away with her grandfather. She's always been my best friend! We went to school together. She and Andrew were childhood sweethearts! Why are you so interested in Jenny?'

'How very cosy!' Theo said expressionlessly, ignoring her question. 'Why did Jenny live with her grandfather?'

Yvonne pulled up her skirt, fastened it, and came out of the dressing room. 'Because her parents were dead. Her mother died while she was very young. I don't know exactly what happened to her father. I think he died in Paris before the war. He used to travel a lot; he was in France and Italy a lot. His employer was rich and wrote travel books.'

'I see.'

Theo busied himself in shaving. He could stand easily on his artificial leg. Yvonne watched him with pride. The conflicting feelings generated by the half-lovemaking earlier had dissipated.

'Did he bring anything interesting back from Italy?' Theo asked nonchalantly. 'From Venice, for example?'

Yvonne turned to look at him, saw the way the cut-throat razor was edging over the line of his jaw and on to his neck. 'I don't know, Theo. He always brought her a present. She had a doll in national costume and a cuckoo clock and other things. I remember she had a mask. It was something he brought back. She drew a picture of it in school one day, but when I asked to see it she couldn't find it. I think her grandfather hid it!'

Theo cursed. A small ooze of blood trickled down his neck. Yvonne had to prevent herself from rushing to staunch the tiny wound. He watched her in the mirror. 'It's only a scratch!' he said coldly. Then he added in a pleasant voice, 'Why did he hide it — the mask?'

Yvonne shrugged. 'How do I know? Maybe he thought it frightened her! Maybe it was valuable. She was a bit weird in those days. Once she told me she had been grown up for as long as I could calculate years! She had a great imagination, wrote wonderful essays . . .'

'What kind of essays?'

'Oh, the sort of thing where the heroine has much to overcome!'

Theo stopped shaving and stared at her fixedly from the mirror. 'But she's a dear,' Yvonne added hurriedly. 'And she and Andrew are very happy!'

Theo resumed shaving. 'How do you know they're happy?' he asked out of the corner of his mouth as he scraped the cut-throat underneath his chin.

Yvonne chuckled. 'What a silly question! Of course they are!' Then she thought of the new melancholy she had seen in her brother's eyes, of Jenny's pallor, and for the first time it occurred to her that perhaps everything between them was less than idyllic. She glanced back at Theo and added with less certainty, 'At least I think they are.'

When he was dressed, Yvonne asked him what he would like to do. 'We could take a taxi somewhere . . . walk a little if you feel up to it.'

'Yvonne, if you will forgive me, I need to be alone for a little while . . . Perhaps you would like to do some shopping, get yourself a few things for the journey: some clothes, whatever you like. There are almost certainly no shops in Bally-shane.' The tone in his voice brooked no opposition.

Yvonne looked around for her hat in dismay. She felt like saying that she should have gone up to London with his mother and sister if he did not want to be with her on their first full day together.

'I'll go for a walk,' she said. 'I have a few things to buy, anyway.'

He handed her a roll of banknotes. She took it and stared.

'Fifty pounds. So much?'

'We're not paupers, you know!'

When she was gone, Theo had taken the lift down to the lobby and asked the porter to get him a taxi.

Chapter Nine

'You are enslaved to Satan. You have caused milk to sour and cows to miscarry and have hindered men in their conjugal activities.'

The witch dared to smile. 'So fine and haughty an inquisitor can believe such nonsense!'

Journal of a Witness

Dee's parents seemed strangely shaken by the talk of Kilashane; she changed the subject and chatted with as much enthusiasm as she could muster, telling them about Laura and about the flat, but obeying her father's injunction not to elaborate about the problems with her boss: 'You know how easily your mother gets upset . . .'

Supper consisted of a chicken and ham salad with homemade mayonnaise and, afterwards, lemon meringue pie.

'You should be trying to save,' her mother said, when Dee told her, between mouthfuls, how much they were paying for the flat. 'Four pounds! It's not Christian for people to charge so much for a roof!' She reached for the serving dish and put some more chicken on her daughter's plate.

'Thanks, Mam.'

'Eat up every bit of that. You need building up! You've lost weight!'

Dee smiled. 'I know!' Since she had taken the job in McGrath, her skirts had become loose, and the days of having to watch what she ate seemed over. But she knew that her mother, who could remember a time when TB scourged the country, was beset by old perspectives, even though she knew perfectly well that, thanks to inoculation, tuberculosis was a spent force.

'You should bring Laura down to stay.'

'I will.'

'What is she working at?'

'She's a production assistant in Telefís Éireann.'

Mr McGlinn raised his white eyebrows. 'Good for her! The whole country wants to work in Telefís Éireann. Does she know Gay Byrne?'

'She sees him around!'

Her mother sighed. 'I've watched "The Late Late Show" every Saturday since it started! Maybe Laura could get tickets for us and we could go to Dublin for the day?'

'I'll ask her.'

There was silence for a moment. Dee felt the sudden tension; she glanced at her father and noticed that his eyes were fixed on his plate. He seemed uneasy. It occurred to her that her parents had not addressed a single word directly to each other during the whole meal.

Then her father said sardonically, breaking the

silence, 'You should hear what our new curate, Father Dunne, says about Telefís Éireann!'

Dee looked at him. 'I can make a good guess. "A hotbed of sex and communism"?'

He smiled. 'That's a fair résumé!'

'The hierarchy has always seen Telefís Éireann as a threat. The business of the bishop and the nightie was a case in point,' Dee said.

Both her parents laughed. Her mother laughed guiltily, because the business concerned sex and was a trifle wicked, her father in spite of himself. She was referring to the episode of 'The Late Late Show' where some newly-weds had been invited to divulge what they had worn on their wedding night. One bride said she hadn't worn a stitch. The Bishop of Galway had fulminated at the incredible immorality of it, had denounced the programme. 'How do you stand it in your island?' Colin had asked Dee when she had told him about it. 'Letting crazy old buggers make life unfit to live?'

Now her father avoided embarrassment by changing the subject. 'What's your friend Laura like?'

'She is white, female, Irish.'

'Thank you, Dee!'

She looked at her father and grinned. 'Laura is lovely. She would talk the leg off a pot! She has straight blonde hair which is very fine, and she has one grey eye and one blue. She is naturally slim; she reads a great deal — history and philosophy and romantic novels — and likes to stay awake until all hours. She has an aversion to mornings!'

'She sounds a dear,' her mother said. 'Does she have a boyfriend?'

Dee had been waiting for this query. It was a way of raising the subject. She would then progress to the real question — was Dee seeing anyone?

'Yes. His name is Ted.'

There was an interrogative silence. 'Nobody on the doorstep for me at the moment, Mam,' she forestalled her.

'What about the boy you knew in London — Colin?'

'He writes.'

'Oh, he doesn't come to see you or anything?'

Dee shook her head. For a moment a longing for Colin subsumed her. For a moment she thought how nice it would be to have him there at table, to go for a long walk with him in the twilight. She saw his lopsided grin, heard his funny, acid commentary. 'No. We keep in touch. That's all.'

Her mother looked disappointed. Dee was well aware that her mother wanted her to marry and settle down, preferably with someone who had a good job which would make it possible for her to have babies right away. Said babies would then have the benefit of a besotted grandmother.

'Well,' Dee said cheerfully, 'tell me what's been going on down in this neck of the woods.'

Mrs McGlinn sighed. 'Nothing much.'

'We have the same breezes from the sea and curlew cries in the evening,' her father said, to show that the peninsula had wonders which could not be sneezed at, 'but we miss you.'

'How are the O'Dwyers and the McDonnells?'

'They're grand. I see them at Mass every Sunday. They're missing the boys at agricultural college. Father O'Shea was asking for you. I told him you had a great job.'

Dee thought of the kindly parish priest who was much loved by his parishioners. 'Oh, Dad. Don't go around telling people that!'

'Why not?'

'It makes me nervous!'

Her mother smiled indulgently. 'Credit where credit is due,' she said decisively. She glanced at her daughter with a smile. 'I'm sure your employers know calibre when they see it.'

Dee thought of Charlie and felt the word 'calibre' was a little out of place. She glanced at her father who raised his eyebrows.

'Actually, we did have one bit of excitement,' he said. 'I forgot to tell you. Poor old Billy is dead.'

Dee sat back in her chair. She was shocked and sad. The long finger of mortality reached out and touched her. Old Billy had been around for as long as she could remember. She had half expected him to go on for ever. Ballyshane would not be the same without him.

'What happened to him?'

'Ah, he went very queer in himself. He said he had been up at the old house and had seen a ghost. He was going around telling this to every-one for a day or two, and then there was no sign of him.'

'That's not unusual for Billy — going miss-ing,' Dee said.

'No. But the poor creature was found at the bottom of the cliff at Carraigh Point a day or two after he was last seen.'

Dee was silent. In her mind's eye she saw Billy's poor broken body on the rocks. She would never see him again, or hear his queer old rambling, or watch him scramble into the woods, or shake his fist at the crows.

'It's horrible!' Dee whispered.

'He was always wandering around Kilashane,' she said. 'I used to see him going in and out of the woods. It will be strange without him!' There was a moment's silence.

'Funny thing, though,' her father said. 'There was a man — a city man I'd say — down here for his funeral, asking questions about him, about where he lived. He said he was a cousin, the last of his family.'

'I see. I didn't know he had any family! Did they tell this man where he lived?'

'Father O'Shea showed him the cottage.'

Dee smiled. 'They didn't show him his tree? He nearly always slept up his tree.' She giggled as she said this. 'Slept up his tree' had a certain ring to it.

Her mother stared at her sorrowfully, with nothing of the tension which usually marked her face when she spoke of Billy. Her eyes had the far-away look of someone remembering something long gone. 'Poor creature,' she repeated.

'Did Father O'Shea show the man Billy's tree?' Dee repeated. 'It would be a bit of a shock for a relative!' And then she wondered if the parish priest even knew where Billy slept. Her parents knew about it, but she had never heard anyone else mention it. She had never told them that she had often watched him from a hiding place in the wood.

Her mother put back a strand of grey hair. The light glinted on her glasses. She seemed uneasy. 'Sure, why would he do that? He wouldn't want to be upsetting the cousin — or whoever he was. Besides, it mightn't be lucky!'

'Oh, Mam, why not? What possible ill-luck could come from that?' Dee demanded in exasperation. She was impatient with her mother's occasional forays into superstition which, she felt, were at odds with her intelligence.

But as soon as the words were out of her mouth, she knew she had made a tactical mistake. Her mother detected the note of criticism and looked offended. 'You don't know everything!' was all she said. 'You don't know everything!'

Dee bit her lip. Her mother had a knack of being personally affronted by small conversational indiscretions. Dee glanced at her father, saw that he gave an almost imperceptible shake to his head.

Later, as Dee was helping her wash up, her mother told her: 'Your father has been invited again to join the Knights!'

Dee thought of the Knights of Columbanus, the Catholic secret society set up to counter the Freemasons.

'Dad wouldn't be interested in that sort of thing, would he?'

Her mother smiled, briskly drying plates. She was happy to have her daughter back, to be talking the conspiratorial talk of women. 'No. But they have a lot of power, all the same.'

'I wonder, could Charlie be involved in something like that?' Dee asked aloud. She turned to look at her mother. 'Charlie is my boss. He's a bit peculiar. You'd think he was the greatest yob; but he's acute and devious at the same time, and he even speaks fluent French, although he pretended he didn't know a word!'

Her mother shook her head. 'Sure, you wouldn't want to take much heed,' she said in a voice preoccupied with domesticity. 'He's probably trying to hide his light under a bushel!'

Dee heard the clean contact of plate against plate as her mother stacked them in the cupboard and did not pursue the matter.

Dee's father returned, whistled for Ricky, who was in the old easy chair by the cooker. 'Dee and I will go for a dander,' he said.

'Will you come, Mam?'

Ricky hurried after them into the hall, tongue lolling. 'Sit!' Mr McGlinn commanded, and

Ricky obeyed, grinned, panted, and thumped his tail on the floor.

'No,' Mrs McGlinn said, without looking at her husband. 'You go off and enjoy yourselves.'

As they walked away from the house, her father confided, 'I'm in the dog-house. That's why she won't come for the walk!'

'Why?'

'Long story. She wants us to pull up stumps and go to live in Dublin once I have retired.'

'I know.'

Dee walked with her father into the back field, walked along by the Meena, the stream where she used to fish for pinkeens with jam-pots, skirted the meadow by the stone wall until they found the stile to the old boreen. The boreen was rutted, overgrown. It was a track which led on the one hand to the cliffs — to Carraigh Point — and on the other to the main road near the entrance to Kilashane demesne, where there was a ruined gate-lodge. The lodge had been in use as a shop for many years after the big house itself had been left to go to rack and ruin. A woman by the name of Doll Kennedy had run the shop, which had sold sweets and newspapers and a few staples like milk and butter and bread.

As a child, Dee had often gone for messages along the boreen to Doll's, bringing home the bag of sugar and a lollipop for herself, sucking it slowly as she wandered home, taking unconscious pleasure in the tang of the breeze, the sight of wild flowers in the grass and the raucous cry of the gulls. But now she and her father took the opposite route, in the direction of the cliffs and the sea. She took her father's arm.

'How's school, Dad?'

'Holidays soon. Permanent for me!' He sighed. 'But that's life — gone before you know you've had it!' He carried his blackthorn and his tweed peaked cap pulled down on his forehead. Ricky ran along ahead of them, sniffing and piddling and wheeling now and again to chase some imaginary quarry.

Dee surveyed the scenery, from the rise to the cliff-tops a couple of miles away, back to where the chimneys of Kilashane appeared above the trees among the circling crows. She took a deep breath. She loved all of this; she loved the fact that it had changed in nothing since she was a child, except perhaps that a few modern cottages had replaced older ones which had let in the fury of winter storms. She knew the family in every house.

They stopped to speak to Mrs Tracy outside her home. 'It's grand to see you. Come in and sit down. I was just going to wet the tea!'

They declined, but spoke with the old lady for a while. Mrs Tracy's family of seven were grown now and all gone, scattered to the four winds. Her cottage was old, with stout stone walls and small windows and a big open fireplace with a black kettle on a crane. Dee loved this cottage: for the fact that it hadn't changed; for its atmosphere of love and family and acceptance; but most of all for the grace and refinement of its occupant who, although she was old and poor, had the manners and carriage of a queen.

When they moved off Dee said, 'Dad, I love being home!'

Her father did not turn to look at her, but he tightened his arm against his side and squeezed her hand against his jacket. 'I know!'

There was peace. Communion. And because of communion with him she felt it too with the wind and the cry of the gulls and the bleating of the lambs up on the rising land, as though she were herself part of the fabric of this place.

'Would you like me to stay at home?' She whispered this, because she had not meant to say it. She had little option but to go away. There were no jobs in Ballyshane.

'No,' he said.

In spite of herself she was hurt. 'Why not?'

He turned, smiling, to look down at her. 'Because, my darling, there are things you must do. A ship is very snug and safe in harbour, but that is not what it's built for.'

'What am I built for?'

'For life.'

'How do you define "life"?'

He raised an eyebrow. 'Different things to different people. A place where you embark on discovery.'

'What is there to discover?'

He glanced at her. 'You are being disingenuous, Dee!'

'Maybe, but I can't help feeling that the journey of discovery is inward; if so, it can be embarked on without stirring from the chair!'

'That would preclude experience,' he said. 'Without experience there is no map or yardstick, no challenge or stimulus, no surprises, and a growing inability to address reality.'

She thought of Charlie, of Laura, of Colin; of the international Bomb; of apartheid; of the Civil Rights movement. 'It seems to me that it's a perpetual power struggle.'

'Yes. But sometimes, in the midst of all the clamour, something real happens. Sometimes there is love.' She looked at her father in surprise, but his face was inscrutable.

They came to the stone wall where the boreen ended. Beyond it was the cliff they called Carraigh Point, and beyond it the sea. She heard it murmuring, saw the calm blue expanse of it as far as the horizon. Father and daughter crossed the stone wall gingerly, careful not to dislodge a single stone in case the wall itself might collapse. Mr McGlinn had seen people's feet crushed that way in the past.

They walked across the stony expanse of ground to the cliff. The wind whipped Dee's hair across her face and drove the breath from her body. She heard the sea growling at the base of the cliff, and she stood some feet back from the edge, watching the white breakers froth and curl on the rocks far below.

Her father took her arm and drew her back.

'Be careful, child.'

He only called her 'child' when he was anxious, or angry with her, and she glanced at him now and saw the fear in his face. One false step, one moment's vertigo, and the rocks below would have her. There was no margin here for error.

She moved back further to reassure him. Then she asked after a moment, shouting to make herself heard, 'Is this where poor Billy died?'

He nodded.

'Do you think it was suicide?'

He drew her away and back towards the boreen. 'Well, it was either suicide or an accident. The coroner decided it was death by misadventure.'

'But what was he doing up here? Billy knew the peninsula like the back of his hand!'

'Don't try to apply logic. All it required was one small step. If you were in Billy's shoes you might find that step not just easy, but welcoming!'

On the way back they stopped by Billy's house. It was a small, plastered county council cottage, with dirty windows and peeling paintwork. It was enclosed in a small garden surrounded by a cement wall. Wild flowers grew abundantly in the smothering grass: buttercups, thistles, yellow dandelions. There were foxgloves in profusion by the wall.

The iron-wrought gate screeched on its rusty hinges when it was opened. The path was cracked and overgrown with weeds. The front door was ajar.

Dee looked at her father. 'He left his door open.'

He frowned. 'Billy might leave the door open, but not Father O'Shea who locked up after his body was found . . .'

'The lock was forced,' Dee said, noting the splintered wood at the jamb.

They pushed the door and it opened inwards, creaking, and they saw the bedroom to the right and the room intended as a sitting room to the left. Both were completely ransacked.

'Holy Jesus,' Dee said, standing in the tiny V-shaped hall. 'The place has been burgled.'

She turned to her father and saw his expression of astonishment give way to one of gravity. He entered first one room then another. There was a smell of must and decay, old papers, old clothes. But the disorder was intentional. The divan bed was overturned, the chest of drawers had been emptied; the drawers were thrown one on top of the other. The chair was lying on its side. The same story obtained in the sitting room: the old couch had been ripped with a knife, and its cotton-and-horsehair stuffing protruded in thick wedges from the ripped covering. Pictures had been taken from the wall and lay, broken, by the skirting board.

Dee stared around her. She saw that the pictures were either oils or watercolours. She saw that the table in the corner, also on its side, was antique, a mahogany occasional table such as her mother had at home. 'Early Victorian,' her mother had said about it. 'Nice old thing.'

'Could he have done it himself?' Dee ventured. 'I can't imagine anyone around here doing something like this!'

'We'd better tell the guards anyway,' her father said.

As they left, Dee turned to him and asked, 'Wasn't it strange that he had some good things — some nice bits of furniture, old pictures. I always thought he was a complete tramp.'

Her father glanced at her. 'He wasn't always a tramp!'

For a while they walked in silence. Then Dee said, 'What was he looking for, do you think, the person who ransacked the house? Money? Something valuable?'

Her father shook his head as though the question defied him, and he quickened his pace. The night was coming down, the long, slow shadows of summer twilight. It would be dark in an hour or so. In the distance she saw the chimneys of Kilashane, with the crows circling. Their cawing could be heard, carried along in the evening breeze.

'I never in my life saw a place with so many crows!' Dee said, shaking her head. 'I used to take it for granted, but I've never seen anywhere else where the crows congregate like that, circling around and around as though there was something there they were watching out for.'

'It's probably the trees,' her father said; 'they congregate because of the trees! They have their nests there. They're very social creatures, you know.'

As they neared home, Dee asked, 'Dad, do you remember Kilashane when you were small?'

'No. How could I? I was not born on the peninsula. But your mother does!'

'I wonder, does she remember what it was like before the house was ruined, when people lived in it?'

'Have you never asked her?'

'I have, but she always changed the subject. You saw it for yourself this evening at supper. She just gets upset.' Her father's face was soft with sudden love. 'She has memories she doesn't want stirred up,' he said. 'She'll tell you someday. In the meantime, try to make allowances.'

When they got home, Mr McGlinn phoned the police. Later a garda came around to say that they had inspected the cottage, but that there was little they could do; there was no one to file a complaint. The occupier of the cottage was dead and there was no next-of-kin. No one knew what the place contained, or if anything was missing.

'There was a man from Dublin or somewhere, a cousin,' Mrs McGlinn said, and told the garda about the inquiry Father O'Shea had dealt with.

'I'll talk to himself then,' the young garda said, and took his leave.

Before the policeman left, Mr McGlinn added, 'We've had someone snooping around our own house here once or twice of late. But Ricky scared him off!'

The garda took a note and left.

'Why didn't you tell me there's been someone snooping around?' Dee demanded.

'Sure, I didn't think of it until Garda Maguire came. There was someone watching the house one night. I keep the shotgun under the bed now, so if anyone breaks in he'd better watch out!'

Mr McGlinn went to bed after the ten-thirty radio news. Dee's mother seemed in no hurry to join him, and sat in the fireside kitchen chair, darning her husband's socks and chatting to her daughter. She asked about what pictures were showing in Dublin, and Dee said she had been to see *The Sound of Silence.*

'Was it good?'

'Very! There are some lovely numbers,' and she began to hum, 'Hello darkness my old friend.'

In the silence which followed, her mother asked softly, 'Is there no young man you are interested in?'

'No, not at the moment. If you must know, Mam, the only man I've met since I got the job in Dublin who is in the least bit interesting was someone from Brussels, on a business trip to the company.' She sounded surprised, as though this intelligence had only just impinged on her.

Her mother pricked up her ears. 'I hope he's not married!'

'He probably is . . .'

Her mother shook her head. 'Keep away from the married ones! Nothing there but problems.'

Through the open window they could hear the sea. The breeze stirred the curtains.

'Mam?' Dee said softly.

'Yes?'

'Why would it be unlucky for someone to visit old Billy's treehouse? What is it that I don't know?'

Her mother put her work back into the basket. 'Will you leave me alone and not be asking me such questions!' she said. She got up, put the basket to one side and left the room. 'Lock the window before you go to bed,' she called back from the stairs.

Dee sat there in silence for a few minutes. Then she too went upstairs to bed.

She stood by her window for a while in the darkness. There was a path by the side of the house, leading to the garage which her father had had built. On the far side of the path was a row of pine trees. Looking out now from her bedroom window, she thought she saw something move among the trees, a shadow. She stared, transfixed, and then the shadow was gone. There was no sound. She drew back and closed the curtains. I'm imagining things! she told herself. Ricky would have gone mad if there had been anyone there.

She was glad to switch on the bedside light. Her room surrounded her with the mementoes

231

of childhood, with the safe and the familiar. She took the ring off the chain and put it on her finger. It was too big, heavy old gold, and she moved it up and down before returning it to the chain.

She got out the cardboard box and looked at the diary, opened it, taking up the faded sepia photograph. Caught in yellowing monochrome, the two girls stared out of their time-frame into the future.

Dee wondered what the burglar of old Billy's house had been looking for. She wondered what the burglar had been looking for when her flat in Dublin had been given a going-over. She wondered what the prowler had been seeking from her parents' home. It was a good job, she thought, that the ring had not been in the flat, otherwise the burglar would have found it. And then it occurred to her that there was nowhere it was really safe. She put it back on the chain and hung it round her neck.

She had a problem. Charlie had asked to see the ring and she had promised. But Charlie was not what he seemed, and she did not trust him. She wondered if she should tell her father about the ring and about Charlie's interest in it. It struck her suddenly that she could get a replica made. Charlie would never know the difference. She could ask Dan Brady down at the forge.

Chapter Ten

'You caused men's souls to turn from grace?'
'Men's souls,' she said, 'are men's responsibility.'

Journal of a Witness

Dee slept. She stirred and whispered in her sleep. In her dream she was in the grounds of Kilashane. It was night. Overhead the crows kept flying, swooping dark-winged against the sky. She saw their nests in the trees. Why don't they go to bed? she wondered. Why are they always at this caper, going round and around?

The house rose in front of her, but instead of the ruin she knew and had explored, there were lights on and the sound of a piano disconsolately played crept out into the night air. The perfume of honeysuckle came sweet and heavy from a nearby shrub. It was an old dream. In it she hid behind a yew tree, watching the house. She saw the man approach. She had no sense either of surprise and fear. He came towards her across the gravel of the driveway with hardly a sound. She pressed back into the shadows, knowing that he had come from the light and could not see her. But he continued in her direction, and when he was only a few feet away, stopped and looked into her face.

Dee felt the rush of recognition.

'Don't be afraid,' he said.

And then it was suddenly Billy's face which was staring at her, with his twisted mouth and half-baked smile, and she ran back down the driveway while his heavy footsteps lumbered behind her. She found her little shelter of laurel bushes and crept in there, watching Billy lope off towards his treehouse, swing up into the branches of the great beech and disappear among the dark leaves. She looked back towards the house. It was a ruin again, lonely and gaunt. The moment of recognition had gone. She began to weep. Come back, her mind wept. I have something to settle, something to understand. She heard the wind sough in the trees, and the cawing of the crows.

Dee woke and lay very still. Part of her was still in the dream; part of her was awake and evaluating. Her heart was beating very fast.

Kilashane! The house and its surroundings had dominated her childhood. It was her back yard and its mystery was necessary to her life. There was a satisfaction in its mystery, a nexus with her own identity.

She thought of the mask she had found and thrown away. She went over in her mind the heaps of rubble in the hall at Kilashane. Was it under the rubble; was it somewhere in the overgrown lawn?

When the dawn came she slipped out of bed, pulled on jeans and a sweater and quietly left the house by the back door. Ricky was in his basket in the kitchen. He whined a bit and thumped his tail when he saw her. She put a finger to her lips, shushed him, opened the back door slowly to avoid the scratching of the lintel. Then, together, they went around the side of the house and down the road towards the trees and the ruined bulk of Kilashane.

The sun was rising and fiery streaks illuminated the eastern horizon, turning the sea into a great lake of fire. The gulls were up, screeching on the shore and wheeling over the breakers. The peninsula was silent except for the first tweets of the dawn chorus and the lonely bleating of sheep.

Dee passed the remains of the gate-lodge and thought of Doll Kennedy and her shop. Doll had contracted cancer and died. The shop was left to crumble along with the house. The Land Commission had bought the land and divided it among the local farmers.

She arrived at the gate to the demesne, read the wooden sign: DANGEROUS BUILDING: KEEP OUT. The words, painted in black, were barely legible now, and the placard itself was weathered and coming adrift from its moorings. She walked on to the gap in the wall and picked her way over the fallen blocks and debris at the far side, where the thistles and nettles grew together in profusion. The latter were knee-high, and she retraced her steps to the road and broke a small branch from a sally tree. With this she beat a track through the nettles. Ricky had found his own way forward, and when she emerged into the avenue he was there, tongue lolling. In the shadowy solitude she looked up at the canopy of beeches over her head, trees planted two hundred years before, so tall and vast that it seemed incredible that any living thing could grow to such a height. Through the leaves she saw that the sky was pink and grey and she felt the shiver of the fresh wind of dawn. The crows were awake; their cawing had started, and some were idly wheeling overhead.

The avenue turned into the lawn, where once the driveway had described a circle around a central green sward. The weeds — ragwort, dandelion and coarse clumps of daisies — had established themselves. Even the flight of granite steps to the front door had not escaped them; they clung to crevices and insinuated themselves into every crack. She remembered her dream of an hour before. The man had come down these steps and across the gravel driveway and she had hidden behind a yew tree. He had walked with a stiff but upright gait. She looked to the right and saw the three dark green yews, standing like sentinels to the stable yard and back avenue beyond. Down there she had had her bower among the laurels and, further away again, Billy had had his treehouse. She wondered again if she were the only person, other than her parents, who knew he had such an abode. Her mother had always given the impression of being strangely knowledgeable about Billy, without ever being in any way specific, but no one else's parents ever mentioned him, except to say, if his name came up, 'God help the creature', or something like that.

She climbed the steps. The front door was long gone and the hall was sagging and covered in rubble from the floor above. Some of the rotting joists lay among the stones, fallen laths and plaster; others, where they were left in the ceiling, sagged drunkenly. She was afraid to enter the place. Standing on the front door lintel she could see through the gap where the drawing-room door had once been, that its floor had collapsed into the basement. The hall looked as though it, too, was on the point of subsiding. The stairs were gone, except for a few support spars sticking out from the wall. When she looked up she saw the sky and the ivy, which was now creeping down the inside of former bedroom walls. Even the plaster had deserted the old walls in places, and the stones were bare in the early morning light. The fragility of the place was patent. There could be no question of searching the house for the mask.

When she came home Dee found her mother in the kitchen. Her father had already breakfasted and had gone out for the paper.

'Did you have a walk, dear?' Mrs McGlinn said.

Dee told her that she had gone up to Kilashane, and her mother turned from the sink to look at her.

'Kilashane? I hope you kept clear of the house!'

'Of course. It looks like it's ready to fall in.'

'Yes, it must be very dangerous. I don't have to tell you at this point that you must never attempt to go inside it, you know that. In fact I'd prefer it if you kept clear of the place altogether.'

Dee sighed. 'I know, Mam. I can't help being interested in the place, though. I know you don't like to talk about it, but I'm curious about the history of the family — the O'Reillys. Why was the house allowed to fall in? Did they die out?'

Dee wondered why she had never pressed these questions before. She had always taken Kilashane for granted, like a landmark, a familiar spot on the local map, as though the ruin had always been a ruin. She had made certain assumptions as to the family, assumed that they had just sold out and gone, or that their departure, as her father had suggested, was in some way associated with the Troubles.

Mrs McGlinn looked uneasy. It was clear that she regretted her abrupt termination of the conversation of the night before. She put her fingers through her short grey hair in an old gesture, one always associated with malaise.

'Well, I don't know everything about them. I think they used to have a pretty gay time of it in the last century — parties and so on. The house was half burnt in 1919. There was a tragedy and the whole family died in it. The weather finished off the house.'

'What kind of tragedy? You mean the fire?'

'Well, the fire was part of it, but it's not lucky to talk about it!'

'Why?'

'It just is not. Dee, that family were responsible for a lot of pain in my life. I don't want to go into it and I don't want you to visit Kilashane!'

Dee was silent. She was puzzled and inquisitive. She could imagine life in Kilashane at the turn of the century. There would have been coaches driving up the avenue to the hall door, and ladies in long dresses and parties in winter, talk of agrarian reform and the Land Acts and later Home Rule; they would have discussed William Butler Yeats and the embarrassing nationalist beauty Maud Gonne whom he passionately loved. They would have hunted and shot. But why were they responsible for pain in her mother's life?

Her mother sighed and said, as though she knew the direction of her daughter's thoughts and wanted to deflect them, 'The owner was a member of Parliament at the turn of the century. They say he knew Parnell and Tim Healy. He worked for Home Rule, but he never lived to see the 1916 rising. He died abroad.'

Dee heard the crisp crunch of her father's boots as he came around the back. His spare frame appeared in the doorway and he smiled at her. 'Were you out? I missed Ricky and had a peep into your room, but your bed was empty.'

'I went for a walk to Kilashane.'

Her father's face altered for a moment and then held the expression. He took off his boots and put his feet into his waiting slippers. 'It's dangerous there, child,' he said after a moment. 'I hope you didn't try to go into the house. The county council should demolish it before someone gets hurt.'

He took his paper with him into the sitting room and Dee followed him. The room smelt fragrant from the bowl of roses on the table. The window was open and the air was scented with the garden. 'I was just asking Mam about the family, the O'Reillys, about what happened to them, but she doesn't want to talk about them.'

'What did she tell you?'

'She said there was a tragedy.'

'That's right. Part of the house was burnt.'

'Were there many in the family? I've just learnt that the owner at the turn of the century was an MP. I didn't know that!'

Her father sat back into his armchair with a sigh. 'That's right.'

'Did he have children?'

'I believe he had two: a boy and a girl.'

'What happened to them?'

'They died.'

'How did they die?'

'It's not certain. The girl died the night the house was burnt.'

'What happened to the son?'

Her father raised his eyebrows. 'He was really destroyed by the First War. He never recovered.' He hesitated, as though he were uncertain as to whether he should continue.

'Poor fellow,' Dee said. 'What was his name?'

'His name was Theodore.'

Dee frowned. Her mind raced to the damaged leather journal in her dressing table, to the name 'Yvonne O'Reilly', written on the flyleaf in faded ink, and the date. She knew the name Theo recurred in that diary. Why had she never read it properly? Was it really delicacy? A desire not to trespass on someone's private life, even though the person was dead?

No. She was sure now that it was dislike of the musty smell, the sense of a ponderous and oppressive past, the whiff of mortality. There was also the difficulty in deciphering the small, sloping writing.

Who was Yvonne O'Reilly? His sister? His wife? The journal had started in 1919. According to what her father said, Theo O'Reilly was already gone at that point.

Dee gnawed at a nag nail on her index finger. 'Dad,' she asked, 'do you think they had parties and masquerades and things at Kilashane in the old days?'

He looked up at her over his glasses. 'Certainly. They would have socialized a lot. People of that class did. Why do you ask?'

'Just curious. I was thinking of a mask I found there once. I suppose it would have been worn at a masked ball.'

There was a thunderstruck silence. 'Oh, Dee . . . What did you do with it?' he croaked. 'You were warned not to go near the place!'

Dee looked hard at her father. 'I threw it away,' she said. She saw the intense set of her parent's eyes; an expression torn between fear and concern. 'It frightened me,' she said defensively, 'and I threw it away!'

She watched her father's stricken face. 'You didn't wear it, look through it?'

'No. Would it matter if I had?'

'I don't know . . .'

Later, in the privacy of her room, she took out the diary, reopened the musty pages. As always she experienced the sense of intrusion, like someone trespassing in a vault, or illicitly opening the door of a sealed and private place. She turned the pages. Some days there were no entries; some days the whole page was filled and the writing got smaller and smaller towards the end of the page. And some of the pages were so stuck together that they could not be separated without tearing them. The entry for 1 February 1919 met her eyes.

The girl (she is only a girl: eighteen, perhaps) who came to see him today was his sister. Her name is Kate. She is shy and would be plain but for the intensity in her face. But she is also slim and graceful and would look well if she dressed properly. His mother was there also — distressed, but pragmatic.

I could see that for Theo there was anguish at not knowing her, of having to pretend. He so wants to have a sister, a mother; to have roots and identity and a definite past. Maybe if he found them he could build a future. But while he introduced me as his fiancée, he did not defend our relationship or our plans. His mother spoke to me afterwards; she thinks that I am a child with my head full of rot. Because of her, because she is sensible, I felt such a fool. I know I should let him go.

Sometimes he asks me for his ring and then apologizes because I have told him so often there is none.

In the afternoon he talked to the chaplain about the past, about history and the Middle Ages and even about the Inquisition. I found the choice of topic strange. I can see that while he is happy to discuss theology and canon law, and history, the chaplain doesn't seem wildly excited at the prospect of a chat about the Inquisition. I don't think he knows very much about it, or perhaps he does not want to discuss anything unpleasant. I'm curious.

'Why does the Inquisition interest you?' the chaplain asked.

'Why not?' said Theo. 'It's the same phenomenon as the one that caused the war — an institution forcing its viewpoint on the world. There is hideous ecstasy in power of that order.'

I could see the chaplain wanted to get away. 'You must remember,' he said, 'that these events happened at a time when everyone saw the doctrine of the Church as divine and not susceptible to opinion.'

'Wrong,' said Theo. 'Not everyone. The people on the rack for example. What about the people on the rack? What about the women burning? Die for your thoughts, die for your sins. We'll tell you what thoughts you should think; we'll tell you what are your sins.'

The chaplain stood up and moved away, murmuring soothingly. I hope he doesn't think the worst of poor Theo.

When I spoke to my poor lamb afterwards and asked him why he was so interested in history and told him that what happened long ago doesn't matter any more, he just stared at me and shook his head. Then he said, 'I'm caught in some sort of trap, Yvonne. But you won't leave me, will you?'

Then he said, 'You see, I shouldn't have touched the ring.'

Dee put her hand to the ring at her throat. She shut the diary and let it fall from her fingers on to the bed. Then she took the ring from the chain and put it in her pocket, and set out for Dan Brady's forge.

It was overcast. The clouds were coming in from the west and the brightness of the morning had faded. Brady's forge was about two miles away, in the direction of the church. Dee put her head in the door to tell her mother she was going out for a while, then got out her bicycle from the shed and set off.

As she approached the forge, she saw Father O'Shea coming towards her in his car. He stopped, rolled down the window.

'Hello, Dee. Nice to see you back.'

Dee got off her bike. 'Hello, Father.'

'How's Dublin?'

'Fine.'

'I hear you have a great job!'

'It's OK. Keeps me busy!'

'Any boyfriends?'

'Not as such.' She looked into the kindly, curious eyes of the priest — who assumed, as a matter of course, that he had a right to know everything about her life — and wondered what it would be like to disconcert him. 'No boyfriends as such,' she repeated, 'but a married man is interested in me!'

Father O'Shea took a deep breath. He was on home ground here; he had something to sink his teeth into. 'Oh, my poor child, you must keep away from married men!'

'I know . . . But he's a foreigner!'

Father O'Shea shook his head. He got out of

the car. 'A man like that would think nothing of leading you into sin!' he said, intoning the whispered words like holy Scripture.

'Maybe I'm not that easily led, Father!'

'Good . . . You were always sensible! Some girls let romance go to their heads!'

' "Sensible" has a hollow, unenterprising ring to it!' Dee said with a twinkle. 'But I suppose I am fairly practical. The only thing I've ever felt truly romantic about in my life is Kilashane.'

Why are you telling him this? she asked herself.

'Kilashane! A place to keep away from!'

'Why, Father? Why this emphasis on Kilashane as a place to keep away from? Anyone would think that it contained the tree of knowledge of good and evil!'

Father O'Shea frowned, as though her levity pained him. 'Because, long ago, the place had to be exorcized,' he said, lowering his voice. 'That's the reason, Dee. The only place in Ireland where an exorcism has been carried out within living memory!'

Dee stared at him. Here it was. Here was the reason for her mother and father's diffidence. Her own reaction was mixed: part of her was secretly horrified; part of her was flippant and didn't give a damn. 'Well, then, it has been detoxified, so it must be safe. What did they try to exorcize?'

'A spirit,' he said warily. 'A poor, demented spirit!'

Dee heard the sound of summer around her. She looked back at the chimneys of the big house, rising above the distant treetops with their circling black attendants. 'Why was it exorcized?'

'Various reasons, it seems, not the least of which was the state of a young Englishwoman staying there who ran all the way to the presbytery.'

'What was her name?'

'I don't know.'

'Who carried out the exorcism?'

'The parish priest of the time!'

'Is he still alive?'

'No. He died. Why do you ask?'

'Because I have reason to believe that he failed, Father,' she said, turning away. 'I thought it might interest him to know it!'

The priest looked aghast. 'Why do you say that?'

She turned back, gestured. 'Look at the crows! They seem to know something we don't!'

'They're only birds, Dee,' the priest called after her. But she heard the uncertainty in his voice. She thought of Laura and of Ted, who thought she was only a bird, too.

'They underestimate us,' she whispered, directing her gaze back to the wheeling crows. 'They underestimate us birds.' But she turned back as he was getting into the car. 'Father?'

'Yes?'

'Was it only the place that was exorcized? Was

there a person involved?'

The priest seemed to hesitate. 'Ah, don't be worrying your head about these things,' he said, as he got into the car and drove away.

Chapter Eleven

'You are schooled in cruelty,' she said.

'Not so. I serve God.'

'You serve yourself dressed up as God. If you did not stand on my neck, what would you do for stature?'

Journal of a Witness

'You see,' Theo said to Yvonne that night, 'there is perfection in the swell of your little breasts . . .' and he bent forward to lick the tender swell, moving the wet tip of his tongue until it reached the aureole. It was the second night of their honeymoon. Theo had returned early from his private excursion and had refused to be drawn as to the nature of the business which had taken him away. They had had supper together in their room and then Theo had informed his wife that she should go to bed. Yvonne, with pleasurable, albeit nervous, anticipation had complied.

She had undressed carefully in the dressing room, slipping into the lawn nightdress with long sleeves and mother-of-pearl buttons and the pin-tucks on the bodice. But the buttons, six of them along the middle of her chest, had not stayed closed for long. Theo had sat there at the end of the bed, fully dressed, and he had, without moving, commanded in a soft voice she hardly knew, 'Undo the buttons.'

Yvonne obeyed. She blushed but she obeyed. The crimson fired her face and down her neck and along her upper arms. She had not anticipated anything like this; she was again not in control; she opened the buttons on her nightgown while the man, this stranger to whom she was married, slowly inspected her body with the eyes of a connoisseur.

'Theo,' she had whispered, 'don't stare at me like that!' And then he had bent forward until he was lying beside her, and had begun slowly to tickle the soft swell of her bosom with the tip of his tongue.

He spent a long time at it, as though there was no hurry, and then, when her body began to relax into languour, he carefully buttoned up her nightgown and smiled knowingly into her eyes.

'I must leave you for a while, Yvonne.'

She saw the gold signet ring on his finger catch the light. The disappointment was heavy and sour, but she did not show it. She sat up. 'You mean you're going out again . . . alone?'

'Certainly. Do you think I'm an invalid?'

Yes, Yvonne's mind answered, yes, yes, yes. You are an invalid; you are a one-legged man suffering from shell-shock. But, privately, she had to admit that he did not look like a casualty of the war any more and, more particularly, that she did not experience him as a war casualty any more, as someone who needed her love and

250

strength. He stood very straight in his dark suit and tie, notwithstanding his injury; his waistcoat was tailored to his body and the silver chain of his fob-watch could be seen above the pocket. His blue eyes seemed very dark and the short moustache on his upper lip was distinguished.

'I wish you wouldn't! I'll get dressed and go with you . . .' She saw the anger glisten in his eyes.

'I don't think so, Yvonne. I don't need minding, you see, any more!' He stroked her cheek. 'I won't be too long. Try to sleep.'

Yvonne turned her face away. She heard him take his coat from the wardrobe, heard his steps, the uneven steps of a man with an artificial leg, heard the door open and close behind him. She was alone. She lay in a half daze, confused and angry, wondering how the whole basis of their relationship could have undergone such radical transformation. She had married a man who needed her desperately, only to find that he no longer existed; worse, some subtle metamorphosis was beginning in her, some kind of dependency. She was half aware that this arose from his certainty, his new confidence and *savoir-faire,* and by the attentions he paid to her body which left her in a state of unfulfilled expectancy.

Theo negotiated the stairs. He found he could do this more easily now, as he had begun to perfect a way of moving which permitted him to place his artificial leg on each step with a minimum of awkwardness. The stairs led into the lobby of the hotel, and he asked the porter to get him a taxi. It arrived quickly, and he tipped the porter and got into the noisy vehicle.

'Where to, guv?' the cabby asked, and Theo gave his instructions.

Jenny was at home. She was in her sitting room, leaning back among the cushions of the sofa, a book in her hand. Andrew was in bed. He got up very early to go to his job in the City and, except for his evenings out, went to bed regularly at ten, read for a few minutes and then went to sleep. They had been married for some months; the marriage had not been consummated. Andrew's earliest outpourings of affection and passion had degenerated into a kind of stalemate. It was her fault, she knew; something had happened on their wedding night which had put paid to intimacy. At least she believed this, looking back at her reluctance, the sudden desire she had to fling herself out of the window, do anything to avoid his embraces. The repugnance had risen in her like the taste of bile. She did not want him to touch her; she could not bear the prospect that he might touch her. The mediocrity in him disgusted her; she could not endure the tickle of his moustache, the slightly sweaty touch of his hand, the hesitancy he manifested, as though some inaccessible part of him knew and accepted her aversion.

He had taken to following her around after

Gramps' death, and they had quarrelled more than once. Every time he tried to take her in his arms, the outcome was always the same — she with a revulsion she tried unsuccessfully to hide, and he with frustration and then with anger.

'You are making me impotent,' he cried just the other night. 'I can't function! Why do you react like that? You're supposed to love me, to be my wife. You make me feel that I crawled out of the nearest cess-pit!'

Jenny wept at this, but she wept privately. 'Maybe it's growing pains,' she whispered to her husband. 'It must take some time to get used to . . .'

Andrew stared at her in fury. 'It doesn't take time to want to do it, it's human to want to do it — even for women. Yes, even for women. It's natural if you care for someone, if you find them desirable. Oh, Christ . . .' He put his head in his hands and then he straightened, dressed, left, returning later with the smell of drink on him. She was in bed and woke when he came in. He reached for her again, clumsily; she lay inert, willing herself to submit, but her body refused and she ran for the bathroom and retched into the basin. He came out after her, banged at the door, and when she came out, white-faced and smelling of puke, he turned away, trying to hide the sudden spurt of tears.

Resentment increased in him. Fear grew in her. She was married and mismatched; each of them, husband and wife, was a dead loss to the other. She recognized this, but did not accept it. He did not recognize it; he saw it as a temporary hitch, as unreasonableness, as prudery. His anger petered out in the face of her beauty, but each time he tried to make her truly his wife, as he saw it, he had less confidence than the time before. A tacit stand-off had now arisen between them. He frequented prostitutes once a fortnight, and lay beside her every night without touching her. The emptiness of her life had become an exquisite suffering, one which she could do nothing to alleviate or change. The prospect of divulging her circumstances to anyone was itself a humiliation. So she smiled and all the world thought the Staceys were a happy young couple, while in reality a gulf was growing between them which neither of them knew how to bridge. Especially now, especially since the episode concerning poor Fandango.

Upstairs, Andrew was not, in fact, asleep. He, also, was thinking of Fandango. He still did not know what had possessed him. It had been his birthday just one week earlier, the Sunday before Yvonne's wedding, and Jenny had given him a grey silk tie. He had thanked her for it and tried tentatively to embrace her. But she had slipped from his arms and he was left again with the sense of grievance, of torn pride, of hurt. Later, after breakfast, he had seen her go up to the attic and, thinking that he would do likewise, just to talk, to do anything at all which would be normal and companionable, he had followed her. The attic door was closed, and when he had opened it, he had found her sitting with the purring cat in her arms, staring at the portrait of the magician. She had started when she'd realized he was there, and risen to put away the portrait and replace it with a painting she was working on, a streetscape with houses leaning against each other like a row of stacked cards, and thin sticks of people, like wraiths from Purgatory, scurrying through a smog. She had given up her art classes when they had got married, in deference to his wishes, but she still secluded herself in the attic and worked away.

'Jen,' he had said, annoyed at the feeling that he had to justify his presence, 'thank you for the tie. It's exactly the right shade for my good suit! I'll wear it on Saturday to Yvonne's wedding.'

'You're welcome.' She had smiled at him politely, as though waiting for him either to leave or state the rest of his business. He saw that she was wary, poised for evasion should he try to approach her, and very unhappy. He moved forward, intending to look at the painting, but she moved so sharply out of his way that the anger he was trying to suppress began to rise steadily, like mercury on a hot day.

'You don't have to shrink from me, you know,' he said. 'I was only going to ask you what you were calling this piece!'

'I've named it "Modernity".'

'You have depicted a bleak urban landscape here.'

'Do you think so?'

'Yes. I think you have a bleak outlook on life.' Jenny glanced at him. 'But of course, life is often bleak,' Andrew went on. 'Which is such a pity, when it could be wonderful!'

Jenny knew how life could be wonderful for Andrew. If she would squeeze herself into the tiny space that Andrew had prepared for her, life for him would be ecstatic. But life for her would be a suffocation. His perceptions of marriage were set. He envisaged a scenario which was ready-made, safe, certain and comfortable. Her perception of marriage was of a place full of challenge and laughter and discovery, where she could dare to be truly herself; a place with enough love and liberty to take on the world. She instinctively resisted the sense of being press-ganged into something pre-fabricated; she cringed from the trap which would reduce her to a chattel and keep her silent. She was revulsed by the indulgence that stemmed from a man's gratitude for a woman's surrender.

But she knew that Andrew did not understand any of this, that what she felt would only shock and anger him. He had sold himself, lock, stock and barrel to the system; he truly believed in it and could not imagine a life without confines and well-thumbed certainties. She was not able to reach him, and consequently could not share her requirement that life be either authentic or not trouble her at all.

They had stood looking at each other, and

then at the painting, and then Andrew began examining the various canvases she had already completed. He narrowed his eyes in apparent appreciation, but Jenny sensed after a moment that he did not have the first glimmer of what she had been trying to do. He picked up the charcoal sketch of himself, which had been intended as the basis of a real portrait, and suggested jocosely that she might like to complete it.

He had seen at once that she was reluctant, and this went to the quick. Jenny, for her part, no longer had any interest in doing the portrait, because she no longer had any real interest in the subject. The things about him that she had once identified as intriguing — the way he held his head and shoulders with such confidence, the thoughtful slant of his face — she now knew to be attitudes deliberately struck. There was no point in any portrait unless the artist had been involved in teasing out the mettle of the soul. Where was Andrew's mettle? He had pinned himself to the flag of convention. Somewhere along the line he had given away his freedom.

Andrew had stepped back, trying desperately to say something that would sound jolly and inoffensive and make it clear that it didn't matter whether she did the portrait of him or not. But he'd stepped on Fandango's tail. The cat, who had never taken to the new member of the family, immediately gave a hideous yowl, turning on Andrew as he bent down to make amends, and tearing three parallel scratches into the back of his hand, which instantly oozed tiny beads of blood.

Andrew drew back to kick the animal, and Jenny snatched up her cat protectively. 'Leave poor Fandango alone! You hurt him! He didn't mean to scratch you: he got a shock.'

The anger, simmering just beneath the surface in Andrew, began to boil over. ' "Leave poor Fandango alone," ' he mimicked her, sucking at his torn hand. 'You think more about that animal than you do about your husband!'

Jenny put down the cat and came to inspect the hand. 'You should wash it,' she said, but Andrew was already turning away, wrapping his handkerchief around his wound.

'Don't be such a baby, Andrew,' Jenny laughed. 'Let me see it . . .'

Andrew had heard her laughter, saw the cat sitting grinning on her cushions, and had gone away down the stairs in a mélange of violent emotions.

Later, when Jenny was out, he had seen Fandango in the garden from the window of their bedroom. Sudden hatred for the cat burned in him. Hatred for Jenny burned in him. The pair of them, cat and mistress, were making a fool of him. He had taken up the silk tie and gone down the garden, inveigling Fandango behind the shed with pretence of having some tit-bit in the cat's food bowl which he held in his hand. 'Puss, puss, come on. Puss, puss . . .'

Jenny, thinking that he had gone off on some

escapade, had not missed Fandango until the next day. But when he had not returned by the following evening, she had gone into the garden to call him. She'd found him at the back of the toolshed, hanging by her birthday present to Andrew. His eyes were popping and his tongue was sticking out. He seemed quite dead.

She wept bitter, private tears, took down her pet, and removed the strangulating tie. Fandango was stiff as a board, and she laid him on the bench in the shed and covered him with a sheet of newspaper. A grave would have to be dug, but she could not bear the prospect for the moment. She put the tie in an envelope and left it beside Andrew's plate. She did not speak to him or sit down to supper with him. That night she moved into Gramps' room.

He had come to her and wept. 'I'm sorry . . . I don't know what got into me. Forgive me, Jen . . .' He tried to reach for her, but she moved away, stiff end silent.

The next day Andrew had said, 'It's all very well going around with that wounded air. My hand is infected from that animal. I should not have . . . dispatched him, but I was angry and he was only a cat, Jenny. A cat! Not a member of the royal family! When I think of the poor bastards I killed in the war, and no one had a word to say, except "jolly good show". And they weren't cats, Jenny, they were people . . .'

Jenny didn't answer and Andrew decided eventually that she was sulking and that he could outlive any sulk. Jenny went into the garden to deal with Fandango's obsequies, but when she entered the toolshed, the little corpse was gone.

She ran back to the house. 'Where did you put him?' she cried. Andrew seemed bewildered, but she was sure he was acting. He had his coat on and was about to leave for his train. 'I didn't go near him . . . At least not since . . .'

'Well, he's gone. His poor body is gone! I wanted to bury him!'

'Oh, Jen. Let me do that!'

'No! I won't give you that satisfaction!'

Andrew nodded. 'I know. You won't give me any satisfaction!' He looked at her with all the bitterness which burned in him. 'Why don't you ask your stupid magician about him. Run up to him and cast runes or something!' Then he added, 'I'll be late home', and he took up his brolly and strode to the door, shutting it behind him with a clap.

Jenny had stood for a moment in the hall. The house was silent, except for the clock ticking in the sitting room and the first droplets spitting against the window-panes. The loneliness was momentarily intense, but the house was empty and she was queen of its emptiness. She wandered upstairs, turned at the landing to the stairs leading to the attic. The door opened at once. There was little light. It was early and the sky was grey with rain-clouds. The beating of the drops against the skylights was almost companionable.

She glanced at the picture she was working on, but she had no heart for it right now, so she took up the portrait of the magician, so scorned by Andrew. 'Your magician,' he had said. Very well then, that is precisely what he would be. She took a piece of charcoal and wrote on the back of the canvas, 'My Magician'.

But even this piece of defiance had not salved the pain. 'He must have done something with Fandango's body,' she confided, holding back the tears. 'He is a monster! I think he hates me. What will I do? Where will I go?'

Now, in the drawing room, with the embers of the fire glowing before her, Jenny thought of that Sunday two weeks ago. She could not concentrate on the book. Her mind scanned the impasse between her and Andrew, and various possibilities surfaced as the answer to her dilemma. She could leave, get a job. So many women had jobs now; she could apply for admission to a women's college, or work in an office as some kind of secretary. She could go back to art school and get her diploma. She owned the house; she had a small income of her own. There were several things she could sell if she needed money, some good furniture and a few curios, including the old mask she used to play with as a child. To survive she needed only a small amount of food and the economic wherewithal to maintain the house. She could even sell the house and travel.

How would she tell Andrew it was over? What did you say to your husband. 'Thanks for everything, darling; there's the door'? No. And thinking about it she began to doubt herself. Perhaps people overcame these sorts of difficulties and rediscovered their love? Perhaps even the episode over Fandango was one which could be, in time, forgotten? She owed the relationship more than she had given it. That was true. But, she realized, it wasn't so much what Andrew had done, not even so much the loss of her beloved pet, but the fact that he had been capable of such a deed that really troubled her.

Her mind went over and over Yvonne's wedding. It was the strangest occurrence in her life and she wondered if she were really sane. At a safe remove, although it had only been two days ago, she was sure that she was not sane, that something had happened to upset the balance of her mind. She tried to put it down to the stress of her marriage. The fact was that she had felt an intense and personal knowledge of Yvonne's husband, and had felt the pressure of his desire fire her. Only long ago, years before, had she experienced anything like it, and that was when she had rambled with fever and imagined a man inside her head. The whole of that wedding reception she had lived in passionate communion with a stranger: she had known that every time she turned around she would find his eyes on her, burning and hungry. Part of her had wanted to escape his attentions, escape the draw she felt to him as though she had known him all her life; part of her had looked for refuge in decency and all the values she had ever been taught. But it was no use. The whole day had been an exercise in some kind of possession. The possession had continued through the night, for she had woken the following morning torpid with desire.

A taxi drew up and jolted her from her reverie. She paid it no heed, but as the motor ticked over throatily for some time outside, she became curious, rose and drew back the curtain nearest her a fraction. She saw the vehicle outside with its lights on. It was just standing there; no one seemed to be getting out or in. Perhaps it's waiting for someone, she thought. In any event she knew it was none of her business and she let the curtain fall. After a while she heard the cab drive away.

The envelope was in the hall; she saw it as she was going up to bed. She picked it up from the mat, saw her own name, brought it back to the sitting room and tore it open. The writing was crabbed, like an old man's. It contained only one line.

'National Gallery. Tomorrow four p.m.'

She tore the letter into pieces and then picked them up and tried to piece them back together. What did the little missive mean? Who would be at the National Gallery tomorrow at four p.m.? She asked all the appropriate questions; but she already knew the answers.

'I won't go,' she whispered aloud. Then she

shivered. Life with all its possibilities, excitement and ferocity seemed to have come suddenly within reach. She mounted the stairs to go to bed and, on an impulse, looked in on Andrew who was now fast asleep, his paper on the bedside table, his face wearing the rather prissy, self-righteous and wounded expression it had begun to adopt in recent days. She stared at his mouth under his moustache. The lips were pinched in a profoundly irritating 'I'm-going-to-be-boss-one-way-or-the-other' expression. She saw that he was weak, that he had not the courage to face her or himself or the problems between them. He would deal with them by being the wounded party; that way, because there was no answer to the justice of his case, he reckoned he would win.

Jenny went to Gramps' room, drew the curtains, undressed slowly, watched her body in the mirror, her high breasts and long waist, her thick brown hair loose and waving. She turned around to catch sight of her back as the chemise slipped down to her feet. She had a small mole on her right shoulder, the one blemish on her body. She liked the privacy to study her body, to undress with leisure, to feel she owned her own space. She could do this here, in this room where her dear old grandfather had died. He had always parried the question of where he had put the mask. But she knew. She had found it after his death, wrapped in a sheet in the chest of drawers by the window, and had left it there.

Now she opened the drawer, reached in and took the mask in her hand. The grimace of the thing no longer frightened her. It seemed to smile at her knowingly, a smile which encouraged whatever in life was audacious and outrageous, whatever refused the strictures and perceptions of conventional morality, whatever was willing to dare. She remembered the strange voice in her head, 'Obey me and you can come back', until eventually the voice had whispered instead something different — one of the last things, in fact, that it had said to her before it became silent: 'If you will not come to me, then I will come for you . . .'

I was mad, she thought; I was a mad child, suffering from delusions. I used to think all children suffered from delusions, but Yvonne disabused me. But I am not mad any more. I cannot go to the National Gallery tomorrow because of a note through the door.

She turned out the light, pulled back the curtain, and looked out of the window at the street. It was very quiet. There was no traffic. The street lamp under which she had seen Oliver on his night-time rampages so many years before shone brightly. There was no Oliver stalking the pavement now, but in the shadows by the shrubs belonging to the neighbour's garden, she saw something, a form, the person of a man standing perfectly still in his hat and overcoat, watching the window. His face was in shadow. She started as she realized she was being observed, and drew in her breath sharply. She heard Andrew stir in bed in the next room, and she turned her head as he came through the door.

'Still sleeping in here, are you? You're very childish, Jen.' Jenny did not answer.

Andrew staggered off sleepily to the bathroom. Jenny looked back out of the window, but the man with the hat and overcoat was gone. She waited until she heard Andrew go back to bed, and then she put on her wrap, found a candle, and went up to the attic.

The attic was very dark, with a grey-black wash where the skylights let in the night. The candlelight flickered and made the studio surreal; images on canvases assumed identities denied them in the daylight. She held the candle above the portrait of the magician. His eyes picked up the flame and glowed.

'You're the only person I can talk to,' Jenny said in a whisper. 'Someone unknown is playing silly games, inviting me to a rendezvous at the National Gallery. I would suspect Andrew, but he was in bed . . . and it's not his kind of thing, anyway. I cannot sleep . . . I keep thinking and wondering. I can imagine only one person who could have sent that note, and he is the last person I should see.'

She put the candle down and glanced around at the paintings, marvelling at how different they seemed in candlelight, wondering if some day she might do something worth exhibiting. 'I can't go, of course,' she continued, talking to

266

herself now. She glanced at the inscrutable magician, who was locked for ever into his canvas and could go nowhere. For a moment she fancied he disapproved of her reluctance, that he was saying, in effect, 'Why ever not?'

Jenny felt unreasonable irritation. 'Well, if you think I should go, you'd better do something to say so, to prove what a magical fellow you are . . . Something remarkable — like making Fandango come back!'

She had not meant to add the last bit, but it presented itself suddenly and was out before she knew it. She knew that this challenge was impossible, but at least, now that it was out, it would prove that there was no power in her life exterior to herself.

The magician made no answer. The quiet candlelight flickered over him as she picked up the candle and retired down the stairs to her bed.

Yvonne was asleep when Theo returned. She surfaced long enough to recognize that he was back, and then she feigned sleep. The tendrils of her earlier humiliation were still shivering within her, the uncertain desire. She wanted to punish him. But Theo did not essay any conversation or attempt to disturb her. He undressed quickly and got into bed and, very soon, judging by his breathing, he seemed to be fast asleep.

In the morning he told her that he would have to go out again that afternoon.

'We're supposed to be on honeymoon,'

Yvonne expostulated. 'Where did you go last night?'

His demeanour was cold. 'Don't interrogate me, Yvonne. I went out for a while last night. I shall do so again today. I'm sure you will not find it too terrible to entertain yourself for one day!'

And that was that. Yvonne was so annoyed that she wanted to scream, but part of her also was intrigued and stimulated. Who the hell did this man think he was? Who did he think he was dealing with?

He turned to her and smiled, drew her to the bed. 'Shall we continue the lessons?' he asked softly. 'Would you like that?'

Yvonne remembered the rapturous sensuality of his touch. She also remembered that she was very angry and she gathered her willpower. 'No,' she answered.

He stroked the back of her hand. 'Yvonne, I am not free . . . Be angry with me if you wish, but I want you to know that any hurt you are caused is something I would spare you. You married a casualty of more than just the war; we have not consummated the marriage; you have grounds, after a decent interval, for annulment. Do you want to go, leave me?' She stared at him and her eyes filled. She remembered the Theo she used to know, who had begged her never to leave him.

'What would an annulment entail?'

'Oh, just evidence of non-consummation.'

'You mean medical evidence . . . that I'm still virgo intacta?'

'Yes.'

'How horrible . . . doctors prying. It's monstrous!'

'Or you could divorce me. I could . . . arrange evidence!' Yvonne saw her dreams in fragments.

'No,' she wept. 'I don't want a divorce. I don't want an annulment. I want you.'

Theo was silent for a moment and then said gently, 'Well, we shall be off to Ireland in a couple of days.'

Jenny heard the mewing outside as the dawn broke. She got up, threw on her wrap and went downstairs. Fandango was sitting on the kitchen window-ledge, looking in at her through the glass.

'He wasn't dead at all!' Jenny said when Andrew came downstairs and found the cat being cosseted. 'But he's very dirty. He must have recovered and just gone off for a while.' She stroked the cat.

Andrew stood dead in his tracks and the cat turned and regarded him from narrowed amber eyes. Andrew paled. He made no comment, but he declined breakfast and left even earlier than usual for the City.

Chapter Twelve

'Only recant, only repent, and you will find mercy.'

'I cannot bend my knee to imposture.'

'Bend it,' he said. 'Or we will bend it for you.'

Journal of a Witness

On Monday morning Charlie greeted Dee with a frown and a sigh, turning away from her when she came in.

Later he had called her in to his office. 'Well, Dee, did you have a good weekend?'

'It was fine. I went home.'

'You mean down to Cork.'

'Yes, back to Ballyshane.'

'I hope your parents are keeping well.'

'Yes. But my father is due to retire soon. It saddens him.' Charlie moved in his chair, shifted his weight. His face assumed a lugubrious but disingenuous expression of sympathy.

'I'm sorry about that. But, as you know, Dee, I have problems, big problems. The shit has really hit the fan. They've sent Peter Eggli from Brussels. He arrived this morning, so now I'm going to have a bean counter breathing down my neck.' He sighed heavily. 'Such a pity you had to send that report . . .'

'I'm sorry.'

'I may be looking for a new job. He's in with Liam at the moment.'

'I hope it's not as bad as that.'

'It's bad, all right . . . I suppose you didn't remember to bring that ring?' he added casually.

She searched in her pocket and produced the lead replica of the ring that Dan Brady had made for her in the forge on Saturday. He had sent her to get some marl, the thick white clay which lay under the first layer on the bog, and had made a mould from it and then made a lead ring. She had left it in a cowpat overnight to give it a history.

His tone belied his expression: she saw the eagerness in his eyes. 'Here it is!' She put Dan Brady's replica down on the table.

Charlie seized it with initial excitement, then his jaw dropped. 'But . . . this is only lead or something. I thought you said the ring was old!'

Dee shrugged. 'Isn't it old? It looks old to me!'

Charlie glanced at her, but Dee was looking innocent. He scrutinized the signet. 'Hmn . . . strange design . . . Hmmn', he said with an avid interest mixed with uncertainty. 'But I thought it was a gold ring?'

Dee shrugged again. 'What you see is what you get!'

'Are you willing to part with it?'

Dee raised her eyebrows. 'I don't know. Is it worth anything?'

Charlie sighed. 'Probably nothing, but I'll give you a fiver for it!'

'Ten quid,' Dee said. 'I'm fond of it.'

Charlie reached for his wallet.

When he had paid up, he said, 'Mr Eggli seems to have taken a fancy to you. He has suggested that you do a course in the Planning Department in Brussels.'

'He only met me once!'

'Nevertheless, he thinks it would be a good idea if you want to progress with the company.'

'I thought I would be in trouble,' Dee said, 'because of the report.'

'No, I'm the poor eejit who's in trouble . . .'

Then Dee asked, 'Charlie, who was the fellow you told me about — the wizard who lived in Venice?'

He glanced at the ring which was lying on his desk. 'Ah, he was an inquisitor — I suppose you've heard of the Inquisition?'

'Yes.'

'Well that's who he was. He dumped the Church and tried alternative medicine!'

Dee met Peter Eggli again in the canteen at lunchtime. She saw him first and watched him surreptitiously. Brown hair, grey eyes, a demeanour that was friendly and formidable at the same time. American with European edges, or was it the other way around? He projected business efficiency, but moved stiffly, as though coping with a leg injury. She knew he had come straight from spending the best part of two hours with Charlie in Liam's office: that he had not gone out for lunch with them spoke for itself.

Later Liam would enthuse guiltily about what had happened. He had moved up in the world. Thanks to Dee's gaffe he would, from now on, have a 'straight line' reporting relationship with Mr Eggli in Brussels, through the EWL comptroller in Birmingham. Every cloud had a silver lining.

Mr Eggli, to her consternation, came over to Dee's table. 'Hello, Dee. Do you mind if I join you?'

He was wearing a light suit, a striped shirt, and a Rolex watch. His American accent was more pronounced than she remembered. Again she sensed his swift assessment of people and circumstances, his understanding of the necessity of remembering names, of the politician's tricks of making the other person feel they mattered. But, thinking of Charlie, she decided he wasn't going to win her over. However persuasive he thought he was, she was going to see him objectively.

'Do you remember me — Peter Eggli?'

'Of course I do,' Dee said, reddening.

He put his tray down, sat opposite her, and smiled at her across the table. He began to eat and, as he did so, questioned her about her work, her colleagues and her boss.

Dee was uncomfortable. She did not want to

say anything about her boss. 'How do you like it in McGrath?'

'I'm glad to be working here, Mr Eggli.'

'Call me Peter.'

She stared at him. 'Are you American?'

'I'm American,' he said, smiling at her and helping himself to mayonnaise. 'What did you think I was?'

Dee felt her flush deepen. 'I was wondering about your accent, and your name . . .'

He looked at her with raised eyebrows. 'Of Swiss extraction. My grandfather came from Berne. He followed his sweetheart to America. And if you would also like to know about my first name,' he continued to Dee's increased confusion, 'my mother was reading *Peter Pan* around the time I presented myself. I suppose I was lucky she didn't call me Wendy!'

'You don't look like a Wendy!' Dee said, laughter replacing embarrassment.

His eyes, deep-set, dark grey, studied her with amusement. 'That is reassuring!'

Dee willed her face to become pale and interesting, but without noticeable effect.

'Have you read J. M. Barrie?' he asked.

'No, actually. I saw the film of *Peter Pan* when I was small and I hated it. It put me off.'

He leaned towards her. 'Why?'

'It seemed unnatural . . . and I was too young to understand it! Does it appeal to you?'

'I suppose the idea appeals. Which of us would not like to go on for ever?'

274

'To be young for ever or simply to *be* for ever?'

'Both, I suppose.'

'Like reincarnation!' Dee said.

He met her eyes. 'Exactly.'

Dee felt a sudden surge of déjà vu, as though she had sat here before and listened to this man.

'I went to Yale and then I came to Europe to study,' he went on. 'A stint in Tübingen. Then I was drafted — Korean War — and afterwards I joined ITU.'

She frowned. 'But why Tübingen? It seems off the beaten track!' She saw his eyes narrow for a moment, taking her in, glancing for an instant at the chain around her neck.

'Theology,' he said.

'Why were you interested in that?'

'Why not? So many claims are made in its name . . . And you, Dee?' he asked, changing the subject. 'What have you been doing with yourself?'

'Not an awful lot. I come from County Cork; I went to college in UCC, graduated last year. This is my first real job. My life has been insular, I suppose, at least compared to yours!'

He smiled, took a forkful of food. 'Tell me, which part of Cork do you come from?'

'A place called Ballyshane. It's in the Fanagh Peninsula.'

He nodded. 'And there is an old ruin there called Kilashane.'

Dee started. Her sense of privacy was suddenly shattered. The place where she kept her private self, the place where she had invested all the secrecy of her childhood, was known to this stranger.

'Have you seen it?' she asked as nonchalantly as she could.

'Let's say I have heard of it. You know it very well, do you?'

She nodded. 'Yes. It's near where I live!'

She examined her plate. She had hardly touched her food and now she had no appetite. 'What will happen to Charlie?' she asked, changing the subject.

'Charlie?' he said coolly. 'I have his resignation in my pocket.'

Dee gasped. 'Is that absolutely necessary, Mr Eggli?'

He raised his eyebrows. 'Are you feeling sorry for him? I'm afraid it *is* necessary. He committed an accounting fraud.'

As they continued to eat their lunch, Dee saw the sidelong glances they got from the other girls. Two typists at a nearby table smiled coyly when Peter Eggli looked at them. He smiled back. As the big noise from Brussels, he evidently felt he should nod and smile at all the staff; it was part of the job, Dee told herself. But all the same, she was surprised by a moment of territoriality. Why? She was shaken by him, by the quiet familiarity of his address, by his knowledge of her background, by the ruthlessness with which he had scotched Charlie's career. She felt undermined by him. He was everything she did not like in a man, she told herself, cock-sure, ruthless, obsessed with questions of profit and loss. And yet she felt that everything around him came to life, as though he spread purpose and intensity. Including her. He made her feel that she belonged, that she was not an outsider, a loner, that she was different only in terms of definition, idiosyncratic only because she had idealistic perceptions. But he made her feel vulnerable, because he made her feel known.

She watched his hands. They were well shaped and well kept, sensitive hands, she thought with a kind of grudging surprise.

> I do not like thee, Mr Eggli,
> The reason why I canna tell thee . . .

But he had nice hands all the same.

When the lunch was over, he leaned across the table. 'Where do you want to go in this company, young lady? The parent company is big, European headquarters Brussels, world headquarters New York. So you have the world at your feet!'

Dee felt the rush of blood to her face. 'I'd like to do this job well, Mr Eggli. After that I don't know: it's too soon to say . . .'

'Peter,' he said. 'Call me Peter. I suggested to Liam this morning that you might like to attend the Business Planning course in Brussels. It would be good for your career in the company.'

'I'd like that,' she said. 'How long is the course?'

'One week. The company would pay your hotel and travelling expenses, of course. All you have to do is write and ask to be included!'

'To whom do I write?'

'Me. You can write to me.'

Then Dee said, taking her courage in both hands: 'I'm sorry I got Charlie into trouble. He's very good at his job, and does not deserve to be in trouble because of me.'

'It's nice to see you so fond of your boss,' he joked. 'I understand you even gave him a ring this morning!'

'Oh,' Dee snorted, reaching for disingenuousness. 'I sold him an old thing I found. Did he show it to you?'

'Yes. Where did you get it?'

'I have had it since I was a child; I found it.'

'Where did you find it?'

She looked into his face; his eyes bored into hers and then, as though satisfied with what he found, fastened themselves laconically on the coffee spoon. 'In Kilashane . . .'

'How old did you say it was?'

'I don't know; I found it when I was a child.' She looked at him as openly as she dared. 'Why are you so interested. Is it valuable?'

He smiled. 'The original probably is. What you sold him is a copy of course. At least twenty-four-hours old, I would say. Wouldn't you?'

Dee went scarlet. 'I don't know.'

'No?' He leant forward. 'Look, Dee, I'll level

with you. The design on the signet is the emblem of a society which has its headquarters in Luxembourg. It's a society like the Freemasons, but a lot older. The original ring would be worth a lot to them. So if you did happen to find it too, maybe you would let me see it. I could give you an idea of its worth.'

Dee was embarrassed. There was something intimate in the suggestion that she should show him the ring. It would be like allowing him access to the world of her childhood and her fantasies, to the musty diary and the elegant man who limped towards her down the steps in her dreams.

'Are you a member of this society?' Dee asked.

He smiled. 'Do I look the secret society type?'

'Yes.'

This time he laughed. 'It's not so much the gold itself, which would be valuable,' he went on. 'It's the age and the workmanship. It would have particular value for a collector.' He raised his eyes and looked into hers. His were steady, slightly narrowed. 'In fact, you might be better off without it!'

'Why?'

He shrugged. 'What if you lost it? Is it insured?'

'No. What do you think the original would be worth?'

'As an antique — and I think it is several hundred years old — it may be worth a few hundred pounds.'

Dee drew in her breath. 'So much . . . Are you sure?'

'It's a guess,' he said. 'I'm not a jeweller; but as a collector's item they always pay more — it might be worth a thousand. Of course you would have to find the right collector: someone connected with the society I told you of.'

Dee was silent. A thousand pounds. A year's salary. She disbelieved what she was hearing and she distrusted the valuer. Then he added, 'Who owns this Kilashane place, the place where you found the ring?'

Dee blushed. 'No one; it's derelict. I'm not a thief!'

He drew back, frowning, smiling reprovingly. 'My dear girl, I hope I didn't suggest anything of the kind.'

'I'm sorry, Mr Eggli — Peter. I didn't mean . . . I have to go now or I'll be late back.'

He patted her hand. The gesture was both familiar and detached. His hand was warm. The resonance from it travelled up her arm. The contact was powerful; it was as though her body recognized something — as though something in her claimed him for its own. She wondered if he had felt it too. But he seemed unruffled.

'Don't forget about the Brussels course. It will be in August. Brussels is an interesting city with a long history.'

Dee, struggling to distance herself from the electric surge of a moment before, said she would remember, stood up and looked around.

The canteen was nearly empty. The clock on the wall said quarter-past two. She moved quickly towards the glass door of the canteen. She saw her reflection, a young woman in a light grey business suit with a blue seersucker blouse.

Peter sat back in his chair and watched her go. When she was out of sight, he took out his pocket diary and wrote something with a gold-plated ball-point pen.

Charlie was sitting at his desk, dictating to Liz. He looked up as Dee came into the outer office and turned his head away.

Dee went to his door. 'Charlie, I'm very sorry. Mr Eggli told me . . .'

'I hope you're satisfied!'

'Please, Charlie, I did ask him to reconsider,' she said miserably.

All of a sudden, Dee was certain that Charlie was not as disconsolate as he would have her believe. There was something about his demeanour that spoke of someone striving to appear at his wits' end, without actually being there.

'I see,' Charlie said. 'He seems to have taken a fancy to you!'

'No,' Dee said. 'He was just telling me about the Brussels course. It's in August.'

That evening, when she left for home, Charlie shook her hand. 'No hard feelings, eh?'

Dee brightened.

'You should go to Brussels,' he'd said seriously. 'You should go on that course. It's just the thing to set you up! There's a good career to be had in this company if you don't make stupid mistakes like me.' He looked around and lowered his voice. 'But watch Eggli. He's not what he seems!' She frowned. 'And, Dee,' he added, taking the ring from his pocket. 'If you ever find another ring like this — one made of gold, for instance — you will remember me, won't you? You'll give me first refusal?'

Dee nodded automatically in order to get away. She walked down the stairs to reception. Peter Eggli was sitting there on one of the mock leather seats, reading the *Evening Press*. He smiled at her as she approached.

'Hello.'

'Hello,' Dee said. 'I thought you had gone.'

'Are you disappointed?'

Dee reddened. 'I can't be disappointed,' she said with mock severity. 'It was not a matter upon which I had pinned any hopes.'

She saw the interest brighten in his eyes. 'What do I have to do to encourage hope?'

'Hope of what?'

'Of you hoping.'

Dee felt that the conversation was losing the run of itself. 'Hope springs eternal,' she said flippantly, wishing she could think of something truly witty.

He smiled. 'But eternity is such a long time,' he murmured lugubriously, 'like the time it takes to get a taxi in this town.'

'Is that what you're waiting for?'

As though it had heard them, a taxi drew up

outside the door. Peter rose to his feet, reached for his briefcase.

'Come and have a drink with me, Dee,' he said, 'if you've time.'

'I thought you had a plane to catch?'

'Nine o'clock — plenty of time!'

He had had the taxi drop them off at the Russell Hotel at the corner of St Stephen's Green. She had never been in the Russell; it was expensive, a Georgian mansion, the most exclusive hotel in Dublin.

The porter had opened the door with a 'Good evening, sir, good evening madam'. Dee preceded Peter into the hall, and thence into the lounge on the right. There was a huge antique mirror above the Georgian marble fireplace, some comfortable chairs and sofas, and a deep, soft carpet. A waiter came hovering.

'What would you like?' Peter asked.

'I'll be a devil: Bacardi and coke, please.'

Peter ordered a whiskey and soda for himself. When the drinks came they sipped them for a moment in silence. Peter relaxed against the back of the sofa, with an almost palpable exhalation of relief.

'I wasn't looking forward to today,' he said after a moment, 'except, of course, for the prospect of seeing you!' Dee was too surprised to answer. She reached for the little bowl of salted peanuts, selected a few and ate them meditatively.

'You look surprised.'

283

'That's because I am. You hardly know me.'

'On the contrary, I know a great deal about you!'

Dee turned puzzled eyes on him. 'Such as?'

'That you are a very competent young woman, with a quick, fresh mind; that you are a natural for the business of Public Relations. I am sure that you could go far in the company.' Dee relaxed. His interest in her was purely professional. This was proper, but all the same there was the sudden involuntary sense of pique. 'Of course,' he added, 'I also find you very interesting for yourself. The first time I saw you I had the strangest feeling that we had met before! Did you, perhaps, feel something similar?'

Dee's suspicions came back with a vengeance. This was too much. She raised her eyes to his. 'No,' she said. 'I'm afraid I didn't.' It was just as well, she told herself, that he had nailed his colours to the mast. She shouldn't have gone out for a drink with him anyway, but she had thought it might be fun. The next thing would probably be the hand on her knee, or was that too like Charlie? This man probably had a different approach, but the end in view would be the same. She finished the rum and coke in a hurry and said she had to be going. 'Thank you for the drink, Peter . . . Mr Eggli.'

Something like vexation clouded Peter Eggli's face.

'Do you have to go so soon? Are you bored with me? I was going to give you some advice on where you could get that ring valued.'

'No,' Dee said, 'of course I'm not bored. But I really do have to go.'

'Can I see you home?'

'Good heavens, no. It's only six thirty.'

She stood up and he did likewise. He extended his hand. Dee took it and felt immediately the same sensation of resonance, an almost over-whelming certainty that this man had some kind of power over her. The touch of his hand, his skin against hers, had an immediacy, an intimacy.

She withdrew her hand, smiled perfunctorily, and left. When she had crossed the street she looked back and saw him standing by the win-dow looking out at her. He raised his hand in a friendly wave. For a moment there was some-thing about his stance, the way he watched her, that reminded her of the man in her dreams.

She walked to the canal, only too aware of the fumes of Bacardi in her head, and sat on a bench to clear them. She found herself wondering if she had been childish. Maybe he hadn't intended to come on strong; maybe she had misinterpreted him. Maybe she was too jumpy. It was just that she couldn't bear the prospect of being some kind of prey. And then she thought that, as it was ten to one that he was married, she had nothing to reproach herself with. Anyway, she was fed up with all this interest in her ring.

She thought of the flat, empty for most of the evening. Laura would be late home tonight. She was seeing Ted, who seemed to vacillate between making her happy to making her guilty. There was nothing on television. If she focused on Kilashane she could imagine that she was home in the garden; that she was a child again on her swing. Life was like a newsreel: it changed and altered and was largely outside your control. What you encountered, rather than what you willed, became your destiny. Chance determined fortune. And yet you stayed the same, watching everything, touched by everything; all experience was grist to the senses and to the mind which sought to make, of all of it, some kind of sense. Did time flow, or was it illusion? Why was a dream the same in recollection as yesterday's events? All that was left of either in terms of immediate personal experience was the image burned in the memory. If she could meet him in the real world, the man who had approached her in dreams, moving towards her down the steps of Kilashane, maybe then she would begin to feel that she belonged, that the present was her milieu, that she knew and understood the ground on which she trod. She felt that for the whole of her life she had been listening, straining after one pivotal melody, trying to catch a few notes that would clarify the parameters of her existence; but they always escaped just as she thought she had nailed them.

She saw him again, moving towards her across the driveway, his quiet footfall on the lawn, the plaintive notes from the piano hanging exquisitely, crystal-fashion, on the evening air. Her re-action to him had been one of recognition, and, at the same time, imminent flight. Why was it only now that she remembered that he had spo-ken; the words were weary, following her as she blundered through the laurels. 'Don't be a fool,' he had said. 'You fly only yourself!'

If only I didn't feel that something important, something which concerns me, is just out out-side of my reach, she thought. If I knew what it was I could deal with it.

She pondered for a moment on the interest both Charlie and Peter Eggli had shown in her ring. Was it disinterested curiosity, or simple greed — or was it something more?

On the way home, Dee thought of phoning Anna, a cousin who had recently come to work in Dublin, and inviting her around to the flat for the evening. But she found when she got home that she was very tired, and she grilled some rashers and sausages, ate them in solitude while she listened to the radio. Bob Dylan's voice came sweetly over the airways.

She moved her foot in time to the song, waited for the last line of each verse with a thrill of plea-sure at the cadence of the notes, and the words which told the world that 'the times, were a-changing . . .'

The radio crackled and she turned it off, washed up, and then went into the sitting room where she sat by the window with the trade journals and the three dailies, which she had brought home from work. It was part of her job to inspect the papers and highlight items that could be of interest to McGrath. She would cut out the likely articles, paste them up, and distribute this Press review to Charlie, Liam and the regional managers. She would also send a copy to Birmingham, who might, or might not, send it on to Brussels with their own review of the British publications. It was this sort of news circulation which had led to the present mess.

While she worked, she thought of Peter Eggli. There was something about him: he was formidable in some way she had never encountered. Neither spoilt nor diffident, sure, slightly larger than life. But he was ruthless, and she hated ruthlessness.

'He's calculating,' she said aloud to reassure herself. And yet the memory of his touch lingered: the sense that he was not confined by any of the perspectives everyone else seemed to take for granted both excited and intrigued her; it was as though he knew that life was not, after all, either what it seemed or how it was represented, but that it contained layer upon layer of reality which was not generally accessible.

Dee started when Laura turned on the light.

'Christ, you gave me a fright. I thought you were out. What are you doing sitting here in the dark?'

'Just mooning! Did you have a good evening?'

'A mixed bag, you could say.'

Dee turned to look at her usually bouncy friend. 'Intimacy is supposed to create a bond, or is it the other way around?'

Laura groaned, pushed back her long silken hair. She was wearing slacks and a white satin blouse which she had bought in Biba's in London.

'For God's sake, don't get intelligent on me!'

'What did you do?'

'We went to the Paradiso with one of Ted's friends, a guy from Wicklow. *Chicken chez soi.*'

'Was that him or was that what you ate?'

'Very amusing. We ate chicken. The bloke is an academic of sorts. A teetotaller — was wearing a pioneer pin! He's a member of Opus Dei! Doesn't approve of me. I think Ted must have told him we made love!'

They laughed. But when Dee looked back at her friend she saw that she was close to tears.

'I hate being regarded as a whore. You give them something wonderful, and they can't wait to reach for the branding iron. And your man from Opus Dei — all prissy condescension, fleeing genuine experience, eyes fixed instead on manipulation.'

Dee smiled. 'Would you like a cup of tea?'

Laura coughed in exasperation. 'Shit!' she said after a moment. 'I only want life to be fantastic. I will not be broken, I will not be reduced by my own munificence!'

Laura went into the bedroom, and Dee went

into the little windowless kitchen, turned on the fluorescent light and washed her coffee cup. Then she took the chain from her neck and examined the ring in the harsh light, putting it into her pocket.

As she undressed for bed, she whispered to Laura who was lying awake and glassy-eyed.

'Laura, have you a book which might tell me something about the Inquisition?'

Laura pointed to the laden bookshelf in the corner. 'Try the *Larousse Encyclopaedia of Modern History* at the end of the second shelf. It starts about the year 1500.' Dee found the thick book, examined the cover reproduction of a painting by Brueghel the Elder, and was about to bring it with her to bed when the telephone shrilled in the hall. She glanced at the clock on her bedside table. Nearly eleven. She sighed, went into the hall and picked up the receiver, reeled off the number. There was a hiss on the line and then a voice said, 'That's a strong, wide-awake voice. I was afraid you might be in bed!'

Dee tried to place the caller; she knew the voice. 'Dee,' the voice came again, less certain now, 'it is you?'

'Yes, Peter.'

'I'm phoning you from Brussels. I want you to promise me something.'

'What?'

'Even if you have the ring we were talking about — the original — don't allow anyone to buy it from you; don't let anyone see it . . . Don't let

290

Charlie know you have it. This is important, Dee.'

'Why?'

'Trust me. And, Dee, I will be back in Ireland in two weeks' time. Will you have dinner with me?'

Dee drew a deep breath and said with a laugh, 'I don't go out with married men.'

She heard his laughter crackle down the line. 'Oh, Dee, but I'm not married. Does that make it all right?'

'I just thought you might be.'

'So you will . . . have dinner with me?'

Dee hesitated for only a moment. 'OK . . .'

'Ah,' he said, 'such enthusiasm! Goodnight, Dee.'

'Goodnight . . . Peter.'

When she went back to the bedroom, Laura said, 'Who was that?'

'It was someone phoning me from Brussels!'

'No kidding?'

Dee took off her dressing gown, got into bed, picked up the *Larousse Encyclopaedia* and pretended to read.

'Who was it?' Laura repeated curiously, leaning up on her elbow.

'It was a guy by the name of Peter Eggli.'

'The big noise from Brussels? But I thought you didn't like him.'

Dee put down the book. 'Course I don't like him! He thinks he's God. Actually, he scares me a little.' She smiled. 'But . . . maybe I do like him a bit. He's a challenge! I had a drink with him today in the Russell.'

Laura sat up. 'Ye gods and little green fishes. The Russell, no less! You are a dark horse! And now he phones you from Brussels. He must have it bad . . .'

'No, he doesn't. He wants to get his hands on an old ring I found years ago in Kilashane House. It has some kind of arcane value — a collector's item.'

'Have you had it valued?'

'No, not yet.'

'Hmn,' Laura said, 'it will probably turn out to belong to an idol in Katmandu — be worth a bomb. You needn't think this little Belgian is chasing it out of disinterested curiosity.'

Dee smiled. Laura was back on form. 'It didn't come from Katmandu. And he's not Belgian, he's American.'

'Worse again. He won't be put off by the curse . . .'

'What curse?'

Laura changed her voice into a banshee-like wail. 'The great curse of the Green Idol.'

Dee pointed to the door. 'Laura, would you ever shut up,' she hissed. 'Other people in this house are probably trying to sleep.'

Laura looked chastened. 'They ought to know better. Well, you know what I mean. Like Tutankhamen's tomb; the fate that overtook Lord What's-his-name.'

'Lord Caernarvon died from a wasp sting: it got infected,' Dee said in exasperation.

'There was a young man from Tralee,' Laura said meditatively, 'Who got stung on the head by a bee . . .'

Dee sighed out loud. There was no coping with Laura in this mood.

Laura laughed contritely, but suddenly said, 'Christ — did you get your letter?'

'What letter?'

'I put it in the drawer. I put it away on Saturday. I got a fit of enthusiasm and did some dusting!'

'Which drawer?'

'Sideboard.'

Dee got out of bed and found the letter. Colin's writing was on the envelope.

Dear Leprechaun,

Thank you for the birthday greetings. I'm sorry I didn't remember yours, but here they are in retrospect — GREETINGS!

I am glad things are going well for you. ITU is indeed a big biz, and I can see that you will rise to prominence and turn into a raging capitalist. However, I do miss you, in spite of everything.

I have some decent assignments now, where I can ferret with the editor's blessing (you wouldn't approve). If I have occasion to come to the Emerald Isle, I'll look forward to seeing you,

Love,
Colin

PS. One thing which might interest you —
there's a queer bird in ITU — Brussels-based.
He's into some hush-hush organization with
an awful lot of money — source unknown.
Don't have the full dirt on him yet, but I'm
ferreting! (Being insane with my new power, I
intend to do an exposé of some rising stars
when I can get around to it.)

Dee showed this letter to Laura, who sat up to
read it. 'Typical Colin,' Dee said. 'Curiosity
masquerading as idealism, tinged with just the
teensiest soupçon of menace.'

'He'll go far; he sounds lovely,' Laura said.
'But who's this other fellow?'

Dee shrugged. 'Anyone's guess!'

She got back into bed and picked up the
encyclopaedia again. Laura burrowed into her
pillow, as though she had at last determined to
get to sleep at a reasonable hour.

'Laur —'

'What?'

'Did you ever hear of a turncoat inquisitor?
According to Charlie he was a bloke who lived in
Venice.'

'You've got that place on the brain!'

'No, it's just that since the floods last November, there's been a lot of stuff about it .'

'A turncoat inquisitor forsooth!' Laura echoed. 'Not their style! They were all company animals!' Her voice was muffled by the pillows. 'But
there was one odd character who was involved

with the death of a witch called the Lady of Florence.'

'Who was she?'

'Oh, some woman who wouldn't toe the line! A resolute individual, it would seem, one of the very exceptional people who are all principle and cannot be broken. He fell for her, hook, line and sinker! Gave the Pope the shove-off sign!'

'What was she resolute about?'

'She said the Church lied and that she therefore could not serve it! And this, my dear, was a very bold thing to do at that time!'

Dee digested this. 'Is it in this book?'

'No, they hushed it up. Orthodox history is edited. You have to ferret in peripheral sources. That's where you find the best stuff!'

'But it might not even be true!'

'Jesus, Dee, you don't want to spoil a good story for the sake of the truth!' She laughed. 'But seriously, orthodox or otherwise, given the unavoidable bias of the historian, how can any history be the objective truth?'

'Laur —'

'What?'

'Do you believe in reincarnation?'

'No. And I don't believe in mornings either, and you see where that gets me!'

Dee took the hint and turned off the light.

Chapter Thirteen

'What must I do to be saved?'

'Obey.'

'If you depend on my obedience,' she said, weeping, 'it is you who are the slave.'

The inquisitor did not reprove her temerity.

Journal of a Witness

Jenny made her way to the National Gallery. She crossed Trafalgar Square slowly, looking up at the lions she used to mount with such pleasure when she was a child. They gazed out at the urban scurry with the old bronze detachment. She approached the pillared portico of the gallery, tense with anticipation. In her stomach was the empty feeling of someone dropped from a height. At the doorway she turned and was aware, dreamlike, of the traffic coursing around the square and down into Whitehall. In this heartland of the Empire, a boy stood with the *Evening Standard*, shouting out the name of his paper; pigeons clustered in the middle of the square near the fountains, pecking at the crumbs thrown by the visitors, flapping up when disturbed with a sudden clatter of wings. Soon it would be dusk and the lights would come on all over London.

She saw him in the hall with the chambers of

the gallery behind him. Theo stood watching the door, his dark hair brushed back, his eyes intent; he was leaning on a stick. He was dressed in a cashmere overcoat, a hat and a scarf; his hands were gloved. For a moment they stood and stared at each other. She turned and retreated, but his stick tapped rapidly across the tiles and his hand took her elbow as she crossed the threshold.

'Wait. Please, Jenny!'

'I am married to your wife's brother,' she whispered, standing back against one of the pillars. 'Why do you seek me out?'

He smiled like a man trying to placate a child. 'You know the answer, Jenny. It is why you are here.'

'What do you want to say to me?'

He put her hand into the crook of his arm. 'I want to show you something.'

She went with him into the gallery. It was almost closing time. He moved with certainty to the Italian school, paused before a picture and invited her, with an inclination of his head, to examine it.

She looked up at the portrait in its heavy gilt frame. For a moment she felt as though cold, dead fingers wrapped themselves around her throat. It was the magician, her magician, almost as she had painted him. The legend beside the portrait said simply, *Venetian Gentleman*, painted by Cetterini c.1601.' She stood staring. She heard a voice announce that it was closing time. But still she stared. The painting was executed with power; the paint and the sombre colours were old indeed; the hooded eyes were alive and studied her; the long face and nose were the same; the mouth, obscured by the moustache and the goatee, was the same; the difference lay in the execution, not in the subject. She felt the gentle pressure on her arm.

'We must go!'

As she walked back towards the exit she said, 'I did a painting like that; I have it at home!'

'I know!'

'How could you possibly know?' she said, without moving her head. 'Did Andrew tell you?'

'No. I suffer from a surfeit of information.'

She was silent for a moment and then added, turning to look at him, 'You see, he looks the same as the person I painted . . . I don't understand!'

'There are more things in heaven and earth,' he recited, but Jenny interjected crossly, ' "Than are dreamt of in my philosophy." I know, I know. I did *Hamlet* at school, too . . .'

'You probably saw him one day when you were here!'

'I don't remember.'

Jenny shook her head. Of course, she berated herself, it must have been that; I must have seen him. I inadvertently copied the portrait. But I don't remember ever having seen it. I would remember if I had, I know I would remember if I had.

She stopped at a painting, a still life, a riot of roses.

'You like flowers?'

'Of course. Red roses particularly. Gramps — my grandfather — was fond of them.'

At the door she felt faint. 'Something is going on. It is making me ill. What is happening, Theo?'

'Nothing,' he whispered, taking her arm, 'and everything! We are at the door of the National Gallery and we are at the gateway of the future. In a moment we shall go down the steps to to-morrow . . .'

Outside, the moist air was still and heavy with smoke. Theo raised his stick and hailed a taxi. They got in; other vehicles chugged by them in the gloom.

'There will be a smog tonight,' he said. 'It has begun already.'

He gave some directions to the cabbie, and the taxi turned towards the river and down towards Westminster. Big Ben rose in majesty above the Houses of Parliament and the quiet abbey across the street. The taxi moved past the warlike Boadicea, lashing her horses into the uncertain future.

'Where are you taking me?'

'Where I can talk to you.'

He lit a cheroot. The smoke was aromatic; it

made her want to sleep.

'You must bring me home!'

'Right now?'

'Yes.'

He did not answer, but inclined his head. 'Jenny,' he murmured, 'you are confused. But I will bring you home.'

Jenny sat back against the taxi seat. She was exhausted and wanted only to sleep. 'I'm sleepy.'

'Then sleep.'

Afterwards, Jenny wondered if she had been dreaming. She recalled the red-brick block of flats, the lift, the carpeted corridor, a stark sitting room furnished with a chesterfield suite, a bookcase with glass doors, four spoon-backed chairs, a drop-leaf dining table, a small sideboard with decanter and glasses. There was a fire in the grate. The room smelt of polish. The bottle-green velvet curtains were drawn.

'Whose is this place?'

'It belongs to the O'Reilly family. It was home from home for the old man when he was a member of Parliament.

'Are you hungry?' he asked then. 'Would you like to eat?'

'No.'

'Is there anything in the world that I can give you?' She shook her head.

'Will you take off your coat.'

Her finger unbuttoned her coat and laid it on a chair. He threw some more coals on the fire and it hissed. A burst of sooty flame climbed into the chimney. She shivered.

'You are cold. Come to the fire.'

'No,' she answered. 'I don't like being too close to the fire!'

'Won't you sit down?'

She sat on the couch. He poured a drink from a decanter, handed it to her.

'What is it?'

'Brandy.'

She sipped the drink, watching him as he removed his coat and sat in an armchair near the fender. He did not reach for a drink, but watched her, and when she put the drink away she saw that he had taken his fob-watch from his pocket and was playing with the silver chain. The watch moved forward and backwards like a pendulum; she followed it carelessly with her eyes, feeling the warmth spread within her from the brandy, feeling herself sink back into the couch. She felt the fear leave her.

'Jenny, Jenny, Jenny, you are safe. There is no place in all the world you could be safer . . .'

She heard the words without the sounds. She heard her name like a chant. The aromatic smoke, the burn of the brandy, the rhythm of the watch chain, the cadence of his voice, all induced immobility; a state where she was outside the present and the past and careless of the future. She saw without particularly wondering at it that he sat in a circle of colour, while outside it the room was dark. What is wrong with my sight?

came the thought, but it was not accompanied by dread.

She saw how he leant forward, his eyes intense, the pupils very black. 'Tell me, what do you see if you shut your eyes?'

Jenny shut her eyes. She felt the parameters of the present melt. She saw rise rough-hewn walls, the smell of the pitch, the guttering torches fitted into the sconces, the instruments on their pegs. The torturer was stripped to the waist; he had the saturnine face of a southerner, but the inquisitor stood to one side, watching, as cruel as death.

Jenny gasped. 'No . . . NO!' She heard her own voice; the scene fractured; there before her were the green velvet curtains of the London flat, the smouldering fire, Theo, his face very pale, watching her.

'Forgive him . . . He knew not what he did!'

She did not answer.

'She loved him, for all that?' he said. 'Say it, say that in the end she did?'

Jenny turned her head. The tendrils of the fading dream writhed in her mind.

'You are insane,' she whispered. 'How could she have loved him?'

'He began as her adversary, but in the end he knew her to the core. When someone knows you to the core, Jenny, you become bound to him; and he knew himself, too, what he could have been, the layers of his worth if he had sought them.'

Jenny shook her head.

'She became his salvation. You must have seen how he loved her, how he could not let her go!'

'He was damned.'

He shook his head. 'Tell me what you need, what you want. You shall have it . . .'

Jenny did not respond. She was full of a lassitude in which she allowed herself momentary belief in such a promise. She felt like the man dying of thirst who stumbled one day into a cave filled with gems, except that the cave was in the middle of nowhere and he didn't even have any pockets. But she humoured him and answered, 'Happiness.'

His face clouded. 'Happiness is not in anyone's gift. You must choose it for yourself.'

She smiled. 'You see. And you think you're so clever . . . I suppose you imagine I came to the gallery to see you?'

'No? Why did you come?'

She giggled, breaking the tension. 'Because Fandango — my cat — came back!'

They laughed. 'I thought he had died,' Jenny said. 'But there he was . . .'

He listened as Jenny told him the story.

'Your husband, who makes you miserable: he could be dealt with,' he murmured in a voice so low that it was almost inaudible.

Jenny roused herself out of the lethargy which was threatening to overwhelm her. 'No! My mistakes are not yours to undo.'

'What then can I give you. Wealth? Fame as an artist? Tell me.'

'Nothing has any value if it can be had on whim.'

He sighed. 'There must be something you want.'

'I only want to live,' Jenny said. 'Now as then!'

The face before her swam in and out of focus. He knelt beside her and caressed her hands. She felt the way her body responded, knew her breathing had quickened, felt the race of her heart.

'Come,' he said softly, 'and I will introduce you to life.'

She did not answer, and after a while he took her hand, drawing her into the dark bedroom.

When Jenny surfaced late the next day, the sun was coming in through a chink in the curtains. For a moment she did not know where she was, and then she recognized her own room, or rather Gramps' old room; the mahogany wardrobe, the chest of drawers.

'I was dreaming,' she said, already half forgetting, shivering at the gossamer memory of wakening to the touch of his mouth at her breast.

'The mask, my darling. Where is it?'

'I have it safe.'

'Will you give it to me?'

She had hesitated for only a moment. *'No.'*

She got out of bed, threw on her dressing gown, and sat by the mirror. 'What have I done?'

she asked the face in the glass. 'Such a dream! Why did I dream like that?'

It was Sunday. Andrew was at home and she heard his footsteps on the stairs. He came into the room and with a sudden, and now uncharacteristic movement, put his arms around her, pulling her head against his shoulder.

'Oh, Jen, I was so worried. You slept like the dead. I tried to wake you earlier because you looked so white, but I never saw anyone so fast asleep. And you came back late and didn't speak. Are you all right?'

She turned to him. 'Andrew,' she said slowly, 'I think the smog must have poisoned me. And I have had the strangest dream.'

'What was it, the dream?' he asked indulgently, stroking her hair, feeling suddenly tender and masterful, sitting there on the side of the bed with his disoriented and delectable wife in his arms.

Jenny put her hand to her head and he released her. She avoided his eyes. 'Some strange nonsense . . . I don't want to think about it. I can hardly remember it anyway.'

'What would you like to do today?'

'I am very tired. I shall go back to bed.'

Andrew's face registered raw desire. He studied his wife's décolleté in the mirror. Then he moved to the door and turned the key in the lock.

'Good idea,' he said, divesting himself of his clothes and walking naked towards the bed. He

305

lay back against the pillow, watching his wife's reflection in the mirror and surreptitiously stroking his erect penis, as though he were afraid it would disappear. Then he put out a hand to her.

'Come, Jen, I am so hungry for you!'

Jenny looked at him, at his mousy moustache, at his eager face, at his eager member. Everything seemed so simple. Quick love, facile desire, mechanical fulfilment. She felt very tired, knowledgeable, like an old courtesan who could size a man up at a glance.

'I don't think I could bear it, not now, anyway.'

Andrew's face darkened. He did not reply, but he waited until his wife had finished brushing her hair, watching in the mirror the line of her neck and shoulders and the swell of her bosom. Then he got up and seized her roughly by the arm.

'I can't stand it any longer, Jenny. This time we will do things my way! I cannot tolerate being put down by you any longer!'

He dragged her to the bed, threw her down and, after a tussle, entered her roughly, his eyes very bright and the distortion of mastery in his face.

Afterwards he said to her with a note of satisfaction, 'Now you are a real wife.' Then he added doubtfully, 'Jen, you were a virgin, weren't you?'

Jenny did not speak, but she covered herself and turned her face away. He dressed rapidly, hesitated for a moment, as though he might try to reclaim what had been lost by a word of sorrow or love, but there was scorn in Jenny's tense body, and he left the room in silence, shutting the door behind him. She heard his footsteps descending the stairs.

Jenny got up, went to the bathroom to wash, heard from below the sound of Fandango caterwauling. He was in the garden, howling to be let in, and it was clear that Andrew would not permit him entry.

Jenny opened the bathroom window and looked down. The cat stared up at her, mewed again, this time piteously. A sense of suffocation suffused Jenny. For the first time in her life she did not want to be bothered with Fandango; she wanted to be let alone. She went back to her room, locked the door, and wiped the silent tears with the sheet, rocking herself as she used to when she was a child, backwards and forwards as though the motion would dislodge the pain. Soon she fell asleep.

It was early afternoon when she surfaced. The first thought in her mind was that something terrible had happened. Then she remembered, and tensed beneath the bed-clothes with the horror of what had taken place. It was like a nightmare, except that it did not fade on wakening, unlike the dream she had had the night before, which she could only barely recall. In fact, when she tried to think of it, her head began to pain, and all she could see in her mind's eye was a silver fob-watch swaying on its chain like a pendulum.

Suddenly, as though it were a living presence in the room, she smelt the perfume. When she raised her head she saw the single dewy red rose on her bedside table.

The first thought that occurred to her was that Andrew had put it there by way of atonement, but the door was locked. A hot-house rose, she thought, examining its perfection. Perhaps Andrew had another key and had come in while she slept. Perhaps he was smitten with remorse. Perhaps he was trying to say that he was sorry.

Jenny considered this. His repentance was not something which would exact automatic forgiveness. Too much had happened for that. She recognized that she was afraid of Andrew now. That she had contempt for him; that she wanted to make him realize the full enormity of what he had done. But, at the same time, even in the turmoil of her feelings, the extreme nature of his actions made her wonder as to its source. Did he possess a passion which was inarticulate and could only express itself through violence? Was there more to him than met the eye, some place within him which possessed certain kinds of absolutes? Or was he compartmentalized, destroyed by war, so uncertain of who he was that he was compelled to fall back desperately on outrage as a means of stating the reality and significance of his existence?

She dressed and opened the door. Fandango was sitting outside, had managed to get in after all. He smiled up at her and followed her down the stairs. The door of the sitting room was closed, and when she went to turn the knob she found it was locked. Andrew's voice came from the other side. 'Put out the confounded cat, Jenny. The beast is dangerous; I wouldn't be surprised if it was rabid! He tried to attack me again!'

Jenny looked down at her pet. He stood politely, waiting for the door to open. She saw that he was still not as clean as he used to be; that his white socks were a dirty grey and his coat dusty. She thought of the sprightly young Fandango, squeaky clean, who had once danced around the garden.

'Come on, Fandango, out you go,' Jenny whispered, taking the cat in her arms and going down to the back door. 'Stay out for the time being and clean yourself up!'

Fandango leapt from her arms and turned to look back at her as she closed the door.

Jenny went back upstairs and put the rose in water. She waited for Andrew's show of repentance. But it never came. He spoke to her as though nothing had happened.

A couple of weeks later, a letter came from Ireland addressed to Mr and Mrs Andrew Stacey. It was from Yvonne; her careful writing advanced daintily across the white envelope. Jenny gazed at the stamp as she handed the letter to Andrew at the breakfast table.

'Letter from Yvonne. It's her writing!'

'Why don't you open it?'

She opened it, slipping a knife under the flap and extracting a folded sheet of writing paper. The address was given as Kilashane House, Ballyshane, Fanagh, Co. Cork.

'Shall I read it to you?'

Andrew looked up from his scrambled eggs. 'Go ahead.'

'Darlings,

'Well, I'm finally here. I've so much to tell you I don't know where I should begin.

We had an uneventful journey to Holyhead, and then a rather choppy crossing which made both Mrs O'R., Kate and me feel queasy but didn't seem to bother Theo. We stayed in Dublin for a night before catching the train at Kingsbridge to Cork. Then we had another train to catch, and eventually ended up in the smallest station you ever saw, the train being flagged down by the stationmaster with a big red flag. We were met by a cheerful little jarvey with a trap and a brogue so broad that I hadn't the faintest idea what he was saying, although he tipped his cap very politely and welcomed Theo with unfeigned delight. I think the journey made Theo very tired because he was very uncommunicative for several days, but he has improved so much you cannot imagine. Every day he seems to get stronger and he walks better with his poor old wooden leg. (He would hate to hear me calling it that!)

Kilashane House is a big square block of a house, built over a basement. It has a flight of steps to the front door, and a circular driveway and lawn in front of the house. You can see the sea from the bedroom windows at the front of the house. There is a cook, a maid, and a groom of sorts (he's really a general factotum), who lives in a nearby cottage with his little daughter.

I have got to know Theo's mother better and I like her. She was very reserved with me at first, but now she has thawed and treats me very kindly. I'm sure she is heartbroken about Theo's leg, but I think she is so glad to have him back alive that she is coming to terms with his injury. She is only fifty years old and is very energetic, comes for walks with us (myself and Kate) along the country lanes around here.

I don't know what I expected of Ireland. I suppose I thought of it as full of quaint little people, with leprechauns hopping out of every hedge and everyone saying "begorrah". It's not like that. It's full of melancholy. It's in the air; the very land breathes it: melancholy. Oh, don't think I'm unhappy. It is very beautiful here, with the sea and the wild countryside and the great sky; but still I find myself thinking of London a great deal and wishing I felt safe. I mean safe in the sense of being "secure"; in being surrounded by all that I knew and understood. We do have fun here, of course. For example, when I was walking with Kate and Mrs O'R. yesterday, we met the groom, Batty, who was searching for something in a ditch.

"Hello, Batty," Mrs O'R. said in her rather precise voice. "What are you looking for?"

"I'm looking for the lid of me pipe, ma'am."

There was an exchange then as to the merits of praying to St Anthony to find the pipe-lid, and Batty opined that this was a waste of time as the poor-box had been "pinched from under his arse above in the church the other day".

Batty has a weathered face, full of sly humour, and a filthy peaked cap dragged down over his forehead. However, he straightened and complimented Mrs O'Reilly. " 'Tis grand and well you're looking, ma'am."

Mrs O'Reilly sniffed. "I'm afraid I can't return the compliment, Batty."

I expected the man to be abashed, but he looked at her slyly and moved off with the coup-de-grâce, which was delivered under his breath. "Indeed you could, ma'am, if you were half as big a liar as I am!"

I told Theo about the exchange and he smiled. Kate interjected to say that Batty and her mother were old sparring partners. She turned to him then to share some recollection, and he nodded and laughed. But his eyes didn't laugh, and I think he doesn't remember Kilashane as well as he pretends. Sometimes he gets upset in his sleep. But I suppose you can't expect someone to recover from shell-shock just like that! Physically the improvement in him is unbelievable, and I would have great hope if only . . . well, if only the old gentleness was still there. But I'd better not burden you with my nonsense.

You are both invited to come and stay whenever you like. Mrs O'Reilly expressly extends her invitation, as does Kate, and Theo too insists on you both coming. He says he would like to reminisce with Andrew, now that he feels his memory is improving, and would be delighted to show both of you the county.

So there! You must come. You really must. I should be so glad to see you.

Your affectionate sister,
Yvonne.'

Jenny put the letter down.

Andrew looked at her expectantly. 'Well, do you want to go?'

'No.'

'Why not?'

'It's too far!'

'Fiddlesticks, Jen. You're not in your dotage yet. I should like to go. I should like to see Yvonne and even talk to that fearful ass O'Reilly.'

Jenny was silent. She heard the masterful tone in Andrew's voice which he had assumed ever since that Sunday when he had forced himself upon her. She remembered it in detail, the pain and outrage of violation, of being secondary to his requirements. But as he had never mentioned the subject again, she had hidden from him how she had begun to hate him. Strangely

313

enough he had not troubled her since, as though satisfied that he had made his statement.

Eventually he sighed. 'Is she happy, do you think?' he asked in a subdued voice, as though, for a moment, he felt the burden of things between them to be heavy and irredeemable.

Jenny met his eyes and looked away. 'No.'

'It's there between the lines, isn't it?' he persisted.

'Yes.'

Jenny looked around the room and out at the suburban street. A child ran by, driving a hoop before him with a stick. 'She's not just unhappy,' she whispered. 'She's desperate!' and in her own mind she added — like me.

Andrew, looking suddenly anxious, indicated the window with a sharp inclination of his head. Fandango was sitting outside and staring in at him with an unblinking fixity.

'That animal will have to be destroyed,' he said. 'I don't know how he gets into the house, but I woke last night and he was in the room. I heard him breathing, and when I sat up I saw his eyes. They were shining in the light from the street and staring straight at me! And when he is not in my room he sits outside your door!'

'You probably feel guilty about what you did to him,' Jenny said in a voice devoid of expression. 'I don't want him hurt again.'

'We shall decide the issue when we come back from Ireland,' Andrew said in a voice of decision. 'I'm sure the Wilkinsons would feed him while we're gone.'

'He doesn't seem to eat any more,' Jenny observed. 'At least not here. Not since you hanged him!'

Andrew made a gesture of exasperation and left the room.

Chapter Fourteen

'What is your message, woman?'
  'Message? All I have said is that I will not serve.'

Journal of a Witness

It was only the beginning. Much later, Dee, trying to remember every nuance of it, struggling with the sense of something having burrowed under her skin, underneath all her defences, wrote a small poem but never sent it to him. There were surges of conversation and silences, and when she looked up she found him studying her. The restaurant was south of the city, on the coast. They could see, out on the horizon, the intermittent flash of the Kish, hear through the open window the song of the ebb tide.

'I thought you might like to be near the sea.'

'The flat is quite close to it. We can see the Alexandra Basin from the sitting room.'

There were gilt-framed mirrors on the walls. She saw herself from her peripheral vision, saw that she looked shy — which annoyed her, saw the cream-coloured dress she had bought in a rush for the occasion. She was wearing 'gipsy' earrings, golden circles which swung when she moved and which, being 'clip-ons', pinched her earlobes so that they felt as though they were on fire.

Peter perused the menu, murmured something about lobster, and she watched his hands and his face and the movement of his eyes as they scanned the bill of fare. The *maître-d'* came solicitously, made suggestions; they chose lobster followed by Wicklow lamb. He looked at the wine list, ordered a bottle of Antinori and two dry sherries as aperitifs.

'Do you have a regular boyfriend?' he asked with a mixture of curiosity and ostensible diffidence when they were alone again.

Dee reddened. 'Not at the moment.' She shrugged. 'I'll probably die a spinster!' She smiled to show she was joking, playing her part, suspecting that we create ourselves.

He smiled back, or at least his mouth smiled. The humour did not extend to his eyes, which never seemed to change, which seemed to watch everything without being affected by anything, as though he already knew the score, as though he had the lines off by heart.

'Oh, I don't think there's much chance of that,' he said gallantly. 'Here you are, early twenties, with the world at your feet . . . Mr Right will come out of the woodwork and whisk you away.'

Dee looked him in the eye. 'Mr Right? Do you think there's such an animal? I'm not so sure I want him. Marriage does not really appeal to me, at least not for years and years.'

He pursed his mouth, shoving out the lips in a Gallic moue. 'So I've no competition? You ran away so quickly the last time, that I felt sure . . .'

Dee suddenly felt that there was no reason why he should not have competition. 'My boyfriend is in London,' she murmured. 'We see each other infrequently. I met him when I was working there last year.'

'What happened?' he asked gently. 'Why did you come home? Did he push his luck too far?'

Dee was taken aback. She thought of Colin, 'Dear Leprechaun', and suddenly wanted to laugh. She remembered that, when she wore flat sandals, she had to reach up to hold his hand.

'Or maybe he wasn't a pushy type?'

'Oh, he was pushy all right, but not in the way you mean!'

'What did he do?'

'He was, is, a newspaper reporter. I got a letter from him recently. He is doing well . . .'

'Indeed. I might know him. I have contacts in the Press. What is his name?'

Dee raised her eyebrows. 'Colin Weaver. He works for the *Daily Mail*.'

'Is he a good journalist?'

'Dedicated. At least he thinks he is.'

'What do you think?'

'I think he is!'

'Do you miss him?'

'Yes. Sometimes more than others . . .'

'Did you tell him all about your life, about the ring?'

Dee sighed. 'No. He would think I was mental. Can't we talk about something else?'

'I'm sorry.'

Then they talked of work, of Charlie who had left the company.

'What happened to him?'

'He got another job,' Eggli said. 'Did he ever bother you again about . . . Sorry, I didn't mean to bring it up!'

'Yes, he phoned me . . . You phoned me. Why did you phone me, Peter, that night? What is so special about that ring?'

He held her eyes. 'Do you actually possess it?'

Dee fidgeted, looked into the grey eyes across the table. Denial was on the tip of her tongue, but she was weary of it all. The bloody thing was only a piece of jewellery. She would go mad if she had to play any more games.

'Yes, as a matter of fact. I found it and, as you guessed, I made a copy of it for Charlie. I thought it might keep him quiet. So now you know the whole story: confession is good for the soul!'

His face was inscrutable. 'Where is it?'

'I have hidden it,' she said, smiling, adding with deliberate provocation. 'Should I sell it?'

'If you do — depending on how you go about it — many people might get hurt to obtain it.'

The sense of devilment died in her. 'Why?'

'It's a long story. It has the emblem of an old and secret brotherhood. It is supposed to possess occult powers.'

'Pull the other one,' Dee said.

'The other what?' He paused, leaning across the table. 'Seriously. It is associated with another curio which is supposed to possess strange qualities.'

'What other curio?'

'A mask!'

Dee was silent.

'You have never seen anything like that, I suppose — in Kilashane?'

Dee's mind went back to the day she had held it in her hand and had thrown it from her. She thought of Laura and the skit she had invented about the curse of Katmandu. OK, Laura had been joking, but this suggestion of occult powers made her suspect that sanity was in shorter supply than was commonly believed.

But she didn't answer the question. The starters arrived, the wine was sampled and pronounced fit to drink.

'How come you know so much about all this stuff? Where did you hear about it?'

Eggli smiled. 'I was waiting for you to ask that. It dates from my time in the American Army. I was in the Korean War, worked in the Encryption Department. My business was the devising of new codes. For this I studied all the available secret codes of the old world. Venice, being the centre of intrigue, had several such encryptions. It was through study of them that I chanced on all this. Afterwards, through my own investigations, I learnt more.'

'It's strange that you should mention Venice,' she said after a moment. 'I watched a programme about it recently. After the floods last winter — when they were carrying out restoration work — they found a body in some sort of sarcophagus. It was the corpse of a young woman, preserved, except that she had no face.'

He nodded. 'That is so. Does this intrigue you?'

'Yes. Very much. There is something haunting about it. And I would never have thought it possible to inter someone in a place like Venice — for obvious reasons.'

'They bury their dead on a cemetery island called San Michele.'

'There was a design hewn into the sarcophagus. It's the same design as on the ring I found!'

He did not seem surprised by this information. 'Yes,' he said simply . 'That would be possible.'

'Why?'

'It was about that time that the secret association which we have already mentioned had its beginnings.'

'For something like that to persist down the centuries! You make me feel that sinister forces are abroad!'

'Perhaps they are. It depends how you define "sinister".'

'Why are you not in the Army any more?'

He shrugged. 'There's nothing sinister about that. I was wounded . . . and I wanted out anyway.'

'Why did you want out?'

He sighed, but he did not answer for a moment, as though he were scanning the horizons of his personal history. Then he said, 'I began to feel there was more to life than a uniform. I became intrigued by the undercurrents stirring beneath all apparent reality.'

'Such as?'

'Did you know, for example, that about eighty per cent of the universe is composed of dark matter?'

' "Dark matter"? What's that?'

'It's matter in a form which can never be examined.'

'You're interested in physics. I'm afraid I have no grounding in it.'

She ate, drank some wine, knew that his eyes were still regarding her.

'What should I do if I were to chance on this thing?' she whispered suddenly.

He frowned. 'You could let me know . . .'

He studied her and she returned his gaze. 'Why should I let anyone know? You want these things I found. Charlie wants them. If I advertised them for sale half the country would probably want them. And all because some idiots think these things confer power or purpose or some other unearned slivers of importance.'

Dee felt the wine go to her head, turning her diffidence into recklessness. 'I will let you in on a secret, Peter Eggli. I am not what I seem. I am a little mad. I decided to become a witch

322

when I was a child!'

For the first time there was humour in his eyes. She expected him to laugh but he just said quite conversationally, 'Why?'

'Why did I want to become a witch? I learnt about their powers of locomotion. I heard about the benefits of the broomstick. Oh, Peter, why should anyone endure this nonsense? If you like me enough to take me out to dinner, I would prefer it was because you liked me for myself!'

He studied her. 'I know you are a witch!' he said with a disarming show of repentance, shaking his head a little. 'I am uncommonly fond of witches. I am bewitched, in fact. And I do like you for yourself. And it doesn't matter at all about anything else!'

He shook his head in a humorous gesture. The drawl of his American accent was like the wine, heady and novel. Dee was mollified.

'The mask is down beneath umpteen tons of rubble — full fathom five — in Kilashane!'

Eggli narrowed his eyes. The charm had left them and they were hooded in the candlelight. 'Curiouser and curiouser,' he whispered.

Dee watched him, drawn by his intensity. She felt the wine in her veins, the beckoning of trust. 'Peter . . .'

'Yes?'

'I know you'll think I'm crazy — Laura says I have a bee in my bonnet — but I wondered if you had ever heard of this fellow that Charlie went on about?'

He frowned. 'What fellow?'

'The old bloke who lived in Venice long ago — the wizard. I thought you might know, seeing you know so much about that city.'

'What do you want to know?' he asked softly.

Dee looked at her plate. 'I suppose I want to know if he really lived. I want to know what link there is between him — if there is one — and the dead girl they found. Laura was telling me recently about a woman called the Lady of Florence who was tortured by the Inquisition. I want to know all this because I cannot understand why the emblem on the ring I found in Ireland is the same as the one on the sarcophagus in Venice, and because Charlie told me that the wizard fellow concocted this design in the first place. It's a mystery and I want to solve it . . .'

Peter smiled, but it did not extend to his eyes. 'He lived,' he said. 'His name was Mathias Robertus. He was a Jesuit. He took to the black arts because he felt himself betrayed. He wanted power and didn't care how he got it. He wanted revenge. Above all, he wanted the woman he loved.'

'Whom did he love?'

'He was in love with a witch,' Peter said with a hint of irony.

'This so-called Lady of Florence?'

'Yes.'

'The one who died without recanting?'

'Yes.'

'She really lived then?'

'Yes.'

'How did he go about getting her, if she was dead?'

Peter didn't answer for a moment. Then he said, 'That is the million-dollar question . . . They say that he learnt how to access the future; that he's still looking for her . . .'

'What will he do with her if he finds her?'

He didn't answer for a moment and then he said: 'He will bring her back . . . to where it began. Close the circle. Redeem himself.'

Dee felt the chill creep up her backbone. 'It sounds creepy and crazy,' she said. 'What was so special about her anyway?'

Peter sat very still. 'Special? She was a flame in the darkness.' He raised his eyebrows, smiled at the expression on Dee's face.

The waiter brought the dessert trolley. Dee chose an ice-cream selection which she ate in virtual silence. He had fresh fruit salad followed by coffee.

'Don't let it bother you, Dee,' he whispered suddenly, his face creased into a smile of urbanity. 'Old stories are old stories.'

'I'm not "bothered" by it,' Dee said. 'I just want to know what the whole thing has to do with Kilashane. If the ring I found belonged to him, why did it turn up there?'

'The world is a small place. Anyone, a traveller for example, might have found it, brought it home.'

'Well, that's true,' Dee conceded. 'I suppose you've been to Venice yourself?'

'Yes, I first saw it four years ago . . . and nothing was ever the same for me again!'

'Why? What happened?'

But he just smiled and reached across the table to take her hand.

He dropped her home, kissed her fiercely in the dark of the car as she was thanking him. 'Now I shall see you to your door and I shall look forward to your coming to Brussels . . .'

She curved against him. She felt his desire as a presence, a statement. She felt the rasp of his face, the vitality which burned in him, felt how her life's decisions were being assumed for her. She didn't mind. She would go with this current and see where it led. She was braced for rejection, but was unable to withstand hope. If there was any substance in what he seemed to be offering her, it was something she was not free to walk away from. If he was playing games he was a damn fine actor. No one, no one had ever looked at her like that. And no one had ever carried about with him the aura of consequence he did, the aura of understanding. She knew, for reasons which were not apparent, that there was some kind of entente between them.

'You will be careful, won't you?' he whispered as he walked her to the door. Dee, dizzy from a kiss which made her knees rebellious, nodded; and the taste of his mouth lingered. She paused as she shut the door, and saw that he had turned back on the step and was watching the closing door with a preoccupied expression, with intense, narrowed eyes.

'How was the evening with Mr God?' Laura asked.

Dee sighed shakily. 'Dangerous!'

Laura smiled. 'Dangerous nice or dangerous dangerous? Don't tell me, I can see for myself!'

Dee sat down. 'It was as though I've never been alive before . . . at least not in the same way!' Then she added in a sudden rush of mistrust, 'He's very interesting, complex, but I don't know what to think. I'm afraid of being hurried into something. He has me all set up for this planning course in Brussels — I'll be glad to go, of course, but he seems to assume that everything will be the way he wants it!'

Laura gave a small, derisive whinny. 'Where have you been hiding? They're all like that, for God's sake . . . I suppose he has got you to promise him the ring!'

Dee frowned, as though trying to work something out. 'They're not all like that — Colin wasn't — and no, he has not got me to promise him the ring . . . But I have a queer feeling, all the same.' She turned to her friend. 'Do you think I'm safe with this man, Laura?'

'What a question!' Laura studied her. 'You've had too much to drink. Was Mr God taking advantage?'

'No, but I think he may be out for more than

my honour!' She expected Laura to laugh, but she looked grave.

'Your question was answered long ago, by Leonidas at Thermopylae — the guy who held a mountain pass against an army with just three hundred men. Not today, nor yesterday, but truth is always truth.'

'What did he say?'

Laura lowered her voice. 'He said, "We are not here for safety!" '

'What are we here for, then?'

Laura shrugged, yawned. 'War, my darling. We are here for battle! Against ourselves mostly, against indecision, against fear!'

'I don't want battle. I want peace.'

'Go to Brussels,' Laura said. 'When you come back you can decide on the peace. But don't let him talk you out of the ring! Get the damn thing valued first.'

The plane — Sabena — was about one-third full. Dee accepted the *Irish Times* and, as a foretaste of Brussels, *Le Soir*, *'edition du matin'*. The hostess's voice — *'Nous vous souhaitons la bienvenue'* — crackled through the address system after a greeting in Flemish. Looking down from her small oval window she saw Howth, Dublin Bay and the Sugar Loaf disappearing far below. She turned her attention to the newspapers and then the meal. As she ate she felt the pressure of the gold ring against her chest, as though it had been a ton weight. She had brought it to a jewel-

ler who had said she should show it to an antiquary, but she hadn't bothered.

The descent into Brussels National Airport
brought her back to staring out of the window.
She saw the straight, tree-lined roads, a motor-
way, a forest, and a pattern of houses and gar-
dens. The landing was bumpy and the tarmac
wet and shiny. Numerous rabbits strutted happily on the grass, oblivious to the great deafening
bird landing so close to them.

She was booked into the Westbury Hotel. She
had been told that it was above Brussels Central
Station, and that she could get a train direct to
there from the airport. But Peter had phoned to
say he would meet her, and she anticipated this
with a mélange of emotions. She picked up her
luggage and followed the Exit/*Sortie*/*Uitgang*
signs, passed in front of sleepy customs men,
and went into the crowds waiting for arriving
passengers.

He was there.

She saw him at the same time as he saw her.
They both smiled. He took her case and led her
to the car park, drove with a barrage of questions
to the Westbury Hotel in the centre of the city.
As he drove she sat beside him, surrounded by
an unexpected sense of peace.

'You have a reservation for Miss McGlinn?' he
said to the receptionist. 'The reservation was
made by ITU.'

'Yes. Would mademoiselle please fill in this
form?'

Dee complied, checking in her passport for the date and place of issue. The clerk handed her a key. 'Thank you, mademoiselle. Room 1406. Enjoy your stay.'

Peter pre-empted the bell-boy, carried her case to the lift, escorted her to the door of her room, commented with a laugh that the hotel had no thirteenth floor.

'Have you any plans for this evening?'

'No.'

'Dinner at eight — would that be OK? I could show you some of the city.'

'Thank you, but there's no need!' She knew this sounded prim, which she had not intended. In fact, she thought, the way she had said it sounded distrustful.

He frowned. 'There is need. I need to see you.' He seemed, without moving his eyes, to take her in from top to toe. 'I don't want to be a baby snatcher, but I want to see you. Trust me, Dee.' Dee watched him walk away.

Her room looked down on to the empty space in front of the station. It was occupied by a half-sunken car park; on the other side of this stood a black gothic church, the Église de la Madeleine. To the right and as a backstage setting were rows of Flemish gabled houses. Beyond those, at the back of the car park, she could see two spires and a square of roofs. She recognized Brussels' famous Grand Place.

Dee showered, unpacked, changed and, fully

refreshed, descended from her eyrie on the four-teenth floor.

She followed the map through pedestrian crossings, and then down a small side street, until she reached the Grand Place. It was closed to traffic that day. The flower-stalls were being dismantled. Dee examined the richly decorated façades of the ancient guild-houses, read the Flemish name, 'Groote Markt'.

She cut across a corner of the square to an imposing building called *Le Roi D'Espagne*. She had heard of this place, decided to have a coffee there, and walked in, up some wooden stairs and past a stuffed horse. A waiter came along dressed in a white, buttonless waistcoat.

'Un café au lait, s'il vous plaît.'

It arrived and she drank it slowly, watching the other customers, the students, the burghers of Brussels, the general ambience of the foreign. It was hard to believe that only a few hours ago her feet had trodden familiar ground some thousand miles away. She thought of Peter Eggli with butterfly anticipation. 'Trust me,' he had said. Everything in her wanted to trust him. She wanted to make amends. The one person she had ever met who captured all of her imagination — and she still treated him with suspicion. Tonight, she thought, tonight at dinner, I will give him the ring. What do I want it for? She put up her hand to feel it on its chain. I am sick of it; I am sick to death of it! He said to trust him. So I shall trust him. Let him do what he likes with it.

She felt as though a burden had been lifted. A decision had been taken. She would please him and be absolved. There was great pleasure in this prospect, and she sipped the coffee and looked out at the Groote Markt.

She went back to the Westbury by a circuitous route, following the map, taking in the Boulevard Anspach, animated by rumbling trams, the Place des Martyrs, where dirty, dilapidated buildings seemed to be empty, except for those used as warehouses. Here she took a shortcut.

The shortcut was a laneway, cobbled, running between silent, gabled buildings and one or two warehouses. Nobody was in sight. She calculated that she would be nearer the hotel when she came out at the far end, and it was fun to sample the old town. But the lane took a turn and she walked a bit further and then stopped. She felt as though the city had disappeared. All the noise, the background noise of a city about its business, had gone. She was like a time traveller, stuck suddenly in the Middle Ages; but a Middle Ages where everyone had died.

The cobbles rang when she moved. She was no longer sure of the way and turned to go back, but found her progress blocked. The man had emerged from nowhere and stood in the middle of the laneway, his arms on his hips and the dilated joy of the predator in his eyes.

'*Pardon,*' Dee said, trying to push past him. He did not move and he did not speak. But he smiled at her with the unhurried luxury of a cat considering a trapped mouse. He looked like a character from one of the old Dutch paintings; he was peculiarly dressed, had a medieval Flemish face, bulbous nose, and his eyes moved from her and fixed themselves on something or someone behind her. She heard footsteps and turned.

In retrospect it all seemed to have happened slowly. She knew that her perceptions had all been changed. She felt no pain. She saw the dark doorway of the old house open, yawn like a tomb. The floor was stone inside and women and men, dressed like something from a Brueghel painting, moved past her. She tried to scream, but no sound came. They, weary people, in costumes which would have been a joke had they not been so worn and lived-in, seemed impervious to her, as though she had been a ghost. The air was full of smells: manure, sweat, baking bread. She felt as though she knew this place and yet did not know it, like the shifting country of dreams.

'Go limp,' something said inside her. 'If you go limp you will not be hurt.'

She sank to the floor, felt the ring being ripped from the chain, and then the sounds and sights and smells disappeared. She was lying inside the open doorway of a disused warehouse. She saw the wooden beams in the ceiling with a curious sense of detachment, and was aware of the light coming from the door. She mentally vetted herself for injuries, but could find none. I'm alive, she thought. She put her hand to her throat but the ring was gone. She looked around for her shoulder bag and saw it a few feet away. I've been robbed, she thought, but I am alive!

When Dee got back to the hotel there was a message for her. Colin had phoned; it was urgent. She should get in touch with him as soon as possible. The receptionist looked at her with dismay. Was everything all right? Had mademoiselle met with an accident?

'I fell,' Dee said, rejecting the prompting to ask for the police. She felt she could not cope with the fuss. Her head was splitting. She wanted to lie down. 'It's all right. I fell!' But she recognized that there was also another reason. Somewhere at the back of her mind there was a kind of relief that the ring was gone.

Once safely back in her room she examined herself carefully. She ran a bath, vetted herself in the mirror. Her face was grimy where it had come into contact with the ground. Her right wrist was tender and had made her wince when she tried to turn on the taps. She had bruises to both knees and elbows. Her underclothes had not been disturbed. She had not been raped or sexually assaulted.

She got into the bath; she was trembling and the hot water closed over her body like a caress and a benediction. She knew she should report the matter to the police. She had been assaulted and robbed. But her wallet, complete with travellers' cheques and Belgian francs, was untouched in her bag. She couldn't bear the thought of a fuss. And then she remembered that Peter was coming at eight and that she could ask him what should be done. He would be anxious to recover what had been stolen; but for the moment she just wanted to be alone and safe. She stayed in the bath for a long time, letting in more and more hot water and watching her flesh redden.

She thought of Colin. She wouldn't phone him. Not now. In replying to his last letter she had given him the details of her Brussels trip. She had even, to amuse him, told him that she had found a diary dating back to 1919, in which the writer had a friend who had executed a portrait she called *My Magician*. Once she used to call Colin 'wizard': the two terms were similar and the tale therefore worth recounting. But what could be so urgent? If it really was urgent he would phone again.

She got out of the bath, pulled the curtains and went to bed. The phone woke her. Monsieur Eggli was here to see mademoiselle. 'Ask him to come up,' she said.

Peter knocked. When she asked who it was he said, 'Room service', with a mischievous accent. She let him in and saw how he raised his eyebrows to find her in a bathrobe.

'I'm sorry, Peter. I'm not dressed . . .'

His face became hard, watching her face which was bare of make-up, staring at the swelling which had come up on her cheek-bone.

'What happened? What has happened to you!'

She sat on the bed and tried to make light of it. 'I was attacked — nothing too serious — some bruises . . . But they stole the ring!'

Peter did not meet her eyes. His jaw worked and he came to take her in his arms. She leaned her head against his shoulder. 'Thank God you're here,' she whispered, the tears coming. 'I'm sorry for slobbering: it's the shock.'

Eggli did not question her at once. He sat on the edge of the bed and held her. 'Are you sure you are all right? Only bruised?'

'Yes. I had the ring. I was going to give it to you this evening. It's gone . . . Get the police if you want . . .'

Eggli did not move. 'Where did this happen?'

She tried to tell him, became confused.

'Shhh, don't upset yourself. I'm afraid the police are useless. But you may be in danger. You will have to come home with me!'

Dee sat back and looked at him. 'Why should I be in danger?'

'The same people who took the ring may assume you have the mask. You were probably followed back to the hotel.'

'But I'm safe here, aren't I?'

'Darling, this is a hotel. There is no way of vetting who goes where in a hotel of this size. With me you will be safe . . .'

'Darling!' To hear it in his mouth, to hear him address her as such! It came with a package, shivers of pleasure, the scent of the past and a promise for the future. But she shook her head.

'How can I go home with you? What about the hotel — I'm booked in here.'

He smiled. 'You are not in bondage to a hotel! You can always come back tomorrow. And, as for my place, there is no one there. There's only me.' He looked at her, made his little Gallic moue. 'And I promise not to eat you!'

Dee smiled shakily. 'You would find me tough!'

'Would I? Many things, my lovely Dee; gentle, sensitive, but not "tough". Strong perhaps, but not "tough". No, it's not the word for you.' He touched her cheek with his hand. It gave comfort.

'So, will you get dressed now and we can go home. I will cook you a supper. In my own modest way I am quite a good cook.'

Dee obeyed. She dressed in the bathroom and packed her overnight bag. They came out, got into his car and drove away, past the immense cathedral of St Michel and Ste Gudule, gothic, domineering, and very blackened with age.

He drove through evening streets to the suburbs, to his modern house with patio and large garden. There was a certain kind of bliss in trusting him, in allowing him to look after her. 'Trust all men,' her mother used to say, 'but cut the cards!' It seemed cynical advice, the sort of thing mothers would say to create some kind of axiom; the sort of thing, Dee thought, that a woman

337

would say who had never met a man like Peter Eggli.

He put the car in the driveway and led her in by the back door, into a blue-and-white tiled kitchen. He brought her through the kitchen into a hall, showed her upstairs to the guest room. It looked out on a front garden and a suburban road. There was a double bed, an antique wardrobe, a bureau with writing paper, old silver inkwell, a small bookstand with books in French and English. There was a mirror on the wall, and she stared at her reflection, examined the mark on her face which was already beginning to fade. The swelling had abated and this cheered her. Her blue eyes seemed dark, the pupils very black. But her skin had a pallor and seemed drawn.

When she came downstairs, Peter was waiting for her in the lounge, a big room which overlooked the back garden. It had a large fireplace, was furnished with modern pieces and an antique cabinet, richly carved. She sank back into an off-white settee.

'What would you like to drink?'

'Gin and tonic, if you have it.' She remembered the first time she had tasted it; Colin had bought it for her in a London pub. She longed for one, for the sense of the world backing away, for the encroaching sense of the ridiculous. He handed her the drink, iced and with a twist of lemon, poured one for himself. 'How are you feeling?'

'Much better!'

'Good . . . Are you hungry?'

'Not in the slightest.'

'You must eat something. How does poached salmon grab you?'

'Very nice, Peter — but don't go to any trouble.'

'Oh, it's terrible trouble . . .' He smiled, a secret smile. He seemed elated. He is very pleased to have me with him, she thought. Then her own thought followed; I am very happy to be with him. But she knew it was more than that; she knew that she was not just happy. She knew that she was excited to be with him. He went into the kitchen, and when she called after him to ask if she could help, he said she was to stay where she was. He came back, a teatowel over his shoulder, moved a pouffe and made her put her feet up on it.

'Dr Eggli is now in charge; would you like some music?' He moved to the radiogram in the corner, selected Bert Kaempfert's 'Swinging Safari', put it on the turntable. The music danced in the air; she felt the gin waltz through her veins. The soreness of elbows and knees abated. The night was falling outside, encroaching swiftly on the garden, swooping on the patio, held in check against the lighted window. Her body felt heavy, sinking into the cushions of the settee, remembering the events of the afternoon as though they had occurred in another lifetime.

Peter returned with a tray. 'Supper is served, madame!' He put the tray down on the coffee table, handed her a napkin and served her with salmon steak, lemon wedge, side salad. He put a basket of bread in the middle of the table and poured Chablis.

They ate, salmon and salad and, afterwards, little chocolate mousses full of sin. He brought the tray back to the kitchen, began to make coffee.

'Could we have coffee on the patio?' Dee called, thinking that the night air might clear her head.

'Why not?'

When she got up to go out to the patio she found her knees were stiff, her elbows beginning to hurt again.

'Are you in pain?' His solicitude was instant; he moved quickly to help her. She sat outside in the warm night, drank black coffee and let him hold her hand, running his palm along her forearm, touching her knee.

'How do you do it? You made the pain stop. I was wondering if I needed a doctor!'

'You have one,' he whispered. 'You will be better in the morning. Wait and see!'

She leant back and looked into the sky, saw the stars and the half moon dipping in and out of wispy cloud cover. He smoked a cheroot, watching her in the light from the window.

'What you are seeing,' he said, 'are the stars as they were fifty to a hundred years ago. They are so far away that it takes the light that length of time to reach us! We have no way of knowing if the stars we see are even still there!'

'Time fascinates me,' Dee whispered. 'It seems to tantalize us with a taste of life and then shut us away for ever — compartmentalized, slotted into our time frames, our own small cells of experience — while it goes heedlessly on. We are tantalized and then betrayed!'

He was silent. The smoke from his cigar was heady. Then he said, 'Time is only an illusion. It is part of us and we are part of it.'

'Perhaps everything, in fact, is part of everything else,' Dee said dreamily. 'Looking up at the sky I could imagine that!' Then she added suddenly, aware of his proximity, his subdued pleasure in her company, 'Peter?'

'What?'

'Why are you not upset that I have lost the ring? You wanted it, I know you did. It's gone! You say the police will not be able to help. You suggest I might be in danger. Yet you don't seem in the least concerned!'

He blew smoke into small rings which floated like haloes. 'I am not concerned about you because I have you safe. As for the ring, I am so grateful that you escaped unharmed that everything else pales into insignificance!'

He held her hand so tightly that it hurt, leaned back and looked at her. She sensed the mystery in him, the mystery of time and experience — so much that had been lived by him while she was still in pigtails. He knew the world; she was still a novice.

'I am falling in love with you,' she said after a moment. 'It frightens me very much — I used to love someone, but it was not like this!'

'Why should it frighten you?'

'Because I am not in control of it.'

He squeezed her fingers. 'You had a crush on the newspaper man?'

'Colin, yes . . . ! In fact he tried to contact me today.' She glanced at him to see if he were jealous, but other than the drooping of his eyelids, his face did not change. 'Oh,' he murmured, 'what did he want?'

'I don't know. He left a message to say it was urgent. But I didn't phone him back. Colin is an alarmist. He thinks the planet is up for grabs! He sees political intrigues and conspiracies in all major world events!'

'He is quite right.'

'He thinks that power is still filched from the people, notwithstanding democracy.'

'Right also . . . But you don't need this Colin to tell you that. Power belongs naturally with some. For the masses it is something they cannot handle.'

'So you think certain individuals are entitled to rule the roost?'

'Of course.'

'I don't agree with that. It's élitist and reactionary — and unscrupulous. I hope ITU is not imbued with that kind of ethos . . . although, come to think of it, Colin once warned me about someone in ITU he was "ferreting out the dirt on" — that was his expression — someone I should be wary of!'

'What was his name?' Peter asked conversationally. 'I probably know him.'

Dee tried to remember. Had Colin mentioned a name? 'I don't think he gave me a name. I'll ask him the next time I speak to him.'

'Where did you say this paragon worked?'

'*Daily Mail.*'

Dee felt the headache start at the base of her skull. The air had become noticeably cooler; there were goose-bumps on the skin on her forearms. She rubbed her forehead with her hand.

'Headache?'

She nodded.

After a moment she asked on impulse, 'Peter, if I found this mask you mentioned — it must be somewhere in Kilashane — if I gave it to you, what would you do with it?'

He didn't answer immediately, and Dee added, 'The question is hypothetical. I'm curious, that's all. Would you sell it?'

'No,' he said softly, 'the mask should be returned to where it came from.'

'It came from Venice.'

'You seem very sure!'

'I am sure, Peter. You see, I also found an old diary which mentions the thing. I found it in Kilashane. It was a diary belonging to someone called Yvonne O'Reilly. She was told it came from Venice.'

Peter was silent for a moment, and then he

whispered sadly, 'Yvonne O'Reilly? Is the diary interesting?'

'Yes. A window on the past.'

He pulled her to him, cradled her on his knee, her head bent under his chin, his arms holding her, his fingers gently massaging the nape of her neck. For a moment she felt like a child in the womb, surrounded by every possible requirement, tied into his life by some invisible umbilicus.

'Bedtime for you, my love!'

In the kitchen he gave her a tablet — 'It's for the headache; it will help you sleep' — and watched while she took it with some water. Then he came upstairs with her to the door of her room.

'Sleep well. You will be better in the morning.'

He hesitated, as though waiting to see if she would invite him in, but when she didn't he crossed the landing to his own bedroom. He glanced back and she saw something in his eyes, a flash of private speculation laced with triumph. It was only there for an instant. Then he smiled and she smiled back sleepily and shut the door.

It was still dark when she woke, surfacing from the dream, but it held on to her, dragging her down like a drowning person. She knew there was something beside her in the bed and she thought, in her dream-clogged state, that it was a huge black cat. But of course, when she put her hand out, there was nothing there. But the fear would not abate; it seemed to come from a place near her heart, like the source of a spring that welled and spilled through her whole being. The room was dim, but not in complete darkness, thanks to the summer night sky and the light from the street.

It took her a moment to realize she was in Peter's house, that he was in the room across the landing. She got up, pulled on her dressing gown and stumbled across the landing to his door.

It opened easily. She heard his breathing, which suddenly seemed to stop, as though he had wakened and knew there was an intruder. Then she heard his voice. 'Dee?'

She stood still. 'I had a nightmare of sorts — silly of me.' She was shivering with the remembered horror, and also with the sudden shock of finding herself in his room in the middle of the night.

He didn't answer for a moment, and she added in a half panic, wondering what he must think of her, 'I'm sorry. I'm still asleep. I shouldn't have come . . .'

'Of course you should!' He put out a hand and took hers, drawing her to the bed, lifting the covers so that she slipped in beside him. 'Cuddle up,' he said, as though he were talking to a child.

She did. She cuddled against him. At first there was relief from dread, so that she relaxed and her heartbeat returned to something like normality. But after a while the warmth of the bed, the warmth of his arm around her, the naked proximity of him, the stirring of his body against her, induced a state of sexual awareness such as she had not known. It was as though another person lived in her body who knew things that she did not. The touch of his skin and the scent of his breath were a language. She felt the tension ebb from her, felt the desire sweep everything away. She eased off her dressing gown and nightdress and let them fall to the floor.

'I am a virgin,' she whispered.

'I will be very, very gentle.'

Body spoke to body. He caressed her until she could bear it no longer and pulled him down on her. He entered her so gently that the only pain was on the final thrust, when he seemed to have lost control. This thrilled her, his loss of control, his vulnerability, as though he too had to have faith and yield.

'That was irresponsible of me,' he whispered in her ear. 'Are we safe?'

'Safe? Oh, you mean . . . Yes . . . I think so, yes.'

She kissed the hairs on his chest, his face, his neck, slid her hands down his back, feeling the coarse hair on either side of his spine, moved shy hands down to where he was beginning to stir again.

This time the pleasure came in waves, first small, slow surges towards the shore, then breakers rushing in fury, moving upwards, blasting everything from their path, finding her soul, twisting in her brain.

Afterwards she slept as though she had been shot. He lay beside her for some time, watching her face.

She woke fully some time later to the scent of grilling bacon. She put on her dressing gown and went downstairs. The light flooded the patio and the kitchen. The papers were on the table, the *Sunday Times* and *Observer*. He stood by the cooker, turning the rashers of bacon on the grill. The patio table was set with napkins and cutlery, a jug of orange juice. The garden seemed to smile.

'Good morning.'

He studied her teasingly. 'How are you feeling? You look much better. Did you sleep well?'

'Oh, Peter . . .'

He put down the spatula and came to her, held her head against him, ran his hands inside her dressing gown, pulled it down and bent to kiss the back of her neck. She pulled it back, suddenly on the verge of tears.

'I am not taking advantage of you; I am in love,' he said. 'Why are you so upset? Why do you flinch from me?'

'I have a dreadful mark — a scar . . . I don't want you to see it! I have been ashamed of it all my life!'

'You mean that little thing on your arm?'

She flushed. 'I thought you wouldn't notice it in the dark!' He pulled back the sleeve. The flesh of her right forearm was shiny with white scar tissue, the soft flesh underneath pitted and uneven.

'Where did you get this?'

'It happened in the lab in school. Sulphuric acid.'

'Tell me about it.'

'It was an experiment . . . it exploded. I can still hear the sound of the beaker shattering, still imagine the stuff coming at me in the air, as though it happened in slow motion. I thought it would hit my face, but I brought my arm up. Then I just stood there like an idiot, half paralysed, staring at the charring jumper and smelling the fumes. Mother Brid came and shoved my arm under the tap. But the damage had been done. For a while the doctor was afraid it had gone down to the bone.'

He bent and kissed the arm. 'Oil of vitriol,' he said. 'It has an infamous history!'

He turned off the cooker, took her hand, and led her upstairs to his room, drew her down on his bed, wrapped his arms around her. 'You will need a little surgery and it will be fine,' he said. 'We will get you the best plastic surgeon there is and all will be well.'

Her eyes filled with tears. 'My parents were told there would always be a mark, no matter what was done!'

'No. Not necessarily. No mark at all.'

Dee thought that all skeletons might as well come out of the closet. 'My name isn't really Dee, you know!'

'Short for Deirdre?'

'No. My real name is Désirée.'

He laughed gently. 'How lovely; how absolutely perfect! Desired One!' He pushed back her gown to seek her breast.

When she woke she was alone. The curtains were drawn. She was covered with a sheet and bedspread. She heard the sound of water coming from the bathroom.

She got out of bed, looked around for her dressing gown. There was no sign of it. She thought he might have hung it up, but it was not on the hook behind the door, so she opened one of the two built-in wardrobes. It took her a moment to register the row of women's clothes hanging there, a few business suits, silk shirts, dresses, an evening dress in jade green with sequins and cut-away shoulders. On the floor were several pairs of ladies' shoes. On the shelf were a selection of hats and two wigs. While she stared at this array, Dee saw the edge of a silver frame sticking out over the wardrobe ledge. She pulled it towards her and gazed in dismay at the happy trio: Peter with his arm around the shoulders of a young woman who held a child in her arms.

She replaced the photograph, turned back, trembling with the knowledge that what they had shared together had been retrospectively bastardized.

Peter came out of the bathroom, reappeared with a towel around his waist. The smile died on his face.

'Dee,' he said in a tone of command, 'don't

look at me like that.'

'Get me a taxi.'

'Why?'

'Just do!'

'You are being ridiculous. You are not going in that state. What's wrong? What's happened?'

Dee turned on him in fury. 'No one tells me where I can go. Don't imagine for one moment that I have become your possession!'

He raised his shoulders and dropped them. 'Please let me drive you back.'

'Will you get me a taxi or will I phone for one myself?'

'May I see you again?'

She shook her head, went back to her room and dressed, throwing her effects carelessly into her holdall. As she was doing so, he came into the room with her dressing gown. 'This was under the bed.'

Dee could not trust herself to speak. 'Dee,' he said, 'I can explain if you will let me!'

She recovered her voice. 'No! No more lies. I never want to see you again.' When the taxi came she got into it. She knew he waited at the open door, but she drove away without looking back.

The driver watched her in his rearview mirror and saw that she wept. He remembered how she had left the house, remembered the man who had stood at the door, remembered how she had neither looked back nor waved. *'Chagrin d'amour,'* he said knowledgeably to himself, and did not offer any conversation.

When she got back to the hotel she asked if there were any messages. Yes, Mr Weaver had phoned again. Would she phone him at this number as soon as possible. Dee put the number in her pocket and when she had regained her room placed a call. But there was no response at the other end. She was about to call his paper when she remembered it was Sunday.

She lay on the bed, trying to contain the fury of her jealousy. It sprung from the fear that, while she had given truly of herself, he had merely been picnicking; it surged from a certainty of rejection; it burned with self-hatred. 'He said he wasn't married,' she whispered over, as though she were trying to convince some judgmental bystander. 'He said he wasn't.' It suddenly struck her — Colin had warned her against someone high up in ITU. What if it had been Peter? 'I haven't got all the dirt on him yet,' he had said. She also thought of what Charlie had said. 'Don't trust him, Dee; he's not what he seems.'

I want to go home, she thought miserably, burrowing into the pillows. I just want to go home to Ballyshane.

Chapter Fifteen

'Your beauty shall not save you, Woman.'
'Only you can save me, but you will not.'

Journal of a Witness

Yvonne woke early, but Theo had already risen.
She put out her hand but the bed, which was old
— a four-poster with a deep, voluptuous mattress
— was empty. She heard the murmur of the sea;
something she was beginning to get used to, although at first it had disturbed her, seeming almost human with the variety and levels of its
voices.

The light came dimly through the thick
old-gold curtains, and she made out the pictures
— a watercolour, a few prints, an oil painting of
roses in a great bowl: satin petals on the shining
surface of a table. There was a picture of a lady in
a stylized gown, a band around her forehead to
contain her hair, a hound at her side, inclining
dreamily into the distance. The wardrobe by the
window was massive mahogany, inlaid with walnut. There was a long mirror on the door, and
she could see herself in it, or at least see her head
and shoulders and part of the bed. Theo liked
turning to this mirror when they made love.
When they were naked on the bed he would

sometimes regard their reflection in the lamp-light, and she would stare at the sensuality in his face. And then he would suddenly desist, move away from her with a curt apology.

The other furniture in the room was also Victorian, a dressing table in rosewood, a mahogany commode with a china chamber-pot, a thick old Indian carpet, worn through to the weave inside the door. There was a smell of camphor. On the black marble mantelpiece was a small clock, also in marble, supported by dancing bronze nymphets. Last night's fire had died and the ashes in the grate were yellow-white. Rough sods of turf lay in a heap in a brass box by the hearth.

She knew the house now, knew how its old timbers creaked at night, knew the people who lived there: Theo's mother who was reserved but kind; his sister Kate, who seemed so placid but who burned with some kind of private ire; the cook, Una, who was all talk and sense; Brigid the housemaid, who was shy; and Batty the groom, who had a cottage nearby and who was very impertinent.

She had also come to know something of the political turmoil in the county: there was unrest in the air, something covert, like a storm building in silence and waiting to unleash itself.

She lay still, aware of the weight of the blankets, the smooth feel of linen sheets, the lace edging of the pillow-cases and the long bolster. She was wearing one of her modest white night-gowns with buttons at the breast. The buttons were closed. Last night Theo had come to bed very late but he had not attempted to touch her.

Yvonne admitted to herself that she did not know him. She saw how his mother watched him with troubled eyes and his sister constantly attempted to jog his memory with pieces of family history and anecdotal nonsense. Theo would nod and smile and evince recollection, and there was something in his demeanour which discouraged either his parent or his sister from pushing against the barriers of his recollections. If Theo said he remembered something, they let it go at that. If he never volunteered his own piece of childhood history, his own angle on an episode under discussion, no one seemed to remark on it. She had told no one of the night when he had come to bed the worse for drink, with fire-red eyes and acrid breath and had shaken her awake, weeping and babbling: 'For the love of God, do something . . .'

She had cradled him in her arms and then he had fallen asleep. But in the morning he appeared to have no memory of the night before: he was urbane and cool and insisted on having her dress in front of him while he sat up in bed and watched her every move with silent appraisal.

Yvonne had rebelled. 'I don't want to dress while you watch me like that.'

'Why not? Do you think you are here for your little middle-class hesitancies?'

'Theo! I am your wife.'

'And is that supposed to unman me?'

Yvonne felt the anger rise in her. 'Unman you? You don't behave like a real man. You tease and watch me. You neither love me nor make love to me! All you want to do is titillate yourself. I'm a woman, not some sort of light switch!'

Theo's face did not register a response. 'Impressive,' he murmured. 'Come here then and be a woman.' He reached out his hand and pulled her towards the bed, divested her of her knickers and lay on her, entering her roughly so that she cried out in pain.

He did not invite or wait for any response from her body, and when he was satisfied he drew away from her, left the bed, reached for his crutch and went to the dressing room.

Yvonne lay in silence. The tears came. Her mind scanned possible reasons for his behaviour. Was he sexually disoriented; was he frustrated at his inability to find his true self; was he just an insensitive and brutal man? She expected him to emerge contrite from his dressing room, but when he did not, it occurred to her that she was, perhaps, expected to behave like someone conquered, so she put on her kimono and went after him. He was seated, his elbow rested on his right thigh, his head bent low. His fingers gripped his hair.

'That was horrible!' she said.

He looked up at her. 'Yes,' he said. 'I'm sorry. I don't know what came over me. Do you want to go back to bed and we'll see if we can do better?'

He reached up, touched her face, and traced the track of the tears. 'You are angry,' he whispered. 'Shall we see how we can marshal outrage to your pleasure? There is nothing quite like outrage to fuel ecstasy.'

Yvonne drew back. 'How dare you?' she said angrily. 'Sometimes I think you are the devil.'

'No more so than most men.'

'I *loved* you!'

'I know. You thought you could control a man you pitied, a poor wreck of a creature, and therefore you loved him. But, my little dear, was it the man you loved or the control? Was it the power of being able to order his life, to wrap him up and mummify him, or the person trapped and incoherent? Think! Women spend their lives in self-delusion, incapable of facing facts. That is why they are reduced to the status of pawns!'

Yvonne was silent. She recognized the truth in what he said and also the shallowness of the perception. Men did not have a monopoly of the 'facts'. At least half the 'facts' did not belong to them at all.

'You know nothing of women. You judge them by the meagre values of men.'

She was surprised at the bitter rapidity of her retort. In the mirror she saw Theo's arrested expression, and the sudden glimmering of respect.

He smiled. The smile transformed his face, filled it with boyishness. 'You have much to forgive,' he murmured after a moment, taking her hand and putting the palm against his lips. 'Will

you forgive, do you think? Can you forgive me?'
Yvonne's anger melted. She regarded the bent
head in the mirror, the bony angle of jaw, as yet
unshaven, the strong tense neck, the sudden ab-
jectness in his posture. Hope and relief rose in
her.

He was still suffering, and she should be more
understanding. All the training of her life had led
her to proffer understanding.

'Of course,' she whispered. 'Of course I do.'

Theo's face darkened. He looked up and their
eyes met in the mirror. His were full of disappointment and contempt. 'In that case, little girl,
you are an idiot! How dare you forgive the unfor-
givable! Do you not realize how boring, how offensive, it is to be "forgiven"?'

Yvonne stared back at him for a moment and
then she turned and left the dressing room.

'Yvonne, do you think Theo is improving?'
Mrs O'Reilly asked at lunchtime. Theo had sent
word to say he would have his meal in his room;
the three women sat at the dining table and were
waited on by Una.

Kate looked at her mother and then at her
sister-in-law, with the air of one listening carefully for her reply.

Yvonne, who was still tense from the morning's exchanges with her husband, burst into
tears. 'I don't know. I just don't know . . .'

'I didn't mean to upset you, dear,' Mrs
O'Reilly said, drawing back in the chair and

357

looking at her with concern. Yvonne looked across the table at Kate. The latter wore a compassionate expression, her head slightly to one side, and seemed to indicate by the quick glance at her mother and the frown between her eyes that she should not say any more.

Yvonne wiped her eyes and apologized. 'I'm being silly. I'm sorry.'

Mrs O'Reilly let the subject drop. She ate sparingly of the roast chicken, and left the table before dessert, saying she would be in her room, that she had letters to write. The two young women picked at rice pudding and jam before Kate asked Yvonne if she would come to the drawing room.

The drawing room overlooked the circular lawn with its carriage drive, its monkey puzzle tree, its row of evergreen cypresses which shut out the view of the sea, so that you could imagine you were simply in a country house with miles between you and the coast. Yvonne sat on the sofa near the window and watched the rain begin to spit at the pane. The curtains were looped back with satin-like ropes in dark green with heavy tassels, and the curtains themselves were of a heavy green material, shot through with turquoise. The furniture smelt of beeswax.

Kate shut the door and moved across the room towards her with a half smile of apology.

'I don't want you to think that I'm going to interrogate you about your husband. But, Yvonne, Theo was never like this, you know,' Kate said in her quiet voice, while her eyes followed the thin needles of rain slanting into the grass.

Yvonne heard the rolling r's of her sister-in-law's voice, which rose and fell in a way that she had come to love.

'What was he like?'

Kate studied her. 'Gentle and funny and a bit of a boy. He was bossy to me — the elder brother. But he was never . . . like *this*.'

'Like what?'

Kate sighed. 'Forceful, abrupt . . . domineering. Even rude.' She glanced at Yvonne to ascertain if she were offended, but when she saw that she was not she added, 'Was he like this when you met him first?'

Yvonne thought of the first time she had seen him, a thin, lost young man, who liked to quote poetry feverishly, as though the cadence of the sounds gave him something to latch on to; a hero, a man made vulnerable by war. It was his vulnerability which had attracted her. Theo had been perfectly correct in that, but his jibe of the morning still rankled.

'No,' she answered slowly. 'He was sweet; a bit lost, a bit fearful . . .'

'How was he fearful?'

'Oh, he was afraid of many things, starting at shadows, jumping at the rattle of trolleys. I remember that on the day he asked me to marry him . . .' Her voice trailed away in recollection, a recollection which seemed bizarre and which she did not want to express, principally because she felt that her own reaction to it had been silly.

'What happened?' Kate persisted.

'He drew a design on the gravel around us with his stick. As though he wanted to keep something out, or in . . . I didn't realize it until I looked back when we were moving away.'

'What did he draw?'

Yvonne raised her eyes to her sister-in-law's face. 'He drew a pentacle.'

Kate's face was expressionless. 'What did you do?'

'Nothing. But later I came back and rubbed it out with the toe of my shoe.'

Kate started and looked away. 'There was a sort of Theosophical Society in Dublin. He joined it when he went up to Trinity. He used to go to séances. He tinkered in spiritualism. He got involved in it after he became a bit obsessed with something he encountered in his history studies, something to do with the Inquisition. But he was quite cheerful about the spiritualism, referred to it as a joke. He told me once that everything, past and present, life and death, are all interrelated. Anyway, I think he felt none of it could touch him — he was the quintessential student, an observer in a privileged little capsule. Until the last time he came home, the summer before the war . . .'

Yvonne sat in silence, hearing the rain. The turf fire whispered; the wind whistled a little around the corner of the house and moaned up the front steps. Under it could be heard a steady, persistent sound — the heavy, eternal, swish of the sea. She felt a sense of aloneness pervade her, fill all the spaces of mind and spirit. She remembered how Theo had ranted about the Inquisition to the hospital chaplain. She remembered his proposal to her in the shrubbery, and how she had looked into a halcyon future. Suddenly she longed for London, for busy streets, the whirl and clatter of traffic; anywhere away from this place and these people with their eyes focused on the past and on the bitter lees of the human soul. She glanced at Kate, but the latter was staring towards the fire, frowning, seemingly lost in thought. I'm English, she thought. There is something here I cannot access. It is not explicable; it cannot be learned. And what I bring here is wasted. The culture I come from is almost invisible in this place. They are all searching for something else, the zest of the spirit, the twist of the spoken word so that it dances or homes to the quick. Even when they are clowning, they are looking out from under their wretched peaked caps at the poor fool who takes them at face value. I may as well be a Martian. They are polite to their Martian, but that's all there is to it!

Aloud she said, 'Kate, I'm an anomaly here. Maybe I should go home. I don't fit in. I try, but no matter what I do . . .'

Kate turned at once and looked at her, her expression full of dismay. She saw that her sister-in-law was crying silently and she crossed the carpet and knelt beside her.

'Dear Yvonne, I know you must be so home-sick. Please don't leave us. It would serve Theo right, but what would I do? It would be terrible! I think I would go mad!' She paused. 'I know, why don't you invite your friends to stay? Mother has already told you how welcome they would be. Please . . .'

'I have asked them.'

Yvonne tried to compose herself, but the turmoil within continued.

'Is it because I'm English?' Yvonne persisted through her tears. 'I heard Batty going on about what England had done to Ireland. He was whispering, and so full of anger . . .'

Kate stopped, shook her head, smiled; a smile full of humour and a sort of quizzicality which said, 'What's this nonsense . . . ?'

'Batty loves the sound of his own voice. We love you. The sins of the past belong to the past. What on earth have they got to do with you? They have no more to do with you than they have to do with me.'

'They're not in the past,' Yvonne whispered. 'Look what has been going on recently. Look at what the papers are reporting . . .'

Kate took out her handkerchief and sat beside her sister-in-law, offering it to her. 'You're looking for reasons because you are unhappy.' She lowered her voice. 'Your problem is Theo and him alone.'

Yvonne summoned the courage to ask, 'What happened that summer before the war?'

As though he knew he was topical, Theo could be heard descending the stairs, the uneven gait, the small thud of the artificial limb on each step. They then heard him cross the hall, a thump of his stick on the tiles, and then the door was opened and he was framed in the doorway. He stood erect, his palm hard upon the handle of his stick, and regarded the two young women.

'Aha,' he said in a note of cheerful mockery, 'what a charming tableau. But don't stop whispering just because I came in.'

Kate rose. 'We weren't whispering,' she said equably. 'And, even if we were, your good manners should have killed that comment before you made it. You have changed greatly, dear brother, and not for the better!'

Theo smiled, hung his head a little in mock contrition. 'And you, dear little sister. Were you always so acerbic? Did you usually address your brother, your elder brother, in this fashion? Is there no change in you?' When Kate did not answer he added, 'I thought I would go riding. I was wondering if my lovely wife would care to accompany me?'

'You can't go riding!' Kate said flatly.

'Why not?'

'You could meet with an accident!'

Theo's face darkened. 'A cripple can meet with an accident at any moment,' he said. 'So can you, for that matter. But I am going riding.'

He turned to Yvonne. 'Will you come? I will

show you how to ride.'

Yvonne looked at Kate. Panic rose in her. She did not want to go riding. She was afraid of horses at close quarters. But she did not want to cross Theo, not yet. Allowances were still to be made; patience was to be exercised as a force, as a means to an end. Let him think it was submission.

'All right,' she said. 'But will you wait until the rain stops?'

'Give her one of your habits,' Theo commanded his sister, and Kate rose and indicated to Yvonne to come with her.

'Don't ride if you don't want to,' the latter whispered when they reached the landing. 'Don't let him bully you. He can't ride either with that leg; but he'll have to find that out for himself!'

In the stable yard, Batty came forward to meet his master, tipping his cap and making some comment about the weather.

'Grand soft day, Master Theo.'

The rain had eased, as though it had agreed some kind of truce for the moment, and the day had brightened marginally. The air was washed and smelt of soft earth and new green things. Batty was uneasy in his master's company, looking for the old easy badinage and not finding it. Theo had visited the stables only once since his return. He had barely spoken. Batty felt he did not even remember him. Yet now here he was, dressed in jodhpurs and boots, looking for all the world like someone eager for the hunt.

'I'm going out for a bit of a gad. I want to teach Mrs O'Reilly how to ride. Do we have a lady's horse?'

'Miss Kate's grey — Polly — you remember her . . . she's good as gold. Will you be able to — ?'

'I will,' Theo said curtly. 'Saddle up . . . my usual animal!' Batty turned aside and then glanced back at Theo from under his dirty peaked cap. 'My usual animal!'

'You mean Caesar, Master Theo?' he said, indicating a chestnut hunter who was munching hay and staring out at them haughtily above his half door. 'But he's desperate frisky after the winter. Do you know — he wouldn't let anyone ride him when he was lent out by your mother while you were at the war. The O'Kellys sent him back and said he was a jade.'

Theo did not seem interested.

Yvonne appeared in a black riding habit at the back door. She hung back, watching Theo as he tried to mount the horse. He got his left leg in the stirrup and was helped up by Batty, but almost came to grief trying to fling his wooden leg over the horse's back. Batty came to the rescue, and when Theo was mounted, Yvonne came forward nervously across the yard.

She saw the chestnut hunter champ on the bit and skitter under his rider, his hooves ringing off the cobbles. Theo put his hand on the animal's

365

neck and he quietened, quivering along his flanks. Yvonne obeyed Theo's instructions and went to the mounting block, where Batty told her to hold the reins in her right hand, put her left foot in the stirrup, grasp the saddle, and jump on to the mare's back, hooking her right knee around the saddle 'crutch'. She obeyed. Her face was strained and her body was tense, but she complied with all instructions and then sat while Batty shortened the stirrup leathers and tightened the girths, thumping each horse in the stomach as he did so to make it exhale.

He turned to his master with a grim face. 'Ye can't ride with that leg, ye'll take a fall,' he blurted as Theo urged his mount forward, calling to Yvonne to follow. 'Ye'd be better off with a side-saddle.'

'God damn the fellow,' Theo said under his breath as they moved off. 'God blast his impertinence.'

Yvonne looked back at Batty and saw that his face was full of genuine concern, followed by open, smiling, admiration. He loves him, she thought with surprise. Batty, crusty and all as he was, sarcastic and all as he was, loved his master.

After a while, Theo turned to his wife and saw the discomfort with which she tried to sit up straight; her body was twisted by the sidesaddle.

'How are you finding it?'

'It's hell,' Yvonne said crossly, feeling that she had exhibited enough forbearance for one day.

'The small of my back is hurting. It's hell.'

Theo smiled grimly. 'It may be unpleasant, difficult, unusual, a source of backstrain, demanding new skills, but it is not "hell". Of that I can assure you.'

'How do you define hell?' she asked, trying to read what she could see of his face, and thinking of what Kate had told her earlier.

He was silent for a moment. 'Hell is wherever I am. I carry it with me.'

'Who are you, Theo?' she asked suddenly. 'Whom have you become? Why do you carry hell with you?'

He turned his head to look at her. 'My, my, we do take life seriously, don't we! What would you like me to say? That I am the devil incarnate? That I am suffering from some personality disorder? Or perhaps I am simply myself, and you, my dear Yvonne, cannot accept me. Have you thought of that — that you cannot accept me?'

Yvonne was silent. She felt the anger rise inside her. How dare he answer her question by shifting the entire responsibility for their relationship on to her?

'I am not an acceptance machine,' she said coldly. 'You would do well to remember that!'

Theo glanced at her. 'No,' he said gently after a moment. 'You are the best and bravest of women. Do you think I do not know? Except that I am not necessarily swayed any more by either the good or the brave!'

Yvonne watched him without turning her

head. She saw the tic at his mouth, and when she glanced at him she saw that he was frowning. She immediately assumed he was trying desperately to recall some time or thought or act which had brought them together.

'I do love you, Theo, and not for any of the reasons you might scorn. But I also have a duty to myself, and I will remember it.'

He smiled. 'You had your chance to leave me, and you refused,' he said reasonably. 'You shall not have it again!'

Yvonne sat as straight as she could. Inside something was screaming, Love me! Why can't you love me? Here I am, young, pretty, your wife. I have trusted you; I have left my family, friends and country for you. I am a stranger here and I need you. Why have you changed? What is to become of me?

Theo seemed to be immersed in a brown study. He sat with his shoulders back, his elbows close to his sides, his old tweed hacking jacket hugging his lean body.

'Don't love me,' he said softly, as though he had been able to hear her thoughts. 'Don't love me and don't trust me!'

'If I can neither love nor trust you, Theo, I cannot stay with you!'

He turned his head. 'You cannot go either! You see, I have taken you prisoner!'

Yvonne tried and failed to see his face. He rode a little in front of her, so that all she could see was the back of his head.

They were approaching the parish church. It was built of limestone, had a small spire and a bell. Beside it was the graveyard, dominated by a huge crucifix, on which the dead Christ was nailed, bleeding at breast, wrist and ankles. Yvonne surveyed the scene in silence. She saw the Celtic crosses and the old slabs and the long grass and here and there the poppies, bowing their scarlet heads.

'Are your people buried here?'

'Yes. There is a crypt which bears the family name.'

'Shall we be buried here?'

He started. 'I thought you were a Protestant!'

Yvonne did not pursue the question. 'Is there a Protestant church?'

'About eight miles away.' He pointed with his riding crop. 'In that direction. Altogether, about thirteen miles from the house. Do you wish to attend the service there?'

'Perhaps sometime. But I am quite willing to go to Mass with you if you would like it.'

Theo gave a derisive snort. Yvonne heard the footsteps approach behind them and, turning, saw it was a priest.

'Hello, hello,' he said heartily to Theo. 'I've been meaning to call.' He looked curiously at Yvonne. 'And this must be your lovely lady?'

Theo stiffened. 'This is my wife, Yvonne.'

'I'm very pleased to meet you,' the priest said, reaching up and taking her hand. 'Everyone is talking about the lovely young bride Master

O'Reilly brought home.'

Yvonne said, 'How do you do, Father?' She studied the small, rotund priest, but saw that his eyes were searching and that the fact that Theo could not remember his name and that he had not addressed him as 'Father' had not been lost on him.

'I hope you're not forgetting to come to Mass on Sundays!' he said to Theo with a wry smile.

The mare lunged suddenly for the grass in the ditch, and Yvonne felt the reins being torn from her hands. She retrieved them before they could fall over Polly's ears. She glanced at her husband and saw that his eyes had narrowed and were regarding the priest with cold speculation.

'When I want mumbo-jumbo I'll ask for it!' he said coldly. The priest took a step back as though he had been struck, but he frowned and his eyes narrowed. Then he turned on his heel and walked away.

Yvonne sat miserably, watching the black-clad back retreating towards the presbytery. How much more of this, she wondered, would Theo go on dishing out?

'Why were you so offensive?' she whispered. 'He was just trying to be friendly.'

Theo gestured in exasperation. 'Those fellows are all presumption. Next thing you know he'd be calling on me.'

After a moment, Yvonne asked, 'Are you going to show me the crypt?'

'No!'

When they moved off again, Yvonne said, 'Theo?'

'Yes?'

'Let me go!'

'You don't mean that,' he said, without turning his head. 'And even if you did, you know the answer. Besides, I need you here!'

They returned to the house in virtual silence. Theo dismounted easily in the stable yard, and Theo put up his hand to help his wife. She stood shakily, holding on to his arm for support.

'My back is killing me!'

He looked into her eyes. His own were hooded, veiled behind black lashes. 'We overdid it for the first lesson. What you need, my little Sassenach, is rest.'

Chapter Sixteen

'You are enslaved to the Evil One.'
'I refuse all enslavements.'

Journal of a Witness

Theo became autocratic, ruled the household with a voice which was never raised; even his mother seemed afraid of him. He said constantly that Yvonne was poorly, that she must keep to her room, that she must rest.

He was even more insistent on this after the parish priest had visited. The latter came on the day following their meeting with him at the graveyard. Theo was out at the time and the priest, introduced by Mrs O'Reilly as Father Keane, was entertained in the drawing room. He drank sherry, spoke to Kate with a certain badinage, under which concern of some kind was discernible, and asked Yvonne if she had enjoyed her ride of yesterday.

'It was my first time on a horse,' Yvonne said. 'I'm still stiff . . .'

He smiled. 'Ah well, it takes a bit of getting used to.'

Mrs O'Reilly rang for tea and Una brought it, with buttered slices of rich boiled cake. The priest was appreciative. Yvonne saw how assiduous her mother-in-law was as hostess. Yvonne was too sensitive to assert her own position, but she was glad that the priest had called, because he brought with him a breath of the outside world. He talked of parish matters, the illness of one of the tenants who had contracted scarlet fever, the draining of a certain stretch of land, the events in other parts of the country. He sat near the fire and seemed in no hurry to go. And Mrs O'Reilly was evidently in no hurry for him to leave; she seemed to hang on his every word.

'How is himself?' Father Keane asked eventually. 'I met him yesterday with his good lady here, but he didn't seem to have much of a welcome for me.'

Yvonne flushed. 'He hasn't been himself for some time,' she said and then, feeling immediately that she was in no position to speak in relative terms, knowing Theo as she had for such a short period, added, 'Well, I think he's changed, but I really have only known him for a short time. He's changed since we first met.'

The priest turned to his mother. 'Do you find him changed?'

Mrs O'Reilly glanced at Kate. 'I find him so altered as to almost be a different person,' she said after a moment in a hollow voice. 'He is not like my son. Sometimes I think the war took my boy and left me a changeling!'

'How was he after you came back from Italy?'

'He seemed unusually quiet,' she said. 'But I

put that down to his father's death. And then the war came and he was gone to it before I could look around.'

'Did you bring anything back with you from your travels — anything unusual that could have fired his imagination?'

Mrs O'Reilly seemed surprised. 'I brought back various purchases: some clothes, shoes; and presents, souvenirs.' She looked at Kate with raised eyebrows. 'Did I bring back anything which could have precipitated — ?'

'No,' Kate interjected. 'Of course you didn't.'

'And your late husband?' the priest continued. 'Did he acquire anything strange.'

'Not that I know of. He was very involved with some old story he encountered while we were abroad. He had long discussions about it with Monsignor Dillon, who travelled with us.'

'Was that Jim Dillon from Limerick?' Father Keane demanded, and when his hostess nodded he added, 'We were at Maynooth together. Well, well! Small world!'

'What makes you ask about all this?' Kate asked the priest. 'Why should anything my parents might have acquired on their travels affect my brother?'

'Well,' Father Keane said, 'I don't know whether you realise it or not, but Theo became very caught up, even obsessed, with some historical event — something which happened in Italy a long time ago — which he had chanced upon during the course of his studies. He used to question me about it because the details were lost. He said the Church hid the truth of the matter. When I did some private research, I found this to have been true, but there was a compelling reason . . .'

'What reason, Father?' Kate demanded. 'Why should the Church conceal anything? I thought it was the bastion of truth!'

'Because, in this case,' Father Keane said mildly, 'it involved someone — an ordained priest, a very troubled soul — whose spirit was thought to be still at large. Some things are better left in peace.'

'Where was this "troubled soul" supposed to have come from?' Mrs O'Reilly asked in a low voice.

'Venice.'

There was silence for a moment. Mrs O'Reilly frowned and sank back in her chair. Yvonne thought of the ring Theo always wore, which Kate had told her had been sent to him from Venice. She wanted to mention it, but a glance at Kate, who seemed to be struggling with some demon of her own, kept her silent.

'Why was he a troubled soul?' Kate demanded after a moment, 'this fellow whose spirit is supposed to be still at large?'

Father Keane gestured. Yvonne could see that he was uncomfortable with the subject and sorry that he had raised it. 'He lived in troubled times,' he answered.

'Was he a good spirit or a bad spirit?' Kate demanded with an arch expression and a trace of mockery.

The priest regarded her without expression. 'Well, my sources say that anything which belonged to him would bring . . . very bad luck, would even be . . . dangerous.'

'Dangerous in what way?'

'In so far as it would alter perception, change the way people think, affect their grip on reality.'

He studied Kate's scornful face for another moment. 'You see,' he added, 'he was probably one of the most evil men who ever lived.'

When Father Keane was leaving, Yvonne overheard him say to Kate, in a tone half-way between paternalism and gentle remonstrance, 'Will we be seeing you at Mass next Sunday, Kate?' Kate was pale, but her face assumed a haughty expression which Yvonne found incomprehensible, and then she turned away.

Yvonne followed the priest down the steps and spoke as he was about to get into his trap. 'Theo's father did send something back from Venice to him,' she whispered. 'He sent him a ring. Kate told me. He always wears it now. It has a strange design: an M with serpents, a face like a mask.'

She saw the priest start, saw how hard his face became. 'Get it from him,' he murmured. 'Get it from him for everyone's sake.' He fastened his eyes on something behind her, and when she turned she saw Theo coming across the lawn.

The priest seemed to make a deliberate effort to collect himself. He nodded to Theo. 'Be careful,' he whispered to Yvonne as he untethered the pony. 'Remember I'm here if you need me.' Then he got into the trap and was gone.

'What did he want?' Theo demanded, staring after the trap as it disappeared down the avenue.

'Just a social call,' Yvonne said unsteadily.

'No such thing with these fellows,' Theo said silkily. 'I told you he'd descend on us. I don't want to see you talking to him again.'

This injunction suited Yvonne very well. The more she thought about the priest's conversation, the more bizarre the content seemed.

After that, Theo was suspicious and increasingly domineering. And yet, sometimes there was something else in his manner, some hint of the Theo she had first known, like an echo or the scent of something loved and lost. It was as though she had contracted to marry one person, and had got his radically different twin brother instead. She mourned for the one, but in spite of herself she found the other challenging and increasingly fascinating. He possessed a vitality which made her feel she had spent her whole existence in a vacuum. And although, when they were together, she found her perceptions challenged, her pulse faster, her mind racing, she knew that something was wrong. She slept half the day and would wake to sleep again. 'Yvonne is not well,' he would say to his mother in the mornings, and she would order a tray sent up and then come herself to inquire how her daughter-in-law felt, her unspoken question as to the reason for her indisposition hanging between them in the air.

'What is the matter?' Kate had asked straight out, coming in with her lunch tray. 'Are you expecting?' Kate's voice was always low on these occasions, as though she were afraid of being overheard. For a few days Yvonne had indeed thought she might be pregnant, but was disappointed.

However, when a letter arrived from London to say that Jenny and Andrew had accepted the invitation to visit and would arrive the following week, Theo's demeanour softened. He acquired a muted air of satisfaction, but, when the day of their arrival came, he refused to allow his wife to accompany him when he went in the trap to collect their guests at the station. He gave the weather as an excuse. 'You'd catch cold; you're looking peaky anyway.'

'I'm not peaky. Haven't we macintoshes?'

But he was not to be persuaded.

It was a terrible day. The driving rain drenched the lawn and the gravel driveway and puddled in small pools. The peonies which had bloomed in a sheltered corner were battered by the downpour and dropped blood-red petals on to the grass. The wind whipped through the monkey puzzle and bent the cypresses, which swayed this way and that as the gusts changed direction.

Yvonne got up after Theo's departure and dressed in anticipation of the visitors' arrival. When she saw the trap return from the station, driven by a grim Batty who had his head down against the wind, she went downstairs and out into the driveway to greet her brother and oldest friend. The downpour had stopped and she ran out of the front door and across the wet gravel to where Batty was reining in the pony. There they were, Andrew and Jenny, in dripping macintoshes. She felt like crying; the emotion rose in her throat and she tried to stifle it, but her eyes filled as Theo handed Jenny down and Andrew stepped down behind her. In some strange way she had begun to suspect that they no longer existed, that nothing existed outside Kilashane, except the elements.

'Jenny!'

Jenny was wearing a hat, and a double-breasted navy blue coat to match which could be glimpsed under the mac. She had got thin, but she seemed excited — by her journey and by the elements, Yvonne assumed.

For her own part Jenny *did* feel well, almost triumphant, like someone released from irons and allowed to feel the wind and see the sky. Her face was polished by the squall and she was laughing, tasting the rain in her mouth, tossing over in her mind the knowledge that Theo was here, that he was just Yvonne's husband who had collected them at the station, that she need never have worried. She embraced her friend.

'Yvonne, I can't believe it . . . I thought we would never get here. Secretly I believed that you had gone to live on another planet.'

'I felt the same,' Yvonne said. 'But here you are!' She gestured at the wind in the treetops. 'And you have been accorded a special introduction to Ireland!'

Jenny looked around, her eyes dwelling on the house and the sweep of the drive. She raised her eyebrows and smiled. 'It's all rather grand, isn't it?'

Yvonne saw it through Jenny's eyes. It *was* all rather grand, and for the first time it occurred to her that she had something here to be proud of. A fresh gust of wind sneaked through the shelter of the trees and lifted Andrew's hat into the air, where it sailed away for several yards before being caught among the branches of the monkey puzzle tree. Everyone laughed.

'Don't worry,' Theo said. 'Batty will fetch it!'

Batty, who had put up the step, shut the door of the trap, and was about to carry in the luggage, did not seem overly enthusiastic, but he nodded, put down the two heavy suitcases, and stood underneath the monkey puzzle as though his mere presence would encourage the tree to yield up to him the spoils of the storm.

'Get a broom or something, you imbecile,' Theo shouted at him, and Batty threw his master a sidelong glance, muttered something to himself about it taking one to know one, and went off around the corner of the house into the stable yard.

Yvonne kissed her brother as he stood staring after his new felt hat. Andrew, in turn, was staring after the disappearing Batty and muttering darkly, 'Blighter doesn't know his place!'

'He's a bit of a character,' Yvonne said, slipping her hand through his arm and drawing both him and Jenny to the steps where Mrs O'Reilly and Kate had come to meet them.

'You remember Jenny and Andrew?' Yvonne said.

Mrs O'Reilly and Kate shook hands with their guests, and hurried them indoors, shivering and commenting on the unseasonable weather. Theo came in behind them, moved with his staccato stride across the hall. He raised his voice for Brigid, and she emerged from the kitchen to take the wet overcoats. Yvonne brought Andrew and Jenny upstairs to show them their room. She paused at the return of the stairs and looked back: Mrs O'Reilly and Kate had already disappeared into the drawing room, but Theo was standing very still in the hall below, looking up after his wife and their guests, and it seemed to Yvonne that his face was feral; his expression — eyes narrowed, lips drawn back — was like that of someone mad with grief and hunger. He looked away immediately, avoiding his wife's gaze, and followed his mother and sister to the drawing room. The moment had not registered with either Andrew or Jenny. Neither of them had paused to look over their shoulders.

The guest room was papered in old flock wall-paper, a succession of small blue flowers on a light blue background dancing diagonally across the walls. There was a double bed with a thick eiderdown, an iron bed with brass bedsteads. The furniture was Victorian, a heavy mahogany wardrobe, a dressing table with an inlaid mirror. There were a few framed embroidered pieces of birds and flowers on the walls and, above the mantelpiece, an oval mirror in a mahogany frame reflected the light from the window.

Jenny shut the door. 'How have you been?' she asked, turning to Yvonne who had gone straight to the fireplace and was putting a few more sods on the embers. 'I . . . I mean, we have missed you so much! Are you quite well. Theo was telling us on the way back that you haven't been yourself!'

Yvonne turned. She looked from her brother to her old friend, standing there so concerned and normal. 'Of course I'm well,' she murmured with an apologetic half laugh. 'I've been a bit tired of late. It was all very strange, particularly at first. Being married and being here; but now that you've come, everything seems all right again. Everything seems . . . sane.'

'Sane?' Jenny repeated, more to herself than anyone else, and she went to stand at the window, looking out at the roofs of the stables and beyond them to the churning of the distant breakers as they drove towards the shore.

'Were you very homesick?' Andrew asked, studying his sister as though to assess the state of her health. 'Jen was worried; your letters worried her. She said you sounded desperate . . . between the lines, that is.'

Jenny gave her husband a reproachful glance, and Yvonne made a moue of self-deprecation. 'I'm sorry . . . Was it so obvious? But yes, I was homesick.'

Andrew moved to the window, stood beside his wife and surveyed the scene outside. Jenny left him to it, moved from him as though she could not bear to be so close to him, and went to sit on the bed. She reached out her hand for Yvonne's, pulled Yvonne down beside her.

'Is Theo good to you?' she whispered.

'In his way. But he's not the same Theo, Jen. I hardly know him.'

'Why? How has he changed?'

Yvonne glanced at her brother and lowered her voice. 'Well, you probably find him greatly improved compared with when you saw him at the wedding,' Yvonne answered slowly, as though trying to find the right words to convey the subtlety of the metamorphosis. 'He's confident, healthy and assertive, even though his memory is still far from perfect. But as far as I'm concerned, his whole personality has undergone some sort of fundamental alteration!'

Jenny was silent. Then she said, 'You haven't fallen out of love?'

'No,' Yvonne said, keeping her voice very low.

'Quite the contrary; he is so strange and . . . in some ways compelling, that part of me is fascinated, and part of me is afraid, and part of me is angry. I cannot pity him as I used to . . . But I do not think he loves me any more.'

Jenny did not answer. She looked across the room at Andrew, who was still leaning against the shutter and watching the world outside the window, as though the scudding clouds and the momentum of the waves had mesmerized him.

'He was always a mad bastard,' he said without turning his head. 'I told you so at the time! These Irish fellows are all a bit strange: too much superstition at an early age and not enough common sense. When we were in the trenches he used to spout bits of poetry and shout in his sleep!'

'He's still a very restless sleeper. Sometimes I think he doesn't sleep at all!'

Andrew inclined his head towards the window and the sea. 'I didn't know you were quite so close to the waves.'

There was a knock at the door.

'Come in,' Jenny said. The brass knob turned and the mahogany door opened silently. It was Theo, wearing his quizzical smile. He moved across the threshold, inquiring genially if everything were all right, and would they join the family in the drawing room for tea when they were ready? His voice was mellower than Yvonne had heard it for some time; it had lost its subtly dangerous register. He seemed to her to be exercising some kind of restraint, to be flexing the muscles of his will; the low-keyed resonance of his tone seemed to stem from this discipline. His presence filled the room; he was immediately the focus of all eyes and an absolute attention which had nothing to do with the civility due to one's host.

Yvonne wondered, not for the first time, how he did it. He filled every place he was in, effortlessly, as though he were the centre of gravity and everyone else mere matter, drawn to him willy-nilly. She saw the way Andrew regarded him with the reluctant reverence men pay others of their sex whom they perceive as formidable. Jenny sat on the edge of the bed, her smile a little fixed, but Theo did not look at her. He leaned on his blackthorn stick, forceful and urbane.

His spirit is formidable, Yvonne thought with yearning, trying to identify what he possessed that was so compelling. It is powerful and multi-faceted. I want him to love me. I want him to see me. Things could be good if he would see me.

Theo looked at his wife and gestured politely that she might care to come down now and allow her guests to get their bearings after their long journey. He stood with studied elegance, despite his leg, and she went towards him with sudden pride, glad to be his wife, glad to show him off to her brother and her friend.

'See you downstairs,' she said lightly, and she preceded Theo out of the room. He followed her, shutting the door and beginning the descent of the staircase, leaning on the heavy oak balustrade with one arm, and tucking his walking stick under the other. Yvonne waited, wanting to be there if he needed her help, sensing even as she did so that it was the wrong move. She should run carelessly down the stairs, behave as though he didn't exist; the more she burdened him with love the more he would dismiss her. If she treated him with cheerful indifference he would see her perhaps as a challenge. But that would be to treat him with less than she felt for him, and she had not lived enough to have learnt how to marshal artifice. She felt like a pawn, someone he shifted around for his personal ends, but the reaches of whose spirit did not inspire enough of either respect or turbulence to generate passion.

'Please,' he said with irritation. 'Don't wait for me. I know that I'm disabled, but I'm not a bloody invalid!'

Yvonne glanced at him. 'All right.' She wanted to add that she was only trying to help, but she merely quickened her pace and entered the drawing room, leaving Theo to his methodical descent of the stairs.

Una had brought in a tea tray, a plate of small ham sandwiches, another of biscuits and a 'devil's food' chocolate cake which she had baked that morning. Tea was in a silver pot. The room was warm from the fire, and the occasional rattle of the window-panes and the bluster in the chimney did not now seem other than the friendly idiosyncrasies of a friendly house, coming alive with the presence of old friends.

Theo fed the fire with dark brown sods, some of them 'hairy' with remnants of ancient, desiccated root systems; then he took up the brass tongs and scraped the warm ash from the front of the embers so that it fell between the iron bars of the grate. He was taciturn, but he turned as the door opened and Andrew and Jenny entered. Jenny had changed to a grey dress which was both elegant and understated. She seemed even slimmer than formerly; her face seemed thinner, too, now that it was no longer glowing from the rain.

Theo turned and moved a pace to welcome his guests.

Mrs O'Reilly moved on the sofa, indicating that Jenny must sit beside her; Kate asked how they had found the journey and, with a glance at Yvonne, began to pour the tea. Theo went to the sofa table, offered drinks. Yvonne handed around the cups, offered the sugar and the sandwiches. Una cut the cake and with a flat, 'Will ye be all right now, ma'am?' to Mrs O'Reilly, disappeared back to the kitchen with the tea-pot.

Andrew sat on a straight-backed chair and accepted a whiskey and a small, tri-cornered sandwich. Both Jenny and Yvonne sampled the chocolate cake, which was rich and black, with a butter-icing filling liberally mixed with sherry.

'Have you been to Ireland before?' Mrs O'Reilly asked and when Jenny shook her head and Andrew said they hadn't, she murmured that she hoped they would enjoy their stay.

'How do you find Ireland?' Kate asked, and Yvonne suppressed a smile, knowing the rejoiner Andrew would once have given, 'Go north and turn left.'

But today he was all gravitas: 'We find it beautiful,' he said diplomatically, 'but different.'

Listening to him from her perch on the sofa beside the older woman in the black dress, Jenny felt a kind of contempt. How articulate, she thought. How original. 'We find it different!' Couldn't he think of anything to say except some trite comment like that? Of course it was different. Foreign countries were always different, and this place was foreign.

'How is it different?' Kate rejoined.

'It's restless,' Jenny said, searching for the words to describe what she felt. 'It pretends to be placid but it's really in some kind of ferment.'

Mrs O'Reilly's eyes dwelt on her for a moment. 'Quite true,' she said. 'Politically things are in turmoil; spiritually it's much the same as always: a country searching for its soul.' She looked at Andrew. 'This is a much less set society than the one in England. You must realize that and not jump to any easy assumptions. There are no people here who genuinely "know their place", for example; the currency of status is really based on respect, not on class.'

Andrew flushed, remembering his earlier

comment about the groom. 'I see,' he said uncomfortably.

'Stature is merited, not inherited,' Theo quipped, smiling. 'But I'll give that petulant Batty a boot up the transom for his impertinence.'

'You two must have a lot to talk about,' Kate interjected cheerfully. She included Theo in the movement of her hand. 'Weren't you at the Front together?' Watching her, watching how her eyes never left the faces of the two men, Yvonne was certain that her sister-in-law was not as relaxed as she appeared, that she was too watchful, that her welcoming demeanour was brittle.

Theo was sitting on the seat on the brass fender, watching the faces in the room. His eyes lingered on Jenny, sitting there with her cup of tea, dressed in her fine grey worsted dress with the white collar, her brown hair arranged softly.

He knew Jenny. And Jenny knew him, was aware of his eyes and his face and the way he sat so straight, the peculiar quality of judgmental languor he possessed. She recalled something which made her face burn and forced her to study the inside of her tea-cup.

I must be mad, she thought; I am insane, riddled with fragments of dreams masquerading as experience. I must not look at him. She avoided his eyes. She took little part in the conversation and sipped her tea thoughtfully.

I never slept with him, she told herself insistently; it was a dream. Perhaps I should not have come; perhaps we should always run like cowards from confrontation, from anything which would rub up against uncomfortable perceptions; but I have come.

She raised her head and, as Andrew was describing an incident in the trenches where shells had whistled and exploded beside a private soldier acting as barber to his jumpy mate — ' 'Old still or I'll 'ave your blinkin' ear off', the intrepid barber had told his subject — and as this was recounted to the mirth of the company, Jenny, as though she could not do otherwise, moved her head and looked into Theo's eyes.

Yvonne felt, rather than saw, the exchange.

'Old Theo here used to have nightmares,' Andrew went on, his tongue loosened by the spirit in his glass, 'about a mask. And about coming home to a silent house . . . He was a great one for poetry.' He laughed. 'I learnt quite a lot from him.' He turned to his wife. 'Jen, do you know what he said when I showed him your picture, told him your name? He said,' and here Andrew's voice assumed a recitational lilt which was not entirely free of personal malice:

' "Jenny the brown, Jenny the brown.
Give us Jenny to burn or drown . . ." '

Jenny started and looked at her host.
Theo's face darkened. 'What rot . . .' He turned to Jenny, 'Your husband is possessed of

390

great powers of invention!'

There was silence. Andrew's drunk, Yvonne thought. Two whiskies on an empty stomach. The rhyme is in appalling taste. She glanced at Theo. He had put his empty whiskey glass on the mantelshelf over his head and was twisting his gold signet ring around and around on his finger.

Outside, Batty was waxing peevish.

'In the name of the everlasting God,' he muttered as he laboured to dislodge the visitor's hat from the monkey puzzle tree. He was holding a long varnished pole with a hook at the end, which was used to open and close the tall windows in the house. He poked at the hat with this implement, and the wind did the rest, dislodging it, so that it flew another few feet, like a perverse parrot, and landed on another branch a bit lower down. This time Batty was completely successful in his efforts, and the hat fell to the ground where it rolled off towards the cypresses, across the flowerbed with its bleeding peonies, driven headlong. When Batty succeeded in retrieving it he was breathless and in a foul mood.

'Themselves and their hats!' he exclaimed darkly, grasping the offending garment and bringing it into the kitchen, where he reached into a drawer for some brushes. The hat was wet and covered in bits of clay from its journey across the flowerbed. Batty regarded this with a certain grim satisfaction. He glanced at his barefoot daughter, Molly, who had dropped in on her way home from school. She knew Una and Bridgie well, and she hated going back to an empty cottage, and she liked to read the books available in the big house. She was now reading a children's book which Una had, with Mrs O'Reilly's consent, borrowed from the library for her. It was a slim book with illustrations, about a boy called Aladdin who had found a magic lamp. Molly called at Kilashane every afternoon to continue with the story, and she read it in a half trance, so fascinated by it that she was like one dead to the world, her bare feet tucked underneath her in the big old kitchen armchair.

Una came into the kitchen with the tea-pot and commenced to replenish it.

'Glory be to God,' she said, putting the silver pot down on the hob while she poured boiling water from the big aluminium kettle which was sputtering on the hottest part of the range.

'But Master Theo cannot take his eyes off Mrs Stacey! You'd think he'd never laid eyes on a woman. And his wife in the same room, half afraid to look at him!' She stopped abruptly, suddenly remembering that little Molly was curled up in the armchair in the corner with a book. She shook her head, drew a deep breath and sent it back into the world as a sigh.

After she had gone back to the drawing room, Batty finished his restorative work on the hat and brought it into the hall where he left it on the table. He stood for a moment in the hallway, listening to the voices from the drawing room, lingering when he heard Theo's low tones and shaking his head.

That night, Andrew said to Jenny as they lay in bed, 'Maybe it's because he lost the leg . . . I mean, how do they do it?'

'Do what?'

'Christ, Jen . . . Fuck — how do they fuck?'

'It's his leg that's gone,' Jenny said. 'And don't be so crude!'

'But it must be . . . bloody queer, all the same.' He put his arm around her, moved his hand and fondled her breasts. 'I have two legs; three right now . . .'

Jenny, who wished with all her might that she and Andrew had been allocated separate rooms, pulled away, and when Andrew followed her with his hands she said, 'I have a headache, Andrew,' and slipped out of bed.

Her husband made a sound of exasperation. 'God damn you, Jenny Stephenson,' he said in a low, sibilant whisper.

She did not reply. She went to the window and pulled back the curtain. I think He already has, she thought. I do not deserve this torture. Suddenly she wished she were back in her attic studio, with her paintings around her and the portrait of her magician as focus for conversation. She had gone back to the National Gallery, remembering what she thought was a dream, to see if she could find the painting of the *Venetian Gentleman*, but the space it had occupied was filled by a different picture. She spoke to one of the attendants, who said that the paintings were often changed to make way for others, and if she could give him the name of the artist he would check the matter for her. But Jenny, suddenly afraid that her 'dream' would turn out to have been reality, declined this offer.

I wish I had my magician, Jenny thought, looking over the nighttime vista of Kilashane. She realized with wry amusement how this sounded, and added to herself defensively, I need to talk; I need to be understood.

There was a half moon. It emerged from behind some clouds and silvered the fury of the waves. She saw the sea. She saw the roofs of the stable below her and the yard to the left which was dense with shadows. But as she gazed into the night she also saw something move. It was down in the yard near the coach-house door, where the shadows were deepest. It came forward into the shaft of the moonlight and Jenny saw that it was Theo. He had his head raised. She saw his white shirt. His face was in semi-darkness, but his head was raised and was staring straight into her face.

Chapter Seventeen

'There is more God in my fingertip,' she said, 'than in all your edifices.'

She tried to hold her hand up, but the strength had left her.

The inquisitor wept.

Journal of a Witness

'Dee, wake up!'

The words swung in and out of consciousness. 'Your father's waiting to drive you. Do you want to catch the train or not?'

What train? Dee wondered in the moment where sleep was shattered and consciousness had not reasserted itself. What does the train matter? If I do not sleep I will die.

It had been another sleepless night, listening to the soughing in the plantation, afraid that if she went to the window the shadow, which she sometimes saw when looking out the window, would be there again. And then, towards dawn, she had dozed.

She had come home for the weekend; scuttled back to safety, run to the shelter where all her anxieties seemed silly and childish. Once home, Dublin, Brussels and McGrath seemed almost a figment of the imagination. She had gone back to work after her aborted trip to Brussels, but liked to get back to Ballyshane at weekends as often as possible.

She had thought of leaving McGrath. She could not stay in a company in which he held a key position. She told all this to Laura who said she should cop herself on. 'Why should you leave a good job just on his account?'

'I know. But I can't forgive what happened! I can't bear to feel myself part of the same outfit.'

'What you can't forgive,' Laura said, 'is yourself. Why don't you give yourself permission to be human, to make mistakes. No one has ever lived who did not make mistakes. Are you still in love with him?'

'Of course I'm not!'

Laura sighed. 'Is that the reason why you mention him in your sleep? You're at it almost every night! Dream about him by all means, but for goodness' sake don't run away!'

Dee thought about this. The job was blossoming for her. There was a new managing director, who ran a tight ship, streamlined the operation; business was booming. Why should she run away, after all? She could always dismiss her experience with Peter Eggli as a fling, as unimportant. She could assume the private mantle of a woman of the world.

This was the theory. But the reality was something else. She realized eventually that she had invested something of herself in their brief relationship something which was obscure and ab-

solute. The thought that she had allowed herself
to have been touched at that level by a philanderer was abhorrent. It felt like rape. It filled her
with the desire to punish herself in some way, so
that she would never again endure a betrayal.
But in all the other areas of her life — in her
work, in her hunt for a car, in her and Laura's
search for a new flat — there was only success.
She had a salary hike; she found a two-year-old
Volkswagen at a bargain price; they got themselves a beautiful flat in Ballsbridge for a rent
which could only be described as ridiculously
low. It was as though everything was conspiring
to comfort her, as though what ailed her could
be healed by a string of fortuitous circumstances.

But there was still the niggle of Colin. She had
not succeeded in contacting him on her return
from Brussels. His paper said he had been sent
abroad on an assignment. And then a parcel had
come from him. Opening it she found his letter
first of all, and had read that before unpacking
the rest.

Dear Leprechaun,
Here is something I thought you might
appreciate. I bought it in a jumble sale, part
of the junk from someone's attic — a lady
who died recently and who had various
paintings and odds and ends in an attic
which she kept boarded up. As you had
witching ambitions once I thought it just

the thing (belatedly) for your birthday.

Ha, ha!

Hope everything is going well for you. They're sending me to Hong Kong — my first foreign assignment. I tried to reach you in Brussels to tell you all this, but you were evidently gallivanting. I'll contact you when I get back!

Dee opened the present, which was swathed in felt and layers of corrugated cardboard. She drew it out of its packing with astonishment. It was a portrait in oils — canvas stretched on a frame. The face was that of some old-fashioned gent, goatee beard, black costume, ring on his hand. The eyes were hooded and were both fierce and sad. She looked for the artist's name. The picture had not been signed, but the back of the canvas was inscribed with the legend, 'My Magician'.

'Gives me the creeps!' Laura said. 'Your Colin has a funny sense of humour. What are you going to do with it? I don't want your man staring at me from the wall!'

So Dee had left the magician in the corner, considering a discarded poster of the Beatles.

Now, in the fresh new morning, she shook her head, trying to shift the focus of her interests and perceptions back to the real world, away from the reality she had just inhabited and which was receding from her with the speed of an express train. In that apparent reality — in the dream —

she had emerged from the cellars in Kilashane, where she had been buried in a new fall of debris. Although half choked by plaster dust and bleeding from scratches, she had managed to fight her way out. She saw the man in evening dress standing at the edge of the woods, watching her. He made no attempt to help her but, when she was out, he came towards her across the gravel. She was uncomfortably aware of her dishevelled state, and knew that however desperately she might desire it, she was not fully visible to him; that he saw only her fight to live and that it displeased him. He had something in his hand and raised it as he came towards her in a priestlike gesture. And all she could remember after that was waking to her mother's voice telling her about the train. She wanted to get back into the dream; she knew something had happened in it which would explain all the malaise of her life.

The clock said nine-thirty.

'Feck . . .'

She flew out of bed, dived into the bathroom for a quick shower, then got dressed. Her mini-skirt was black. She put on a black cotton polo-neck which hugged her torso, slipped into her platform sandals with the cork soles, and thumped down to the kitchen. She stared at herself in the hall mirror; she had had her hair cut and it swung forward a little on either side of her face, from a short back which was cut into the nape of the neck.

The radio in the kitchen was blaring. Helen

Shapiro was melodiously informing the world that just because she was in her teens and still went to school she wasn't anyone's fool. Dee used to sing the song herself. 'Don't treat me like a child.' Her father had laughed until he was weak. She had been fourteen then.

'What are you laughing at?'

'Nothing, darling, nothing,' and then he was off again.

Dee had looked at her father and felt sorry for him that he was so old with nothing to look forward to. Now she hadn't got anything to look forward to either. Peter Eggli had written letters to her saying that he loved her. Dee had torn the missives into pieces. Piss off, Casanova, she hissed to herself.

Dee knew her mother was in bad form this morning. This was evident from the silence and the compressed lips. Her mother seemed to be suffering from depression; she had withdrawn into a silent world of her own and did not converse much with her daughter. The result was that her father had also retreated into a pained silence. He occasionally tried to crack a joke, to jolly his wife out of her determined gloom, but to no avail. Now her mother put Dee's fry, which was being kept warm in the oven, on to the table.

'The rashers are all dried up!'

'It doesn't matter, Mam.'

Her mother sighed. 'And I wish you wouldn't wear those dreadful sandals . . .'

Dee looked down at her platforms. 'I know,'

she agreed. 'They do look a bit thick, but they make me taller.'

Her mother sighed again.

'I'll throw them out if you like.' Dee said this placatingly. She hated her mother to be in bad form. She sensed the constrained tenor of her life. Her father's retirement was a fait accompli; he obviously had no intention of leaving Ballyshane. If the matter was mentioned he changed the subject, cracked a joke, looked a little sheepish and uneasy and sidled off to read his paper. It was a clash of temperaments. Dee knew he lived for the sea crashing on the black rocks, for the wild cry of the birds, for the people he knew so well, for the sea wind which came full of bluster down the chimney on stormy nights. Dublin would choke him. She also knew that her mother still thought she was young. She had found her corner in the ocean of time, had stood still within it, busy with her domestic cares, and life had washed over and past her almost without her noticing. She still yearned for the city, for the lights, the theatres, the cinemas, for the gaiety she had never known. The young girl hidden behind the façade that time had etched into her face, was calling in the promises made by her husband in his youth.

Dee knew that her father would not budge, and that he felt guilty. But she instinctively sided with him. She knew her mother would be lonely in Dublin, and that it would not fulfil the expectations generated by an era of her life which was long gone.

'That man!' Mrs McGlinn said in exasperation, picking up a bundle of newspapers which her father had deposited on the back table. He tended to keep the papers until he had read each one of them from cover to cover, and then he would make a bundle and leave them in the kitchen.

'He only thinks of himself . . . Never a moment's thought for anyone else. Year after year of slaving in this house and still he leaves the old papers on the back table. Always waiting for someone else to clean up after him.' She sighed again.

Dee ate her breakfast in silence, put the dishes in the sink and, when her mother said peremptorily, 'Leave them, you haven't time,' she left the kitchen with a hurried, 'I'll get my stuff, Mam.'

Her mother nodded. 'Year after year,' she continued, 'till I'm blue in the face!'

Dee found her father sitting on the stairs outside the kitchen door. He put a finger to his lips.

'What are you doing here, Dad?' Dee demanded in a whisper as she passed him by on the stairs. He looked vulnerable. He smiled a little sheepishly and indicated the kitchen door.

'Just listenin' to what am goin' on in dat stockade!' Dee recognized *Treasure Island*. He had read it to her at night, many long-ago nights when she was so small she only filled half her bed and he had seemed larger than life, omnipotent, the nearest thing to God; when she had felt his love for her like a great warm cloak wrapping her up.

Now she felt so touched that tears stung her eyes. She looked back at her father as he sat there, listening to the complaints from the kitchen, his grey head bowed. I love you, Daddy, she thought. I love you more than anything in the world!

In that moment she decided that the train could go to hell. It was Sunday. She would go to Mass with her parents, spend the day with them, and phone the office in the morning and take the day off. She would go back to Dublin tomorrow on the evening train. She thought of her car and wished she had brought it home. But it was being serviced.

Still, things were simple when you made your mind up. She was entitled to take a day off.

They drove to Mass in the Morris Minor, a bit battered from years of faithful service, but still robust. The church was a mile and a half away, where the peninsula began to merge into the mainland and the sea no longer sounded as though it were master of the world. Father O'Shea, in gold and white chasuble, stood before the altar and intoned, ' "I will go unto the altar of God." '

' "Unto God who gives joy to my youth," ' Dee answered silently, listening to the responses of the congregation and remembering the Masses of her childhood and teens when everything had still been in Latin. Because it was in Latin it had been mysterious, arcane, even mystical. Now it sounded almost mundane. Did God give joy to one's youth? She knew she should be happy, but she was becoming afraid of sleep. In it she might find herself lying weeping in Peter Eggli's arms, or still in the old demesne with the crows overhead. Give me joy, God. Let me never dream again of Kilashane.

The church smelt of candlewax and incense. She studied the stained-glass windows, the figure of Christ and his mother; she studied the brass plate screwed into the back of the pew in front of her: 'Pray for the soul of Brigid Murphy, Ballyshane.' She smelt the soap on the freshly scrubbed bodies around her. She saw how rough the farmers' hands were, how leathery and dry, how tough and broken the nails. Families knelt together, father in his best suit, mother in her best dress, children — one, two, three, four, sometimes five — all well behaved, neat, ostensibly devout; like fireflies they were here for a season and then became names screwed into the backs of pews or carved into gravestones.

Father O'Shea gave his sermon. Dee didn't listen. They were nearly always boring. She thought of the fun they had had years before, when she was eight, and old Billy, to the intense delight of the congregation, had wandered into the church and inquired with a shout, 'Mother of God, will he ever shut up?'

Billy had come to Church only sporadically,

404

but when he did the children present nurtured furtive hopes of some entertainment. He would shout a verse of the psalms: 'Take not away my soul with the wicked, nor my life with bloody men.' Or he might thump the back of a pew and call out, 'I have walked in my innocence. Redeem me. Be merciful . . . to me.'

Except for the giggles of the young, no one pretended to heed him. There was compassion for this wreck in the parish of Ballyshane.

Dee surfaced from her reverie when Billy's name was actually mentioned; the priest referred to his death a month earlier and asked the congregation to join in prayers for the eternal repose of his soul.

Billy was dead, his cottage ransacked. But whoever had ransacked his cottage would have known nothing about his real abode, his treehouse in Kilashane.

She went to Communion; it was more than an hour since she had had breakfast, otherwise it would have been a sin. She bowed her head and felt the thin, unleavened wafer sticking to her tongue, already dissolving by the time she regained her seat.

Will I go to Kilashane today? she asked dreamily, as though the God-in-her-mouth should answer.

A 'holy picture' fell out of Dee's missal. She bent to retrieve it. It was of a beautiful madonna by Murillo, in the act of ascending to heaven. Her face was that of a very young woman, pretty and vapid as holiness seemed to require. The legend underneath said 'Immaculada'. She was immaculate, untouched. Not like me, Dee thought, feeling again the anger at her plunder; not like me.

On the back of the picture, her old adversary Treena Casey had written, 'In rem. of our last day at Alma Mater. It seems rather awful going out to fend for ourselves.'

Treena had gone to the same boarding school; they had patched up their differences, glad to have a familiar presence in so much newness. There had been a fashion in the last week at school of handing holy pictures to one's friends, suitably autographed, for remembrance. She hadn't seen Treena for a long time: she had gone to England to a teacher-training college and now had a job over there.

When Dee replaced the picture in her missal, the page opened at the place where two rose petals were pressed, still velvety, dry and almost purple. Billy had given her a rose once when she walked by him after Mass, following her parents to the car which was parked a little way down the road. He had leaned over the wall into the presbytery garden, broken off the perfumed bloom, and handed it to her as she passed, his arm jerking with the sudden spasmodic movements which afflicted him, his limp as he moved towards her very pronounced. She had been ten then.

'Keep the petals,' he mumbled in her ear,

'lucky petals.' As he moved away he had added in a voice so low she couldn't be sure she had heard him correctly, 'Remember me . . .' On a whim she had pressed the petals. But most of them had been lost, and the two remaining ones between the back pages of her prayer-book were all that were left.

'What did Billy say to you?' her mother had asked as they drove home that day.

'Nothing. He gave me this rose,' and she held it up, still splendid with its beauty and beaded with the rain of the morning.

Her mother had looked at her father and he'd glanced back at her, but from her seat in the back of the car Dee could not see his expression.

Now, thinking of poor Billy and the dead rose, she felt overcome with a kind of melancholy. I will go to Kilashane today, she thought, fingering the sad, dried mementoes of a summer long past. I will go to Kilashane. I wish everyone and everything didn't die.

Father O'Shea turned to the congregation. 'The Mass is ended,' he said. 'Go forth in peace.'

'I fled Him, down the nights and down the days;
I fled Him, down the arches of the years;
I fled Him, down the labyrinthine ways
Of my own mind . . .'

Dee murmured to herself that afternoon as she walked towards the old demesne. The poem had been in her mind on and off for the past few days.

The crows were still circling over the ruin. Such sombre birds, grey-black beaks, black feathers, how many of them wheeling and cawing above the treetops?

She had changed out of her mini-skirt into dark blue jeans and runners. It was fine and sunny. The black cotton top soaked up the sunlight. The cows raised their heads to look at her as she passed. The bleating of sheep came from the higher land towards the west. In the clover the bees were busy, furry little bodies on a frenzied nectar hunt, their droning heady with intoxication. The river, the Meena, was a shallow affair now, in keeping with the lowered water-table, and it too sang over the stones. A kingfisher flashed by in startling blue and was gone.

Her father had looked up from the Sunday papers when she said she was going out for a walk. He didn't offer to join her. He was in his armchair, over-replete from the roast beef, and her mother was still wearing her air of injury.

'Take Ricky,' was all he had said. 'He could do with a bit of a dander.'

She entered the demesne through the old gap in the wall, over which the brambles were now growing in thick, green-leaved interlacings, their wicked little thorns aggressively erect. She pushed them aside with a stick and crept through the gap. The old avenue was overgrown with summer weeds; the gothic gateway at the half-way mark looked older than she remembered, and was now almost completely smothered in ivy. Ricky lifted his leg and anointed a rusty hinge with pee.

It was cool under the green canopy, almost a different world from the bright September day. Here there was bracken, the pungent smell of wild garlic.

'If you go down to the woods today,' Dee whispered to herself under her breath, afraid to break the waiting silence, 'You'd better go softly . . .'

She paused, stood quite still beside the bole of an ancient beech, suddenly aware that someone else was in the demesne. She heard the sounds of footsteps, muted on the soft loam underfoot, scuffling for a moment through undergrowth. She moved a fraction and saw that, some distance away, a man was moving through the woods in the direction of the house. He was wearing green wellingtons and was moving purposefully, although something in his gait, the manner in which he transmitted his weight to the ground, spoke of stealth. She could not see his face, but his clothes, a pale jacket over flannel trousers, suggested that he did not belong to the locality.

Dee felt a sense of outrage, as though some burglar had violated her home. She was so used to having the entire run of the demesne, and the solitude and privacy that went with it, that she felt she had acquired rights. For a moment she wanted to confront the intruder and ask him to explain himself, but reflection made her realize that she had no standing whatever to warrant such peremptoriness. So she contented herself with watching him, moving a little from one tree to the next so she could observe his actions without being seen. Ricky had disappeared a few moments before in hot pursuit of a rabbit and so, for the moment, she did not have him to contend with.

The man moved across the overgrown lawn, across the driveway, and up the granite steps to where the front door had once stood. Before him yawned the collapsed hallway, the view of the old basement kitchens, the broken stairs, now completely rotted, the pieces of balustrade hanging from the fallen landing, and up, through the whole height of the old, roofless house, he could see the bare stone chimney from which sprouted a healthy sally tree like a television aerial. He stood and stared, turned his head this way and that, as though trying to ascertain whether it was possible to safely enter the decayed building. Then he turned, retraced his steps, moved around to the side of the house towards the ruined stables, and disappeared.

Dee followed. She kept to the shelter of the trees, skirting behind the old monkey puzzle tree and over to the left where she could see the approach to the stables. The man was moving about in the stable yard; she heard the clump of his rubber boots on the cobbles and the creak of rusty hinges as he opened the coach-house door. She knew the coach-house was empty, except for a couple of old wheels, a battered carriage lantern, and a three-legged stool which was thrown in the corner and festooned with cobwebs. She wondered if the man were a thief. But the surviving treasures of the big house had been taken by persons unknown: fireplaces, mahogany doors, antique furniture which had survived the fire and the elements.

Ricky came bounding through the wood, panting, long tongue lolloping. The rabbit had given him the slip, but he was in fine fettle after his run. He gave a cursory bark of recognition, wagging his tail furiously.

'Shut up, you eejit,' Dee whispered to the dog in exasperation, but she knew the intruder in the stable yard must have heard. In a moment came the squeak of the hinges and then the sound of the boots and then the man stood in the archway, staring straight at her. He held himself with a certain raw arrogance, but the expression on his face was wary. He took in the girl and the dog at one glance and turned his head fractionally to examine the rest of the lawn, the overgrown forecourt, the line of trees, and what he could see of the driveway. Then he approached her, walking slowly, his eyes fixed on her. Dee was glad she had the dog, but she took an instinctive step backwards. Ricky growled. The man gave a half laugh, turned up his palms and stopped.

'Hello,' he said.

'This house is dangerous,' Dee said. 'There's a sign . . .' She waited for him to answer, and when he did not she added, 'And you're trespassing!'

'And you're not?'

His accent was foreign. He was not English, but he might be French or German or Dutch. He had fair hair, blue eyes and sallow, sun-slicked skin. His eyes were very close-set and alert, and the smile on his mouth disclosed uneven, stained teeth.

Dee ignored the rejoinder. 'What are you looking for?'

He shook his head. 'Nothing. I just wanted to have a look.'

'There are plenty of big old houses where tourists are welcome. This one is only a ruin.'

'I can see that! But I'm curious about this one!'

'Why?'

He gestured. 'It's off the beaten track. Do I have to have reasons?' He laughed again. 'Who are you, anyway — pretty girl like you? Some kind of sentinel? A spirit of the woods?'

'I live locally,' Dee said.

'So you know this place well?'

'Yes. I've known it all my life.'

'I see.' He seemed thoughtful. 'You wouldn't like to show me around?'

'No. I have to go home and there is nothing to see.'

'All the same, I bet you came across some interesting curios during your explorations here — when you were a child, and so on,' the man continued after a moment.

Dee reddened with anger. Here it was again. She thought of the diary and the photograph. She smelt a subtle kind of danger, though she did not know why it should be there in the shaft of sunlight in the middle of the afternoon.

'This place was destroyed long before I was born. Everything of value was taken one night while I was still a baby: the furniture, the fireplaces, even the doors.' She watched the man before her. 'Were you hoping to find something in particular?'

He took a step nearer and stared into her eyes, watching her reaction. 'Actually,' he said very softly, 'I was looking for a mask!'

Dee dragged her eyes away from the predatory gaze. She looked up at the window of the room where she had first seen the ring glint by the hearth. She thought of the insignia of the ring. She thought of the mask, which she had flung from her, surely now buried in the basement.

'I can't help you,' she said with a shrug, aware that her face was turning livid. 'What kind of mask?'

He followed her gaze to the first-floor window, glanced at her again, and at the dog, which lifted back his lips and hissed at him. 'I'm not sure. Just a fancy I have. Well, I'd better be off, I suppose,' he said. 'Nice meeting you, Miss . . . ?'

'McGlinn.'

He hesitated, then smiled. 'But perhaps I should tell you why I am really here?'

He retraced a couple of steps. 'I am vetting this property for the new owner. So you see, I am not a trespasser, but you are!'

She watched him walk away down the avenue. Then, running, she caught up with him. 'Wait . . . Who is the new owner? Who wants to buy Kilashane? What is he going to do with it?'

He raised his eyebrows. 'So many questions! He intends to build a hotel here. The builders will arrive in a few weeks!'

Dee recoiled. 'Horrible!'

He shrugged. 'Not horrible. "Progress", I think, is the word. He will shift away all the rubble, but will keep the old walls. He already has planning permission. The house will look much as it did in its heyday, but there will be an extension for weddings and so forth. The grounds will be tidied up; there will be a car park. If adjoining land can be acquired, there will be a golf course!'

Dee's jaw dropped in dismay. The place would be ruined. She studied the face before her. 'Why did you ask me about a mask?'

He raised his eyebrows, but his eyes gleamed. 'Do you know where I might find it?'

She shook her head, and he moved away down the avenue and raised a hand to forestall any further questions.

When he was gone, Dee walked into the stable yard and then into the coach-house. The few things there had been moved; a wooden cupboard on the wall had had its locked door forced to disclose some rusty tools. The man had been in the old barn as well, and also in the loose-boxes, because the doors hung outwards. She felt grief-stricken. She had sensed the urgency in him, the almost feral imperative. He had rooted around where he had no right to be, disturbing and disarranging what had been left for years in isolated peace. Who would want Kilashane?

She looked into the future. The bulldozers would arrive; trees would be felled to open the sea view. The rubble would be dug out of the basement and sifted for 'curios'. A modern damp course would be laid, new floors would materialize, new doors and windows, a new roof. There would be a lounge bar in the silent space now open to the elements. The bedroom where she found the ring and the mask would become guest rooms, decorated with too much money and not enough taste. Kilashane would lose its soul.

The thought flashed into her head of old Billy's cottage and the way it had been ransacked after his death. There couldn't be any connection . . . And then she thought of Billy's treehouse, down in a dell in the deepest part of the woods. He had built his bower in the embrace of an old beech. It was not easily visible, especially in summer. It would probably be an early casualty of the forthcoming 'progress'.

She whistled for Ricky and began to retrace

her steps. The afternoon was yielding to early evening and the crows were particularly raucous as they set about returning to their billets for the night. She wondered if the man had gone away, or if he was still somewhere in the woods, watching her.

Ricky came to heel eventually, and she hurried back down the weedy path to the gothic gateway, and thence to her exit point in the demesne wall. She looked up and down the road, but could see no sign of a car nor any vehicle which might have belonged to the new owner's agent. He must have gone, she thought. She drew a sigh of relief; she was out of the woods and she was safe. She sat on a stone and looked out on the water, trying to disentangle her emotions. Why did she feel safe because she had left the demesne? It was the first time in her life that it had contained any threat for her, but then she realized that the threat had not emanated from the place itself, but from her own reaction while talking to the stranger. She closed her eyes, feeling the heat of the late afternoon sun on her face, and the sea breeze which came in sporadic eddies and lifted tendrils of her hair. She remembered with sudden and unexpected clarity what had been happening in her dream that morning, before she had awakened to her mother's warning about missing the train. Because she was exhausted, she had obeyed the man in evening dress who had come towards her, holding the mask in his raised hand. She had lain on the woodland floor among the ferns and the blackberry, and he had gently placed the mask on her face. It was so extraordinarily and unexpectedly heavy that it crushed her into the earth; she felt her head being forced down among the roots, smelt the loam, heard the insects, knew it would be impossible, with that weight on her, to rise again. And, throughout, she also sensed the silent rain of his tears.

It took Dee a moment to recover her composure after this sudden recollection. She thought of the stranger in the demesne and what he had been seeking. She thought of Peter and what he had told her. If the mask could be found she should find it and put it away where no one would ever locate it again.

I will come back later, she assured herself as she walked home. If there is something hidden here and can be found, I will find it.

But it will be dark later . . . Courage . . . courage, she told herself, echoing her father's phraseology. Whatever was to be found in Kilashane, she was the one to find it, not the stranger with the stained teeth who had been so full of covert rapacity.

As she walked she felt the evening sun on her back. She watched a few yachts from Cobh harbour tacking far out on the sea. Near the cliffs she saw the occasional dark head bob in the water: the seals, the 'sea people', were looking up at the land.

Chapter Eighteen

'If your dogma be from God, prove it!'

'My lady, you know I cannot!'

'All this,' she whispered, 'and not a jot of proof.'

Journal of a Witness

I should be able to analyse it, but I can't. If I did not care so much for him, I could wriggle out of it, tell myself that he is mad; leave him, perhaps, and go back to England. There is no life to be had here, unless you are content with the sea and the countryside and the feeling in the air. There is humour, but sometimes I find it goes to the quick. It is too subtle for me, too sly. I pity Kate: no young men, no romance; just books and the company of her family. She is far too intense and seems pathetically glad to have visitors.

And as for religion, I find the statues outside the parish church idolatrous, the crucifix in the worst of taste. The parish priest is well meaning, but since my stolen conversation with him my mind is agitated. I would like to talk to the protestant rector, but the Rectory is some distance away and I suppose Theo would try to prevent me going. He has become very possessive, wants to know all my movements. I suppose I could cycle — I will have to cycle, especially after last night.

I determined last night that I would try to talk to Theo, try to banish the unease generated by the recent superstitious talk with Father Keane. If we could talk sensibly, laugh together as we did in Hurleigh Hall, I would feel so much better.

Theo had been reading in the library. He came to bed late. I had blown out the lamp, but I was not asleep, and I spoke to him when he came into the room with his candle. The flame shivered and cast shadows on his face. He seemed pent up with some sort of excitement, the kind of thing you can detect in the presence of someone twisted with tension. He was carrying a book, a heavy, blue-bound tome, and he put it down on the blanket chest. I spoke to him. 'Theo, you're very late . . . !'

I watched him in the mirror as he turned his head in my direction. 'Aha, my little Sassenach is still awake. Maybe she would like to read to me while I undress?'

I hate it when he calls me his little Sassenach, yet in another way I like it. I want to be 'his' — in the way that women do — because he represents possibility, energy, movement, all the doors which may be opened. Women are mad to endure so much, but they are impelled to it by strictures. There is life, of a kind, in madness.

'What do you want me to read?'

He took the book from the blanket chest and

put it on the bed, lighting the lamp beside me. The shadows retreated and he picked up the heavy volume, opened it and handed it to me. I sat up, put pillows behind my head, raised my knees and laughed as I propped the tome against them. Like a fool I was glad that he wanted something from me. He was silent, watching me. I read the lettering on the binding: *The Catholic Encyclopaedia.*

'Open it at page six hundred and seventy-seven,' he murmured, watching me.

I obeyed. We were sharing something, and this made me happy; it seemed to open the possibility of a real talk. The heavy black print on the page said 'Witchcraft'. I read a little, saw mention of the Inquisition.

'Do you know what that was, little Sassenach?' he inquired.

'Of course I do!'

'What was it?'

'It was the torture of persons the Catholic Church regarded as heretics . . .'

'Very good,' he murmured. 'You surprise me. So much erudition in a Sassenach. What do you think of it?'

I ignored the provocation. 'Torture?'

'No, the institution . . . the power to subdue.'

'It is an impertinence. How can any human agency properly deem itself dictator of what others should and should not believe?' I was sorry I had spoken. I do not know how much of a Catholic Theo actually is.

But he smiled and turned away to the dressing room. 'Human agency?' he muttered as he went. 'They claim it is Divine — which is handy.' Then he echoed, 'An impertinence? Indeed! But there is great pleasure in impertinence, in bending the will of others to one's own . . .'

'Shall I go on?'

'By all means.'

So I read. 'The abstract possibility of a pact with the devil and of a diabolical interference in human affairs can hardly be denied, but no one can read the literature of the subject without realizing the awful cruelties to which this belief led, and without being convinced that in ninety-nine cases out of a hundred the allegations rest upon nothing better than pure delusion.'

Theo laughed. 'You see. This is what they are saying now! Their infallibility has changed its spots.' He laughed again. 'But it's a bit late now, isn't it!'

'What is the matter, Theo? What damage are you talking of?'

'Damage, destruction, other people's. And mine! And mine! Why must you be so stupid?'

'I am not stupid, Theo. But you are cruel!'

'Yes . . . I am instructed in it and I cannot escape it.'

I calmed my anger and tried to deflect his train of thought by murmuring something about the horrors of bigotry. 'Religious bigotry has been responsible for more bloodshed than any other force.'

Theo came back to bed, removing his leg as the last act and letting it fall to the floor, appearing to cope with his injury through violently overt contempt for it. Then he turned to Yvonne, took the book, and put it on the bedside table.

'I do not think you nurture any love for our holy mother the Church,' he said, 'and this is very wrong of you!'

'Theo, you know perfectly well I am not a Catholic.'

'You are a bit too puritanical for your own good, little Sassenach. And you do not bow to the will of your husband. I will have to teach you respect. And pleasure! There is pleasure in submission, especially when it is against the will.' He stared at his wife. 'Take off your nightgown.'

'No, Theo. Not if you ask me in that tone of voice.'

He was silent for a moment, fixing her with hooded eyes while a smile played on his lips. Then he moved, pinning her to the bed, hitching her nightgown, holding her down. Yvonne struggled and tried to throw him off, but once he had achieved penetration she found the task impossible. She expected that it would end almost immediately, this violation, like it had before, but he lay, whispering in her ear, gentling her, stroking her, hardly moving except to tease her nipples with his lips, and after a while the sexual tension generated by his adamant presence within her sought release. Against the wavering dictates of her will, her body succumbed to pleasure and, eventually, volcanically, to her first orgasm.

Afterwards he said with some satisfaction, 'You were bucking like a horse!'

Yvonne sought refuge for the turmoil of her emotions, but Theo turned his back and was soon asleep. She lay, searching the darkness with her eyes. You should not turn your back on me, she thought. You should not treat me like this. There is a limit.

But no matter what she whispered, she felt she had lost some part of herself. There are too many persons in one flesh, she thought and they are at cross purposes. She wept in silence. I cannot face them tomorrow, she thought. I cannot smile and pretend any more.

In the morning, Jenny woke early, wondering for a moment where she was. It was still dark, and the black bulk of the wardrobe seemed to be the one in her own bedroom, except that that would mean the position of the bed had been changed. While she was puzzling this out, the heavy, swishing sound of the sea reminded her of where she was.

I am in Ireland, she thought in a rush of wonder, in Kilashane. I am in his house.

Andrew was asleep, snoring sporadically. He was very warm and she moved away a little from contact. She remembered the night before; his rage and his hurt and her own hatred which was beginning to corrode her. She had tried to sleep in the armchair, but in the end, being very cold and uncomfortable, had crept back to bed.

I suppose I should grit my teeth and think of England. When we go home, perhaps, I should try again. I cannot live with him and hate him.

And then she thought, I do not really believe that. How can I 'try' what I know will make me ill? Why should I live with him when I hate him?

Mrs O'Reilly did not get up for breakfast. Theo was in the dining room when Jenny came down. He made to rise from his seat and Jenny said uncomfortably, 'Please, Theo, don't . . .' The wind had died and the day was dry, with patches of sunshine coming in sudden bursts through the window. Then the intensity of the light would fade as the clouds moved to obscure the sun. Theo had the folded paper beside him.

'I'm afraid there's been some more unfortunate business. A couple of RIC constables were murdered yesterday . . .'

Jenny helped herself to scrambled egg, made some appropriate noises in response. The turmoil in Ireland was outside her understanding. Neither did she understand why her heart had begun to beat very fast as soon as she came into the room. In his presence she felt a sense of discovery, of danger, as though all the barriers of her life were either transparent or non-existent.

'Is Yvonne up?' she asked. 'I thought she

424

might come for a walk. I'd like to see the locality.'

'Yvonne said she would keep her bed,' Theo answered. 'I think that's the term they used in the good old days. But I will show you the locality. Do you ride?'

'No. I've never been on a horse in my life.'

'There's always a first time.' He smiled. 'Are you game?'

The door opened. 'Is she game for what?' Andrew asked, coming into the room.

'For a ride,' Theo said and, seeing the expression on Andrew's face, stopped.

'A ride?' Andrew said with a bitter laugh, 'A ride of all things! Jen game for a ride? I'm afraid she's not, are you, darling Jen?'

Jenny glanced at Theo who narrowed his eyes, but deflected her husband's prurient tone and closed the looming silence with, 'And you too, of course, Andrew. I thought you might like to see the area on horseback. The roads are mostly boreens from here on down the peninsula, so it's better on horseback!'

Andrew filled his plate and sat down. 'No,' he said after a moment. 'Don't see myself as a horseman. Never did. I'll stay, Jen too. She hasn't the nerve.'

'I will go riding with pleasure,' Jenny said sweetly, borne on the surge of fury at her husband's licence. How dare he allow himself crude sexual innuendoes at her expense. 'I don't know how, Theo, so I hope you will be patient.'

Theo smiled. 'I will be all patience. We need only walk the horses.

'What will you do?' he asked, turning to Andrew.

'Smoke, read, walk around — that sort of thing!'

Kate came into the room.

'You'll look after him, won't you, Kate?' Theo said, and his sister smiled while she ladled out eggs and bacon.

'I'm starving . . . Look after whom?'

Andrew looked up at her, raised quizzical eyebrows. 'I'm afraid he was referring to me.'

Kate laughed, glanced around the table. 'Where's Yvonne — not up yet?' Her smile died, and she cast a careful glance at Theo. She turned to Andrew. 'How am I supposed to look after you? You look grown up enough to me!'

'Yvonne has a headache,' Theo said evenly. 'One of these migraine things of hers. Jenny and I are going riding. That leaves you and Andrew to entertain each other.'

'I'm sorry about Yvonne,' Jenny said. She turned to Andrew. 'I never knew she suffered from migraine!' But Andrew just shook his head. How should I know? his demeanour suggested. How should I know about women's things? Women were always getting things. And they were especially good at headaches, he thought sourly, chewing his bacon and looking sideways at his wife, whose eyes were very bright. Why is she glowing? he wondered. She has nothing to glow about. She denies her husband and her nature. It's not natural . . . not natural. Then he thought, this bacon is damn good. He glanced surreptitiously at Kate and thought she looked damn good too.

'Is it all right if I go up to see her?' Jenny inquired after a moment. She was regretting that she had committed herself to going riding, and was seeking a way out. If she could spend the time with Yvonne, try to soothe her, even sit with her . . .

Theo shrugged. 'If you like, of course . . . But she generally needs to be left in peace when she is suffering . . . makes the pain worse when people are present or try to talk to her! She needs a dark room for a day or two. She said to tell you this. She was sure you would understand!'

'Oh,' Jenny said, 'I see.'

She glanced at Kate, but the latter was frowning at her brother, her brow knitted as though there was something here which didn't add up.

'Jenny hasn't ridden before, but I can see she's a good sport!' Theo said. 'Poor old Yvonne was in such a funk when I tried to teach her.'

Kate did not answer. 'You can wear one of my habits,' she murmured, looking into Jenny's face, 'if you really want to go. They're a bit old fashioned; I hope you won't mind! There's several pairs of ladies' boots, all old as the hills, but still serviceable.'

'She can always ride astride,' Andrew said. 'I'm sure that would suit her!'

Jenny reddened with vexation.

'Not in this neck of the woods,' Kate said softly. 'What would the parish priest say?'

'Oh, the wickedness of it,' Theo murmured mockingly. 'The mortal sin of it; the hell for all eternity of it; the mad, power-crazed nonsense of it. A woman astride a horse; a woman with her legs spread; life with its legs spread!' He stood up. His face was suffused with anger. 'I detest the parochialism of religion and its great and petty tryannies!'

When he had left the room, Kate turned to Jenny. 'It is good of you to humour him. He seems a bit overwrought. But do not go riding unless you want to.'

'It would be a novelty for me,' Jenny said. 'I would like to try it.'

'Shall I come with you?'

'Only if you wish. I shall be all right.'

Kate smiled at her; her eyes were without mirth. But she glanced at Andrew and met his eyes.

Later, in the stable yard, Batty had the horses waiting: Theo's chestnut, Caesar, and the 'lady's horse', Polly, formerly ridden by Yvonne.

Theo got into the saddle with no help from his groom. Jenny stood on the mounting block and obeyed instructions. Theo told her how to hold the reins and Batty looked on in covert disparagement. But she got the hang of it quickly. There was nothing to holding the reins. But what did bother her was the fact, which she appreciated immediately, that she had no control at all if the horse should bolt or trip or do any of the dangerous manoeuvres she knew these animals were capable of.

'All set?' Theo asked. 'We'll just walk for a bit.' Batty went to open the gate, and the two horses walked under the limestone arch and took a left turn towards the fields.

'There's a boreen over here which will bring us out near the cliffs . . . Are you comfortable?' He turned his head to watch his guest.

Jenny held herself erect. She was nervous, but after a little while she began to enjoy the feeling of being on horseback, the tension at the small of her back, the contact of the stirrup at her foot and the saddle tree inside her right knee, the breeze at her face and neck. She watched the forward motion of her mount's head and it occurred to her that riding was mostly a matter of balance.

'I'm fine,' she called back, 'but I feel I have to rely on balance, that I have no control!'

Theo laughed, waited for her where the path became wider. 'Of course you have no control. Side-saddle is a hobble: women are so good at wearing them! In fact, they are so good at wearing them that whole cultures are distorted to accommodate this amazing facility.'

Jenny was stung. 'I'm not,' she said. 'I'm not good at being hobbled! Are you always so provocative?'

He smiled with sudden charm. 'Do you find me irritating?'

'I don't know you well enough for that.'

They moved side by side in silence. Then he said very softly, 'But I think you *do* know *me . . .* !'

Jenny turned to him. 'I do not. I never saw you in my life until the day of your wedding to Yvonne.'

The day returned to her: Yvonne at the altar, the sight of his head and profile, the rush for the door and the violent retching.

He sighed, turned away to gaze around him. 'Look,' he said, gesticulating as they emerged from behind some trees, 'there are the cliffs up to your right. This side of the peninsula slopes down to the shore.'

Jenny examined the panorama. The breakers flung themselves in fury at the beach, tore at the dark rocks, flinging white spume high into the air and receding with a sucking, rending motion as the small stones clashed in the undertow. High above the water, the seagulls wheeled and cried their harsh, lonely song. Away to the right she saw sheep grazing at the rise to the cliffs and the stone walls dividing each field into squares which looked about as big as postage stamps.

There were a few cottages, with half doors open to the morning. A woman fed chickens in her yard and stood up straight to watch the riders pass by.

Theo's horse began to trot, and Jenny's followed suit.

'Oh,' she gasped to herself, trying to ignore the discomfort of a motion which would have flung her up and down if she had not been anchored by the saddle tree.

Theo glanced at her. 'I'm sorry. You would find a canter more comfortable side-saddle, but we will leave that until another time.'

He reined in Caesar, who danced under the restraint, eager for a gallop. 'I will never hurt you. I will never allow you to be hurt . . . again,' he said gently, without changing tone, and Jenny did not pretend that she had heard. 'Do you hear me?'

Jenny glanced at him, frowning. 'Do you hear me?' he repeated patiently, as though addressing a child.

'Yes. I heard you . . . But . . . I do not understand why you should concern yourself with my welfare. It is hardly a concern of yours. And, if you will forgive me saying so, I would ask you not to pay me so marked an attention, particularly in your wife's presence. She is my friend!'

Jenny felt that she had acquitted herself well by this speech. She flushed with the effort of having said it, and barely glanced at her host from the corner of her eye. He sat watching her, and the horses walked on.

'I am hungry for you, Jenny. I have some certainty in me about you . . . You are my truth.' He looked across at her. 'And I am yours. So you can scuttle away home if you like, if you take fright. But you will come to me somehow, somewhere. You might not know why, but you will come. You might hate me, but you will come. There are things to be resolved. There is no middle ground in this, and no escape.'

Jenny was silent. The act of listening to his voice, which came at her through the wind with a softness at variance with his usual biting sarcasm, made her feel she belonged to some elemental dimension.

A strange peace subsumed her. I will do what I must do, she thought. He is mad. I cannot encompass the madness, although it answers the absolute in me. I will do what I must.

He gestured towards the beach; the sunlight glinted on his gold ring. 'The path gives out shortly. Would you like to dismount and take a walk along the beach?'

He got down first and put up a hand to help her. Then he tied the reins of both horses to a nearby hawthorn, and led the way across a rocky space to the shore.

He took her hand; she used the other one to anchor her hat, which was straining against the hat-pins. The water frothed raggedly up the beach.

'Jenny,' he said, leaning towards her to speak into her ear, 'I asked you for the mask. You remember, I came to you when you were sick . . . Long ago, when you were a child. I came to you often in those days. I said I would come back for you.'

Jenny had the feeling that she had been swept into some deadly charade. She tried to remember the face of the man she had seen through the mask all those years ago. She felt Theo's hand draw her behind a huge boulder, which gave some shelter.

'I don't understand. How do you know?' Then she thought: Of course, Yvonne must have told him, and she tried to remember how much she had told Yvonne. 'Oh, Theo, why do you tease me like this? You know perfectly well that none of that is possible!' She had to shout to make herself heard above the wind.

He smiled. 'Not only is it possible, but it has happened. What makes you so sure that time is linear? Everything is possible, Jenny. I learnt that. But I need the mask.'

Jenny pulled away from him. 'You are talking madness . . .'

'Will you send it to me?'

'No. If it really is an artefact with some kind of power — as you seem to suggest — why should I not use it?' She thought of the day she had looked through it and what she had seen. But she had been very young and the memory was indistinct, more a taste than a vivid recollection. 'What makes you assume that everything has to gravitate to you?'

'You cannot use it, Jenny. You don't know how, or what it is capable of now that I have found you. It must be restored to where it came from!' He lifted his left hand and thrust the gold ring towards her. 'They went to certain silly rounds to hide this, you know; wrapped it up with charms, like a fortune-teller's toy, and put it on the hand of a statue they made of me. That was supposed to contain it. But they forgot who had made it.' He lowered his voice. 'The mask, however, is another matter! You may rest assured I would never hurt you or allow you to be hurt again!'

Jenny looked at the furious sea. 'So you keep saying . . . But I can tell you this — that I will not be hurt by you, or anyone else for that matter, because I will not permit it, and not because of your arrogant munificence! I have my own business in the ritornello of the years.'

Theo looked at her and smiled. 'You always had,' he said in a voice full of contained passion. 'I love you!'

'You have a wife you should love!'

He ignored the comment. 'I will follow you always; even if you escaped me now, Jenny, it would not be for long! You would return and so would I. There is something to be resolved between us! You have forgotten, but I cannot. There will be no peace until it is!'

'Theo, let us go home.'

He bowed and they moved back up the beach to the horses. As they mounted they saw little Molly Moloney, Batty's daughter, who was walking barefoot along the boreen, disappear into cover behind a stone wall. 'That child sees everything,' Theo said. 'Maybe she will be my chronicler!'

'Tell me,' Jenny said after a moment, 'what is

the meaning of the mask — since you seem to know so much! So many strange things have happened since first I found it. It is only a thing, after all . . .'

'It is more than that. It was generated out of anguish.'

'Are you telling me it's magic?'

He looked at her. 'You can call it that if you like. Anyone who finds it is changed for ever. Once the world was full of magic, you know, full of magicians.' He smiled at her. 'So tell me what you want, Jenny.'

'I want to be free.'

He was silent, as though the answer displeased him. Then he said, 'Be sure of one thing. I will follow you, no matter how many people you become or how many years you try to escape me. The years mean nothing. I need who you are. What happened must be undone. Do you think you could love me?'

'Love is earned,' Jenny said, trying to stem the sense of alarm. 'In the end it has to be earned!'

'I wonder. It has to do so much with resonance, with necessity.'

'It has to do with respect.'

'I respect you,' he said. 'If you remembered anything you would remember that! It was because they respected you so much, feared you because they respected you, that the deed was done . . .'

Jenny didn't know what he talking about. 'You have a wife such as few men could hope for,' she said. 'As for me, I have yet to find my niche in the turmoil of eternity. Claiming me with power will not persuade me. I live with someone who subcribes to power. I am bored to death by power!'

'What do you want?'

'I told you — to be free!'

'If you were free,' he said slowly, 'you would not look at me; you would not spend hours talking to a magician in the attic. If you were free, I would lose you for ever.'

Jenny felt the movement of her mount and the rush of the breeze. She straightened her back. Yvonne had told him a great deal, it would seem, and this surprised her. But then Yvonne had been alone and removed from her family and friends, with no one but him.

She humoured him, trying to penetrate the tangled coils of his thought. 'If you would lose me for that reason, you never had me, Mr Magician. What does your love mean, after all? Does it give me the power to be myself, or does it seek to bind me to your perceptions, your requirements, your terrors? Does it seek only to use me as leaven for your own emptiness? Why do you really want me?'

Theo turned to look at her. 'Because I honour you. Because you belong to yourself.'

Jenny laughed. 'And that is anathema?'

'It is rare. It is something I must have or die.'

'Die then, Theo. I am not your keeper.'

Theo smiled. 'You are delicious,' he murmured. 'But I will not die. I will live for you! I will undo it all.'

Jenny was tired. It seemed suddenly like a silly game. She looked through the trees and saw that they were nearly home. But when she turned to look at him again, she saw that the tears were pouring silently down his face.

Chapter Nineteen

'Why do they fear me?'
'Lady, they fear the truth.'

Journal of a Witness

Batty listened to the suggestions one of the men made about the fate of Kilashane.

'They can stuff it up their jumpers!'

He sat back in his chair. The turf fire behind him in the open hearth was oppressively hot, sending out aromatic puffs when the wind changed, making everyone's eyes water. 'Good for the eye-juices, anyway,' someone offered, wiping his eyes.

'Nobody burns Kilashane,' Batty repeated. Molly was sitting at the table beside him and working on her homework; he stroked her hair. 'Molly, child, go to bed now!'

The girl smiled at her father, put down her pencil, lit a candle and took it and the copybook with her to the adjoining bedroom, shutting the door.

'Are you thinking of Mr O'Reilly?' inquired Pat Keegan, the blacksmith. He sat at the far end of the scrubbed deal table in Batty's kitchen, enjoying his position of belonging to the inside group, the men who were going to forge a new

Ireland. 'Sure he's gone from bad to worse. He asked me the other day how all the gombeen men were in what he calls "Paddysland". He shows no respect for anyone and none for his country.'

Batty pulled on his pipe and regarded Pat with ostensible patience. 'He's as mad as a March hare,' he said equably. 'One Master Theo went off to the war, and another came back. That's the truth of it!'

The men smiled. They all knew Theo. Some had fished with him when they were children, spending long summer afternoons on the banks of the Meena where the trout were sometimes obliging and sometimes not. A few had joined him in later years on the shoots for pheasant and grouse in the woodland at the neck of the peninsula. But Theo was a landlord, and although a Catholic of old Irish stock, his suspected Unionist loyalties made him a target. The big houses were a target. A proud and angry people, accustomed to hiding their shame at being tenants in their own country under sarcasm and melancholy, felt the changing tempo of the times and knew that theirs had come.

'You'll run into trouble if you don't obey orders — if they give the order,' someone ventured.

'Trouble is right!' Batty said. 'Kilashane is the only employer in the townland. What do ye think we will do if it is gone? Make daisy chains? Is that what ye want?'

Pat and the rest of the men conceded that Batty had a point. Most of them worked in Kilashane as farmhands, and most had cottages on the estate, with a few acres, for which they paid nominal rents. The income for the big house was being generated by the rearing of beef cattle and lambs for export. It was a mystery how the O'Reillys, being Catholic, had managed to hold on to their lands right through the Penal times when Catholic lands were confiscated; it was whispered that the devil had put a mark on the place so that the English had left it in peace. However much the English liked to throw their weight around, they were reluctant, for some reason, to involve themselves more than was strictly necessary with the powers of darkness.

'Didn't he play cards with the company one night and only disappeared when someone noticed he had a cloven hoof!' Batty's father had told him long years before.

Batty, young, impressionable and afraid, had gasped, 'How did he disappear?'

'No bother to him. Wasn't he the divil? Up the chimney with him in a flash, cracking the hearthstone . . . You can see it in the drawing room in the big house to this day!'

'Why would the divil want to play cards in Kilashane?'

Batty's father had thought for a moment. 'Looking for souls,' he said. 'Looking for excitement. Bored stiff, maybe . . .' He shook his head.

Batty had checked the accuracy of his father's

story. Sure enough, there was a crack on the hearthstone. But he had his reservations about the 'divil'.

Batty's father had worked for old man O'Reilly. He was proud to work for a member of Parliament, a friend of Parnell, the uncrowned king of Ireland. He was a man who liked to travel, and Batty remembered how he had taken his wife on a tour of Italy some years before the war. He had died there, in Italy, in the city of Rome.

Batty enjoyed his position as general factotum in Kilashane. Some called him the chief steward, but as there was no other steward, the title was a bit incongruous. He looked after the books. Mrs O'Reilly was the final fiscal authority, and he presented the books to her. She knew he was honest, but she checked them carefully. Between the two of them, Kilashane was being kept on the rails, diminished in fortune from its heyday, but viable still.

Batty often wondered about Mrs O'Reilly. She was still relatively young, handsome, but, it seemed, committed to widowhood. She was a fine lump of a woman, he told himself, as he watched her examine the books with her head slightly to one side, and her brown hair, greying at the temples, piled up on the top of her head. Batty had been widowed two years previously, and he chafed at the waste of his own lusty life.

'Isn't there any decent man would do you, at all?' he asked her one day towards the end of the war. 'A woman needs her pleasure!'

Mrs O'Reilly did not look up from the books, but a small, tight smile creased the corners of her mouth.

'Batty, are you for marrying me off?'

'Not at all, ma'am. It's the waste I was thinkin' of. There's many a grand man that does be starvin' for female companionship . . .'

'I'm afraid I can't help them, Batty! Would you be thinking of anyone in particular?'

Batty heard the edge to her voice, notwithstanding the smile. 'No offence meant, ma'am.'

'None taken, Batty.'

After that, Batty consoled himself with the whiskey. There was a cask in the cellar, laid down by the old man some years earlier, and Batty had drilled a hole at the bottom. This hole Batty stopped with a cork, but he helped himself to the fiery spirit at night, before he headed for home. On his way back to his cottage, he was frequently overtaken by an inexplicable weakness of the legs, and would end up in the ditch. Sitting there in the deep, damp grass he would enjoy the afterglow, sometimes bursting into enthusiastic song. Local people who heard him wondered at the great pay he must be getting to be drunk every night of the week. Others, who didn't know the source of the midnight singing, swore they heard the banshee. But the whiskey did not last, and when he had finished the cask Batty filled it up with water.

'Sure they'll never know!' he told himself.

' 'Twas a sin, stuff the like of that going to waste with no one to drink it!' But now Master Theo was home, and Batty lived in dread that he would call for some of his father's whiskey and find out about the inverse miracle.

So there was only one thing to be done: drain the water from the cask and fill it with poteen, the illicit distillation made from potatoes which had a potency in the region of one hundred per cent. He cut it with some water and cheap sherry, and because he had accidentally poured in too much sherry, he adjusted the taste with a tincture of iodine.

Since his return, Master Theo had taken over the running of the estate himself, leaving only the books to his mother. He paid the men in person once a week, sitting in the loft of the barn, a drawerful of money beside him, and the men would come to him one by one through the trap door and sign for their wages. He had given Batty a revolver and told him to stand behind him with it while he paid the men.

'With the unrest in the country and all that, I don't want to take any chances with Paddy-the-Pale-Patriot!'

Batty laughed privately, and the men of the local IRA tried not to smile as they saw their commandant standing behind their employer with a loaded revolver.

'Poor bastard,' they said, loving him for the incongruity of it. 'Sure who would hurt him anyway? Isn't he harmless for all his carry on?'

From her vantage point in her bedroom, Yvonne watched her husband return with her friend. He was laughing, but without the cruel twist to his mouth which he employed with her. He glanced at Jenny with open, candid love. There was no mistaking the expression, or the way her eyes moved back to him, the small smile. Everyone knew it now. Batty, who came to take the horses, knew it; Kate, who watched the pair from her quiet, personal remove, knew it. Mrs O'Reilly surely knew it; she watched them at table with a disquiet which was evident to everyone except them. Andrew watched them too, but he drank so much whiskey before and after his meals that he was in no condition to make any coherent protest.

Watching them, Yvonne felt she would give her immortal soul to change places, to have Theo look at her like that, smile with that utter intimacy, reach for her hand as he did for Jenny's when he helped her to dismount. She retraced in her mind the events which had led to this impasse; she remembered Theo in the nursing home. He had been churlish then, but sweetly so; lost, vulnerable, a man who did not know where next he should put his feet. Now he lorded it around the countryside and the people treated him like God, although it was clear that they looked askance at him being constantly in the company of a woman who was not his wife. She could see this in the eyes of every person

they met when they drove out together, the polite greeting, the sham obsequiousness, the shift
of the eyes from him to Jenny to her. She was his
wife, and this humiliation was her lot. For a moment she thought of what the parish priest had
said, what he had exhorted. Get the ring from
him, indeed! How was she to accomplish that?
The ring never came off Theo's finger; if she
tried to prise it off while he was asleep . . . She
shuddered at the possible repercussions. No. He
would have to be ill, in a weakened, insensible
state, before anything like that would work.

She tried to talk to Jenny. 'People are talking
— about you and Theo!'

Jenny seemed so thunderstruck that Yvonne
was instantly mollified, instantly descending on
her own readiness to think ill of her friend.

'You mean . . . ? Oh, Yvonne, I shall not ride
with him any more. I'm blind . . . I've been blind.
Oh, I shall not ride any more with him. You
should have come with us!'

'I hate riding,' Yvonne said. 'I hate riding and
I hate his comments when I try, and I hate the
way he looks at you and I hate being the wife of
someone who loves someone else and, most of
all, I hate loving someone who loves someone
else!' She turned away.

Jenny was silent. 'We have done nothing
wrong,' she said after a moment. 'I am very sorry
that I have caused you pain. I will talk to Andrew
and we will go home tomorrow.'

Yvonne started. She saw Theo's face in her

mind's eye; she imagined his fury. She saw her own loneliness. 'No! He treats me as if I am a figment of my own imagination. If you go home, he will be terrible! Worse!'

'You could come too,' Jenny said. 'Come back with us to London. There is something here I do not understand. Why cannot we all go away and leave it behind? You and I could go away together . . .'

Yvonne laughed bitterly. 'It cannot be left behind. And he cannot be left behind. He is the one thing in my life that I utterly require. His cruelty is a kind of absolute. It scorches to the bone. I am addicted to it. I need it almost as much as I need his love!'

She turned and walked away. Jenny watched her stiff movement down the landing. She ran after her. 'Yvonne, I don't know what is going on here . . . Theo is mad. Is there no one we can talk to, no one you can talk to? Something will have to be done!'

'I am the one who is mad,' Yvonne whispered. 'I let him get away with everything. The parish priest, Father Keane, ascribes his behaviour to some superstitious rubbish; he said I must take away his ring. He seemed frightened . . . How can I talk to him, a man who clearly believes in shibboleths? Anyway, there is no easy way of getting the ring.' She shook her head. 'No! I will deal with this in my own way!'

Jenny let her go. I must leave, she thought. I must go back to London and face reality. But first I will talk to Father Keane. He may know more than Yvonne thinks. And he is the only person outside the family to whom it would be possible to talk about this. He is the only chance there is . . .

That evening, for the first time, Mrs O'Reilly began to talk of Venice. Dinner was over and she was with her guests in the drawing room and, as she had the beginnings of a cold, had been prevailed upon to accept a whiskey. She drank it in tiny sips, but it was clear that the spirit was making itself felt, for her eyes became bright, and a dull flush mottled her usually pale face.

She had asked Jenny about her parents, and Jenny had said her father had been secretary to a man who wrote and travelled — Sir Michael Philips. 'He was in Italy before the war and then he went away to France. He died in Paris.'

'I was in Italy many years ago with Theo's father. It was our last holiday together.'

'What did you do?' Jenny inquired politely. 'I have never been there.'

'There is much to see . . . Venice, for instance, is a city of great art treasures, some of them dating back to Roman times. The four horses over the loggia of St Mark's basilica, for example, came from Constantinople. The lion of St Mark in the square of that name came from Persia. The Venetians were originally people fleeing persecution, who established themselves in the salt marshes of the neck of the Adriatic and, becoming enriched through their command of the spice and salt trade, built a city. They built it on water, on piles sunk into the mud, and developed it into a city state which became a model for the world. I met people there, a couple by the name of di Robenico, who told me quaint stories.'

'What kind of stories?'

Mrs O'Reilly sighed and looked at her son. Theo appeared to be in a brown study. 'About the past, long years ago when people on the Continent fled to Venice to escape persecution. There was a young woman, for instance, who was said to have preached some kind of heresy and been persecuted by the Inquisition. Her inquisitor tried to save her in the end — but it was too late. It was a love story; I suppose you could say a sort of myth.'

'What was her heresy?' Yvonne asked.

Mrs O'Reilly shook her head. 'Who knows? But the thing was a scandal of the time, for when she was dead he resorted to black arts to bring her back, to restore her to life! He deserted the Church and hid her corpse in Venice so that they should not burn it.'

There was silence in the room. 'But she was dead,' Kate said.

The fire settled; the dog moved, pricking up his ears, and then subsided, his head between his paws.

'Death,' Theo said softly, without turning his head, 'is an invention of the blind!'

Yvonne looked at him with an anguish which was full of resentment.

'The Church said she was a witch,' Mrs O'Reilly added. 'They had a great number of them in those days.'

Kate watched the candlelight flicker on the faces around the table. 'Indeed! Every woman who had a thought in her head, or a single requirement for her own fulfilment, was a witch!' She flushed. Andrew looked at her and smiled into his whiskey.

'Did he find her?' Jenny whispered into the silence. 'Did he contact the dead girl?'

Mrs O'Reilly widened her eyes, shrugged. 'It's only a story. They say he learnt the arts of possession, that he had a ring invested with some kind of power . . . But how can you contact the dead?' She paused. 'Signore di Robenico also told me there was something else of the bizarre in his possession; something he made with the devil at his shoulder!' Mrs O'Reilly glanced around the table at the expectant faces, looked at Kate.

'What was it?' Jenny demanded.

'I don't know. Some kind of catalyst.'

'This di Robenico fellow — what was he like?' Theo asked suddenly.

Mrs O'Reilly seemed to tense. Her knuckles whitened for a moment on the glass in her hand. She avoided her son's eyes and stared into the fire.

'He was tall,' she said in a voice devoid of emphasis.

449

'Did he fancy himself a descendant of this inquisitor?'

'I don't know. But I do know he was avid to find the source of a rubbing your father took during one of his nocturnal walks in Venice. He said it was of the signet on the magician's ring. But your father could never locate the place again.'

Kate made a sound. Theo stared at her across the room. He rose, walked across the room to his mother, his stride uneven. He held out his hand. 'What do you think of that ring, Mother? Have you ever seen that signet before?'

She stared at it, put her hand abruptly to her throat. What was it Salvatore had said? She strained to hear his voice again. Some kind of warning. 'If your husband has found it, he must not keep it. He must give it up; he must get rid of it, carissima . . .' She remembered suddenly what Father Keane had told them in the course of his recent visit.

'Papa sent it to him from Venice,' Kate said in answer to her mother's unspoken question. Mrs O'Reilly closed her eyes and sat back in her chair. She was looking tired and bitter, like someone who had been defeated.

Later, in their room, Jenny said to Andrew, 'Let's go home.'

Andrew drank his whiskey. 'Why? It is comfortable here. The booze is astonishing. Your lover is mellowing, Yvonne is quiet, the winsome

Kate is not entirely out of reach, and one of the wenches in the dairy is semi-accommodating. The drawback is our hostess, who insists on boring us blind with her travels. But, who knows, I may even get to like Ireland!'

Jenny began to shiver. 'Are you cold?' Andrew asked conversationally. 'Throw another few sods on the fire. Have a whiskey. This Irish whiskey is powerful stuff — never came across anything like it in my life! Take your clothes off and seduce your husband . . . Ah,' he added, hearing Theo's staccato step on the stair, 'why not take them off and seduce your lover?'

Jenny heard the slow steps. In a moment he would be on the landing. 'He is not my lover!'

Andrew sneered from the armchair. 'You expect me to believe that!'

She turned to him. 'It is true. But, Andrew, I am desperate . . . Take me home. Take me away from that man!'

But Andrew only laughed. 'What has he done to you? Seduced you without due care and attention? Are we feeling a little sore? Don't worry: practice makes perfect. But I am not going home and you are staying here to reap the benefit of what you have sown. We shall stay for the harvest of your iniquities.'

'He is quite mad. We are all drifting into madness!'

'Rot!'

Jenny listened as the halting steps passed their door. 'Andrew, I must go. I must find something

I have at home: a mask!'

Andrew smiled. 'You mean the enamelled affair in silver? The dear lady and her reminiscing have made you jumpy.'

'But,' she whispered, 'how did you know about it?'

'I am not a fool, nor as blind as you take me for.'

'I have to destroy it . . .'

Andrew found this very amusing. He laughed again, got up and went to the window. The sea was silvered by the moon and it marched towards the shore in serried waves.

'Why are you always . . . baiting me . . . ?'

Andrew considered her pale face. For a moment he wanted to weep with loss. What had gone so wrong for them? Why had things turned out the way they had? He knew she was special; he wanted to deserve her; he knew she was talented and private; he wanted her love and admiration. He wanted the warm beauty in her as the place where he could warm his soul. But he had lost the hope of it and now was trapped in a burrow he had dug for himself. He did not know how to extricate himself. It was too late. So he plunged on with the superciliousness he had adopted as armour. Pride came before all. For it, he had raped his wife and hanged the pet she loved, and still he had not won. What did you have to do to win?

'You see, my dear, I took the liberty of bringing the mask with me . . .'

Jenny stared at him. 'You mean you have it here?'

'I did have it,' Andrew said. 'But I gave it to Theo.' He gestured with his hand. 'I gave it to him today, in fact, after you returned from your little ride. He did seem so uncommonly interested.'

Jenny stood very still. 'You have betrayed me,' she murmured.

Chapter Twenty

'She hath seduced her inquisitor,' his Eminence said. 'Her beauty is the Devil's tool. Relieve her of it in God's name!'

The witch screamed when they brought the oil of vitriol.

Journal of a Witness

Mrs O'Reilly sat with Kate in the drawing room. She was tired. The weariness seeped through her, so that every limb felt heavy. I am getting old, she thought. But I was not old that summer of 1914. I was not old in Venice. I was not old the first day I took the gondola to that house. I wore a veil. It was evening and he was there to take my hand at the water-gate, bend over it. *'Come sei bella!'* Then he murmured, *'Sono un uomo ferito'*, a wounded man.

He led me across the mosaic floor, up the marble stairs. There were echoes. The house was empty, the bedroom baroque. He loved my body with a totality I could not have dreamed of. Afterwards there was no guilt, just elation, as Eve must have felt when she ate of the tree of the knowledge of good and evil. But I felt worried coming back to the hotel, although to no purpose. Bernard was as immersed as always.

He looked up from his papers long enough to register that I had returned. 'Nice time, dear? Good. Good.'

Later I asked him about the ring, and I knew he was lying. But I could not find it, although I searched for it next day while he was out with Monsignor Dillon. Yes, I played the snake in the grass to Bernard, the husband who would practically knock me down to get at another snippet of that wretched story, just as he had brushed by me with his papers all our married life.

'*Te adore,*' Salvatore would say, his eyes full of worship, and, '*Bellissima, bellissima,*' as each piece of underwear came off. How strange and delicious it was to cast off invisibility, to discover so much, to allow myself to live.

Kate stirred. 'I suppose I should go to bed, Mother.'

Mary O'Reilly came out of her reverie. She regarded Kate and wished that the child were prettier. It would not be easy to marry her off. Men didn't take to serious women, unless they were beautiful. The days of plenitude at Kilashane were over, so she would not even have a hefty dowry.

'You're looking very pale. Are you all right?' She lowered her voice as Kate nodded. 'Are you weary with entertaining?'

'No, I'm fine, Mother. I went for a long walk today and I'm tired.'

'Where did you go?'

'To the church. To visit Father's grave.'

'On your own?'

'No,' Kate said after a moment's hesitation, 'Andrew came with me.'

'Was that wise?'

Kate shrugged. Something in the gesture perturbed her mother. 'I trust he behaved like a gentleman!'

'Oh, yes. He spoke to me of London and suggested we run away together! You see, he is in love with his wife, but in thrall to himself! I let him kiss me; I wanted to see what it was like!'

She saw how her mother's face became set, then vulnerable, as she revised her initial reaction of outrage. 'Were you always wise, Mother?'

Mrs O'Reilly caught her breath. 'Wisdom is distilled from the stuff of one's own life,' she said after a moment. 'None of us is wise to order, not even mothers! But one thing I am sure of — it would be the height of folly to allow that man to play with you. You know that as well as I do!'

'Play with me! Of course I do! I also know that I live so silent a life that I am sometimes unsure as to whether I am alive at all! It seems to me that everything is surrounded by such strictures, such half truths, that one is slowly strangled.'

She regarded her mother's stricken face. 'Never mind. There are things to be done, even by a plain Jane . . . Tell me about Father. Wasn't he the wisest of beings? I used to feel resentful that he died! The day his coffin came back was the worst day of my life! But at least you had your last holiday together!'

'Your father?' Mrs O'Reilly said wearily. 'All wisdom and no understanding. I can tell you this now. He became withdrawn and obsessive on that last holiday. In fact, I was angry with him. It was supposed to have been a second honey-moon, but instead he spent his time talking to that dreadful Monsignor Dillon, who ate and drank his way through Italy. Grovelling to a gross man like that so that he would gain access to some Vatican archives! He was fired with some quest he would not share with me. He wouldn't trouble me with it, he said, patting my hand.'

She paused. 'I was sick of having my hand pat-ted. Perhaps I should have stayed in Italy.' She sighed, shut her eyes, and added softly, 'Perhaps I am the one who should have died there!' Kate heard her mother's voice become unsteady.

'Did Father ever speak of me in Italy?' Kate whispered.

Her mother did not take up the question. She shook her head and murmured, 'I have con-fessed, but it does no good!' She remembered the monsignor's prurient eyes, and how he had shifted in the seat, his crotch giving the lie to his grave, sacerdotal face. 'You must not let that man kiss you. It is quite improper!'

Kate shrugged defiantly. 'What do I care?'

She remembered how Andrew had squeezed her breast, and she had felt such a surge of life and lust that she would have let him have her, right there on the grass. 'I don't care, Mother. He is a man I could take to. His wife does not understand him . . .'

'The old story, Kate. The old story!'

Kate compressed her lips. Her mother watched her and said in a voice full of emotion, 'Darling, will you not turn back to the sacraments, to the practice of your religion? Why do you cut yourself off from the source of God's love?'

Kate's mouth tightened, and her mother saw this and desisted. 'But it's a long walk,' she added, referring to Kate's walk earlier that day. 'You could have asked Batty to drive you — cycled.'

Kate smiled and said she had preferred to walk, and her mother rang the bell. Una came with a lamp and carried it up the stairs, although there was one already lit in the landing which threw shadows through the banisters and on to the walls, picking up colour in old paintings. Kate stayed behind in the drawing room and looked into the fire.

The house quietened. Theo and Yvonne were in their room, Jenny and Andrew in theirs. Outside a thin rain fell. Una came into the drawing room before she went up to bed.

'I'm off now, Miss Kate. You won't forget to riddle the ashes into the grate before you go up, and put up the fire guard?'

Una always asked this question. She had a terror of being burnt in her bed.

'Don't worry, Una. I'll see to it.'

Una's steps sounded heavily in the hall, then receded as she disappeared through the door to the kitchen stairs.

Kate's mind was feverish, full of the images and memories conjured by the talk she had had with her mother. She remembered clearly her parents' last holiday: she had been fourteen then, and Theo six years older. She remembered the day a letter came for him, followed some time later by a parcel. But her father, whom she loved, had not written to her from Italy. When her mother wrote he contented himself with a postscript, asking how his little Platypus was. But he did not write himself, and he did not send her a present.

On the day the small parcel came for Theo, she had watched jealously while he opened it, taking out a packing of folded newsprint and a pair of heavy glass paperweights. But in the middle of the packing was a small morocco box, and inside that was a heavy gold ring.

Theo had laughed, held up the ring, examined it in the palm of his hand, murmured, 'So this is what he was talking about . . .'

Kate was filled with the certainty of some kind of conspiracy between her brother and her father, something from which she was excluded. A sense of worthlessness pervaded her. Theo was treated as though he mattered. She was a 'platypus'. Once she had looked in the dictionary to see what the word meant. The horror of the definition — 'an aquatic, egg-laying mammal, having a pliable duck-like bill, webbed feet and sleek grey fur' — had frozen her heart. She had avoided mirrors after that. It was no use telling herself that she was pretty. She knew, Papa knew, everyone knew that she was not.

'Are you going to wear it?' she had asked her brother who, since he had gone up to Trinity, affected English mannerisms. He slipped it on the ring finger of his right hand and took it off again.

'Wear it! Dear infant, the thing is a bit sudden.' He put it back in its little box and slipped it into his pocket.

'Do you want one of these paperweights?' he asked then, examining the objects in blue glass. 'Not my style!' Kate had shaken her head. 'Not mine either!' she had said.

The following day — Sunday — she had gone to Mass in the trap with Theo. She had been wearing new gloves, which Una had bought for her in Cork the week before. She had listened to Father Keane intone his way through the Mass, watched through her lashes during the elevation of the Host. Every other head in the church was bowed. *Domine non sum dignus,'* the priest said, and she had bent her own head.

On the way home in the trap she had realized that she'd left her gloves behind.

Theo had been annoyed. 'Why are girls such scattered little creatures?' he'd inquired irritably as he turned the trap around. 'All the way back for a silly pair of gloves!'

The church was empty. Everyone had gone home to their midday meal. Kate approached the pew at the front, but there was no sign of the gloves. She wondered if the sacristan had found them, and she glanced up at the door of the sacristy, which was on the other side of the altar, and stood open. She moved up the steps and crossed the sanctuary, forgetting that it would be out of bounds for women, entered the small room where the surplices hung against the wall. An altar-boy, still in his surplice, was putting something into a drawer. He turned with a start.

'Did you find a pair of gloves?' Kate asked.

The boy looked around, saw a pair of white gloves on the side table, indicated them. 'Are those they?'

Kate nodded. The boy grabbed them and shoved them at her.

'Get out quick,' he said with a smirk, in which the power to offend with impunity played for an instant, 'before Father Keane comes back and finds a girl in the sacristy!'

Kate felt as though she had been struck. A girl in the sacristy! A contamination! She saw herself instantly as something unclean, as less than she knew herself to be. She took the gloves and left. She carried the smirk with her. If she had met the boy anywhere else he would not have dared to offer her an affront, or even wished to. She sensed the significance of what he had said as greater than the words. A boy with grubby fingernails who picked his nose and played with his private parts was giddy with licence because he stood in a sacristy. Had she been beautiful he would not have said it. They hated you for being female, but would endure and flatter you, while hating you, if you blinded them with beauty. Without it you might as well be dead.

Theo had asked her why she was so quiet, and she had told him.

He had laughed. 'Is our little platypus feeling peeved? Is she cross? Does she find the order of things irksome?'

Kate had turned angrily to look her brother in the face. 'Not irksome, Theo. Intolerable! And I'm not a platypus!'

He'd raised his eyebrows with a suppressed chuckle. 'Dear me . . . !'

Don't laugh at me, Kate had thought.

Later that day, when Theo had gone out riding, she had gone to his room, found his tweed jacket, and searched the pockets. The little box was still there with the ring inside. She took it away to her own room, played with it for a while, hid it beneath the chest of drawers in a cleft above the carved wooden leg. It took him a day to realize that it was gone.

'Where did I put that confounded ring? Did you see my ring — the one Father sent me? I thought I left it in my pocket.'

'No.'

He was upset. 'He'll never forgive me if I've lost it. Are you sure you didn't take it?' He grabbed her shoulder. 'Come on, Katy. Don't play silly games!'

'I'm not playing games.'

When a second letter in her father's writing came for Theo, she had intercepted it and brought it to her room.

> Hotel Superiore,
> Via delta Sistinaia,
> Rome

> 22 July 1914

My dear boy,

You will by now have received my letter and also the ring of which I told you. I have misgivings about the latter and feel that I acted precipitously in sending you so strange a curio, chanced upon in such strange circumstances.

We have visited Florence and now are in Rome. Monsignor Dillon has left us, disappeared into the world of the Vatican. He has been an excellent travelling companion and, thanks to his kindness, I have experienced more of the nuances of this extraordinary country than would have been otherwise possible. To assist my researches into the circumstances concerning the matters I raised in my last letter to you, he kindly searched in the Vatican library and found something of great interest.

His find was a letter in the Vatican archives

from a priest of the Inquisition, requesting the Pope to revoke the excommunication of a lady called Agnes of Florence. His letter to the Pope requested that steps be set in train for her beatification.

The Pope refused. He pointed out that the Church could not be seen to have erred, and that the woman's death was irrelevant. He also said that the woman deserved excommunication. It seems that, after this, the priest forsook his faith and took to magic. I suppose torture is unsettling! (Forgive my little joke.)

The correspondence is in Latin. I did not see it, of course, but the good monsignor made a copy. It bears the date 1601. The whole point of my writing about it to you is that the letter from the inquisitor is sealed with a signet, and the design is that of the ring you now have, or should have, in your possession. The monsignor assures me this is the case. He has compared the rubbing I made with the seal on the document.

He tells me, with some disparagement, that the inquisitor is said to be still searching for the woman he loved. In this he is recounting an old story — a piece of superstition, which we would call a *pishogue* at home. It is all nonsense, but I am sufficiently superstitious to wish I had not sent the ring to you. So I would ask of you only one thing: I beg of you, do not wear it. Put it away in some hidden place where no one will find it and return it to me when I come home. I have heard such strange tales about its owner that I am anxious you should have no close contact with anything of his.

You may say that he is dead and that all the troubles of the era he inhabited are past. But passion and injustice have a way of marking the very air around them, and of reverberating down the years.

I will see you soon. I am still 'under the weather' from an intermittent fever but, God willing, will have recovered my health by the time I set foot again in Kilashane. I am tired of our journey and the heat of this country which taxes my endurance. I begin to feel old. There are many things which burden my spirit. In addition your mother seems to have lost her *joie de vivre,* and has not been herself ever since we left Venice.

Your loving Father.

PS. Give our fond love to little Platypus.

Kate still had the letter. Theo had never known of it. Father had not come home alive. He had died in Rome and his remains were brought back and interred in the family vault near the church at Ballyshane.

Now, as she stared into the dying fire in the drawing room, she thought of Theo's reaction when she had handed him the ring at his wedding reception — how he had flung it across the

465

room. The guilt she had felt then, the guilt she felt now, intensified around her until the whole room seemed to echo with accusation. It's my fault, she thought. It's all my fault.

She thought of Theo, who had become half mad, even dangerous. She thought of Yvonne, trapped and desperate. She thought of Jenny, beautiful but fey, who did not understand Andrew. If you don't want him, she thought, why can't I have him? She thought again of Theo, who could not take his eyes off Andrew's wife. She thought of her mother and her secret pain, hinted at for the first time this evening. She thought again of Andrew, because she could not do other than think of him, whose foreignness she coveted, whose devotion she desired, but who was in love with his wife and without the courage to be vulnerable. She thought of herself. She thought of the past, where she was a shadow, a platypus to the father she adored. She thought of the present, full of secret hungers and insecurities, herself doomed to spinsterhood in a house full of casualties.

'It is time,' she told the fire. Time to end it. Time to end it.

Chapter Twenty-one

'I pray God I may never witness such scenes again. They restrained the inquisitor and made him watch. It was he who screamed at the dissolving flesh, for the woman had fainted.'

Journal of a Witness

Dee took out the diary, sat on her bed, tucked her legs beneath her and read.

Theo is full of some kind of triumph. I know him well enough now to realize that. He ignores me, seems to be caught up in a private world of insane intensity. Maybe I was wrong ever to deem him compos mentis. There is something here that smacks of a diabolic assertion, an inverted energy. Sometimes I am sure that I myself am going mad.

Jenny was pale as a sheet today. She assures me there is nothing between her and Theo; I do not doubt her honesty, in so far as she means that her honour is still intact. But there is more to a relationship than a roll in a feather bed, as I have found out with such cruel certitude. There is something between Theo and Jenny which is not wholesome, which is symbiotic in the extreme. He seems to live just for the purpose of turning his head and finding her there. What other plans he has I do not know. I would not put anything past him at this point.

Kate is quieter and quieter, although given to sudden comments full of brittle gaiety. I think the arrival of Jen and Andrew, on top of my addition to the family, has been very exhausting for one so unused to company. Andrew is fawning all over her; he seems to have set his cap at seducing her. But Theo does not appear to see this — I expected him to jump to his sister's protection: family honour and so forth. Kate herself seems impervious. I certainly do not want my brother to dishonour my sister-in-law. Sometimes I think he hates his wife. This is very sad. I feel something has disappointed him beyond measure. What has happened to the innocent world we used to inhabit when we were children?

I saw Theo with something in his hands earlier today. It was a curious antique, a mask with a strangely haunting expression.

'Where did you get that?' I asked.

'It came from Venice,' he said. 'All the way . . .'

He laughed and put it into a gladstone bag. Then he left the room and took it with him. He has an office down in the basement, and I can only suppose that he has taken it there.

I recall Jenny once saying that she had a carnival mask, but this thing did not look like a carnival. I suppose it is something that has been hidden in this house since the year of dot. There are so many things here which are old and evocative.

But I hear the dinner-gong and had better go down. I observe the rituals of the household. No one knows what I feel. But I know. I feel a murderous rage. I wake in the morning with it. I feel it when I look at him. Violence fills all my imaginings. My feelings fill me with terror. I married in rush of generosity and have been betrayed by it. Theo thinks this generosity is inexhaustible, that I will be there for him no matter what. He thinks that, because I gave it, he has acquired a right to it. He thinks that it never has to be earned. He thinks I am some sort of cornucopia which needs no nourishment. He is centred on cruelty. It is his oxygen. He fulfils it in me. But a reckoning must come. It is like truth and cannot be avoided. I will not spend the whole force of my life in propping up my own destruction.

Dee turned the next page but it was empty. She leafed back, teasing at pages which were stuck together. They did not yield, and when she tried gently to force them they tore. There was nothing else to be learnt from the diary.

She ran her thumb along the inside back

cover. She had noticed how the marbled blue backing page was unstuck. It gaped and she smoothed it down. But as she did so she felt what seemed an undue thickness underlying the lifting backing sheet, as though a sheet of paper had been inserted between it and the back of the cover.

She gently inserted her middle finger, and felt the edge of a paper, a folded sheet which had obviously been introduced at some time. She got her nail file and used it to carefully separate the backing sheet from the cover, lifting out the small document which had been folded in four.

My darling Yvonne,

I cannot bear that you look at me with such coldness. I am leaving tonight, alone. You must understand that Theo is not sane (forgive me for saying it), and that there has been nothing between us which would stand in the way of our own old friendship. He now has my mask, a curiosity Papa brought me once from Italy. He asked Andrew for it when the latter mentioned it to him at your wedding, and Andrew brought it here without my knowing. He has given it to him. It has some significance for him and may fuel his derangement, may act as some kind of catalyst. If you can get it, hide it, do away with it, but separate him from it at all costs.

Andrew scoffs at what I try to tell him. He finds my anxiety hilariously amusing.

Dear Yvonne, you have been the best friend of my life. There are many things I do not understand, but I have determined to escape the focus of so much need. But our spouses are full of it. It is a need which is not so much of the body, but of the mind and the spirit and their sense of stature, of who they are. It is complex and terrible and they will satisfy it at any price. I may sell the house in London and go abroad. Do not concern yourself with me, but have a care for your own safety. I would love to have your company if you wished to tear yourself away from what is happening here and come with me.

Forgive me for having brought you unhappiness. Do not tell Theo what I plan to do. He would follow me. He will try to follow me anyway.

Your loving friend, Jenny

Dee put the letter back into its hiding place. She lay back against the pillows. She glanced at the clock. It ticked officiously and told her that in an hour the crows at Kilashane would be up and circling. But she knew one thing. Whatever had caused the ruin of Kilashane could not be explained by just the Troubles.

Dee left Ricky whining in the kitchen as she set out for Kilashane. 'Not now, Rick. I have to be very quiet . . .'

The moon was up and the night was full of the sea. She was wearing the jeans of earlier in the day, tennis shoes and a jumper. The boreen and the fields were dry, but the moonlight magnified things, made the familiar unfamiliar, transformed Mrs Brady's donkey into a monster as it moved suddenly behind a hedgerow, screaming out its ancient hee-haw to the night.

The demesne itself was shrouded in silence. She pricked her hand with the thorns of the blackberry at the usual entry point, sucked it and tasted blood.

Were it not for the fact that she was so familiar with Kilashane, she would have been lost. The canopy of trees blocked out most of the light from the night sky, so finding her way depended to a large extent on memory. Added to this was the fact that Billy's treehouse, where she was headed, was in the depth of the woods surrounding the ruin, and therefore she did not have the benefit of the avenue or the other pathways laid down long ago.

She plunged through the bracken, woodbine and scutch grass, caught her foot in some ivy and tripped, picked herself up. The moonlight came down through gaps in the trees, silvering patches of the woodland floor, catching a drift of bluebells and the silver bark of a birch. There were small scurrying sounds; a badger, black and white stripes unmistakable, moved into the shadows on her right, and her heart, which had skittered for a moment, resumed its normal beat.

An owl hooted in the near distance. It occurred to her how alive everything was; while she slept each night the natural world was about its business. But how larger than life the night world was; how keen the senses! Her eyes could see quite clearly where there was any moonlight at all; her hearing was alert for the smallest sound. And yet she was only in a place which she had known all her life, a place where most of the very contours in the ground were familiar to her. She heard the small stream, a tributary of the Meena, trickling over its stones. This meant that she was not far from Billy's hideaway; he used to drink from the stream and eat the watercress and cow parsley, and the young nettles. Sometimes she had watched him beating them against a tree to knock the stings off them, while he muttered to himself, looking up from under his bushy eyebrows, like some kind of simian creature checking for predators. On one such occasion he had seen her, while she crouched not far off, hidden by brambles. He had started and then stood very still, never taking his eyes off her, beginning to move towards her like a man who would surprise an enemy.

She had been frightened, but only for a moment, because Billy suddenly stopped, grinned, and turned back to what he had been doing. She had realized then that he'd known who she was and that he trusted her. She was never afraid of him again. She might see him in his comings and goings in the woods, and he might see her, look at her, and pass her by with some awkward gesture of recognition. Occasionally he spoke, with rhymes and ramblings of poetry, but the most he had ever said to her was the verse from Swinburne:

'Let us go seaward as the great winds go,
Full of blown sand and foam; what help is here?
There is no help, for all these things are so,
And all the world is bitter as a tear.'

And, of course, the time he had stopped her outside the church and given her a rose.

'He's not mad,' she had told her mother. 'I think he's just very, very sad!'

Billy's treehouse, hidden in the fork of a beech and made from planks nailed together, was still there and almost invisible. The moss and ivy had overtaken it. To anyone but the strictest observer, it looked as though it were part of the tree itself. The only evidence that the tree functioned as anything else was the remains of a rope ladder, which Billy had used to climb to his home. This ladder was now tattered and rotten: as Dee walked around the tree, feeling with her hand against the bole, she realized in dismay that it was useless.

She turned her back to the tree and looked around. The shadows pressed on the small forest; there was a susurration of the wind as it moved in the branches above, a song turning to a roar when a strong breeze came in from the sea. But that was above her head. Down here, on the ground, was the smell of the woodland, the wild garlic, the small rustlings, the little song of the stream.

She returned her attention to the rope ladder. It was definitely rotted beyond any possibility of using it, and its slimy strands were unpleasant to the touch. Billy, she thought, if you can hear me, help me. It is not that I want to trespass. But I do want to know.

She looked up into the great tree above her, saw the swoop of the branches against the dark sky. She leant against the tree, pulled at the ivy which surrounded the bark, wondered if she could climb it, because some of it was very strong, wrapping the trunk in a web of tough stems. Some of the leaves came away in her hands, emitting a pungent smell.

But as she felt with her hands around the bole, something hard and cold met her fingers. It was a piece of metal driven into the trunk. Further investigation revealed that there was a series of these, placed like steps up the trunk and hidden in the ivy. So Billy didn't use the rope ladder. He had hammered in a means of reaching his small abode which would not succumb, as the ladder had, to the years. He had used mower tines, the strong fixed teeth of a mowing bar.

Dee put her foot on the lowest bar, pulled herself up by grasping the ivy, and then stood on the next tine, and so on until she was at the fork of the tree; the gaping door of the old shack that Billy had made for himself was straight in front of her. The foliage swayed as Dee moved. The door creaked on old hinges with a sound which she felt must have travelled right through the wood.

The interior of the treehouse was perfectly dark, and gave off a thick, musty smell, so strong that it caught in the back of Dee's throat. She could hardly bear to enter. But she moved into the small space where old Billy had lived, and began, with nervous hands, to feel her way around the walls.

Everything seemed to be covered in mould.

Her feet encountered what might have been a mattress, and also a bundle of clothes. She turned and almost fell over something which clattered. She had brought a box of matches, and fished them out of her pocket, lit one. The small flare lit the room, showed the disorder of rags, the battered saucepan and aluminium kettle, the chipped mug and plate, the enamel basin. The match burned down to her finger, and she shook it out and lit another one. Again she barely had time to look at her surroundings before the match was spent. She knelt in a corner, groped beneath a pile of rags. A rat came out of its habitat and fled, squeaking, across the floor. She cried out in disgust, lit another match. Then she repeated her investigations in the other corner of the room. Again she found nothing. Her hands encountered spider-webs, some old papers, a cardboard box with a pair of mouldy shoes. Why am I here? she thought. Rooting around in the debris of someone's life. There is nothing in this place.

She lit another match, but as it burnt out she glanced above her head at the roof. Set directly into the wooden ceiling, now rotted, was a face of extraordinary power, staring directly down at her from blank sockets, the mouth a rictus of cold appraisal. One glance and she knew she was staring at something of incomparable value, carefully wrought, ancient, something she had once picked up and thrown away. The burning match slipped from her fingers and, still crouching, she reached over her head for the mask.

She moved as quickly as possible through the wood. She felt the curio she was clutching underneath her jumper, like something that burned her. She could not believe she had found it. The sounds of the woodland she hardly noticed.

But, stopping suddenly in response to some unconscious warning, she heard something behind her which did not fit the pattern of an animal's movements.

The knowledge that what she had heard was footsteps, froze her where she stood. It was unmistakable to someone who knew woodland sounds as she did; the noise of a human footfall on the woodland floor, however muted, was a relatively deliberate business, incapable of the swift, silent relocation of an animal. The footsteps had stopped, but as she moved forward again, the footsteps began to do likewise, again as though they were pacing her. She looked behind her, but saw nothing except the outline of the branches against the sky, the small shafts of moonlight here and there and the shadows.

She began to run. She remembered Brussels, the cobbled lane, the man with the Brueghel face, the weird sensation of intruding on the past, the theft and the sense of plunder. She imagined for a moment that he might materialize from the trees. She raced through a clearing, dived behind a tree. She leant against the tough bark to check back the way she had come. After a moment she saw a form emerge in silhouette, before disappearing again. It was too dark for it to be recognizable, but it was certainly human. The thought of some stranger, following her, inching towards her in the darkness, galvanized her. She turned and, heart hammering, began to run, her feet crashing into the undergrowth, her mind feverishly scanning what she remembered of the terrain, desperately trying to work out where the nearest point of exit was.

But her foot caught in some ancient root system which pushed itself above ground and she fell. She heard the voice calling, 'Dee, Dee, are you all right?'

'What were you doing in Kilashane in the middle of the night, young lady?' old Doctor Meehan demanded. He was leaning over her, inspecting the wrenched ankle, which he pronounced to be nothing worse than a sprain. It was morning. The light slanted through the half-drawn curtains and the birds were singing. Her ankle was swollen and felt as though it were on fire. Her father had knelt beside her on the woodland floor while she cried with pain; then, having ascertained that only her ankle was hurt, had gone back to the house to fetch the car, had brought her home. But he had taken away the mask.

'Why did you follow me, Dad?'

'Why do you think, Dee? I couldn't sleep and I heard your footsteps and Ricky whining. It occurred to me suddenly that you were going to Kilashane. It's not safe there at any time. Why on earth did you want to go at such an hour? Your obsession with the place is unhealthy!'

Now Dee told the doctor that she had gone to Kilashane because she had been unable to drop off, and had thought a walk would make her tired. He had shaken his head, told her to drink hot milk in future, bandaged the ankle, given her something for the pain, and told her it would make her drowsy and that she should sleep.

She slept for hours, and when she woke her father was sitting on the edge of the bed, looking at her with an expression half-way between love and sheepishness. When he saw that she was awake, he shut the door and returned to sit on the edge of her bed.

'How are you feeling, darling?'

'It hurts, Dad, but I'll live.'

He handed her a letter. 'This came for you.'

Dee looked at the airmail envelope with the Belgian stamp. She saw the writing. She wanted to tear it up, but she put it on her bedside table.

Her father reached over and stroked her hand.

'Dad, what did you do with the mask?'

'I want to talk to you. I have a confession to make.'

Dee stared up at him, the leathery jowls, the deep-set blue eyes, the wonderful white tangle of his eyebrows. 'What kind of confession?'

'Darling, the truth is — I have disposed of it!'

Dee sat up. 'What did you do with it?'

'I . . . threw it into the sea at Carraigh Point!'

'You threw it into the sea? I don't believe you!'

'I acted for the best.'

'You should have asked me, Dad,' she whispered, sinking back into the pillows. 'I found it. I wanted it.'

'It was bad luck . . .'

'How do you know?' she demanded angrily. 'Surely you don't believe in superstitious gobbledygook!'

Mr McGlinn sighed. 'I do know. I know from your mother. She used to frequent the big house when she was a child. Her father was the groom in Kilashane.'

'Are you serious?'

'I am serious!'

'That means my grandfather was Batty, impertinent Batty! I read all about him in a diary I found there years ago. And she must have been the little girl who liked to read in the kitchen!'

'Batty's real name was Bartholomew Moloney.'

'What happened to him?'

Her father looked unhappy. 'It's a bit of a story, but your mother will tell you. Where's the diary you found?'

'I'll show it to you later.'

'Dee — you were told not to go into the place! Did you . . . find anything else there? Such as a ring, for instance?' Dee regarded her father with a frown. She could not understand his sudden interest, his sudden knowledgeableness.

'Oh, Dad. Of course I had to go there, especially after the warnings. I was boiling with curiosity! And I did find the ring; I know a bit about it. But I haven't got it any more . . .'

There was silence for a moment 'What did you do with it?'

'It was stolen from me in Brussels!'

'Dee, are you telling me the truth?'

'Of course I am.'

'How was it stolen?'

'I was taking a short cut and was attacked. I had the thing on a chain around my neck and they ripped it off!'

'Were you hurt?'

Dee remembered the bruises, remembered Peter's hands, remembered the supper and the breakfast which wasn't, remembered everything. She shook her head.

'Did you report it to the police?'

'No.'

'Why not?'

'Someone told me not to bother, said the police could do nothing!'

'Who told you this?'

'Someone in ITU — a bloke who was out for himself; I don't want to talk about him.'

Mr McGlinn looked at the letter. 'The writer of that letter, perhaps?'

'Perhaps!'

He looked from Dee to the letter and back. 'Well, if it's gone, it's gone!'

'Dad, do you know something I don't? It's not like you to believe in *pishoques*.'

'All of these things are harmless in themselves. It is the use of them as a focus for the powers of the mind that creates the problems. That ring had a history!'

'How do you know?'

Her father hesitated before he answered. 'You should ask your mother.'

'It's no use asking her. She won't tell me. You know, Dad, I used to dream of a man in evening dress who came down the steps of Kilashane towards me.'

'Did you ever . . . go to him?'

'No.'

The door opened and her mother came in carrying a tray. She smiled at Dee and deposited the tray on her knees.

'Molly, will you tell Dee about your father?

About what happened in Kilashane?'

Mrs McGlinn glanced at her husband and looked away. He got up and left the room.

'Please talk to Dad. Your anniversary is tomorrow. Is this how you are going to be for the rest of your life?' pleaded Dee.

Her mother's mouth tightened. 'Matters between your father and me are between us, Dee. As for Kilashane — the truth is, what happened made me sick, as though something in me died. But my teacher was kind and told me to write down everything I remembered of that night. He said it would help me.'

'Did you . . . write down everything?'

'Yes.'

'Have you still got what you wrote?'

'Yes.'

'Mam, can I see it?'

'I would rather you didn't. It rakes up the past. It is so far away and long ago that it might have happened on another planet. I have tried to put it behind me.'

'*Please.* I really need to know about it.'

'If I had told you the whole story long ago, would it have prevented you from scouring Kilashane yourself? Would it have prevented you from getting hurt?'

Her mother went to her room and Dee heard a drawer being opened and closed; then she reappeared with a child's copybook. The brown cover was a little mottled, the edges stained. Dee opened it very gently, saw the large, childish writing, the legend at the top: Mary Moloney, Kilashane, 20 May 1919.

The avenue was full of little stones and I kicked some along with my toes. I knew I should not have come up the avenue. Dada says we have to go in the back way.

He hadn't come home the night before. I was hungry. They might give me food in the kitchen, I thought. Bridgie always gave me food when I came. I had finished the book, but they wouldn't let me read any more until the visitors had gone. They said I was in the way.

I saw the master coming out of the house. I went up on the grass and hid among the trees. The grass was damp and I liked it on my feet. I stayed watching. He came down the steps. I heard music.

I saw Miss Kate through the drawing-room window sitting at the piano. The master was wearing a black suit with a white shirt. He walked across the lawn, smoking. I saw the smoke from his cigar twirling up into the air.

I was sure he had seen me and I was afraid. But although he looked at me, he just walked around for a while, as though he was thinking of something. He leant on his stick with his right hand and held the cigar with the other. I looked at the upstairs window and saw a face. It was Mrs Yvonne, the English lady the master had married. She watched him and then drew back and I could not see her face any more. Then the music stopped. I saw one of the visitors, Mrs Stacey, standing by the piano, talking to Miss Kate. The master turned to the window. Then he went into the house.

I went around by the side walk to the back door, keeping among the shrubs. I saw Mrs Yvonne walking quickly towards the clump of trees near the stables. There are trees there with red berries. The birds can't reach them here because they are afraid of the magpies who live in the beech tree and who don't eat berries. I forget what the berries are called, but Dada said I must never eat them. Mrs Yvonne stopped and picked the red berries. She took a paper bag out of her pocket and she put the red berries into it. Then she went back to the house by the kitchen door.

I waited for a while before I went around to the kitchen. I was hungry but I did not want Mrs Yvonne to see me. Una was there. She told me not to be annoying her. She said she was busy. But I saw Bridgie coming out of the dairy and I said I was hungry. She said hasn't your Dad bin home? I said no. She said to come back to the kitchen and she gave me bread and jam. They were busy getting the dinner for the gentry. I saw the big copper full of soup. There was a roast of meat. The smell was lovely. Una told me to go away and not be under her feet, but Bridgie told me to come with her. She brought me into the dining room. There was a table set with silver things. But Bridgie said I could stay under the other table, which was covered by a white cloth, if I behaved myself.

The legs were thick and had carvings. The floor was shiny and almost black. When I peeped out I saw the ceiling. It had bunches of plaster fruit in the corners and there was a big mirror over the fireplace.

The company came in. They sat down at the table and Bridgie began to serve them. She brought in the soup and they began to eat it.

The master was quiet but there was another man, Mr Stacey from England, talking loudly. He had a big moustache. He was talking funny, like Dada when he drinks too much. The ladies looked nice. There were small embroidered holes in the tablecloth that I could look through.

Bridgie brought in the meat. The smell made me hungry, but I stayed where I was. I knew Una would kill me if she knew. There was vegetables all steaming and nice and plenty of spuds in a big dish. My tummy began to rumble, but the men were talking and they didn't hear. I watched their faces. Mrs Yvonne was very quiet. She had red hair and very white skin. Mrs Stacey was lovely with dark eyes and brown hair. Miss Kate and Mrs O'Reilly watched the master. None of the ladies spoke very much.

When the meal was over, Mrs O'Reilly got up and the ladies followed her into the drawing room.

Bridgie put the whiskey on the table in the

486

dining room — they had it in a nice bottle, with a glass stopper — and then she went away.

I waited. I wanted to get out from under the table. My legs were cramped. I heard the music from the drawing room. I knew it was Miss Kate at the piano. She is always playing 'The Last Rose of Summer'. We sing it in school sometimes. She stopped playing for a moment and I heard the voices of the ladies. I heard the drawing-room door open and close and then the front door opened and closed very quietly.

The master seemed in great form. He pressed more whiskey on Mr Stacey. He began to talk of the war and Mr Stacey laughed a lot, but it was like a man who really wanted to cry. I wanted to leave and find Dada, but I could not get out until they did, so I waited. After a long while the master said, 'I suppose we'd better join the ladies.' He got up and went to the drawing room. 'Where's Jenny,' I heard him ask. 'She's gone up to bed,' Mrs O'Reilly said. Then they shut the door. Mr Stacey stayed in the dining room. He left the table and went to the leather armchair in the corner and sat there, just drinking and drinking. His face got very red and then he threw his glass into the fire and fell asleep.

The master came back into the room, just as I was sneaking out. He looked at me and said, 'What the devil are you doing here?' 'Nothing!' I said. 'I was looking for Dada.' 'You won't find him here. He's probably in the cellar drinking his remarkable whiskey!' He spoke to Mr

Stacey, but he was dead drunk. He rang and Una came. He asked her to knock on Mrs Stacey's door, but she came back and said there was no answer. This made him jump. He went upstairs himself, so fast you wouldn't think he had a wooden leg, and opened her bedroom door. When he came out he was very angry. 'Where is she?' he said to Una, but she didn't know. Then Mrs Yvonne came out of the drawing room. 'She's gone,' she said. Her voice was very quiet and kind of dangerous. 'You will never find her now!'

Master Theo just stared at her. 'Indeed? You fool! What do you know of what I can and cannot do!'

I went down to the basement to find Dada. The floor was stone and very cold. I was tired and wanted to go home. But I could not find Dada. When I heard Master Theo coming down the steps, I hid behind a chest. When I peeped out I saw I him sitting at his table. He was wearing something on his face, a white mask, and he was turning his head right and left as though trying to look in some far-off directions. Then he started to mutter, 'Come back; oh, come back. You know you cannot escape me for long.'

I slipped from behind the chest and ran for the stairs. Mrs O'Reilly, Mrs Yvonne and Miss Kate were in the kitchen. The mistress was saying to Mrs Yvonne, 'You must take that ring from him tonight. Father Keane was talking to me about it today.' Then she looked at me. 'What are you doing child?' I said, 'Looking for Dada, ma'am. But the master is below with a white mask on his face.'

'He is becoming more and more deranged,' she whispered. 'He will have to be put away if this goes on!' We heard the master's step coming up the basement stairs. He came into the room and said, 'So you would lock me away, Mother? Your own son?' He had the mask in his hand.

'Give me that thing, Theo,' she said.

'What?' he asked. 'What are you talking about? This poor little mask? It's mine. I can't give it to anyone.' Then they looked at me. 'You were wearing it down below!' I said. 'I saw you!'

He stared at me and laughed. 'Everywhere I turn you are under my feet, watching me, watching my every move. But you will not be a child for ever. You will live to know your own defeats.'

The fire started during the night. The smoke killed them all, except the master. Dada saved him. But he died himself. He got the master down the stairs and went back for the others, but it was no use.

They put the fire out, but the house is all ruined. The rain has got in and it is standing there looking awful and I am very lonely for my Dada.

Written by Mary Moloney, aged eleven.

Mrs McGlinn sat on the bed while Dee read.

When Dee had finished, she looked up at her mother with her eyes full of tears. 'Why did you never tell me this?'

'Oh, Dee, I wanted to forget! You can't blame me for that. I nearly succeeded too, but some things stay so fresh that the merest glance back at them brings the whole episode into the present!'

'So they're all buried down at the church in Ballyshane?'

'Some of them are in the Protestant graveyard — Andrew Stacey and his sister, for example.'

'What about Jenny?'

Her mother shook her head. 'She never came back. They never found her. Nobody saw her at the station. She simply disappeared. So now you know . . . It's because of everything that happened that no one will go near the demesne.'

'She probably went back to England.'

'I wonder. I often think about the stretch of high bog near the house. Anyone trying to cross it might never be found!'

'Who started the fire?'

Her mother raised her shoulders and dropped them. 'I don't know. Some people blamed the IRA. All I know is that I was orphaned by it, and the man I blamed for it all wandered around the peninsula for the rest of his life. You can understand now why I hated you talking to old Billy.'

'I never saw him with a ring!'

'I know. Someone took it from him that night, or perhaps he gave it up. He was very sick afterwards, like someone who had been poisoned.'

'Father O'Shea told me the place had been exorcized!'

'So I've heard. I knew nothing about it at the time.'

'What happened to Theo?'

'He spent the rest of his life looking for his wife, peering into strangers' faces. You knew him yourself, old Billy.'

'Why did Dad not tell me who he was? I did ask him.'

'I think he didn't want to upset you,' her mother said softly. 'There's something horrific about someone spending his life wandering demented in the ruins of his former home, searching for his bride. Once he asked me if I had seen her. "Yvonne, where is Yvonne?", and quoting lines of poetry: "Love is a bitter sea, barren and deep." ' She looked away. 'In those days I thought that love was everything!'

There was silence for a moment.

'Mam,' Dee said, 'will you make it up with Dad? I can't bear to see you torn apart this way!'

Her mother sniffed. 'He's happy enough. He keeps himself busy. My feelings don't seem to bother him. He was able to chat and laugh with a visitor today.'

'Oh, who was that?'

'A foreign-looking man. He arrived at the door asking for your father. They went off for a walk together.'

'Foreign? What did he look like?'

Her mother shrugged. 'He was of medium height, had sallow skin and a foreign accent.'

Dee remembered the man she had met in the demesne. 'Mam, did this man, the foreigner, wear a beige jacket? Did he have stained teeth?'

Her mother shrugged. 'Yes, I think so. Do you know him?'

'No. But he knows me.'

Later, Mr McGlinn's voice could be heard on the phone; then he came upstairs. He entered the room like someone uncertain of his welcome, glanced at his wife.

'Dad,' Dee said. 'I want you and Mam to make it up!'

He smiled at his wife, rubbed his hands together as though they were cold. 'I've news for you, Molly,' he said, with the look of someone who couldn't bear to keep his news to himself. 'I've sent off a booking deposit on a flat in Dublin. It's in a new apartment block about to be built in Ballsbridge! It'll be our anniversary present,' he added.

Mrs McGlinn gasped. Her mouth trembled as though tears were not far off. 'Where are we going to get the money for that — unless we sell the house?'

He put his arm around her. 'Leave that to me. I've been putting a bit by for years, and there's my gratuity. This way we can have the best of both worlds — go to Dublin, see the shows, see Dee, and then get out when we've had enough!'

Dee stared at her father. She sensed immediately that her father had sold something, maybe against his better judgement, maybe in spite of himself, and Dee thought she knew what he had sold.

He did not meet his daughter's eyes.

'Who was the foreigner Mam saw you talking to today, Dad?' she asked.

'Who . . . foreigner? Oh, you mean the tourist. He was looking for directions!'

'I see,' Dee said. 'That wasn't what he was looking for when I met him yesterday in Kilashane!'

But her father's face darkened and he went away downstairs. Her mother followed him, calling his name.

When her parents had gone, Dee tore open the letter with the Belgian stamp.

Dee, my darling,

I try to phone, I write. But I am banished. I know that you believe the worst of me. But I am not the worst. This is not a recommendation, just a fact. And whatever you might think, and I know you think ill of me, I am not given to light pronouncements of love. I need to talk to you. I need to see you.

I am coming to Ireland on Friday the

twenty-sixth. My flight gets in at five-thirty. Will you meet me?

Peter.

Dee tore this letter up, tried to move her leg, and lay back suddenly with the throbbing in her ankle.

'Piss off, Casanova,' she whispered bitterly. 'Save it for the wife.'

But words were only words, and the wound and the longing were still the same. He had accessed her self, her reality; she had given with trust. He had trailed all that in the dust as the trappings of some kind of concubine. He could do that because society smiled on men who preyed. He had a wife, a wardrobe full of her clothes, a child who smiled into the camera. He had all that and he was still a predator, a liar, and ultimately a thief. He had obtained by false pretences.

But think what she might, her body remembered; and some yearning, inaccessible, stubborn part of her mind remembered with love. She thumped the pillows behind her, reached out again for the bits of Peter's letter. She held them in her hand and wondered if she could sellotape them back together. Then she heard the voices in the hall and her mother's step on the stairs followed by the footsteps of a second person. She stuffed the pieces under her pillow. 'I'm sure she'll be delighted to see you,' her mother was saying. The door opened and her mother entered, followed by Father O'Shea.

'Hello, hello, how is the patient? I met the good doctor earlier and he told me about your mishap — wandering in Kilashane in the middle of the night!' He shook his head. 'You young girls are a restless generation . . .' He smiled with genuine kindness, but there was a frown lurking between his eyes. Mrs McGlinn excused herself, saying she had something in the oven, and Dee invited her visitor to sit down. He confined himself to badinage for a couple of moments, and then came straight to the question which perplexed him: 'What were you doing in Kilashane, Dee? Why on earth would you want to go into that place in the middle of the night?'

'Why not?'

He sighed. 'I think we've had this conversation before!'

Dee cast her mind back to the last time she had spoken to him, when he had told her how Kilashane had been exorcized.

'It's an important place to me, Father. You see, I found a few things there long ago which sparked my imagination.'

'What kind of things?'

'Oh this and that. A diary, for instance, which belonged to a woman called Yvonne O'Reilly — and a photograph.' She looked at the frowning face before her. 'Did you ever hear of her, Father? Yvonne O'Reilly?'

'Of course I heard of her! I knew before I came to this parish that there had been an exorcism, and I found out as much as I could as to the reasons why it had been performed. That's part of my business as the parish priest: you can't be a good priest without knowing a good deal about your flock's history!'

'So you know they were a very strange lot up at the big house?'

He nodded. 'I found out everything I could about them. Some things didn't add up, but they certainly seem to have been beset by a sequence of tragedies.'

'Why was the exorcism really carried out?'

'The parish priest of the time was nervous. The family had been abroad and the son at the war. But he came back apparently possessed. His family were frightened . . .'

Dee took a deep breath. 'Did you ever hear of Mathias Robertus, Father?'

He sighed. 'Of course I did, Dee. He is one of the skeletons in the Church's closet, not so much because of his apostasy, but because of the shameful circumstances which provoked it. He certainly did acquire some kind of odd power . . .'

'Was he a very evil man?'

'Evil?' Father O'Shea intoned. 'It's all a very long time ago. I'm not so ready to describe people as evil!'

'What do you say he was?'

'About the man himself, only this — and it may surprise you, Dee, if you imagine for a moment that priests are incapable of the same fierce human emotions as everyone else — I say only that the poor creature was in pain . . . that his heart was broken.'

Dee thought for a moment and then she asked, 'What were the shameful circumstances surrounding his apostasy?'

'I found an account of it . . . It seems that Father Keane — he was the parish priest at the time — wrote to a Monsignor Dillon in the Vatican. The latter had travelled with the O'Reillys when they went on a tour of Italy that fateful summer of 1914. Father O'Shea had discovered that Theo O'Reilly had the ring of Mathias, that his father had sent it to him from Italy, and he thought Monsignor Dillon would know something about the circumstances of the find. It is clear from their correspondence that the monsignor suspected something strange had occurred, because his travelling companion had developed such an intense interest in the circumstance surrounding the apostasy, and had a rubbing of the ring itself. The two priests had known each other as seminarians, and their correspondence was conducted on friendly terms. The monsignor sent a translation of an almost contemporaneous account dealing with the interrogation and torture of the Lady of Florence which was kept in the Vatican archives.'

'Will you let me see it?'

'Why not? I'll send a copy of it.'

He stood up, warned her to make sure she rested, and left as suddenly as he had come.

Chapter Twenty-two

'What say you now, Inquisitor?' his Eminence demanded when the work was done. 'The witch will need a mask to hide behind.'

The inquisitor's wrath was like to madness, but he was powerless and lame from his shackles.

I could see that the Cardinal feared him and, when he was gone, being sick of so much pain, I set him free.

Journal of a Witness

It was Friday evening at Dublin Airport. It was the breathing space, the evening which made the week's work worth while. Dee was glad she had not given up the job, a prospect which now seemed to have been generated by childishness, by some sort of assumption that another person's space ranked before her own, by an inability to allow that she might make a mistake and simply shrug it away.

The atmosphere in the workplace had changed: Charlie's frenzy had been replaced by calm and more efficiency. Liam was buzzing with his own success: he had been given a pay rise and invited to join the company in England. He had also been reconciled with his girlfriend, and they were about to announce their engagement.

Dee congratulated him; he asked her to the canteen for a coffee.

'You never told me how you got on in Brussels!' he said. 'Would you recommend the planning course?'

'I left early,' Dee said. 'I met with an accident.'

'Really? You never said a thing! What happened?'

'Ah, it was silly. I fell, hurt myself. Nothing too serious, but enough to spoil the week. I went home to Ballyshane so recover.'

'Poor you! I did think you were a bit taciturn when you came back. And recently you hurt your ankle!'

'Yeah. I must be accident-prone!'

'Did you meet Eggli in Brussels?' The question came innocently out of the blue. She searched Liam's face for disingenuousness, but he had the same candid, open look as always.

'I bumped into him.'

'Poor bugger has great resilience. He's filthy rich, of course, which is probably a help, and he works hard, and work is a great anodyne; but I still can't help feeling sorry for him.'

'Liam,' Dee asked after a moment, 'what are you talking about?'

He stared at her. 'Didn't you know about his accident? Where do you think he got his stiff leg?'

'I don't know about his accident.'

'It happened on the autobahn. No room for error in the fast lane there!' Liam tightened his mouth. 'His wife and little son were with him!' He gestured with his hands. 'She was killed outright. The kid lingered for a few days.'

Dee sat bolt upright. 'When?' she whispered. 'When did this happen?'

'About three years ago.'

She had excused herself and gone to the ladies'. It was empty. She leant against the windowsill and put her head in her hands. The moment of their parting was vivid. Peter's face, in retrospect, suddenly proud and drawn.

'Oh my poor darling,' she whispered in a ferment of self-hatred, 'my poor love. Why didn't you tell me?'

Dee was driving her new Beetle. She approached the airport car park with relief. The traffic from town had been heavy; it was rush hour, the roads were wet. She, with a visitor to collect and an array of attitudes to reorganise, was on tenterhooks.

But she recognized that, compared with her usual self — the self which moved between work and the flat like an automaton — the persona she now inhabited was full of prospects and excitement. Peter was coming. After her conversation with Liam she had answered his letter and said she would meet him. She needed to see him. She needed absolution. She was appalled at what she had almost thrown away. In the days since she had learnt the truth about his accident he had assumed romantic proportions of a heroic nature. Various heady memories lingered: his arms under the stars while he soothed her headache; his tenderness; the passion of his lovemaking. Weighed against the pros, the cons — the fear of plunder, of being out of her depth, the suspicion which had dogged her view of him — seemed childish.

It seemed to her that life was a current into which one plugged oneself occasionally, as privilege, as moments of grace. For the rest one simply existed, acting on automatic, relying on the habits which took one through the day. She did not want to wake up when she was seventy and know that she had been too proud or too cautious to allow herself to live. Better to be chastened, better to be bowed, better even to be broken by life than to let it simply pass by.

She sat in the car and looked out at the darkening airport; up there in the control tower behind their grey-green glass were the flight controllers at the nerve-centre of this complex hive. She was early; she watched people coming back to their cars, putting luggage into the boot, smiling, eyes shiny, radiating pleasure. Theirs was the rawness of suppressed emotion, love, reunion; tight rein on forces which could disclose the truth, or part of the truth, could crack the private masks.

She looked at her watch. Ten minutes to go. She got out, locked the car, and walked towards the arrival terminal through a fine drizzle, arranging the scarf to protect her hair. Rain would make it frizzy, spoil the effect. She had been to the hairdresser's at lunchtime. The brown hair swung heavily, shining and perfumed with a light spray. She was wearing fluid make-up, had lined her eyes and burnished the lids. All to permit her to plug into as much life as possible, to gather the day.

She went through the door and stood at the back of the waiting knot of people, one eye on the arrivals monitor, the other on the clock. Somewhere out there a plane was dipping towards the runway, undercarriage down, poised for the miraculous judder of contact, the roar of reversing engines. He was here now, on her soil, her ground, out there in the mist. The legend on the monitor opposite the flight number changed to 'landed'. She felt the tension release in her, felt the mounting excitement replace it.

Peter Eggli came through the glass doors with an expression of optimistic inquiry. She watched him for a moment, saw him scan the waiting crowd, saw his eyes swivel instantly to where she was waiting, almost as though he knew where to look. He smiled, a closed smile of elation, lowered his head. He looked distinguished, she thought; he looked interesting. He did not look like the man she had privately dressed up in the motley of the philanderer.

Dee waited. He approached her gravely, lifted her hand to his lips. 'Thank you.'

She felt overwhelmed. He did not square with any of her projections; she felt that she had dissected him with a child's scissors. She felt she was too young, her perceptions too immature, to have seen him properly. So, apart from saying 'Hello!' with sudden shyness, she walked with him in companionable silence to the exit.

'Shall we get a taxi, or are you mobile?'

'I'm mobile.'

'I'm booked into the Shelbourne . . .'

'This is my latest acquisition!' Dee said with diffident pride, unlocking the passenger door of her car.

'Have you named her?'

She smiled. 'No. Do you think I should?'

'Only if you want.'

' "Dee's Destrier", or something like that?'

He laughed, got in. She sat in the driver's seat, changed into her driving shoes, tossed the other ones into the back, put the key into the ignition.

He reached across for her, caught her in his arms, pulled her close. 'I would like to take you out for dinner. Where would you like to go?'

'Oh, Peter, I'm not hungry. Come back to the flat and I'll make you something. Laura is out this evening and I know how to cook the odd steak when I put my mind to it!'

He smiled. 'Am I forgiven?' he whispered in her ear.

'Was there something to forgive?'

As forecast, the flat was empty. Peter took off

his coat and hung it carefully in the hall. She remembered his house in Brussels, how neat everything was. She offered him a sherry and he accepted it, sat by the gas fire and sipped. Dee put on an apron, took the fillet steaks out of the fridge, peppered them and put them down to fry. The oil sputtered and a few hot specks hit her hands. 'Ow,' she said, pulling back.

'Are you getting charred in there?' Peter's laconic voice said.

'No. Just assaulted.'

'What are we having?'

'Steak au poivre.'

'So you can cook. What else have you not told me?'

'Plenty!'

He laughed, came into the kitchen.

'You can set the table if you like,' Dee said.

He took the cutlery and did as he was bid. Dee put a soupçon of cognac into the pan and set it alight. The flames burned with an instant's blue flare and then died. She dished up the steaks, took the salad out of the fridge, put the garlic bread in the oven.

'I'm a bit disorganized, Peter. The garlic bread will be ready in a minute. Will you open the wine?'

Peter took the red wine, a Côtes du Rhone, and applied the corkscrew. 'I have never seen you domesticated.'

'Aha, think of what you have missed: the amazing multifaceted Dee McGlinn!'

She rescued the garlic bread from desiccation and they sat down to eat. She glanced at him thinking, I am so shy I could die.

When the meal was over, and the dessert of apple pie demolished, she made the coffee and sat back in a haze of pleasure, looking at him, loving him, the way he sat and moved, his dark grey eyes and the aura of the masculine and the mysterious.

'I'm sorry, Peter!'

He raised his eyebrows. 'For what are you sorry?'

'For being a cow! I only heard the other day about your family . . . About the accident. I cannot tell you how badly I feel!'

His face closed. 'Do you mind if I don't talk about it?'

'Of course . . .'

He sat on the couch, drank his coffee, ate a few chocolate mint wafers.

'How long will you be in Ireland this time?'

'That depends on you. My first meeting is on Monday. I came today specifically to see you!'

Dee was sitting on the hearthrug, watching the hissing in the gas fire. The light from the chianti-bottle lamp was mellow; the fire warm; the rain, which had started while they were dining, came in a squall against the window.

'We belong together,' he said. 'You know that, don't you, Dee!'

'I do!'

He looked around the flat. 'I often imagined

what your apartment would be like.'

'It's much better than the last one. We were very lucky to find it!'

He got up to look at the books on the mantelpiece.

'They are mostly Laura's.'

He cast his eyes over the pictures, saw the posters propped up in the corner. 'You like the Beatles?'

'I used to. Now I prefer Simon and Garfunkel.'

He examined the sketch of St Stephen's Green which Laura had done at school and brought back as decoration on her last trip home. He looked at the print of *The Bog at Allen*, with its sunset and its hues of autumn. He turned the canvas which Colin had sent her around.

'Who's this?' he asked, and then he read aloud from the charcoal legend on the back. 'My Magician!'

Dee laughed. 'Colin sent it to me. He bought it at a jumble sale in London!'

He considered it. 'It's quite well done. But why do you leave the poor fellow in the corner? Why not hang him up where he can see everything!' He lifted the portrait up against the wall.

Dee looked at the magician and his inscrutable eyes. She suddenly knew she did not want the picture on the wall, not even to please Peter Eggli. 'Laura can't stand him,' she said. 'He gives her the creeps!'

'How is this Colin of yours?' he demanded

darkly, putting the picture down, but so that it faced into the room, 'this chap who sends you paintings from jumble sales?'

'He's in Hong Kong.'

'Good. I hope he stays there!'

'You don't have to be jealous of him, Peter.'

He smiled, moved towards her, and stretched beside her on the hearthrug. 'I am jealous of him. It is an emotion I am not used to . . .' He bent swiftly and kissed her lips.

Dee felt his weight. She felt his tongue in her mouth. She felt the wine in her veins. She felt his hand suddenly at her breast, but so gentle, so slow, so full of temptation.

'Do you love me?' he said, when they drew apart. 'I want you to love me. I am vulnerable too. I need you!'

Dee pulled him down to her, cradled his head against her shoulder. 'In all my life,' she whispered, 'I have never known anything like this. You have become my obsession, Peter Eggli.'

He did not answer. When she looked at him she saw his face was tender, but his eyes were open and were staring across the room at the magician.

He sat up, leaned back against the armchair, drew a cheroot out of his pocket. 'Do you mind if I smoke?'

'No!'

He lit up; the smoke wafted through the room. She drew the heady cigar smoke in through her nose. 'Tell me,' he said, 'about Kilashane.'

And when she didn't answer, he added, 'Never mind. Tomorrow will do. You're tired. I shall go now, my darling.'

He ground out the cigar, leant over and kissed her, then stood up and went to the hall for his coat. Dee drove him to the Shelbourne.

'Tomorrow,' he said. 'Where shall we meet? Shall I come to the flat?'

Dee thought of Laura on Saturday morning, soaking up sleep, lounging around the flat in her bathrobe. 'I'll meet you in Bewley's — Grafton Street,' she said. 'Ten-thirty!'

He caressed her cheek with his hand. 'OK. Sleep well.' She watched him disappear through the swing doors and then she turned for home.

The morning was fine, but the air was cool — the first crisp harbinger of autumn. She parked in Stephen's Green, walked down Grafton Street, followed the scent of fresh coffee and found herself in Bewley's. He was sitting at a small corner table, reading the *Irish Times*. Every now and then he raised his head and looked at the door. She watched him for a moment, caught his eye and crossed the room. A pretty waitress in black and white, with a little white cap, came to take their order.

'Tea for me,' Dee said. He ordered coffee for himself, and some croissants.

When the waitress was gone he reached for

Dee's hand. 'Morning becomes you!'

She smiled, pushed back her hair. 'No. It's you. I can't believe you're here! I'm half afraid you might be a mirage!'

'Is that what you think of me,' he asked with a mock wounded air, 'a trick of the light?'

She squeezed his fingers. 'You seem substantial enough.' She indicated a mirror on the wall. 'You can even be seen in the mirror.'

'Which means?'

'That you're not Dracula!'

He laughed out loud. 'That must be a considerable relief!'

'Yes.' She twinkled, teasing him. 'A girl can't be too careful!'

Dee knew that she was still on a high, treading the clouds at their reunion, relaxed as she had never been with him. All her misgivings had turned out to be absurd. She was a provincial miss with a set of provincial attitudes which required drastic surgery. But she was a woman first. She was a woman who had met a real man, her man; a woman who knew and loved him; a woman who was loved in return. Life brimmed, overflowed. The tea and coffee arrived. The croissants were warm. She buttered one and savoured the mouthfuls.

'Have another one.'

'Ah, no . . . they're lethal!'

'Make a martyr of yourself!'

She giggled, but when she looked at him his eyes were suddenly full of pain. 'Peter — is

509

something bothering you?'

'No . . .'

When they were finished, he suggested a walk. They strolled up Grafton Street, pausing to look in Weir's. The window displayed its shining wares: engagement rings, eternity rings, necklaces, gold bracelets. She didn't want any reminders, so she pulled away and he came after her, taking her hand in silence.

They passed the Grafton Cinema, moved along to Stephen's Green. She led him across the road and under the Menin gate, with its tragic list of the dead carved into the stone of the archway. The Latin legend announced that it was a fine and proper thing to die for one's country.

Peter spent a moment looking at it. 'First War humbug!' he said.

Dee put her hand through his arm. 'Let's look at the ducks!'

The ducks were duly inspected. The drakes were vivid in startling blues and greens, while the hens were dowdy little things, but they all toppled over when the humour took them, and stuck their pointed tails in the air.

'I love it when they do that!' Dee laughed.

They sat on a bench, very close, very warm, although the air was nippy with a promise of things to come.

He asked conversationally, 'Tell me — how things are in Ballyshane?'

Dee sighed. Here it was again. She didn't want to be grilled on Kilashane. The things she had found there were gone. But to please him she decided to tell the whole story.

Dee told him everything: the track down to the shore, the boreen to Carraigh Point, the demesne, the old house, the treehouse where she had found the mask.

He held her hand firmly. She told him of the stranger she had met in the demesne. She told him that she had returned that night and found a mask in the treehouse, the same one she had discovered years before.

'What have you done with it?'

'Dad took it.'

'What did he do with it?'

'He said he threw it into the sea.'

'Do you believe him?'

Dee hesitated. 'I don't know. He seems to have met the foreigner who talked to me in the demesne, and the next thing he had money for a flat in Dublin. My mother wanted to move there,' she added in explanation, 'but he didn't, so they have compromised with a *pied-à-terre* in Ballsbridge.'

He didn't seem surprised by this. 'I see,' was all he said. 'I see.'

She turned to glance at him, but he had inclined his head and she could not see his face. 'I'm sorry it's gone, if you wanted it. But I'm relieved, too, Peter. I had the weirdest feeling while I was carrying it.'

'What was that?'

'I thought it was alive. It felt hot!'

511

'It was night,' he said, 'you were being followed. A lot of adrenaline was coursing!'

'Yes, I know that. But the mask seemed to live.'

Then she talked about the plan to turn Kilashane into a hotel. 'Who do you think would want to try something like that? It's far off the beaten track!'

'The man you met,' he said, 'was probably sent by the secret organization I told you of. They would want Kilashane only for the chance of locating the mask. If they have it now, it may be a long time before Kilashane is developed.'

She glanced at him, knitting her forehead, trying to read him, fighting off returning suspicion.

'But how would they know? You are the only person I told about the mask!'

He smiled. 'Do I detect a hint of distrust? Do you think I sent him? Do you imagine that I bought Kilashane for the purpose of sifting its rubble?'

Dee shrugged. 'No, of course not. You make me sound very silly. But I didn't tell anyone else, so how would they know?'

'Well, Dee, you told Charlie you had found the ring there. Don't you think he was capable of putting two and two together?'

'So he was a member of this organization?'

'Of course, or one of its offshoots. Men have a fascination with secret societies. If you think about it for a moment, you will realize how you are surrounded by them: the Freemasons,

Knights of Columbanus, Ancient Order of Hibernians, Opus Dei, Orange Order; while abroad there are others such as the Priory of Sion, P2 in Italy, and many more. Not to mention the ones sanctioned by government, like the KGB and MI5, and, on a criminal level, organizations like the Mafia. And if they just happened to be all interconnected at some level, what do you think you have then?'

'What would we have?'

'Assume for a moment that the leading lights of each of these secret societies had formed a society of their own, focused on something, such as an occult artefact, as a kind of logo or mascot, with common global banking interests. What you would have then would be the most exclusive secret society in the world.'

Dee was silent. Then she murmured, 'You make me feel that everything is circumscribed by underground machination.'

'What's to stop it? It allows for manipulation, for power.'

'It's frightening!'

'Only if you don't understand it.'

'And you do?'

He smiled again. 'Perhaps. I am older than you. I have seen more of the world!'

'Sometimes I feel that you are ancient!'

'Ancient? Me?'

She laughed. 'So Kilashane may be left undisturbed after all . . .'

'It's possible. But remember that it would

have a definite appeal of its own. People like to get away; in fact they are in perpetual ferment, seeking the new and the mysterious, seeking something that matters, seeking peace.'

'Do you need to find peace?' Then she thought of the tragedy in his life and added, 'Sorry. Silly question!'

'I find it with you.'

He pulled her against him. She felt the crackle of his trenchcoat and nuzzled her head into his shoulder and under his chin. Around them was the sound of rippling water, the sudden agitated flurry of mallard and the sad, giddy free-fall of the first leaves of autumn.

'Will you come away with me?' he asked. 'Will you marry me?'

She did not answer for a moment. 'Dee . . . Désirée,' he said slowly. 'Will you give me an answer?'

She did not raise her head from his shoulder. 'I know the answer, but I need to be sure of it. Give me a few days.'

Later he talked of where they might live. 'I will sell my house and buy another one if you like . . . We could go skiing in winter. There's the forest of Ardennes near Brussels where we can walk, where we can ride. Would you like that? Where shall we go on honeymoon?'

He was filled with suppressed excitement. Then he added before she could respond, 'I know where we shall go on honeymoon; I have just the place in mind!'

Dee was surprised by the sudden sense of being taken over, crowded, deprived of a vote. She felt, in what seemed to her afterwards to have been a graceless moment, like a sapling that would be grafted on to another tree while her own limbs would be lopped.

But when she went back to the flat she felt bereft, as though life was essentially full of silence, and as if Peter held the key to sound, to challenge, to stimulus — and to all the colours of a kaleidoscope.

She told Laura. The latter was the only one who knew of the débâcle in Brussels and the subsequent developments.

'I'd grab him,' Laura said. 'When do you think you will meet a man like him again? Think of the life you could have with him! But don't let that be the deciding issue. You know this guy and I don't!'

On Sunday night, Dee dreamed that she and Peter were making love, and that, in the midst of their passion, he was suddenly taken away from her, drawn back and down a long tunnel which echoed with his voice. She woke in desperation, in a fever of loss, and then realized, with returning consciousness, that all was still well. He would be going away in a few days. If she refused him, that was all that would be left of him — the echo of his voice. That evening she and Peter drove into the mountains, where she accepted his proposal of marriage.

He took a small box from his pocket and opened it. Inside was an engagement ring — a ruby surrounded by diamonds. They sat in the car above Lough Dan and saw the night deepen and the stars come out and still they waited, reluctant to return to the city, reluctant to stir, simply holding each other.

Laura was still up when she got in. She blew her breath out in admiration. 'Wow! That must have cost a bomb!'

'I don't know what it cost and I don't care!'

'This calls for a celebration!'

Laura produced two beers from the fridge and said a little wistfully, 'Here's to your happiness, Dee. When am I going to meet the paragon?'

'Tomorrow.'

Later, as she was undressing for bed Laura said, 'By the way, there's a piece in today's *Times* about the missing corpse.'

Dee stared at her. 'What corpse?'

'The one you were so interested in! The one found and lost in Venice! The body of the young woman who had no face.'

'Oh . . . What about her?'

'They've found her!'

Dee stood still. 'Where did they find her?'

'She was in a new grave on the cemetery island. The director became suspicious when he saw it, because it was not accounted for. So they exhumed it, in case it involved a matter of foul play. It was her all right, but badly decomposed; even her nice silk dress. Her necklace, predictably enough, was gone. But one other odd thing —'

'What?'

'She was wearing a mask!'

'What kind of mask?'

'Enamelled silver.'

Laura turned around after a moment and asked, 'Dee, are you all right?'

'Of course I'm all right,' Dee hissed, 'but I never want to hear another word about that business!'

Laura shrugged, looking at her curiously. 'Fine by me!' She folded the paper and put it down.

But when Laura was in the bath, Dee took up the paper on the pretext of doing the crossword, and found herself turning to the international news page. The piece on the missing corpse took only a small boxed-in space. She scanned it furiously, saw that, in addition to what Laura had read out, there was an addendum recounting an interview with an old Venetian who swore that the discovery of the missing body with the mask meant only one thing: 'The sorceror Mathias Robertus is coming back!'

Dee smiled to herself. 'And they say the Irish have fey notions!' she informed the print of *The Bog at Allen*. She glanced at the painting Colin had found in the jumble sale. It was still there, staring into the corner at the discarded poster of the Beatles, the charcoal scrawl 'My Magician' across its back.

Next morning there was a letter for Dee. She opened it hastily on the way out to work and then threw it down on the hall table.

'Who is it from?' Laura asked.

'More of this stupid business,' Dee said with an exasperated sigh. 'It's from the parish priest at home. He said he would send me some details about that queer business to do with the Inquisition, and here it is . . .' She held out some densely written pages. 'He's gone to the trouble of copying it out himself. He makes me feel guilty.'

'Aren't you going to read it?'

'No. Not now, anyway. I've had enough of this!'

'Do you mind if I read it?'

'Please do.'

When Dee had gone off to work, Laura took up the letter.

The Presbytery,
Ballyshane.

Dear Dee,

Further to our conversation, I'm enclosing copy of the translated account of those events we discussed, as promised. It was attached to a personal letter from Monsignor Dillon, dated June 1919, thanking Father Keane for his missive and referring to old times. He said he was very disturbed by the news that the ring of Mathias had been sent to Ireland, and hoped he had not done wrong in satisfying the curiosity of Mr O'Reilly.

I hear you are engaged to be married, and wish you every blessing on this new chapter in your life. I know that now you will have other more important concerns than the strange circumstances surrounding Kilashane.

God bless you, John O'Shea, P.P.

Laura glanced at the attached, densely written pages, remembered she would be late for work, folded them and put them away in the drawer of the hall table. They remained there, unread, and were eventually forgotten.

The witch, Agnes Galletini, was Venetian by birth, and was reared in that city where her father, a merchant, conducted his business, trading in glass, silks and spices with the Orient. On one of his journeys he was entertained in the house of a Musselman in Constantinople where, chancing to glimpse that gentleman's beautiful eldest daughter, he persuaded his host, after all the usual delicate negotiation attendant on such a matter, to confer on him her hand.

After her marriage, this lady embraced our Christian faith.

The couple had two children, a son and a daughter, both of whom were baptized into the Church. Their father, who was uxurious in the extreme, suffered his wife to retain a learned Circassian slave, a eunuch, as tutor for her son, and was so foolish as to permit the boy's sister to attend the lessons. The result was that the girl became versed in Mathematics and the Classics, and other subjects unsuited to her feminine station, among them Arabic. This may have seemed unremarkable to the father, used as he was to that language in his trade with the Orient, but it was the unfortunate circumstance which was to seal her doom.

The mother of these children died in childbed with a third, and stillborn, child. Her husband did not remarry, contenting himself with a mistress, and he engaged no female chaperon for his daughter, who was allowed the run of his library and the society and instruction of the Circassian slave. This person taught her the use of herbs as remedy for human ills and, in this lore — which is demonic if not practised under the auspices of our Holy Mother — she became proficient, as she is reputed to have done in other diabolic sciences in which she was instructed by the same slave.

Being of great personal beauty, Agnes was eagerly sought in marriage, but seemed unwilling to embrace that state, preferring to remain a virgin. Her father did not compel her in this matter, and indeed seems to have failed utterly in his duty to mould her understanding and bend her will to the submission which should adorn her sex.

When the witch was twenty, her father and brother were both lost at sea, killed in the same tempest which was, doubtless, engendered by the wrath of God. With them were lost her father's ships and their cargo, which loss decimated his estate and forced his executors to sell his house in Venice, in order to satisfy his creditors and provide a small competence for his daughter. With only her Circassian slave for companion, she left the city and made her way to Florence. There she was permitted to settle in the hills of Fiesole, a place of great beauty to the north of the city, once favoured by Etruscans and Romans, and famous for its flowers. She acquired a small villa and devoted her days to private study, of what demonic nature can only now be guessed at. But her beauty attracted attention, and her apparent modesty and retiring disposition attracted respect. Such is the gullible propensity of human nature without pastoral guidance.

How it first emerged to public knowledge that she was proficient with herbs is not known, but the devil has ways of insinuating himself into the confidences of honest people. Soon she was acclaimed as a worker of miracles, but she attributed these only to her herbs, saying that our mother the earth had given us whereof we might be cured of all our ills.

When the Cardinal di Garanavo went to see her, she offered him a herbal infusion for gout, which proved so uncannily efficacious that his suspicions were aroused. He spoke to her of God and our Blessed Mother, astonished to find in a Christian woman so little piety or subservience. Her mien was open and seeming innocent; but he knew how Satan works his wickedness. When he asked her where God resided on earth, she answered, with seeming candour, that He resided in the veins of all creation, and she was not persuaded that she had erred even when reminded that God lived in the Tabernacle and that the world was the province of the devil.

Worse was to ensue, for when his Eminence warned her, as became his priestly office, that she was possessed with evil spirits, she said coldly that he lied. The cardinal knew then that his suspicions were well founded, and he ordered his servants to seize her book in which she had written the recipes for her charms and spells. It was in the Arabic tongue, with heathen runes and symbols, and although she protested that she used that language solely in order to preserve the results of her private researches, his Eminence knew that the Father of Lies but spoke through her, for he had such experience of witches that he knew one at a single glance.

He had the book burned and the witch arrested by the Inquisition. Mathias, the sternest of them all, was her inquisitor.

Mathias had seen her once, collecting mushrooms and other vegetation, in the woods of

Vallambrosa, and had been struck by her extraordinary beauty, her youthful grace, and her air of dignity and freedom. He was zealous at first to redeem her, thinking her but a simple soul who had been misled, but when she proved obdurate and too proud to receive correction, he proved unequal to the task. Through Satan's wiles he conceived a sinful passion for her, and would have released her but that the cardinal intervened. She died from her torture, which was inflicted to correct her sins, and was as fearful as man has ever visited on woman.

Mathias's anger at her fate made him as one possessed. He was eventually excommunicated and sought by the Inquisition, but was never apprehended, slipping out of every net with inhuman cunning. In the full flush of his unrighteous ire at the woman's fate, he compacted with the devil, who is said to have promised him revenge, giving him a mask with which to cover her obliterated beauty in the tomb. He hid her body in Venice and studied whatever black arts would serve to bring back her soul.

Epilogue

The train was hurtling through the night. Plush seats, mellow light, curtained windows, good food and wine: Mr and Mrs Eggli were off on honeymoon.

In retrospect it seemed whirlwind, the wedding in University Church, her mother smiling through her tears, her hand on her father's steady arm, the organ playing Wagner. Laura was there with Ted in tow; Liam attended with his fiancée; there were some colleagues and old friends from college days, her two aunts, friends of her parents and a few cousins. Peter had surprisingly few guests, just a few colleagues from ITU and no relations.

'I'm an orphan,' he had explained with a lugubrious expression, 'and an only child to boot!'

Dee had invited Colin, but he had been posted on another assignment; he had sent regrets and said a present was on the way — something else he had bought in the same jumble sale in which he had acquired the magician's portrait. 'I bought it on impulse. I thought you might take to it!'

They had the reception in the Russell Hotel. Upstairs in the suite overlooking the Green, she had stood beside Peter and greeted their guests,

524

the first social act of their married life. Dee watched her parents. She knew they were pleased, glad that her life's course was settled and prosperous. Peter had gone out of his way to charm them. Her mother had whispered to Dee afterwards that she was sure she had met him before. 'You must be imagining things, Mam. How could you have met him before!'

But while her mother was excited with the preparations for the wedding her father did not meet her eyes. He had changed, become quiet, lost his *joie de vivre* in some way. His eyes now tended to follow his wife, who was overjoyed with the Dublin flat.

When Dee went to change into her going-away clothes, her mother came with her. 'Are you happy?'

'Deliriously. Peter surrounds me with attention, with everything he thinks I would like. But sometimes I'm afraid it's all too perfect, as though I will wake up some day and find it was all a dream!'

'It's natural to feel like that! This is your life's adventure! Where are you going on honeymoon?'

Dee laughed. 'I don't know. He says it's a surprise!'

She had been glad to get out of her wedding dress, toss her bouquet to waiting hands in the hall of the Russell, make the dash to the airport to catch the plane to Paris.

'Are we going to spend our honeymoon in Paris? There are so many places there I would love to see with you!'

He smiled. 'No. Not Paris!'

It was only when they were boarding the train in the Gare de Lyon that she realised they were on the express to Venice.

She turned to him. 'Peter, darling, why are we going to Venice?'

'Aren't you pleased?' he asked anxiously. 'I thought it would be romantic. We can change our minds if you don't like it!' But the whistle had blown and the train was already pulling away, leaving the platform and the station and then Paris far behind them.

They had a double compartment to themselves. They had locked the door and made love, lying sleepily afterwards in each other's arms until it was time for dinner. When they were dressed and about to go to the dining car, Peter took something from his case. It was a morocco box and inside, on satin silk lining, was a double row of pearls. 'Your wedding present.'

Dee drew in her breath sharply. The pearls were large and the clasp magnificent. 'Thank you! It's beautiful. Is it old?'

'Yes. I've had it restrung.'

He took it from the box and put it around her neck. She saw herself in the mirror, her bobbed hair shining, the pearls lustrous above the scooped neckline of her new silk dress. He moved back to examine her. 'Splendid!'

At dinner he leaned over the table. 'You will adore the city,' he said. 'It is like nowhere else on earth! You will come out of the station straight on to the Grand Canal. You will be surrounded by an ancient living construct, a city spun out of dreams. The church of San Simeone Piccolo will face you across the lagoon. If you follow the canal round to your left, you come to the Rialto Bridge, first constructed in stone around 1591. There was a competition to find the right design, you know!' His eyes were bright, as though he were talking about events of yesterday. 'Everything that is secret and potent in the human psyche finds a home in Venice.'

She sighed. 'Once I wanted to go there very much. But after all this business to do with . . . with the curios I found, I began to wonder . . .'

'What did you begin to wonder?'

'Whether my mother could have been right. Whether these things did carry with them some malediction, like —' she thought of a conversation she had once had with Laura — 'the business to do with Tutankhamen's tomb, something like that . . .' She saw his jaw tighten, but when she tried to look him in the eye he looked away.

'You're surely not susceptible to that kind of crap, Dee,' he said with a teasing voice. 'Venice is a city well worth seeing, a mysterious and private place! There are palaces and virtually inaccessible private houses and dim waterways and small hump-backed bridges. There are little squares, which are silent and empty at night! It is a fantastical city, just right for lovers.'

'But doomed,' Dee whispered, feeling suddenly oddly upset. 'Like Atlantis and Mu it is doomed . . .'

He made no effort to comfort her, only looked at her with a strangely expressionless face.

She drank champagne to quell the sense of malaise, much more than she should. She felt the pressure of his foot against hers under the table, felt the touch of his hand, knew that he never took his eyes off her. His concentrated attention was such that it was a relief, when they returned to their compartment, that Peter excused himself, saying he was going into the corridor for a smoke. But the smell of the cigar permeated into the compartment.

She sat down to steady herself, wondering why the wine had gone so wildly to her head. Her focus had become disjointed, so much so that her surroundings seemed to have fractured. She put her hand up to the necklace at her throat. The pearls were warm. She thought suddenly of Colin and how he would joke if he saw her. 'The tipsy leprechaun.' His present had arrived the day before her wedding when she had been in the bath.

'A parcel for you,' her mother had called.

'Open it, Mam.'

There had been the sound of paper being torn, and then silence.

'What is it?'

'I don't know what to make of it. It's a dress, a black velvet dress with a bustle — the kind of thing you would wear to a fancy-dress party! It smells of mothballs! It seems to be the genuine article; no zips, just hooks and eyes up the back!' She had come out of the bath and inspected it, laughing.

'I thought you might have fun with this!' Colin's note said. 'So here it is.'

She thought how she had never asked Colin precisely who in ITU was the 'queer bird' he was 'ferreting out the dirt on'. There had been no further mention of him, and she had discounted her silly suspicions.

She had told Peter about the dress and he had smiled. 'You must wear it. You must let me see you in it! Anything elegant, anything so redolent of the past, is bound to suit you!' he had said.

Dee began to feel dizzy. If I rinse out my mouth, she thought, I will feel better. But, searching in her overnight bag, she realized that she had forgotten to pack toothpaste. Peter's bag was beside hers. She opened it, found his sponge bag, rooted around for his toothpaste.

Her fingers felt the small square box, and she took it out. It was of tooled leather. She flipped the lid. Inside was a gold signet ring. She stared at the familiar design on the signet, the letter M engraved with twining serpents. She remembered how it had been torn from her neck in Brussels by a man dressed in a leather jerkin and knee breeches who seemed to have come straight from the Middle Ages. She looked around, her heart sinking, a dread coming up to meet it from the soles of her feet. She stared at the communication cord, as though it was her last link with the world she knew. It was there above her head, but she could not rise, was not sure that she wished to rise. What did time matter anyway? She was part of past and future, as he had told her once.

The train screamed as it entered a tunnel. She heard his steps, his returning stiff gait, and then the opening of the compartment door. He smiled a little; his eyes seemed very dark, very sad, but his mouth was triumphant behind the small smile. He took the ring from her and slipped it on his finger, covered her mouth with his, murmuring, 'My darling, I will explain everything.'

We hope you have enjoyed this Large Print book. Other G.K. Hall & Co. or Chivers Press Large Print books are available at your library or directly from the publishers.

For more information about current and up-coming titles, please call or write, without obligation, to:

G.K. Hall & Co.
P.O. Box 159
Thorndike, Maine 04986 USA
Tel. (800) 257-5157

OR

Chivers Press Limited
Windsor Bridge Road
Bath BA2 3AX
England
Tel. (0225) 335336

All our Large Print titles are designed for easy reading, and all our books are made to last.